SCENES FROM MARRIED LIFE

AND

SCENES FROM LATER LIFE

Works by the same author

SCENES FROM MARRIED LIFE

AND

SCENES FROM LATER LIFE

WILLIAM COOPER

E. P. DUTTON, INC.   NEW YORK

Published in the United States by E.P. Dutton, Inc.,
2 Park Avenue, New York, N.Y. 10016

Library of Congress Catalog Card Number: 84-70466

ISBN: 0-525-24258-9

OBE

10 9 8 7 6 5 4 3 2 1

SCENES FROM MARRIED LIFE

This book is dedicated to
My Wife

CONTENTS

Part I

Part II

Part III

Contents

PART I

ON A NO. 14 BUS

'P.S.A.,' said Sybil, in a tone of amiable comment. She was looking through the window of the bus and I had my arm round her.

Startled, I followed her glance. The bus was going along Piccadilly — I was on my way to seeing her off at Euston — and I judged that her glance was directed towards one of those huge-windowed shops which in London appear to be indispensable for selling motor-cars, though there is no evidence that fewer motor-cars are sold per financially eligible head of population in say Aberdeen without them. P.S.A.? Or was it B.S.A.? That rang a bell — it was the make of bicycle I had ridden when I was a schoolmaster before the war. A ridiculous idea. There could be no B.S.A.s among Hillmans and Austins and Bentleys, in fact there was no connection between them other than in my imagination, where, when a provincial schoolmaster astride a B.S.A., I had imagined myself writing a novel which could sell enough copies to buy me a Bentley, or for that matter an Austin, even just a small Austin.

I could see no letters P.S.A., nor B.S.A. In fact I could see no three-letter group anywhere on anything.

'What on earth does P.S.A. stand for?' I asked.

Sybil half-turned to me and said: 'Pleasant Sunday Afternoon, of course.'

I burst into laughter. It was appreciative laughter. Just before getting on to this bus, Sybil and I had been in bed together. My appreciation was enormous.

Sybil was an unusually pretty girl. She looked remarkably like Marlene Dietrich — Marlene Dietrich when young,

3

though Sybil was now about thirty-two. Sybil was aware of the resemblance and plucked her eyebrows accordingly. Above her wide-open blue eyes, they rose in two hyperfine arches, which, when she was talking to you, wiggled in a remarkable manner. I was fascinated by them: I could never understand why they did it.

'I thought you must have seen the letters on a shop-front,' I said. 'I was looking for them everywhere.'

At this Sybil turned away thoughtfully. The fact which I might have remembered, thereby saving myself some trouble, was that Sybil was so short-sighted she could scarcely see the shops. There was a pause while we went round Piccadilly Circus, and then she turned back to me and, with her eyebrows wiggling, said:

'Joe, do you think I ought to wear contact lenses?'

Like a fool, I replied: 'I should have thought a pair of specs would have done just as well.' Having bits of glass against one's eyeballs seemed to me creepy.

Sybil's expression was not a hurt one: it was an uncomprehending one. Contact lenses were something she could envisage: spectacles were not. I realised why not, by reference to a concept which originated from a friend of mine named Robert, who knew Sybil well. Robert was convinced that in her inveterate perusal of women's magazines Sybil had succumbed to the propaganda that any woman can be beautiful by following certain rules of make-up — 'Glamour Tips' was what Robert was convinced they were called, and he believed that there was a fixed apocalyptic number, actually forty-four, of them. Robert, I realised, would have understood at once why Sybil looked uncomprehending — not that he did not understand everything at once, being that sort of man: I revered him for it. Robert would have understood that contact lenses were numbered among Sybil's Forty-four Glamour Tips, whereas spectacles were not.

'Perhaps you ought to have contact lenses,' I said, to get on the rails again.

4

'Yes,' said Sybil. 'I can't see very much when I'm out.'

'How much can you see?' I said, thinking of her when she was in.

Sybil looked through the window again. She read out the name of the play that was then on at the Globe Theatre, *The Lady Is Not For Burning* — the year was 1949. As the letters were a foot high and only a pavement's width away, I said:

'If you look at the people on the other side of the road, can you tell which sex they are?'

Without hesitation, and with what seemed to me a touch of characteristic complacency, Sybil said:

'If it's fairly clearly marked.'

I laughed, and then something, perhaps actually looking at the people on the other side of the road, made me speculate on how the world looked to Sybil. Very, very different from how it looked to me. The difference visually was obvious — whatever my moral defects were, I had pretty good eyesight — but that was only the beginning. Not only did Sybil see the world differently from me with the outer eye: the truth was that after knowing her for years I had no idea *what* she saw with the inner one.

I had known Sybil off and on for fifteen years. She worked as a librarian in the provincial town that I came from. I repeat, as a librarian. Sybil looked so like Marlene Dietrich that you might have thought she would never have had a book in her hand, that nobody would ever even have shown her one. Not a bit of it. Once during a lull when we were in bed she recited the whole of one of Hamlet's soliloquies — and not the '*To be, or not to be*' one, either. I was amazed.

Sybil was a mystery to me. After knowing her for fifteen years I had to confess that I had not the faintest idea what moved her immortal soul, what made her tick. Nor had Robert. We used to discuss it with persistence and chagrin. You may think I was in a better position to solve the mystery

5

because she had slept with me and not with Robert. Well, no, you are wrong there, I think.

Anyway, the generalisation that you will penetrate the mysteries of somebody's nature if she sleeps with you is a shaky one at the best of times, and in the case of Sybil it was simply non-operative. There she lay, for example, happily reciting one of Hamlet's soliloquies. Amazing, but not exegetical.

'What does Sybil want out of life?' Robert would ask me. When propounding a question to which neither he nor I knew the answer, Robert always safeguarded his own self-esteem by aiming the question at me.

I told him I had heard her say she would like to be a film star.

Because it was out of the question for her to become a film star, Robert looked at me as if he thought I were reporting her untruthfully. It was not possible for Robert to believe that aspiration could exist so independently of action: in Sybil they existed together without the slightest mutual influence — they appeared not to cause each other a scrap of bother. Sybil went on her way imperturbably. Sometimes I thought conceitedness might have been the source of her imperturbability, but she never seemed particularly conceited.

Then Robert and I argued about whether Sybil wanted to be married again. Robert wanted to know if she wanted to marry me, and when I said I saw no signs of it, that between Sybil and me marriage somehow did not come into it, he looked neither satisfied with my reply nor dissatisfied. He said: 'H'm.'

Sybil and I were friends who had slept together off and on for years, the off spells corresponding on my side to the times when I was in love with someone, and on her side to the spell when she was married. The latter, alas, was short. In 1943 she married a willowy, dashing young man in the Parachute Regiment, and he was killed at Arnhem. After that she went

6

on working in her library, helping to support her mother. There were always men about the place who wanted to marry her, and no one was more in need of a guiding hand, literally, than Sybil. Sybil standing on the pavement looking for a bus-stop was a sight so heart-rending that any man who saw her longed to drive up in an expensive car and carry her away. Yet she did not marry.

Marriage and widowhood had made no difference in Sybil's attitude to me: failure to marry and confirmation in bachelordom had obviously made no difference in my attitude to her. Sitting in the No. 14 bus that November Sunday evening, we might just as well have been sitting in a provincial tram soon after we first met. Oddly self-possessed yet diffident, in some ways ineffably remote — not to mention others in which she was deliciously contiguous — with beautiful eyes picking up next to nothing and eyebrows wiggling like antennae, she gave me no clue whatsoever to what made her tick. She never had. She never would.

That Sunday evening was almost the last time I ever saw Sybil, so that I have had ten years to recollect her in tranquillity. Still no clue.

The bus fetched up at Euston and we went into the station. Euston is dark at the best of times and, on this particular evening, night had come early, coldly and wintrily, wafting into our nostrils fog flavoured with sulphur dioxide. We were in no hurry. We went through the classical entrance into the forecourt, where the lights were burning without seeming to make the slightest difference to the degree of illumination. A faint shadow had crossed both our minds, for a glance at the clock had reminded us that although time was passing it was still too early to get a drink.

How often I had entered this station, just before seven o'clock of a Sunday evening! *Autre temps, autre femmes,* I reminded myself in a sprightly way — that suddenly fell flat . . . I was reminded of *autres temps,* some years back, when I had thought I was all set to get married.

7

'Damn this station!' I must have said it aloud, because Sybil said:

'Yes. It isn't as nice as Paddington.'

We went on to the platform and found that the train was in. It was always in. I put Sybil's case on a seat and then we strolled down the platform. The faint fishy, appley smell was too poignant to be borne, I thought. I really wished I might never be seeing anybody off from this station, from this particular platform, ever again. I said to Sybil all the same:

'How soon can you come and see me again?'

'Not till after Christmas, more's the pity!'

A porter beginning to slam the doors at the top end of the train took us by surprise. It was time for Sybil to get into the carriage.

When the train had gone out I made for the bar, which was now open, and ordered a large whisky. It may sound as if I had fallen into a bout of *tristezza* consequent on the pleasures of the afternoon, but to my mind it was consequent on something of much longer duration, and not pleasurable either. To ward it off I drank the whisky quickly and ordered another. I paused. And then inspiration suddenly hit me in the way a large whisky does.

There was something wrong with my life, and my predicament at this moment expressed it perfectly. Having just seen off Sybil, what had I got to go home to? An empty flat. At my age — I was thirty-nine — what had all other men got to go home to? A cosy house with a wife in it and some kiddies. What a corny dream-picture! I thought, and yet what an attractive one! (For the moment I disregarded the fact that if there had been a wife and some kiddies in my flat I should have been lucky to get out for a solitary whisky, let alone to see off at Euston, *con tristezza* or *con allegria*, some such girl as Sybil.)

A romantic bitterness about my fate temporarily overcame me, in the deserted bar. When I was young I had not

8

wanted to get married. And now? At that question my
spirits slipped a notch lower. I began my second whisky.

As my colleagues in the Civil Service would have put it, I
'reviewed the situation'. What a situation! And what an
awful review! For fifteen years I had slept with someone
whom I comprehended so little that somehow marriage just
never came into it. Like ships that pass in the night, Sybil
and I, for all the passing and re-passing which practically
amounted to a regular service, were still a couple of ships,
lone in the night. I was still lone in the night. Was it, could
it possibly be, that there was something wrong not with my
life but with *me*? When I thought that, I felt something deep
in my psyche like the fall of ice-cream on teeth that have just
been scaled.

'Joe,' I said to myself as I drank some more of the whisky,
'it's bad, very bad.' I meant the prognosis was bad.

Mine was indeed a predicament — in Robert's idiom, a
predicament and a half.

Remembering Robert made me decide to explain my
latest view of my predicament to him. Of course he knew
all about it, as he knew about everything else. The trouble
with our predicaments, especially when they are painful,
incapable of resolution, even tragic, is that we are just a bit
proud of them, just a bit attached to them. Though Robert
knew all about mine already, I had every intention of ex-
plaining my latest view of it even if I bored the hide off him.

I made my way out of the station and caught a No. 14
bus going in the opposite direction to the one I had come on.

'Terminus,' I said to the conductor heavily, but meaning
it literally. I was living at Putney.

9

CHAPTER II

TALKS WITH A FAT MAN

HARRY was one of those active fat men who are really more muscular and less fat than they look, though that is not saying much in the case of Harry, whose shape came as near as makes no matter to a globe. And like the terrestrial globe, he seemed to be always spinning. When he approached you, moving bulkily on light, strong feet, a whirling gust of air preceded him — it was the outskirts of a vortex at the centre of which you saw Harry, sweating profusely and fixing you with a beady, eager, inquisitive look.

Harry was a distant cousin of mine. (Exactly how distant was something that he and I — unlike members of the aristocracy, to whom, with titles and large sums of money in the offing, such calculations seem to come like second nature — had never bothered to work out.) Though our families saw little of each other, Harry and I, between the ages of fifteen and eighteen, when he was going to a country grammar school and I to a town secondary school, had been companions for pursuits involving bicycles, box-cameras, air-guns, tents and suchlike; pursuits frequently commended by parents for promoting healthy adventurous instincts in boys, and often undertaken by boys chiefly as a means of getting away from parents.

I still possess a small terracotta Roman bowl, artfully stuck together with Seccotine, that Harry and I ought to have handed in to the local museum of antiquities. I also keep an old photograph of both of us, taken by another boy and somewhat imperfectly 'fixed' by the look of it, in which Harry misleadingly appears as lithe, broad-chested, and quite un-globe-like. Globedom, as in those dried Japanese flowers which you drop into a glass of water, was then securely hidden in the comely packet of Harry's particular type of physique — a type which he and I nowadays referred to with professional facetiousness as the Pyknic Practical Joke. The joke was comic enough when played by the Deity on Harry, but was seen by us at its most comic when played on a young man who married a beautiful, lithe, broad-chested girl, in whom was hidden, as in one of those Japanese flowers, etc. etc. etc.

Harry, I may say, was surviving the joke with over-high blood-pressure but admirable grace. I found him more fun now than I had done twenty years ago, not because his nature had changed, but because I suppose I had meanwhile learnt how to find people entertaining. Boys have a dim time of it because they have so far learnt only how to find each other useful. Anyway, I was glad when Harry reappeared in my life.

One day the telephone in my office rang — by this time I had become a Principal in the Civil Service — and it was Harry. Our boyhood companionship had lapsed when I went up to Oxford to read science and Harry went to Manchester to start becoming a doctor. Throughout the last twenty years I do not suppose I had seen him more than half a dozen times. My sense of family was strong but of the passive, non-visiting, non-corresponding kind. It was not activated by a feeling that if I did visit and correspond I should be overwhelmed by moral approval of my goings-on. Harry's and my family was sprinkled with Methodist ministers, my father being one of them.

I felt nothing but pleasure when Harry rang me up that day to say he had got a job in the Medical Research Council and had bought a house in Putney. I was ready to take up our friendship just where we had left off.

But the first time Harry and I met again, I realised that it was pure illusion on my part to think that anything had been left off where he was concerned. There was no lapse, no blank, no absence whatsoever of contact from his side. Harry seemed to have a complete dossier of everything I had done during the last twenty years.

At this point in my story I have to make my chief revelation about Harry's nature. About Sybil I remarked that I had not the faintest idea what moved her immortal soul, what made her tick. There was no such mystery about Harry. His mainspring was visible to everyone. What moved Harry's immortal soul can be named in one word — curiosity. I have never in my life known anyone to come anywhere near Harry's level for being moved so constantly, so powerfully, so magnificently by curiosity. It shone in the beadiness of his bright hazel eyes; it whirled in the warm gust of air that preceded him; curiosity, fat, energetic and insatiable.

'Good gracious!' I exclaimed when I first saw him come into the room — we met at my club — not having expected him to be anything like so globular. His waist measurement must be his biggest, I thought with stupefaction.

Harry looked at me shrewdly for a moment, and said in his quick, fluent, high-pitched voice:

'You're greyer than your photographs show, aren't you, Joe?'

I could not think where he had seen a photograph of me. As for being grey — it is very hard to realise how much older one is looking. Whenever I was at the barber's and a wad of hair fell in my lap, I always had a job not to exclaim: 'Is that *mine*?'

Harry, I observed, had not much hair at all now. He had a globe-shaped head, over the top of which his fine-textured, straight, mouse-coloured hair could scarcely be said to hide the pink of his scalp. He had a shining, intelligent face, in the middle of which sat a snub nose. With the years' accretion of flesh round them, his eyes looked smaller than they used to, not quite puffy, not quite baggy, but somewhere in between the two. He took out a handkerchief and wiped a few drops of sweat off his forehead before he sat down.

'I suppose,' he said, when he had sat down, 'getting turned down in marriage, that last time, must have taken a lot out of you?'

'How in God's name do you know all about that?' I said. After all, I had hardly told my parents anything about it, and I presumed our family was his source of intelligence.

Harry said: 'Oh, I pieced it together . . .' His tone might have been thought apologetic as well as explanatory. But his complexion gave him away. I noticed the sudden tinge of a blush. It was a blush of triumph, of pure triumph.

I stared at him.

'I was sorry to hear about your bad luck.' While he was saying this, his eyes seemed to enlarge with sympathy, and he looked at me with intimate concern.

Harry's feeling was not in the least put on for the occasion. His curiosity was linked with unusual empathy. Looking at him now I realised that when we were boys I might have been unaware of what he was like but I had not been mistaken in choosing him for a friend.

'It's the sort of thing that happens to one,' I muttered, looking down.

'I wonder . . .' he said. His tone stayed on its high, honeyed pitch. 'Don't you think you attract that kind of bad luck?'

I looked up pretty quickly at that.

'There's the internal evidence of your novels, you know,' he said. And again he was unable to keep the triumphant look off his face.

'I don't write my novels to provide the likes of you with internal evidence,' I said, trying to hide my huffiness by grinning.

'I think,' he said, without the slightest flicker in his friendly concern, 'they're very good novels. Especially your last one.'

I should like to know what I could say to that.

Anyway, all this happened a year or more before the evening I described when I saw Sybil off at Euston. It is relevant because instead of going home to my empty flat that night, I went round to Harry's house, which was only a quarter of an hour's walk away. It was Harry and his wife, Barbara, who had persuaded me to quit the dilapidated square in Pimlico where my most recent disaster in love had happened to me, and to start life afresh in Putney. Energetically they had found me a flat and supervised my removal. I was grateful to them. I did like the change. Also, I had been constantly troubled by the prospect of my Pimlico landlady giving me notice.

I strolled along the dark, bosky by-roads from the bus-stop, feeling encouraged by the prospect of being offered something to eat at Harry's. I was hungry.

Harry opened the front door to me, silhouetted like a globe against the light from inside the hall. A whirl of air left me standing as his high voice receded down a corridor.

'Come into the kitchen, Joe. Barbara's out, so I'm getting my own supper.'

In the kitchen I could readily see that for myself. There stood Harry, with drops of sweat on his forehead and an apron tied round his equator, preparing an omelette. On the top of the table were a piece of Gruyère cheese from which a teacupful had been grated, a saucerful of chopped chives, and the broken shells of no less than four eggs.

'Are the children still up?' I asked, looking at all this.

'No,' said Harry, taking a cardboard crate of eggs out of the refrigerator. 'Can you eat more than two of these? They're rather small.'

In a moment the smell of hot butter rose from the stove, and the sweat began to run down into Harry's eyes. His movements were deft and quick.

'I'm hungry,' I said.

'I expect you must be,' said Harry, and added lightly, *en passant*: 'Did the train leave on time?'

I could not help laughing, but as he was busy with the omelette he did not notice.

'Platform 17, I suppose,' he said.

'No,' said I. '12.'

Harry spun round, and his astonished look of 'How-could-they-have-changed-the-platform-without-my-knowing?' rewarded me in full. Had the omelette not been sizzling deliciously in the enormous frying-pan that he was holding in front of him, I think he would have whirled off to the telephone instantly to ring up Euston. Suddenly an elephantine glint came into his eye.

'I know why it was!' he said. And he produced on the spot an inordinately convincing explanation of the change.

Having already had my full reward, I considered this was pure bonus. (It had been Platform 17, of course.) I said:

'Let's eat, Harry!'

Harry divided the omelette, and while I took out of the oven a long French loaf that had been warming up, Harry drew two glasses of cold water from the tap over the sink — he drank very little alcohol, under the impression that so doing would keep his blood-pressure down.

We began to eat.

In view of his questions about Sybil's train, you may think Harry's curiosity would have led him to begin quizzing me about the events of the week-end. That would have been a journeyman's method. Harry was a virtuoso. His method was to pick up a detail here, a detail there — the more improbable the quarter the better — to throw in now and then a shrewd guess or a sharp bit of deduction, and then to 'piece them together'. It was only then that professional pride allowed him to ask a direct question, just to prove to himself that he already knew the answer anyway.

Harry did not mention Sybil again that evening. What we began to talk about, while we were eating the omelette, was my job. I have remarked that I was a Principal in the Civil Service. I worked under Robert, who was an Under Secretary, and most of my job was interviewing people. I saw large numbers of them, and, for both human interest as well as professional use, I needed some scheme for classifying them. Nobody can look with detachment at a large number of his fellow human beings without noticing that when two people of approximately the same physical shape turn up they show resemblances to each other in temperament. Some particular kinds of temperament go with some particular kinds of physical shape. Part of the fascination of my job, the claim it had on my imagination, was the search for a generalisation, detailed and well-ordered, about these things.

Harry was interested, professionally as a doctor, privately as Harry — curiosity moved both of us, in this field at least, with the same power. Our discussions lasted us well into the stage of the meal when we were eating delicious cold apple-pie.

However, Harry's curiosity could not be confined indefinitely. I suppose I might admit the discussion had come to an end, but during the following pause I was still thinking about it. Suddenly, sweetly out of the blue, Harry dropped a question. About Robert.

Now my having told you Robert was my boss, my intimate friend of twenty years' standing and my literary comrade-in-arms as novelist — we were fighting to liberate ourselves through Art from the Civil Service, Robert having already half-won the battle and gone on to part-time — has not told you all. It has not made clear how important to me Robert's continued presence in the Civil Service was. Robert was the creator of his own job and of mine. I had reason to believe that if he resigned his job, mine would disappear.

The question Harry dropped, sweetly from the blue while he stood by the stove making our coffee, was:

'Is it true Robert's going to resign from the Civil Service at the beginning of next year?'

CHAPTER III

LUNCH IN A TEA-SHOP

THE effect of sleeping on a troublesome idea is, as every sound man knows, to flatten it a bit. One puts it, like a crumpled pair of trousers, under one's mattress, and oh! the difference when one brings it out next morning. If one is lucky. But then sound men *are* lucky.

Next morning, in the ordinary light of day as contrasted with the dazzling night of Harry's imagination, I saw that Robert simply could not be intending to leave me in the lurch. In my opinion, though not in his, Robert had many faults; but lack of responsibility for his friends was not among them. I had been momentarily swept off my feet by one of Harry's *ballons d'essai* — it suddenly occurred to me that if one ever actually saw a *ballon d'essai*, it would probably look like Harry.

So I got up that Monday morning feeling refreshed by the week-end and looking forward to my work. I did not want my job to disappear. I liked it. I was fascinated by it. Also it kept me from starving.

Robert and I were employed in a department of government that got scientific research done on a big scale. Large numbers of scientists and engineers were involved; and looking after those we had, together with trying to lay our hands on more, was a task and a half. During the war, when anybody who could do a job well got a chance to do it, Robert had taken that task and a half upon himself with great success — and, I should like to add, with my devoted assistance.

If you know the Civil Service only in peace-time you would expect such a task to fall to the lot of the department's establishments division. Though our department had a perfectly competent establishments division, with a brace of perfectly competent Under Secretaries at its head, Robert had got agreement after the war for continuing his job as head of a separate, semi-autonomous directorate. Though his directorate was closely linked with our establishments division, and one of their Under Secretaries was technically Robert's boss, we were, well, not *of* them. Robert, as a novelist, was a creative artist: there was indeed more than a touch of creative art about his Civil Service set-up.

The set-up had obvious advantages for us, but it required hypnosis to make any advantages for our establishments division obvious to that division. Many of them asked themselves how Robert managed it. In the first place he was a man of hypnotic personality. In the second, he had made himself a pretty high reputation and none of his immediate seniors was anxious to take the responsibility of losing him to the Service. Nevertheless, at the end of 1949, when the Service had shaken down to something more like its pre-war regular self — had shaken down far enough for many a regular Under Secretary to have completely forgotten that he was in his present post through irregular entry or promotion during the war — the touch of creative art about our present set-up was becoming over-apparent. And one has to remember that although Mankind has always had Art about the place, there is no evidence that Mankind could not have got on without it. My job of interviewing scientists and engineers and making decisions about their futures was one that quite a few people in our establishments division would have liked. And I have to admit that I had only Robert to hypnotise them into agreeing it were not better so. You see why it was very important indeed to me that Robert should not resign for the time being.

All the same, when I set off for work that Monday morning, Harry's question was not high on my list of things to talk to Robert about at lunch-time. I was thinking mostly —

and not unnaturally, if it comes to that — about Sybil. It was a bright November day and I strode down Putney Hill cheerfully singing under my breath. After all, I had come to Putney to start life afresh. Something brought the tune of 'Sweet Lass of Richmond Hill' into my mind, and I tried to fit in words to denote myself.

'Brave Lad of Putney Hill' commended itself insistently because it was so obvious. Yet its Housmanesque ring, I thought, was so wrong. I was neither young nor bucolic, and offhand I could not recall any occasion that had shown me to be brave. I passed the traffic lights and the Zeeta café, and noticed the usual haze drifting up from the river. The buses flashed a particularly inviting red, while their bile-shaded luminescent posters were more evocative than ever of nausea. Suddenly I caught sight of myself in Marks & Spencer's window, and my unconscious mind got the better of me:

'Smart Chap of Putney Hill!'

Unbidden — I would certainly have turned my back on them had I known they were coming — the words attached themselves to the tune, and the image of a Smart Chap attached itself, horribly, to me. It was not what I thought I was trying to look like at all. 'I don't look like a gentleman,' I thought. 'All well and good, because I'm not a gentleman. But a smart chap! . . . There are all sorts of other things one could look like. But no, not that!'

I passed Marks & Spencer's pretty quickly, I can tell you. And it was with relief that I heard a high-pitched, honeyed voice calling behind me:

'Joe!'

It was Harry, overtaking me. We often met at this time of day and travelled to work together.

'You're looking very dapper this morning,' he said.

I did not reply. I simply did not reply. And on the way to London we discussed neither my appearance nor the question of Robert's plans for getting out of the Civil Service.

We read our newspapers. But all the same, he did, merely by his presence, provoke my concern. I decided that I would put the matter higher on my list of things to say to Robert at lunch-time after all.

Robert and I usually had lunch together and we usually went to a tea-shop. Practically all our colleagues went to our canteen, with an air of loyally all keeping together — as if they were not together enough in their offices! — and in the canteen chewed over indiscriminately, but with apparent satisfaction, a mixture of bad cooking and office shop. Robert and I frequented a café where there was not the slightest likelihood of our meeting any of them.

Our behaviour was, of course, completely contrary to the Social Ethic, which tells you to be as other men are. Now in my experience men are more tolerant than they are often made out to be. They do not mind your not being as they are. What they will not tolerate is its *showing*. And here I must point out a great difference between Robert and me. When Robert and I sloped off at 12.45 to our tea-shop, *something showed in me*. There was no doubt about it. But in Robert? Did our colleagues realise that if I had not been there he would guilefully have excused himself from chewing over toad-in-the-hole and shop? They did not. That is the way life is.

I will tell you about me. At the end of the war, when Robert set up his directorate, we had been asked if we would care to be made permanent civil servants. In two minds, but politely, I had filled up a form I was given for the purpose. And in due course I got a reply, Roneo'd on a slip of paper of not specially high quality, measuring about four inches by six, and beginning thus:

MISC/INEL

Dear Sir,

The Civil Service Commissioners desire me to say that having considered your application for admission etc. . . .

And ending thus:

> They must, therefore, with regret declare you ineligible
> to compete and cancel your application accordingly.
>   Yours faithfully,

It was a mistake, of course. Of course it was a mistake. I got an immediate apology from someone higher up the hierarchy than anyone I had had an apology from before. But was it a mistake? Had something *showed* already?

MISC/INEL. Miscellaneous/Ineligible, it stood for. The letter I thought I might, as a literary artist taking on the style of a petty official, have invented. But not MISC/INEL. That was beyond me. That was the invention of an artist in his own right: it had the stamp of uncounterfeitable originality, the characteristic of striking through to a deeper truth than its creator comprehended. MISC/INEL. It could not be a mistake. Through that slip of not very high quality paper, measuring about four inches by six, I saw my epitaph, composed by a delegated member of the company of men and inscribed on everlasting, distinctly expensive marble.

> Here lies the body of
> ### JOSEPH LUNN
> Who though admittedly
> A Great Writer A True Friend
> A Perfect Husband and Father
> Must in The End be classed
> ### MISC/INEL

Actually the MISC/INEL letter settled my flirtation with permanency. My two minds about becoming a permanent civil servant became one, and that one said No. I asked myself what on earth I had been thinking about. I wanted to be a writer. If it came to that, by God, I was a writer.

The battle that I referred to earlier, the battle for the day when I would be nothing else but a writer, was on.

So much for that. Back to the story —

'Give my regards to Robert,' said Harry, as I got out of the bus — and then, never short of a *ballon d'essai*, he loosed off: 'Not forgetting Annette, of course.'

He wanted to know whether Robert was going to marry Annette or not. I said: 'Sure, I will,' in an American accent.

When I got to the office, there was Robert sitting on the edge of my desk, reading a proof-copy of my next novel. He glanced up as I came in and I saw that his face was pink.

'This is very good,' he said, although he must already have read the book five times. He had a characteristic muffled, lofty intonation that gave enormous weight to everything he said, but the pinkness of his complexion gave evidence of something other than weight. Robert was prudish, but that is not to say he was not just the faintest bit lewd. He shut the book, and looked at me with eyes that were sparkling. 'It's very good indeed.'

If that is not the sort of literary comrade-in-arms you want, I would like to know what is. What a friend! And what a book he was reading!

'How was Sybil?' he said.

'Very well,' said I. 'How was Annette?'

'Very well.' He glanced away, through the window — not that he could see anything through it, as it faced on a dreary well: modestly Euclidean, I have always felt that an internal circumference, so to speak, would be shorter than an external one; yét our office-architect had contrived to put at least twice as many windows looking inwards as outwards.

Robert said: 'We went to the Zoo,' in a tone which stressed the cultural, rather than the erotic nature of the expedition.

'Oh,' said I, 'we stayed in.' I let it go at that.

There was a pause for reflection, very satisfactory reflection.

22

Robert, sitting on one haunch, was swinging his foot to and fro. He looked like Franklin D. Roosevelt. I am sorry to have to say, within the space of describing three of my friends, that two of them looked like world-figures, and I will not do it again with any of the others. But it would be absurd for me to let Sybil's resemblance to Marlene Dietrich stop me saying Robert looked like F.D.R., because he did. F.D.R. without the gap teeth. Robert had a massiveness of body and of head that nevertheless gave the impression of a certain lightness. Like the best kind of cake, he was big without being heavy.

It was the same with Robert's temperament. Essentially he was a man of *gravitas*. His temperament was massive and complex, deep-sounding and made for great endurance. From the time when I first got to know him, when he was my Tutor at Oxford, I had sensed his *gravitas*. Yet it was *gravitas* leavened, I am happy to say, by extraordinary wiliness and charm, and by the occasional flash of unpredictable private fun that put you in mind of a waggon-load of monkeys — than which, incidentally, Robert was much cleverer. Much. Robert was as clever as, if not cleverer than, a waggon-load of high civil servants.

It will be apparent to you that I was still in the attitude towards Robert of an undergraduate bowled over by his Tutor, an attitude causing constant irritation to my nearest and dearest, but a source of great satisfaction, not to mention use, to me.

On we go. But not very far. My telephone rang. It was our P.A. (short for personal assistant) saying our Senior Executive Officer wanted to speak to me. While she was putting him through, Robert said:

'Who is it?'

I told him. 'He's got on to me because he wanted to speak to you and you weren't in your room.' I held out the receiver towards him. 'You can speak to him here.'

'He probably wants you in any case.'

23

I hesitated at this display of extra-sensory perception. He who hesitates sees the other man nip gravely out of the room before he can get another breath.

The day's work had begun. I had some people to interview, and Robert had his usual Monday morning commitment, which was a conference with the Under Secretary, Murray-Hamilton, who was technically his boss, and Murray-Hamilton's Assistant Secretary, Spinks. (Perhaps I ought to explain the titles. In the worlds of commerce and industry, your secretary is your subordinate: in the Civil Service, not on your life. Rating in the hierarchy goes up thus: Assistant Principal, Principal, Assistant Secretary, Under Secretary, Deputy Secretary, *Secretary*!)

I was glad to be in my own shoes and not in Robert's. By a mischance that was tiresome to say the least of it, Murray-Hamilton and Spinks strongly disapproved of me. The last thing I would have proposed for my own good was a morning with those two: I did everything I could to keep out of their way. Yet I say this with some ambivalence of feeling. I disapproved of Spinks — 'Stinker Spinks,' I called him to myself — but there was nothing remarkable about that as he was pretty thoroughly disliked by everybody in the department. On the other hand I approved of, even liked Murray-Hamilton. He was first-rate at his job and furthermore he had — what was unusual among senior civil servants — a brooding, reflective look . . . I had not the faintest idea what he was brooding or reflecting about, but I felt drawn to him by his look.

When I met Robert at lunch-time, he did not show signs of having spent the morning with marked enjoyment. He sauntered along the Strand beside me in an abstracted mood, and at a street corner he bought an *Evening News*, which he began to read as he walked along. The pavement was crowded and he covered the rest of the journey by a sort of 'drunkard's walk', bouncing obliquely off passers-by. The morning sunshine was dimmed by now, and a thin mist, very

November-like, seemed to be clinging round the roofs of the tallest buildings. We went into our tea-shop and ordered our usual ladylike snack.

Throughout the meal Robert read his newspaper, so I got no opportunity to refer to any of the topics I had waiting. And when finally he put it down — Robert did not fold up a newspaper when he had finished with it: he just quietly dropped it over the arm of his chair — I saw the heavy, thoughtful look he usually wore when he was irritated or displeased.

'What's the matter?' I asked.

'Nothing of any particular interest.'

I watched him, waiting. His large, light grey eyes appeared to be focussed on his cup of coffee and he was frowning. Suddenly he said:

'Actually there is.' And then he looked away from me. 'I'm fed up with being sniped at by these people.'

He meant Murray-Hamilton and Spinks. I said:

'What about?'

He turned to me.

'You.'

There was a pause.

'What have I done now?' I said.

Robert promptly leaned over and picked up his newspaper again.

'Just general,' he muttered in a tight-lipped way that indicated he was not going to say anything else.

He started to read again.

CHAPTER IV

DINNER WITH TWO DOCTORS

HARRY's wife, Barbara, was a doctor, too. She was intelligent, good-looking, and well-disposed towards me. In manifestation of the latter she had a way of giving me a look that indicated I-know-you-better-than-you-know-yourself.

I told myself I could have taken it more readily from a man than a woman. After all, I conceded, I actually had taken it from at least one man over a period of twenty years, namely from Robert. Of course you may think there was something wrong with me rather than with Barbara — you certainly may if you happen to be a woman. But that does not alter the fact that I found the look hard to take, above all when Barbara gave it me while declaring:

'*You*'ll never get married.'

You see what I mean?

Harry had married slightly above him, both socially, which may or may not be all to the good, and financially, which is beyond all doubt beneficent. Harry and I were quite simply petty bourgeois: Barbara's father, now dead, had been a provincial lawyer of considerable substance, and a portion of this substance had already come down to Barbara — that was how she and Harry came to have such a large house. Her mother, who stayed with them sometimes, was even slightly grand in her manner: she used to take Barbara to race-meetings, which to me, in spite of seeing the Irish dregs of Shepherd's Bush pour out of trains from Newbury at Paddington, always smacked of the idle rich.

At this particular time Harry and Barbara had been married eleven years and had begotten three children. Barbara was about the same age as Harry — they had first met when they were medical students. She was a brisk, energetic woman, with the sort of trimness of body that active women often have, though she was now thickening at the middle. She had a longish face, whose length she enhanced by sweeping her hair up at the sides. Her complexion was unusually fine and very fresh in colour, slightly freckled, and her eyes were a clear, light hazel. They were large, clear, knowing eyes.

'Barbara's a strange girl,' Harry used to say to me.

The first time he said it I was amazed. Active, strong-minded, confident and direct was what she seemed to me. Above all, direct. But when he had said it to me on several occasions, I got over my amazement to the extent of being able to note what *his* emotion was. The look in his eyes was not as usual shrewd and inquisitive: it was sentimental, indulgent . . . Barbara seemed strange to him, I realised, because he *wanted* her to seem strange.

The explanation? Harry was, I think, born to be a faithful and devoted husband — I had in my time come across quite a few men who were clearly born to be the reverse and Harry reminded me of none of them. I turned over in my mind the idea that Harry's curiosity played the absorbing part in his life that sexual adventurousness played in theirs. His wife, to Harry, had simply got to be someone around whom his curiosity could play. Whereas to me she looked like a woman destined to be a local councillor and a Justice of the Peace, to Harry she had got to look as mysterious and enigmatic as the Mona Lisa.

'Barbara's a strange girl,' he said. He was always looking away from me when he said it, clearly meditating on goodness knows what subtleties of mind and convolutions of temperament in his loved one.

I nodded my head. The revelation was mad, but oddly

appealing to me. I could not help liking him all the more for it.

So there you have Harry and Barbara. Oh yes, I have not told you yet that Barbara, as well as running a house and being a mother, also had a part-time job at a children's clinic on the other side of London. I had a feeling that although she found no difficulty in knowing adults better than they knew themselves, children did present her with certain problems. Whether that made things better or worse for the children was a question upon which I used to speculate.

The occasion when Barbara gave me her I-know-you-better-than-you-know-yourself look and simultaneously said '*You*'ll never get married' was the first time I went to dinner with her and Harry after I had gone to live at Putney — uprooted from dilapidated Pimlico, mark you, with her exhortation and Harry's assistance, in order to re-build my dilapidated life. Even if Barbara did know me better than I knew myself, might not she spare me, I wondered, the knowledge of my doom? Might not she and Fate keep it to themselves, as Fate did when operating on its own? Apparently not.

Still, I liked Barbara. And I liked her cooking. I really looked forward to dinner with her and Harry.

The next time I went to dinner at their house after the night Harry asked me if it was true that Robert was going to resign from the Civil Service, Barbara was going to cook a duck. I was very partial to duck. All previous looks and questions were forgiven and forgotten.

Over dinner Harry and I got down, as usual, to a fine professional discussion about classifications of physiques and temperaments. We were recently completely *épris* — if you can use that word about scientists — by the ideas of an American named Sheldon. He seemed to us a master man, not without reason: he had got over the two hurdles which had previously floored everybody else at the start of their operations in 'typing' physiques, namely how to measure up a physique reliably, and how to cope with the obvious fact that it was not a 'type' anyway but something in between.

Harry and I could scarcely wait to start trying out the ideas for ourselves. You cleared the first hurdle by photographing the physique you were proposing to 'type' in a pre-defined posture from the front, side and back, and then you made your comparative measurements from the photographs. You cleared the second by regarding this individual physique as a blend, in different proportions, of your chosen 'types' — the rounded fat man, the cubical muscular man, and the linear skinny man. From your comparative measurements you could make a quantitative assessment of the blend. Quantitative! The thing was beginning to look like a science.

But that was only the half of it. The same idea was paralleled on the side of temperament: in the particular temperament you were proposing to type, you made a similar quantitative assessment of the blend of three 'type' temperaments, these 'type' temperaments being the temperaments that characteristically went with the 'type' physiques. The whole thing tied up, was our verdict.

'It's maddening,' said I, 'that *we* didn't think of it.'

'It's like all the best revolutionary concepts,' said Harry. 'So obvious, so simple!'

You can see how *épris* we were.

At Harry's dinner-table we were concerned not so much with the phon and antiphon of praise as with the prospect of getting down to business on our own. We were agreed that we had got to devise some means of trying out Sheldon's 'somato-typing'.

'If only you could get the M.R.C. to set you up with a research unit!' I said to Harry.

Harry looked at me with baggy bright eyes.

'But surely you,' he said, 'in your job, have all the people we need for it. You've got them all there, simply on tap.'

29

I looked back at him. And well I might! You see, when one refers to physiques in medical society, one is not thinking of their being clothed. I imagined our engineers and scientists being invited, after I had questioned them on their technical life-stories, to go into an adjoining room to be photographed in the stark — from three viewpoints!

'Do you want to get me hounded out of the Civil Service altogether?' I said. I was not thinking what would happen if the *Daily Pictorial* got on to it. I only needed to go as far as thinking what would happen if Murray-Hamilton and Spinks heard of it.

For a moment Harry held his large round head on one side. Barbara intervened.

'Couldn't it be combined with a medical examination?' Sometimes Barbara, instead of saying the most peculiar thing, baffled one by saying the most sensible.

'Not in this set-up,' I said firmly.

Barbara gave Harry a glance, but I did not feel inclined to explain to her.

We had finished our dinner and Barbara said: 'Shall we have our coffee in the drawing-room?'

We went into the drawing-room. The house was Edwardian, massive and ugly but spacious. Harry and Barbara had done it up very agreeably in the first post-war fashion, which was called 'contemporary'. This evening a fire was sparkling in the grate; lamps were glowing in the right places for comfort; and Barbara, wearing a black dress and a big topaz and diamond brooch which set off the colour of her eyes, looked unusually handsome. I said to her:

'That roast duck, Barbara, was simply——' and I made a gesture such as I thought I had seen Italians make in restaurants to indicate that food was delicious.

Barbara laughed. And then she blushed.

I drank my coffee thinking how pleasant life was.

In a desultory way we began to gossip. I scarcely noticed it when Harry first mentioned Sybil. He said he supposed she was coming up to London at Christmas, and I was feeling too relaxed to tell him he was a few days wrong. He was sitting fatly in an armchair whose legs splayed outwards. He was smiling.

'I suppose Robert asks you if you're going to marry her,' he said.

I grinned.

Barbara leaned forward and said to him:

'Does Robert really ask that, do you think?'

'I was saying I *supposed* he did,' said Harry. 'After all, Joe's mother asks me every time I see her.' He glanced at me sideways to see how I took this gambit.

I took it with stupefaction: I knew that it would be unlike Harry not to go and see my mother whenever he went to his own home, but that he was on these terms with her was something that I had not even considered.

Harry was quick to see the effect. He went on with a happy smile:

'Only last week she asked me if you were going to marry "your Sybil".'

This instantly conveyed verisimilitude. The prefix 'your' conveyed without a doubt that my mother had said it, since it evoked the particular tone — unintentional, I ought to say — with which my mother always seemed, to my sensitive ears, to refer to any of my young women.

'Did *she* think I would marry Sybil?' I enquired.

Harry shook his big, globe-shaped head. 'I think she's thought for some time now that you've missed the boat.'

'Missed the boat!'

Harry leaned his head against the back of his chair, and said nothing. Barbara said nothing: there was clearly no need for Barbara to say anything.

After a while, Harry said pensively:

'I like Sybil.' He paused. 'I never understand her.'

I said: 'Nor do I, for that matter. I don't really know her even after fifteen years.'

'And that,' said Barbara promptly, 'doesn't affect your relationship with her?'

You will recall my predicament as I saw it on that night of self-revelation in the bar at Euston. I said to Barbara:

'Not an atom!'

Barbara regarded me.

'There's a very definite split, there,' she said, 'between comprehension and function.'

'I see what you mean,' I said. Suddenly I was delighted, as a lewd transformation of her words occurred to me. 'You mean between knowing and doing.'

Barbara looked mystified. 'Perhaps,' she said firmly.

I turned to Harry. I could see that he was thinking about something else. He said:

'I suppose Robert has in mind whether you're thinking of marrying Sybil——'

I interrupted: 'I'm not thinking of marrying Sybil!'

'—because of his plans to marry Annette.'

'*Is* he going to marry Annette?' said I.

Harry looked at me triumphantly and sympathetically. He said, in a high sweet voice:

'Well, *isn't* he?'

I said nothing now. You see, when Harry told me Robert was going to leave the Civil Service, I was disturbed for the practical reasons that I have since explained. When he told me Robert was going to marry Annette, the disturbance was just as serious but much less worthy of a decent man. Robert and I were comrades in the unmarried state, and my first response to Harry's remark was to foresee another kind of desertion.

I picked up my coffee-cup and held it towards Barbara, asking if I could have some more coffee. And I looked at

Harry, wondering if he knew exactly what sort of dismay his inquisitiveness caused me. He was a clever man, and I had a strong suspicion that he did know. By nature Harry was generous, kindly, devoted — a good man. Yet I could not help thinking that he was also a devil.

CHAPTER V

A COCKTAIL PARTY AT ANNETTE'S

ANNETTE was a sweet girl. Her father was a high civil servant, a very high civil servant indeed.

At that time, Annette was living in her father's flat. She had just come down from doing a D.Phil. in Oxford. Yes, she was quite young, about twenty-five, I suppose, against Robert's forty-four — he was five years older than me. She was young, pretty and clever. The reason I have said she was sweet was that, granted that there is a strain of the cruel, the uncharitable and the ill-disposed in all of us, in Annette it was unusually weak. She was charitable, nicely balanced, quickly stirred to sympathy; in a word — sweet. Robert was very fond of her, and that did not surprise me.

Annette was living in her father's flat while she made up her mind what career to go in for. She was taking her time, partly because she was serious about it and partly because — here, alas, I display my own uncharitableness — in my opinion she had fallen in love with Robert. A feminist would say that a woman's falling in love ought not to make her less serious about choosing a career. I say that if it did not make Annette less serious, certainly it made her slower. Annette's choice seemed to me to show distinct signs of hanging fire that were not to be associated with intellectual or moral difficulties over deciding between becoming say an Oxford don or a Wapping schoolmistress. It did not worry me, of course. Nor did it appear to worry Annette: she seemed pretty happy.

Robert and I went to a cocktail party at Annette's. (It was called 'drinks at six-thirtyish' — the word 'cocktail' was going out.) Robert seemed pretty happy as well. He had been on another cultural expedition to the Zoo with Annette at the week-end. Though Annette's father retired to his house in Berkshire from Friday to Monday, Annette stayed in London, having the flat to herself.

Robert and I went straight to the party from the office. It was a wretched, sleeting night, and the flat was in an area just north of Hyde Park that was salubrious but inaccessible by bus.

'We'd better have a taxi,' I said. 'I'll pay half.'

'No. Why should you?' said Robert. I told you he was pretty happy.

Annette opened the door to us. Before she had come to live in the flat her father had had a servant, but Annette had insisted on dispensing with her.

'Hello, darling,' said Robert, and gave her a hug of noticeable warmth before taking off his overcoat.

Annette stood back — she was a short, sturdy girl — and looked up at him. Her eyes were shining with amusement and pleasure.

'You can't pretend he isn't spontaneous, in spite of all they say about him,' I said to her.

Annette shook her head. Her hair was straight and cut plainly in a bell-shaped bob: when she shook her head one expected to hear a sweet lucid peal. She took hold of Robert's hand for a moment.

'Come in,' she said.

I thought: 'Well, there you are . . .' and took off my overcoat.

We went into the living-room, which was L-shaped, the walls of the foot of the L being covered with books, and the walls of the stem, which included the windows and the fire-place, being panelled with a light-coloured wood. Annette's father was both a scholar and a traveller, and the objects of decoration in the room were chiefly small pieces of classical statuary. Between the windows there was a statue of a

35

woman, headless and draped, which I should like to have owned.

The party was for Annette's friends, and though Robert and I were the only two civil servants there, also the only two novelists, we were not the only two men who were more than ten years older than Annette. A very satisfactory state of affairs, I thought: the world was all the better a place for the existence of girls like Annette. There were, of course, some young women of Annette's age. I saw a girl I had met there before, a painter from behind the Fulham Road, and one of Annette's Oxford girl-friends who did philosophy too. Still better a place! I recognised some of the men — they were chiefly academic persons, philosophers, some sociologists, and a young scientist whom I had once interviewed for a job. I noted that Harry was not there, or, as I put it to myself, had for once not managed to get in.

Perhaps I ought to have explained before that there was a connection between Harry and Annette. Harry had discovered that Annette's brother, who was a doctor, had been a house-surgeon at the hospital where Barbara had done her clinical training. Though Harry and Barbara now looked on him with the special contempt they reserved for anybody who had become a gynaecologist, this did not diminish Harry's use for the connection or his satisfaction with having unearthed it. I may say that for Harry this passed as a strong connection. When he saw that Annette was a figure in my life and Robert's, he would have found a connection, even if it was that the housemaid Annette had dispensed with happened to be the illegitimate grand-niece of the organist at the church where my father preached his first sermon.

Half an hour later, to make a change from talking to people, I went over to have another look at the statue that fascinated me. I put out my forefinger and drew it lightly, for the sensuous experience, down the folds in the drapery. Then I looked at my forefinger, the receptor of that experience. It was black with dust. There was a good thick layer of dust on the top of the table on which the statue was standing. There was also a pile of books, new books. I picked up the top one and opened it — a review slip fell out and floated down to the floor.

'Are you really going to read that?' It was Annette who spoke. She was standing beside me, laughing.

I retrieved the review slip and put the book back on the pile. It was a philosophical work.

'Is it any good?' I asked.

'I haven't read it yet. I'm going to review it.'

I looked at her with curiosity, as one does at any young person who is going to be entrusted with passing a professional opinion upon a matter of serious import. My interest switched from curiosity to approval. Annette was pretty and her complexion was beyond compare. She never wore any make-up, and there, in all its incomparableness, was her complexion exposed as it might be to one's forefinger. Fine, clear, high-coloured, and glossy with the sheen that comes from heartily washing it with soap. Her lips, without lipstick, were simply red. I did not know why Annette saw fit never to use make-up, but I never felt inclined to question the result. I brought my mind back to her books.

'Have they all seen,' I asked, referring to the authors, 'the great truth that metaphysics is bunk?'

This was my standard joke, for what it was worth, when I was talking to Annette. She belonged to an up-to-date school of philosophers whom I habitually referred to as the 'metaphysics-is-bunk' school, out of what Barbara would have called a distinctly ambivalent attitude. Though I felt that any school of philosophers ought to be treated with irreverence, I was far from sure that I did not think metaphysics was bunk myself.

I had never got over a crucial moment in my young manhood, when, hearing my father proclaim his favourite text, 'God is Love', for the I-don't-know-how-manyth time, I

37

suddenly realised that it did not mean anything to me and I could not see what it could mean. This was a shock. 'God is Love' — I kept thinking and thinking about it, focussing on the word *is*, which now appeared so incredibly between the other two. The only circumstances, I kept thinking pigheadedly, in which God and Love can have *is* between them is not if God is a person and Love is what we all mean by love, but if God and Love are words, merely words.

I had never got over it. Some words were only words: my father's favourite text was a piece of literary algebra. Of course I had been subsequently shown the error of my thought, but it had permanently coloured my approach to metaphysics.

'We don't say metaphysics is bunk,' Annette said. She laughed as if she were amused by my joke, but did not hesitate to correct me just the same. 'We just think there aren't any platonic essences that many of the words we use in metaphysics would have to correspond to — if they were going to have the meaning we've chosen to give them.'

'H'm,' I said, not committing myself to agreeing with her — or understanding her, for that matter. Yet, you can see how, when I was talking to Annette, though I might have been shown the error of my thought I was not entirely convinced by the demonstration.

'Such words as Truth,' I said, doing my best to fall into the swing of things.

'Such words as Truth.' She shook her head, and her bell of hair swung to and fro.

At that, something made me think of my father's second favourite text: 'God is Truth.' Oh dear!

However, I have to say that it was a comfort of sorts to have a young woman like Annette, clever as paint and much admired in academic circles, to assure me that some of the words of which I had never been able to grasp the common use, such as my father's, could with advantage cease to be used in that way.

'Now, what are you two talking about?' Robert interrupted us.

'Scarcely anything,' I said. 'We've only just started.'

Annette looked up at Robert. I could have removed myself to the other end of the room without her noticing. Robert returned her look. I thought they must be intending to get married.

At that moment I noticed Annette's father in the doorway. He glanced round the room as if he were not certain whether to join the party. I heard Robert say:

'Darling, there's your father.'

'Oh yes,' said Annette.

One might have expected that Annette would hasten across to her father and that Robert would remain with me. On the contrary, it was Robert who lost no time in going across to Annette's father. Annette stayed where she was.

'I hope somebody will give Daddy a drink,' she said.

I laughed at her idea of a hostess's functions. Annette was oddly shy about some things, and entertaining was one of them. She liked having parties and got as far as inviting the guests, but at that point she seemed to get paralysed. I did not understand why, though I felt it might be connected with shyness. And yet, was it? Was it really shyness that made her go without make-up and appear at this kind of party wearing a shapeless woolly jumper and skirt?

'Oughtn't you to go and give him one?' I asked.

'It's all right — Emma's giving him some sherry.' Emma was the painter from behind the Fulham Road. Her name was Margaret, but she was always called Emma. She was a big girl, wearing a sweater and trousers, these, paint-stained, being the current uniform of her set. There was a scruffy-looking man with her in an identical outfit. I had never seen them dressed, at any time of day, in anything different; and pointing to the two of them, I said to Annette:

'Do they take those things off to go to bed?' thinking they looked as if they slept in them.

39

'Emma doesn't go to bed with *him*,' said Annette. 'I mean, not now. Or at least only now and then.'

'Oh,' I said. 'Oh.'

It was only asking for difficulties, to try and explain now what I had originally wanted to know, so I paused, and then said:

'There seem to be some sociologists here.'

Annette said: 'I don't think I should really like to work with sociologists.' She explained thoughtfully: 'The trouble with all the social sciences is that their laws are reducible to laws of individual psychology. It means they lack the autonomy that the physical sciences have.'

'Oh,' I said. I had been trained in the physical sciences — in physics, to be precise. Her remark sounded favourable to me, so I said 'Oh' again, more enthusiastically.

I looked at her, and found that she was looking at me. Her eyes were a clear bright brown. Her cheeks were glowing.

'Annette,' I said, 'you're a sweet girl.'

She said shyly:

'I do want to marry Robert. Do you think there's any chance?'

CHAPTER VI

THE RECURRING SITUATION

D ID I think there was any chance of Robert marrying her — well might Annette ask! I told her, Yes, of course, but I did not see fit to prolong the conversation by discussing the length of the odds. As Robert had reached the age of forty-four without getting married, it was obvious that he was not the sort of man who takes to matrimony like a duck to water. And though he stood in no danger of being written-off, like me, he did lay himself open, clearly, to the charge of being reluctant. Poor old Robert.

In fact there was more to it than common reluctance, in Robert's case. We had discussed it a good many times. In the past he had fallen so deeply in love as to overcome common reluctance. But on each occasion the girl had been so odd, so eccentric, or even so crazy, that somehow the upshot, partly through her own actions and partly through a final move for self-preservation on Robert's part, had been no marriage.

Suspicious, that! you might say. Why did he not fall in love with someone who was sufficiently ordinary, sufficiently uncrazy — after all, there were lots of pretty girls who came into that category — to be marriageable? The only answer Robert seemed able to find was that they, the ordinary, uncrazy ones, did not seem to him so fascinating.

In the present situation, though, the fact seemed to me that Annette, while eccentric enough to be fascinating, was sufficiently uncrazy as not to be likely to hit him on the head with a bottle of whisky or take an overdose of aspirins — two of the deterrents to matrimony which had come his way in the past. There was definitely a chance for Annette, I thought.

It appeared, the following day, that Robert thought the same thing. He came into my office first thing in the morning, and sat on the corner of my desk.

'That was a very good party, last night,' he said.

I said it was.

He paused, and then said in a different tone:

'I don't know what to do. Ought I to marry Annette?'

I did not reply. Throughout our lives we had often asked each other's advice on matters of this kind. We had never taken it.

I was thinking what to say. We had never taken each other's advice in the exact form in which it was given: what we did was something tangential, something based on what the other advised, but modified by our own impulses, sensible or otherwise.

'She's a sweet girl,' I said.

Robert said: 'Of all the women I've known, she's easily the sweetest.'

'What's holding you back?'

He shrugged his shoulders and did not answer for a long time. I just waited. He said:

'It's hard to say. Some sort of instinct about the future. It's rather hard to place it exactly. Annette's easily the sweetest girl I've ever known, but that doesn't mean that in some ways she's not very' — he tried to find the right word — 'self-concerned. For instance, she attaches much more importance to some of the decisions, in particular the moral decisions, she makes than I ever should.'

'Isn't this part of the current fashion among philosophers?'

'If you mean is it something that has nothing to do with her natural inclinations, I think the answer is No. I think the fashion suits her rather well.'

I thought it over, and said:

'But isn't this all a bit theoretical? I don't see why it should cause any special practical difficulties.'

'Nor can I. And yet something tells me it will.'

'Then don't marry her!' I said, knowing this was the last thing he wanted me to say — his last sentence had ended in 'will'.

Robert laughed and stood up.

'Do you happen to have that file about revised salary scales?' he said in a completely different tone, lofty and rather official. 'It would be a bit of a help if you'd clear it pretty rapidly.'

I was delighted by the change. It was one of Robert's gifts to have at his finger-tips, so to speak, the capacity for chameleon-like transformation.

'Spinks is asking for it,' he went on. 'He seems to think you're holding it up.'

'I'm *not* holding it up!' I said. 'It only came in yesterday.'

Robert shrugged his shoulders and went out of the room.

'Really!' I shouted at the door as he pulled it to behind him.

I began my day's work by dealing immediately with the file about revised salary scales. And, in case you would like to know, I wished Spinks could get sacked.

During the next few days I did not see very much of Robert. It was on the following Sunday afternoon that he turned up unexpectedly at the club to which we both belonged. He knew that I was likely to be there, because on Sundays I usually spent the day at the club to save having to get my own meals at my flat. I lunched with about half a dozen members who enjoyed bachelordom in various degrees of confirmation ranging from that of elderly specimens of my own species to that of middle-aged married men whose wives had left them. Afterwards I took my manuscript to the library to work, and they mostly went into the reading-room to sleep.

At tea-time I had come down to a small central room that

was the Piazza San Marco of the club, normally astir with gossipers having tea or drinks but to-day deserted. It would have been cosy had there not been so many doors always open for people to go through to other rooms. Lights were shining over pictures lent by members of the club, but the chandelier in the middle of the room had not been switched on. I was sitting beside the fire, munching a piece of anchovy toast and reading the novel reviews in the previous Friday's *Times Literary Supplement*. Someone came in and I looked up. It was Robert.

I exclaimed with surprise.

'I thought I'd find you here,' he said, sitting down at the other end of the sofa I was sitting on.

I held up the *Times Literary Supplement* and said:

'You'll observe that I'm keeping up with literature.'

Expecting that, as usual when he found himself having a casual meal with me, he would pick up a newspaper and read, I began, for once, to read myself. A servant brought in a tray with Robert's tea on it and put it on a small table in front of him. Robert poured a cup of tea and then said:

'I'd like you to put that down for a moment, if you will.'

He was looking both solemn and excited. He said:

'I came to see you because I wanted you to be the first person to know that Annette and I are going to get married. We decided last night.'

'That's excellent!' I cried, and shook him by the hand. 'I'm delighted. I hope you'll be as happy, as happy as anybody can be!'

I really was delighted. And I really did feel, suddenly, unutterably wretched. I was devoted to him, I had been whole-heartedly wretched on his behalf when he was having disastrous love affairs — in fact the occasions of the whisky bottle and the overdose of aspirins had been not funny but bitterly serious — but now, when he was going to be happy, I was not whole-heartedly delighted. Envy, the most unpleasing and the most common of emotions, suddenly caught

44

me. In the midst of thinking how glad I was for him, I wished, yes, I wished it were *I* instead of him.

Robert was watching me. I remembered well his once having observed epigrammatically that it was easier to sympathise with one's friends in their defeats than in their victories.

'I thought you would,' I said, meaning 'would marry Annette'.

He laughed. His laughter sounded confident, relieved and faintly rueful. 'There's a difference between thinking one will and actually doing it.' His glance seemed to become more penetrating. 'As you'll discover for yourself.'

Of course he knew I must be wishing it were I. I said: 'Robert, do you think I *shall*?'

'Think you shall what?'

'Do it?'

He did not answer me immediately. Then he said: 'That depends on you. On what you make up your mind to.'

'Make up my mind to?' I said. 'Surely one doesn't make up one's mind to something, just like that. . . . It's got to arise from one's nature. . . .'

An elderly member with a stick made his way slowly through the room, greeting us as he passed. We smiled at him — in the ordinary way we should have encouraged the poor old man to stop — and then we waited for him to go.

As soon as he was through one of the far doorways, I said to Robert:

'One's behaviour falls into a pattern that arises from one's nature. The reason the pattern gets fixed is because one's nature is pretty fixed, though we don't like to think it is.'

I was referring to a theory Robert and I had of human behaviour, which depended on what we called the Recurring Situation. It was particularly easy to identify in people's sexual lives. Time after time we had seen our friends, not to mention ourselves, embark on a sexual gambit which might superficially look as if it were something new, but

45

which, as time went on, led to a familiar situation — if it were not leading to it in the natural course of events, the instigator of it seemed to force it, himself, into the familiar shape. We got the impression that for many men there was a characteristic situation to which, from whatever point they started, they always tended.

Sitting beside the fire in the club that Sunday afternoon, Robert and I did not discuss all this because we had discussed it at length many a time before. We had accepted our own behaviour as examples of our theory. Certainly Robert had arrived often enough at the situation of being deeply in love with a woman who was — it seemed to him — just that bit too crazy for him to risk marrying her.

In my own case, the recurring situation was twofold: I always found myself either wanting to marry someone who would not marry me or not wanting to marry someone who would. There was no future in my recurring situation, either way.

'I'm not sure it's so completely fixed,' said Robert.

'What?'

'Either the pattern or one's nature. One can be too rigid about these things.'

'Indeed!' I said, rather as if I were in favour of rigidity.

'Yes,' said Robert.

He suddenly gave me a quick, odd glance that made me pull up. I stared at him and then tried to laugh.

'You're not trying to take my recurring situation away from me, are you?' I said.

Robert shrugged his shoulders.

When I was first describing my predicament, I observed how many of us, poor fish that we are, are rather attached to our predicaments, are even a bit proud of them. We also, I might have added, tend to find them something stable in our lives. Take them away — even, as it might appear for our own good — and we are left faced with . . . we know not what. It is the same with the recurring pattern. We want to get out of it, and yet also we want to stay in it. I do not pretend to be able to explain my own ambivalence — nor the ambivalence of most of the human race, for that matter. Double, double, we are all double. . . .

'I have always granted,' said Robert, 'that there is a recurring pattern. But there are times when it's possible to break out of it.'

Even if his reply might be going to take the ground from under my feet, I said:

'How?'

'By an act of will.'

An act of *will*! 'Like all the best revolutionary concepts, so simple, so obvious . . .'

I did not say anything. I knew it was true. An act of will could get me out of my recurring pattern. I felt as if the ground really had been taken from under my feet. And yet at the same moment I was feeling something opposite. It was a thrill of — what? I had not the slightest doubt what it was a thrill of. It was of hope.

PART II

CHAPTER I

CHRISTMAS EVE IN THE CIVIL SERVICE

THE first and only occasion Spinks set foot in my office —
you can imagine I never went out of my way to invite
him across just for the sake of his *beaux yeux* — was on
the afternoon when we shut down that year for Christmas.
Every Christmas Eve Murray-Hamilton and Spinks did the
rounds of their own people and then of ours on a visit of
goodwill. The members of staff most affected by the prospect
of the visit were the messengers, though I could never see
why, since the only duty that fell upon their cadre was that
two of them should hold the lift doors open while Murray-
Hamilton and Spinks got out. But affected they were: their
bush telegraph, which in the summer circulated up-to-the-
minute Test Match scores, hummed all afternoon with
the current movements, from room to room, of the touring
party.

It was unusual for Spinks to deliver the goodwill message
to me in my own office. At this stage of the Christmas Eve's
proceedings, Robert and I were usually at the tea-party
which our own people held in the room where most of them
worked. This room was referred to by Robert and me as
the big room, and by some of its racier inhabitants, I gleaned
from passing the time of day with them in the lavatory, as the
snake-pit. The room and what went on in it interested me,
but my communication with its inhabitants was supposed to
be on paper, or if it was a personal matter, through our Senior
Executive Officer, who was their boss. At this rate, had it
not been for the lavatory, which was small and over-
crowded, I should never have identified some of our clerks,

let alone — for hygiene is a great leveller — have picked up some of their racier observations.

Perhaps in fairness to the service, I ought to interpolate that Spinks's minion responsible for 'accommodation' was shocked when I made him note how small, over-crowded and dirty our lavatory was, shocked that Robert and I had to use the same one as our clerks.

Anyway, there was the snake-pit having a party and Robert and I sitting in our own offices not invited. And this year it was not a tea-party, far from it. The inhabitants had collected money for drink, and by keeping the collection to themselves had set up a neat basis for excluding outsiders. And why was it, I speculated, as I listened to the sounds of entertainment echo down the corridor, that the inhabitants of the snake-pit wanted to exclude outsiders? There were two possible explanations. The first was that they thought Robert and I were stinkers. The second — this was more than an explanation: it was fact — was that our Senior Executive Officer had got at loggerheads with them.

The chief messenger put his head round the door, which I had left open.

'Mr. Murray-Hamilton and Mr. Spinks have got separated, sir. Over in Registry. That'll be, Mr. Spinks is coming on first. And then Mr. Murray-Hamilton sort of after him.'

Thinking of the lift doors, I said: 'Twice as much work for you.'

A burst of riotous noise came from down the corridor. He wagged his head towards it.

'If Mr. Murray-Hamilton and Mr. Spinks don't get here before long, they'll be dancing down there.'

'Dancing? Will they really?' I said. I was very fond of dancing. Also of drink, too.

'Ar,' he said. Having been leaning a little forward, he now shifted his weight comfortably over his heels. Then he said:

'Have you seen the decorations this year, sir?'

'Yes. I glanced in.'

'Not so good as last year's,' he said.

'Not so necessary,' said I, thinking of last year's tea-party and this year's saturnalia.

'Ar.'

Our conversation went on for a few minutes in this vein, counterpointed by sounds from down the corridor. When he had said they would be dancing in the big room, he had meant it metaphorically, but in point of fact somebody had brought a portable gramophone. We heard music.

'Shall I leave the door open, sir?' he said, when he thought it was time to go back and take his place in the bush-telegraph.

'Do. I should like to hear the music.'

I wondered if they really would dance, and what sort of dancing it would be. When I have referred to saturnalia in the big room, I may have given the wrong impression about its inhabitants. Every year, after the Senior Executive Officer had brought in to Robert their annual reports, Robert said without fail to me in an awed tone:

'You'd be surprised how old some of them are.'

I was not in the least surprised, since the S.E.O. reminded me of it every time I found something to complain about in the work of the office. We had what I agreed was a higher proportion than might be expected of clerks who were past retiring age. In fact I sometimes thought there was evidence for what the S.E.O. was always suggesting, that Spinks's side of the organisation used our side as a dumping ground for crocks and misfits in general. We had our share of them: a walk through the big room confirmed that. Had we more than our share?

'It's one of the results of full employment, Froggatt,' I said. (That was the S.E.O.'s name.)

His expression combined deference with disbelief. He argued that Spinks's side of the organisation were dumping crocks and misfits on us so as to use our resulting inefficiency as a reason for taking us over themselves — the argument had its points, of course.

So the saturnalia that was going on in the big room, under the shade of brightly coloured paper chains, tinsel balls, and squares of cardboard (inscribed with peculiar mottoes) that floated in the air like mobiles, was not an affair of nymphs and satyrs — not unless you are prepared to face the fact that some of us stay nymphs and satyrs till we have one foot in the grave.

> '*I'd like to get you,*' sounded the music,
> '*On a slow boat to China . . .*'

'It would have to be damned slow for some of you,' I thought, having in mind not the aged ones, who were rather nippy, but some of the forty-year-old clock-watchers, who were more bone idle than I could have imagined. Slow! If they had not had all the office-hours in which to do their football pools they would never have got them in in time.

I looked at my watch. Half past five. The sooner Spinks and Murray-Hamilton came in with their Christmas handshake the sooner I could go home. There was no more work to be done — or anything else, for that matter. I wondered whether to go into Robert's room, but thought I had better not as he was doing some re-writing of his next novel. I might have gone into the small room where our P.A. and one or two of her colleagues worked, but I thought they would be busy clearing up the remains of the Christmas tea-party they had loyally given for Robert and me and Froggatt and the H.E.O.'s, in default of our being invited to the saturnalia. I had my own next novel to work on, but somehow I was never able to get going in the office, being inhibited either by files coming in or the likelihood of files coming in — remember that unlike Robert, who was part-time, I was full-time.

The chief messenger's head came round the door-cheek.

'Mr. Spinks has just left the other side, sir. They say he's got Mr. Jacques with him.'

54

I cannot say the news affected my spirits one way or the other. At that particular moment it did not occur to me that the visit could either have any effect or lead to any action. I did not object to the addition of Jacques, for I liked him. He was the minion I referred to a moment ago as responsible to Spinks for 'accommodation'. It seemed to me that, as a civil servant, his talent for execution was well eclipsed by his talent for sycophancy. He was a tall stringy man with large eyes and a pleasant voice; and like all successful sycophants, he was born with a genuine desire to please: if I had to choose between that and a genuine desire to kick people in the teeth, I chose that. Also I judged that while Jacques sucked up to Spinks with natural abandon, he did not in the least care for him as a man.

'Thank you,' I said to the chief messenger. 'Perhaps you might shut the door now. You know . . . it will give them something to open.'

'Ar,' he said with a non-comprehending grin. I regretted the door's being shut, because from down the corridor came the sound of the gramophone playing, amid delighted shrieks:

'A-hunting we will go! . . .'

'What *can* they be doing to that?' I said to him.

He shook his head. 'I don't know, sir.' He was not interested, other than in the sounds as a manifestation, I thought, of the difference between how the upper and the lower orders behaved.

I was left alone, quiet, in my rather large room. I had switched on only half the lights, so as to enhance the dirtiness of the walls which must once have been painted by the Ministry of Works in a shade known to them, I believed, as primrose. My picture on the far wall was crooked, which puzzled me, since the office-cleaners never touched it. Below it the tablecloth formed a long rectangle of dead navy-blue — it was a piece of felt that had been used during

55

the war for black-out curtains: Robert had got rid of his, leaving his table-top bare, but I kept mine as a souvenir.

I sat swinging around in my chair, waiting for the visit.

Spinks and Jacques came in. They looked hearty and bright, and had clearly been fortified on their way at some-body else's party. They brought in a distinctly Christmassy air, and suddenly we all shook hands in one of those waves of *bonhomie* that sometimes sweep unpredictably through a group of men who hate each other's guts.

'I didn't expect to find you in here,' said Spinks, glancing round my office.

'We had a small sedate tea-party on our own,' I said, and explained that we had not been invited to the non-tea-party down the corridor.

I do not intend to describe Spinks, certainly not in any way which might lead anyone in the Civil Service to think this is supposed to be him. I will content myself with saying that he did not look the detestable man he was. Had you met him you might have presumed he was a man whose wife and children were probably fond of him: they were. It would have been a shock to hear that he was the most detested man in our part of the world: he was.

'This is your office?' he said.

As he was also one of the cleverest men in our part of the world, I thought he must either be drunk or so little inter-ested that he did not care what he was saying. He did not look in the least drunk. Jacques, I was happy to see, did look drunk — he rocked slightly and said:

'It's dark in here.' He caught my eye. 'We must do something about it.' His glance moved critically round the walls. 'A coat of paint . . .'

I knew that he would not get them a coat of paint, but I thought it was amiable of him to have said it. You see why I liked him. Spinks was looking at my bookshelf.

'Are these your books?'

56

'Yes.' They were a very odd collection of throw-outs from my flat, ranging from a second copy of *The Tale of Genji* to a first copy of *The Admiralty Handbook of Wireless Telegraphy.*

At this it appeared that the Christmas visit was over. Spinks and Jacques smiled at each other and then at me. Then we all shook hands again and said, 'Well, a happy Christmas,' and they went out of the room. It seemed, as an incident, harmless enough, in fact positively innocuous. I hung about until they had gone, and then went and did a similar round of our own people while I waited for Murray-Hamilton. And that was that.

But was it that? One day in the week after we came back after Christmas, Robert and I were strolling along to our tea-shop for lunch, when Robert said:

'By the way, you'd better get one of those trays for your desk, to keep papers in.'

Let me explain. The Civil Service provided a long compartmented tray for the top of one's desk, the compartments usually being labelled In and Out. (The current joke among bosses was to propose four compartments labelled In, Out, Pending, and Too Difficult.) On the grounds that our P.A. always brought in my work in the morning, always took it out when I had done it, and hung on to anything that was pending till the morning when she could bring it in ready for me to do, I had got rid of the tray. A dust-collector, I thought it.

'What on earth for?' I said.

'I know you do a lot of work, but it makes it look as if you don't.' He was not looking at me.

'To whom does it make it look as if I don't?' I asked. For once I thought Robert could put up with having his evasiveness on this kind of topic punctured.

'Just tell me *whom*!' I said.

Robert put his head down. After a pause he said in a muffled, distant voice:

'As it were Spinks.'

I was too enraged to speak. I have to admit that my immediate cause of rage was not so much Spinks's being beastly as his being beastly on Christmas Eve. On Christmas Eve! The fact that Christmas had little significance, either religious or sentimental for me, affected me not at all.

When we got back to the office after lunch I told our P.A. to get me a dust-collector for my desk and then I spent a few minutes considering Spinks.

It seemed to me that the first fact to take into consideration was that Spinks was going to find it hard to get a lot further in the Civil Service than his present mid-grade of Assistant Secretary. Somehow, somewhere among his seniors, a decision had been come to that he was not going to be one of the successes.

This may seem odd. It seemed odd to me. Yet often I felt that the final verdict on a man's career had been pretty well settled, whether he knew it or not, by the time he was forty. A spell in the Cabinet Office, a spell in the Treasury, and the word must have gone round the reaches above him: 'He'll go a lot further,' or 'He won't.' In a way it was not difficult to explain. Firstly, with the Administrative Class being very small compared with the Service as a whole, the number of bosses was small enough for them all to know each other well, and so for the judgment to get around easily. Secondly, the bosses (*a*) were clever men, and (*b*) took to this kind of assessing and judging with enthusiasm. There was nothing to show that they made many mistakes either. Mind you, they were not without the power to help their own prophecies along: the man who was tipped for success got the more exciting jobs, while the man who was tipped for failure was headed towards some backwater of the Service.

If Spinks had not been so beastly to me, I should have been sorry for him. It seemed to me that he must have been tipped for un-success and was perceptive enough to have seen it — remember that in this particular sphere, men's perceptions have a notable record of letting them down: it is very hard indeed to perceive that you are tipped for un-success.

And what about me? By not becoming a permanent civil servant I had not entered the competition. I wanted to stay where I was, working with Robert, till the day of liberation through the art of letters. I was not to be tipped for going further or for not. As I sat at my desk considering Spinks, I perceived that the two alternatives for which I could be tipped were for being allowed to stay where I was or for being pushed out altogether.

I felt rage again. I recalled Robert's being sniped at about me. Granted that I was by nature MISC/INEL, what, I wanted to know, did I *do* that was wrong? After all, it seemed to me, I was paid my salary for choosing and looking after scientists; not for what I was.

Obviously one of the things I did that was wrong, was not having a tray on my desk.

I ask you . . .!

CHAPTER II

FALLING IN LOVE

THOUGH Barbara had laid it down as axiomatic that I would not, or could not, get married, she and Harry introduced me from time to time to fresh girls. I was never sure what, if one of them caught my attention, I was supposed to do — I sometimes knew what I wanted to do, but that, of course, was a different matter. I usually met fresh girls when she and Harry gave a party.

Harry and Barbara gave excellent parties. Their drawing-room was big enough to dance in; there was plenty of drink; and the guests covered a wide and entertaining range of society. Their 'party of the year' was on New Year's Eve, when they invited, so they said, everyone they knew, irrespective of social status. Certainly the range in social status of the people who turned up was wide enough to make this explanation seem plausible. There were people from the M.R.C. of rank both some distance above and well below Harry's: there were distinguished doctors and probationer nurses, professors and laboratory assistants; and a smattering of people connected with the arts — a painter or two, two or three writers, and some journalists. Also there was a collection of persons whose profession was not clearly defined, to say the least of it. I used to look forward to New Year's Eve at Harry's.

I had not told Harry and Barbara about my new source of hope. The concept of changing one's fate by an act of will — especially when it referred to my fate not to get married being changed by an act of my will, such as it was — was not likely to impress Barbara. I was not certain how much it impressed me. I felt cautious about it. I contemplated my will, such as it was.

Before I went to the party I had been seeing off Sybil at Euston. As well as coming to London, for a few days before Christmas, she had managed to fit in a few days after. Barbara had asked me if I would like to bring her to the party.

'She's planned to go home,' I said, hoping to dismiss the idea.

'Surely some plans are made to be broken?' said Barbara.

'They form a small category, compared with that of plans that are meant to be kept.'

Barbara gave me a sidelong penetrating look. 'Very well, then,' she said. 'Come alone!'

As that was what I had always intended to do, I felt I might now relax to the extent of assuming a mournful expression.

'Always alone . . .' I murmured, as if I were speaking to myself and not to her.

And yet, when I sat in the bar at Euston after Sybil had gone, I felt genuinely mournful. The recurring pattern had just recurred.

'A Guinness, please,' I said.

If I stopped the pattern, in its most immediate sense, recurring, I was not going to see Sybil again. Sybil sitting in buses trying to distinguish male passers-by from female; Sybil standing at bus-stops clutching her beaver-lamb coat round her; Sybil lying quietly on her back reciting soliloquies, long soliloquies, from the plays of Shakespeare . . . all over, all gone.

I have to say here and now that it never for one moment occurred to me that, if I did get married, it need not necessarily be all over, all gone. To men who did not take getting married seriously, to men who could get married at the drop of a hat, it might have, it would have, appeared differently. Not so to me. I took getting married very seriously indeed.

Few men could have taken it more seriously than I intended to take it.

'And a ham sandwich,' I said, thinking that if I were going to drink a lot at the party it would be well to have food inside me at the start.

'The recurring pattern . . .' I said to myself, lifting the glass of Guinness to my mouth. '*Can* I break it?'

By the time the waitress brought me the ham sandwich I was shaking my head even more mournfully. I was back again at the contemplation of my will. It's going to take a long time, I was thinking. A long, long time. There was not a soul, probably not even Robert, who believed I could do it. I ate the sandwich.

All the same, however long it was going to take me to break the recurring pattern, I decided to go home before the party and spruce myself up. There was no need to let everybody know that life had got me down. I put on my newest suit, and a bow tie to indicate that I was more of an artist than a civil servant. Then I walked briskly, if not hopefully, from the block of flats where I lived to Harry's Edwardian mansion.

It was a warm and drizzly New Year's Eve that year, and every so often the overhanging ornamental trees in people's front gardens let fall large drops of accumulated rainwater, plop among the specks of drizzle, on my head. Lights were shining from almost every window of Harry's house, and as I walked up the drive I could hear the sound of dance-music. There was a clutter of cars in the roadway and drive, and I noticed some bicycles propped against the large cast-iron dog, a greyhound I think it was, which stood heraldically beside the front door.

The eldest of Harry's children, a boy of nine looking extraordinarily pleased with himself at being allowed up so late, took my coat from me and pointed out to me where his mother was. Already cheered up by the party atmosphere, I kissed Barbara.

'You look very nice,' I said. She had altered the way in which her hair was done. Instead of being severely swept up at the sides it hung softly and loosely over her ears. Her skin glowed with high colour, and the confidence in her clear hazel eyes was masked by excitement. Active, strong-minded and knowing, Barbara nevertheless had a girlish love of giving parties.

'You do look nice,' I said. Then I felt the rush of air that preceded Harry's whirling up to join us.

'Come along inside!' he said in a high hallooing voice, while mopping his forehead with a handkerchief. 'We've got some pretty girls for you.'

It crossed my mind that, faithful and respectable husband though Harry might be, the pretty girls were perhaps not invited for the delectation of only his guests.

'We want you to dance,' said Barbara. 'We've collected a lot more records for to-night, jivey ones.'

'Why, how did you know? Jive is my second favourite activity.' I thought it was a very old quip.

Barbara gave me a satisfied look. 'I see the connection!' she said.

I went first of all to the room where they had rigged up a small bar and helped myself to a drink. The room was crowded. Standing just inside the door, where I had missed him when I came in, was Robert, talking to a man whom I saw was Harry's M.R.C. boss. I caught Robert's eye and waved to him. Then, having emptied my glass, I had it filled up again and pushed my way through the drinkers to the drawing-room.

Barbara's description of the records was apt enough. As I reached the door I heard a stirring performance of the 'Chicken Reel' coming out of the radiogram. I supposed that although the record happened to have been made a long time ago, it was Barbara's interest in the 'contemporary' that had led her to get it for a party like this. True, in one corner of the room a couple of young men with their hair done in cow-licks — I took them to be lab-assistants — were jiving with their girls: but the rest of the floor was occupied by persons of higher social status indomitably doing the dance they did on all occasions, a sort of walk.

I put down my glass on the nearest ledge and looked round for a partner. Somebody had got to show the flag for persons of higher social status. There was a girl standing quite close to me, watching the dancers while a heavy-jowled man beside her appeared to be advancing the fact that he did not dance as a reason for surreptitiously groping round her waist. I did not blame him. She was dark-haired and comely. Nor did I see why I should not stop him instantly.

'Why don't you dance?' I said to her.

She gave me a surprised half-glance and then laughed.

'Why not?' she said. With a twist she was out of his reach and lifting her hand for me to take hold of. 'I've been wanting to . . .'

She had a pale complexion and she was dressed in a rosy, coral colour. I wondered, somewhat late in the day, if she could dance.

'Let's go over there,' I said, and led her over to where we could congregate with the lab-assistants and their partners.

It was all right—she could dance. A bit too quick on the lead, I thought, but that did not matter: it showed she was anxious to please. I was not looking at her most of the time we danced, because I had been given to understand that in this sort of dance one was supposed to appear abstracted and independent, if not actually schizophrenic. Of course I did glance at her now and then. I was puzzled: she seemed easy-going and relaxed, and yet she was too quick on the lead. How could that be?

The record ended. Before anyone else could forestall him, one of the lab-assistants, both knowing and determined, turned the record over. On the other side was the 'Dark Town Strutters' Ball'.

'Wonderful!' I said to my partner. 'Now we'll really get hep!'

And we did. Her glowing dress spun out this way and that; her short dark hair flopped over her forehead.

'Now!' I cried, flicking her right hand downward behind her waist and catching it on the other side — giving it a spiral tug upwards could send her spinning twice without having to be let go. It *would* have sent her spinning twice without having to be let go, had she not suddenly staggered.

'Oh!' she cried.

She was nearly on the floor before I managed to grasp her. I lifted her. As her head came slowly upwards we looked each other in the face, close to, for the first time. I saw grey eyes, brilliantly sparkling, looking into mine, long red lips twitching up at the corners in chagrined laughter——

I could go on with the description, but I cannot wait to come to the point. We were looking each other in the face, close to, for the first time. I thought:

This one's the right one for me.

Those were the words. I am sorry, but I just did not think anything else. I can see it was a moment that ought to have brought out the highest poetry in me. Grey eyes sparkling, a beautiful mouth, loose dark hair over her forehead, her body panting against mine as I hauled her up from having let her drop on the floor. Oh! the poetry that ought to have surged through me. What did surge through me?

This one's the right one for me.

Oh! the echoes, if it comes to that, of chapel jokes in my youth about 'waiting for Miss Right to come along'.

The girl said: 'I think one of my heels must have come loose.'

'Oh,' said I.

Was it love at first sight? Certainly it was at first sight. But love? Love, love, love . . . Did I hear nightingales singing, waves crashing, bells tinkling, winds blowing? . . . I

65

cannot say that I did. I just heard one of the flattest sets of words I had ever come across, at regular intervals.

This one's the right one for me.

Her glance went swiftly round the room, and then came back to me. She did not say anything. Laughing made two lines, like brackets round her mouth, flash into existence and out again. The flat set of words might have been signalled to and fro between us — was she thinking I was the right one for her?

'I don't know your name,' I said.

'It's Elspeth.'

I said: 'Mine's Joe.'

To my surprise, she blushed. I said:

'We ought to get somebody to introduce us to each other.' I straightened my tie. 'I'm all for the proprieties.'

'I'm sure we can get somebody to introduce us,' she said. 'If you like.'

We were standing at the edge of the dance-floor, and just then the 'Dark Town Strutters' Ball' stopped. A whirling gust of air caught us.

'What are you two doing?' We turned to find Harry's inquisitive eyes moving shrewdly from one of us to the other.

I said we were looking for somebody to introduce us. A look of great cunning came over Harry's face.

'I'll introduce you,' he said.

I thought: He's guessed! Harry's curiosity was insatiable, but that was not to say it was always wildly off the truth.

'Are you,' I said to Elspeth while we were being introduced, 'by any chance Scottish?'

'No. I'm English.'

Harry was not in the least affected by this attempt at diversion. 'I think you two ought to come and tell Barbara you've met.' He said to me: 'Elspeth is one of Barbara's friends.'

I looked momentarily at Elspeth with fresh eyes. She seemed unconcerned by the revelation. Perhaps, I thought, it might be all right — I did not know what had made me think I might be in for some opposition from Barbara.

I said: 'Didn't Barbara mean us to meet?'

Harry burst into laughter. 'Of course. That's what we invited her for.'

Elspeth turned on him. 'Really!' She was blushing again.

I said to her: 'Don't worry!'

She said to me: 'I'm not, really.'

Harry led us through the doorway into the hall. There we came straight upon Barbara and her mother, who must have been keeping an eye on the dancing.

'What happened?' Barbara asked Elspeth.

'We saw you enjoying yourself,' her mother said to me.

Barbara's mother looked like Barbara, only, like many mothers in comparison with their daughters, more so. Her jaw was longer and squarer than Barbara's, her complexion so much higher in colour that it looked permanently weather-beaten. The look of confidence in her eyes was opaque. Battle-axe, I thought. She said:

'It's the first time I've seen that kind of dancing.'

Her smile told me instantly that she had viewed my performance not as showing the flag for persons of a higher social status but as abandoning it to join persons of a lower social status. How could I make her see the truth? At that moment I caught sight of myself in a big looking-glass on the wall behind her — a smart chap, in a bow tie, grinning. How indeed?

Barbara said to me: 'We're going up to my room to see if we can find a pair of my shoes that will fit Elspeth.'

I said: 'But aren't all your shoes the same size?' I had forgotten that in the romantic hope of making their feet look smaller or smarter or both, women buy shoes of all shapes and sizes.

Elspeth and Barbara exchanged feminine smiles instead of replying to me.

67

Anyway, I thought, watching Elspeth go up, she would have to come down. I could afford to wait. The fact of which I was convinced was not one that could alter with time.

For want of something to do, I turned to Harry and enquired who the man over there with the heavy jowls was. 'That's Barbara's *bookmaker*,' he said triumphantly, and went away.

The man was now standing next to a fair-haired girl, leaning over her shoulder and quietly putting his hand on her waist. His jowls looked heavier than ever.

I was going to point him out to Barbara's mother, but found that she had gone. I saw Robert coming out of the room where the bar was: with him still was Harry's boss. He called to me.

'Joe, will you come over here?'

Harry's boss and I shook hands. I reminded myself of the rule Robert had formulated for me to obey when I met bosses.

'We've been having an interesting discussion,' Harry's boss said. He was about my height, a tough, muscular little man with a leathery, grey face and a croaking voice: he used to make Robert and me think of a shark. We liked him. In the strictest privacy we used to call him The Shark.

I nodded my head. Robert's rule was for my self-preservation.

'Very interesting indeed,' said Robert.

I nodded my head the other way. The rule was, of course, to try not to say *anything*.

Robert began to say: 'It was about——'

'I was telling Robert,' said Harry's boss, not being the man to let anyone else speak for him, 'that you chaps are more fortunate than we are in getting supplies of people to do research.' He stared at me, showing his teeth slightly — just like a shark.

I tried wagging my head this time.

Harry's boss gave Robert a glance, as much as to say, 'Is

68

your friend dumb?' and continued, undismayed by my handicap, with his exposition.

'You'll hear it said that our present budget is too small, that the country ought to be spending more than three and a half millions on medical research. So it ought. But if we had more money we should scarcely know what to do with it. We've got plenty of problems we should like investigated, but chaps of the right quality to investigate them don't exist.' He aimed a question mid-way between me and Robert. 'How would you cope with that one? I should like to hear what you'd say.'

I said nothing. I thought Robert must be pleased with me.

Robert began: 'Lunn and I took steps some years ago to ensure that bigger supplies of research people were *made*.'

Lunn and I! He really was pleased with me. He really must think I was increasing my reputation with The Shark.

I was so encouraged that from then on I never looked back. Until Harry's boss shook hands again — 'That was a very interesting discussion!' — I did not utter. As we separated Robert gave me a frankly congratulatory look.

Within five seconds of our actually having separated, Harry was at my elbow. A honeyed voice said close to my ear:

'The Shark's in good form, to-night, isn't he?'

I caught a bright sideways glance coming past Harry's snub nose and said nothing.

'You know he's going to put in for another half million on our budget?'

I could not help it — I burst into laughter.

Harry looked hurt. For a moment instead of whirling he seemed to be quite stationary. Then he picked up.

'I must go and find Barbara's mother,' he said busily.

I stayed where I was. In a little while I saw Elspeth looking in the crowd for me. I called to her. When she joined me I said: 'Let's go and have a drink!'

'I think I've had enough already.'

'Let's dance, then! Will you be all right?'

'If we don't do anything too sudden.'

'Nothing easier.'

I took her on to the dance-floor. The lab-assistant had been deposed from his charge of the gramophone, and low soothing music was coming from it now. A voice crooned.

You are
    The breathless hush of springtime . . .

'Suits me,' I murmured.

Elspeth did not hear.

We did a gentle circuit of the room, quarter turns all the way. 'Did you know that man was Barbara's bookmaker?' I said.

'No. I'd only just met him. Thank you for rescuing me.'

I had rescued her. I brushed my cheek against her hair.

'What a romantic beginning!' I murmured, this time loudly enough for her to hear.

As I went on brushing my cheek against her hair, I was unable to see her expression. You cannot have everything.

You are the angel-glow, crooned the voice, taking a more improbable flight,

    That lights a star . . .

This one, I thought, is the one for me. Just that. Why try to think about anything else?

I had never felt like this in my life before. I had fallen in love before; I had fallen, I have to admit, into bed; I had fallen into ecstasy; and my goodness I had fallen into error. But I saw all of these things now as things else. In the conviction that this one was the right one for me, I had the feeling, quite new, that I had this time cut all the cackle and come straight to one single, stark, wonderful hoss. It was a traumatic experience, traumatically satisfying. I could have gone on doing the quarter turns all night. Elspeth said:

'You don't really have to be quite so un-sudden as this . . .'

70

I dutifully swung into a running turn, which ran us back-wards into another couple.

And now that moment divine, crooned the voice, brought to the foreseeable misfortune contingent upon apostrophising one's love with an inventory, namely having to wind it up,

When all of the things you are,
Are mine.

The orchestra went on playing the song over again without the voice, and we sank back into the quarter turns.

'Isn't this nice?' I said.

Elspeth nodded her head so far as that was possible, seeing that we were cheek to cheek.

'We must meet again.' It hardly seemed necessary to say that.

She nodded her head again, and that was enough for the time being. We must meet again, again and again.

Soon after this it was midnight, and everyone crowded into the room and we all joined hands for Auld Lang Syne. Then Barbara announced that there was food ready in the kitchen, whereupon everyone crowded out again at twice the speed. I lost touch with Elspeth, and expected to find her in the kitchen. When I got there I saw her trapped on the other side of the room with Harry and Barbara's mother.

Suddenly, quite close to me, I saw Annette.

'Has Robert left you on your own?' I said.

Her eyes were bright, and when she shook her head the bell of hair swung to and fro. She had discarded her shape-less jumper and skirt in favour of a party dress that reminded me of what the girls of fifteen used to wear at our school dances: it was of a shade that used to be called apricot. She was wearing no make-up. She looked charming.

'Who was the girl you were dancing with?' she asked.

'Did I make such an exhibition of myself as that?'

'One always notices anyone who falls down,' said Annette.

I burst into laughter, and Annette looked pleased.

'She's called Elspeth,' I said. 'Why do you want to know?'

'I liked her. I should like to know her.'

I could not resist the indiscretion of saying: 'I hope you'll have plenty of opportunity.'

Annette said: 'Are you going to marry her?'

Her tone was simple, sweet, unoffending. I was taken aback.

'Good God! I don't know . . . I've only just met her. Give me a chance.'

'But, surely that's just what you've had. A chance, I mean.'

I hastily crammed a sausage roll into my mouth.

Annette said: 'I should like you to dance with me before you go. You look as if you know what you're doing. I don't.'

'You could have a few lessons,' I said sharply. I had great faith in lessons.

Annette shook her head and looked away. 'I suppose I'm self-conscious,' she said. I cannot say that she looked specially troubled by the thought.

'Anyway,' she said, 'Robert doesn't dance very much.'

'No.' I was glancing through the crowd to see if there was any sign of Elspeth getting free. And I was distracted by the word 'marry' having been introduced into my thoughts.

Suddenly it occurred to me that Annette appeared to think that I really could get married.

'Yes, let's dance!' I said enthusiastically. 'I'll teach you.'

I danced with Annette. There was now no sign of Elspeth. Perhaps she had gone home. Perhaps she felt a little shaken after all. Perhaps somebody had offered her a lift in a car. After I had handed Annette over to Robert, I made a last tour of the house without finding Elspeth. I decided it was time I went home.

As I said goodnight to Harry, I asked:

'What's happened to Elspeth?'

Harry gave me a quick look. 'I thought she was waiting for *you* to take her home.'

I was on no account going to accept that remark for the start of a conversation with Harry. 'I expect she's already gone,' I said, with such decisiveness that it carried me over the threshold and out into the garden before Harry could try another tack.

The drizzle had stopped, but the bare branches of prunus and lilac still dropped their large drops of water on my head in the darkness. I looked forward to my walk home. I was of the opinion that, unlike most of the guests I had left behind at the party, I was sober.

I thought about Elspeth. I was not dismayed by not having seen her again. I could well do without seeing her again that night, I thought. My conviction that she was the girl for me, the one exactly right for me, was quite enough for me to cope with. For the time being I wanted no more. I walked back up Putney Hill just thinking about it.

CHAPTER III

A TABLE AT THE CARLOS

I LET a couple of months go by before I got in touch with Elspeth. What was I waiting for? you may wonder. I will tell you. I was waiting till Sybil's next trip to London was over.

In the days before the war, when I was a schoolmaster, I had had a robust friend who used to prolong his anguish over the passing of an old love until he had got a new love actually ready to get into bed with him.

'I must have continuity,' he used to say — somewhat self-righteously, I used to think.

My own need now was the reverse. I must have *dis*-continuity. It seemed to me as a changed man, as a man now aiming at marriage, improper to get in touch with Elspeth while still 'carrying-on', as my mother would have called it — no doubt did call it, to Harry — with Sybil. As a changed man I was getting curious ideas of propriety, I noticed. But there it was. The recurring pattern had to be broken. I needed discontinuity. And I happened to have previously arranged for Sybil to come up to London in February.

So that accounts for the delay. It also accounts for a final scene in the bar at Euston whose mournfulness exceeded all previous mournfulness. This was, I had decided, really the last time I was going to see Sybil. Is it any wonder I was mournful? Sybil, with the looks of Marlene Dietrich, with the softest of voices and the most touching of myopias, was now gone, gone for good. From now on I was aiming at marriage.

74

I drank a large whisky and considered the prospect. And I considered Sybil again, too. Marriage, I thought . . . the very word was like a knell.

I meant to try and marry Elspeth. I bought myself another whisky and told myself to put knells out of my mind, even though this one was metaphorically ringing a New Year in as well, more obviously, as an Old Year out.

During January and February I kept out of Barbara's and Harry's way. This was not difficult because for part of the time I had to go down to one of our major research establishments and do what was called a staff-review. Instead of being able to dwell on the breathless hush of spring-time and the angel-glow that lights stars, I had to bend my mind to following professional discussions about shock-waves, aspect-ratios and suchlike; which, I can tell you, takes a lot more out of you than thinking about love. It also, I can tell you with the same authority, puts a good deal more into you, too.

I had noticed, before, the therapeutic value of a stay at one of our research establishments. If you lead a life of sexual disorder, there is nothing like a bit of science and technology for putting you straight. In the first place I found it interesting to think about shock-waves and aspect-ratios just out of natural curiosity. In the second place the people who were doing research on these topics had so little intention of discussing anything else that they gave me less than half a chance to maunder privately about my sexual life. I used to come away from these visits feeling a tireder but a better man. Perhaps only a little better; certainly a lot tireder. Still, only a little better, I felt, is *something*. Good for you, science and technology!

Since nobody else I knew could give me Elspeth's address, I had to ask Harry for it.

'I thought you'd want to know it,' he said, kindlily, 'sooner or later.'

I thanked him.

He said: 'I suppose you weren't able to take her up straight away because of being out of London.'

'Yes,' I said, delighted by the thought that his spies at Euston must have failed him for once.

'Elspeth was very disappointed, I think, that night. She was waiting to go home with you. She was up in Barbara's room . . .'

He was looking at me with such an innocent expression, and the speech had gone so smoothly, that a pause elapsed before I tripped, in retrospect, over the test phrase. 'She was waiting to go home with you.'

I tripped, before I knew what I was doing, with chagrin and frank astonishment. I had realised that I was a changed man, but I had not realised I was so changed a man as to be shocked by the thought of a girl being ready to go home with me the first time she met me.

'How did she get home?' I asked casually.

Harry answered in his high, fluid voice: 'We put her up for the night here.'

I felt relief.

In the time between telephoning Elspeth and meeting her I reached a conclusion about myself that could scarcely have been more embarrassing. My reaction to the concept of the girl I proposed to marry being prepared to go to bed with me the first time she met me was the typical reaction of my father and the congregation of which I was no longer a member. I could now only conclude that, having discarded my recurring pattern, which, when all was said and done, was my own invention, I was going to fall back into the conventional pattern of the society in which I had been brought up. Not to put too fine a point on it, I must be going to be *respectable*.

I recalled what I chose to regard as my life of revolt. I had seceded from my father's church, in fact I had seceded from all religious belief; and I had practised my recurring pattern. Altogether a pretty fair score in the way of revolt, as both sides admitted. And now at the age of forty I was thrown back in one sphere at least — I saw no sign of dawning religious belief — to the start. I saw the prospect of courting Elspeth as if we were any two members of the choir, any two respectable members of the choir, that is.

A further thought occurred to me before I met Elspeth again. Supposing Harry had not been lying about her? Horrors! When I sat waiting for Elspeth in the foyer of the Carlos Hotel, where I had asked her to dine with me, one of the questions I most wanted to find the answer to was whether Harry had any grounds for his lie.

The Carlos was an hotel I had frequented since about the middle of the war. It was small and, as far as I could gather, very grand — the sort of place that made Claridge's look rather commercialised: I mean, the Carlos would never have had flags outside, or gypsy music, or anything like that. As a result of my dining there alone when there were air-raids going on, some of the servants had got to know me. And considering how good the food was, I decided it was not as expensive as all that. The Carlos, as I had told Elspeth, not without intent to make an impression, was my favourite hotel.

You may think my attitude to the Carlos does not accord with my having said a little while ago that I was simply petty bourgeois. Not a bit of it. I may have cultivated some of the tastes of persons of a higher social class than myself — who would not cultivate the Carlos, if he had the chance? And I may have modelled some of my behaviour on theirs — I had removed most of the provincial accent from my speech, though naturally I could not do anything about removing it from my physiognomy. But I never really felt that my own social class was any different from that to which I had been born.

Perhaps I can make myself clearer by referring to my political attitudes. I had taken it into my head that the Labour Party were out to try and give the lower classes a

better time of it, the Conservative Party to see that the
upper classes did not lose one jot or tittle thereby. For that
reason alone I could never have voted anything but Labour.
(I may say that I kept strictly away from political meetings
because the sight of M.P.s tended to put me off voting
altogether.)

'The Left is motivated by envy and hope,' Robert had
once pronounced, 'the Right by nostalgia and fear.'

Awful as the whole human race was, I stood by the
side which at least was moved sometimes, in its envy, by
hope.

So there you are. I was sitting in a big high-backed armchair in the entrance hall of the Carlos, not feeling like a
lord. If anything, I was feeling like Charlie Chaplin sitting
in a chair made for Hamlet. I was waiting for Elspeth.
Beside me, on a heavy William Kent'ish table with a marble
top, there was a vase of flowers. The time of year was
spring. The flowers were mimosa. I did not have to wait
long for Elspeth, because she was punctual. She came
through the revolving doors, hatless and a shade less pale
than I had remembered. We shook hands.

She was nervous. And so was I. A handshake, and a
formal handshake at that, was somewhat different from the
last physical contact we had exchanged — I glanced at her
cheek, thinking that my cheek . . . She caught me doing it,
and suddenly we were looking each other in the face again
as we had done when I hauled her up off the floor.

'Let's have a drink!' I said.

'I don't drink very much . . .'

I said playfully: 'I only suggested one, anyway.'

Fleetingly the lines like brackets round her mouth came
and went. She really was nervous, I thought. As we went
past the huge vase of mimosa I saw her notice it with surprise
and awe.

'What a lot!' she said.

'And who's paying for it?' said I. 'Us, of course.'

She succeeded in laughing. I was pretty sure she had never set foot in a place as grand as this before. We both sniffed the mimosa with pleasure, and then I steered her into the big drawing-room, where there were more vases of it. At this she laughed naturally.

While we were having a drink I realised that she looked less pale because on the previous occasion she had been wearing a coral-coloured dress whereas to-night she was in dark green. It suited her: I noticed that her eyes were a transparent blue. No jewellery, no scent. I bet she has not got many dresses, I thought, and found the conjecture touching.

We had a drink, and then another one. Some of her nervousness disappeared, but not the air of mild formality. As you will have gathered, I was on my best behaviour. It became apparent to me that so was Elspeth. Our behaviour at the party, whether it was our worst or not, was a thing of the past, I thought — as also was Harry's deplorable suggestion. I had no doubt that Elspeth was somehow moving along on the same lines as me. Our parents, after they had got over the surprise of our being in the Carlos, would have recognised us as their own son and daughter respectively.

I have said 'our' parents. The way Elspeth and I spent most of our time over dinner was in exchanging information about our careers and our families. Her social origins were not very different from mine.

Elspeth was twenty-five years old and working as a school-teacher in Bethnal Green.

'I'm afraid I didn't go to a university,' she said, blushing, and glancing swiftly round the room as if she were ashamed of something.

I too glanced swiftly round the room. 'I doubt if all these ladies are honours graduates of Girton or Somerville, either.'

She grinned, though she still looked ashamed.

'Where *did* you go?' I asked.

'To a teachers' training college.'

'Did it do you any good?'

'It was very hard work.' She paused. 'So it must.'

I said: 'That's a fine Calvinist sentiment! *Your* father doesn't happen to be a non-conformist minister, does he?'

She laughed. 'No. He's a school-teacher. We're all schoolteachers in my family. You know, at council schools. . . . I've gone the highest, by getting into a senior school.' She was amused. Then she said: '*Your* father's a minister, isn't he? I think Barbara told me.'

I nodded my head.

She was thinking something. I asked her what it was.

'Well, only that ministers' sons either become ministers themselves,' she said, 'or go to the other extreme.'

'Oh!' I cried.

She blushed again and let her table-napkin fall on the floor. I felt as if my reputation must be on the floor in the moral sense.

'You don't know me,' I said.

'No,' said she, looking frightened.

A waiter came and picked up her napkin, and for a while we concentrated on our *hors d'oeuvres* — in my opinion, particularly good at the Carlos.

I reflected on the concept of marrying somebody whose social origins were approximately the same as my own. I was perfectly happy about it. In fact I had never really thought of marrying either above or below me. I supposed I might have thought of marrying above me, as ambitious men did — I *was* ambitious. But I was ambitious as a writer, as an artist. Had I been a publisher or a politician, it would of course have been a different matter: I had noted that politicians and publishers were great ones for marrying into the aristocracy. But I never saw how it could make me write better novels even if I married a Royal Princess. So why worry? I asked myself.

I looked at Elspeth — she happened to be eating a little mound of shrimps in a curry-flavoured sauce that she had been saving to the end — and thought there was no need to worry at all. She was eating slowly and with pleasure. Nice and relaxed, I thought. The right one for me. From bending forward over her plate, a dark strand of hair had fallen across her forehead.

'Well?' I said, when she had finished the shrimps.

'M'm,' she said.

'It's a nice place, this, isn't it?'

She said 'M'm' again.

While the wine-waiter took over, I looked approvingly and proprietorially round the room. It was panelled in a brightish wood that I took to be mahogany. On most of the tables there were small lamps with old-fashioned pink shades and tapering silver vases with daffodils in them. The curtains were of some dark, unstirring colour. My glance was caught by the flickering flame of a spirit lamp that rose up when a chafing-dish was lifted off it.

When we had got started on our next course, I said:

'How do you come to be a friend of Barbara's?'

'We send some of our children to Barbara's clinic.'

'Oh,' I said. Nothing easier to understand after all.

'The L.C.C. always seem to send you a long way from home.'

'What?' I was completely at sea, now. 'They send *you*?' I was trying to work out all sorts of complicated interpretations.

She said: 'No. Barbara.'

I laughed.

'They could perfectly well have found Barbara a job,' she said, 'somewhere near to where she lives, instead of sending her all the way down to our borough.'

I had no views on this. Judged by the heat with which she spoke, Elspeth had.

I said: 'If the L.C.C. had found her a job near where

she lives, you would never have met her.' Anyway, no civil servant would be prepared to judge L.C.C. policy on one example.

'I shouldn't . . .'

I looked at her. 'And so you'd never have been at the party. . . .'

A smile showed at the corners of her mouth. She glanced away and drank some wine. We paused for a little while. Elspeth said:

'Barbara tells me you write novels.'

In the ordinary way I should have replied: 'Yes, have you read any of them?' in a tone which indicated that a negative answer would not be well received. (I never understood why people expected one to smile, if not actually to pat them on the back, when they disclosed that they had never read any of one's books.) I said:

'Yes.'

'I should like to read them.'

I had met this remark before: the correct riposte was, 'Well, what's stopping you?' I said:

'That's the spirit!'

'Actually,' she said, 'I've just finished——' and she named a book I had brought out after the war.

'What did you think of it?'

She smiled shyly: 'I've never met an author before.'

I was interested by that but did not see how it answered my question. Elspeth said:

'I don't know the kind of thing to say about a book to its author.'

'I should just concentrate on praise,' I said. 'Sustained praise, with a touch here and there of flattery.' I recalled a friend, a woman, who, when I sent her a manuscript for her opinion, used to ask: 'Which do you want to hear, flattery or what I really think?'

Elspeth gave a laugh which seemed to absolve her from the need to reply. Encouraged, I said impetuously:

'The book I'm just about to bring out is much better than any of the others.'

'Oh, I shall get it!'

At that moment I thought of my reputation in her eyes. I have to say that the book I was encouraging her to read was on the same lines as this which you are now reading: it was about myself. Only it was about myself before I became a changed man. The moral tone of the book I was encouraging her to read was consequently nothing like so high as the moral tone of this book — after all, if you are behaving respectably, your moral tone cannot help being high, can it?

You see my point. I was sitting there in the Carlos with Elspeth, behaving in the most respectable manner imaginable, namely in the manner of a man who is taking a girl out to dinner with a view to matrimony. The book of mine which was going to come out in the following month was about a man who took his girl out to dinner with a view to *not* marrying her. A reprehensible view. A reprehensible man. I had difficulty in recognising the fact that it was me, even me before metamorphosis.

'What is it called?' Elspeth was asking.

I told her, wishing I had given it one of those American titles like *Now Yesterday* or *Here and Forever* that nobody can remember. Elspeth did not write the title down but I knew she would not forget it.

'I shall watch for the reviews,' she said.

People always said that, rather as if they had some idea that both they and I gained merit by it.

'They may be bad,' I said insincerely.

'I don't think they will.' For all her shyness Elspeth was giving me a sparkling look, quick but direct, appraising but admiring.

'Oh!' I cried. 'I'll let you read a proof copy if you like.'

Elspeth said she would like.

I grinned. 'I suppose you might as well know the worst.'

Elspeth looked down at her plate, which by now was empty, and I saw her forehead go pink. What a wonderful girl! I thought. Just right for me. . . . It only remained now for her to think my novel was the funniest, the wittiest, the most touching, the most truthful, and in some ways really the most profound book she had ever read.

'What would you like to eat next?' I asked, happy enough to buy her the most expensive *crêpes* on the menu or even a whole *bombe surprise* for herself.

Elspeth considered the alternatives and modestly chose to have some *marrons glacés*.

'I love chestnuts,' she said when the waiter had gone, 'but I've never tasted *marrons glacés*.' She smiled. 'We couldn't afford them.' She smiled. 'I still can't.'

I made the sort of tut-tutting noise that rich people make in the effort of trying not to hear what the poor are saying, and said:

'Well, they are pretty expensive.' I did not want her to think I could afford to dine at the Carlos every night, though I guessed she would have found somewhere not so grand less of a strain. 'Actually,' I said, 'I don't think I tasted them till the days when I was an undergraduate.' I had explained to her about my mother inheriting a little money which had enabled me to go up to Oxford — those were the days when only a grand slam, so to speak, of scholarships and grants enabled a boy to go up to Oxford without some other source of money. 'We were quite poor, you know. If there's anything poorer than a Methodist minister, I'd like to know what it is.'

'Yes, but you didn't have five brothers and sisters. I mean, your parents didn't have to bring up six children . . .'

'Six children!' I cried. 'They're not Roman Catholics, are they?' Though I no longer believed in God, I was still a hundred-per-cent Protestant. Generations of nonconformity had endowed me with a blood-pressure that rose at the mere thought of Papism. I could have married Elspeth if she were a Mormon or a Seventh Day Adventist, but not if she were R.C.

Elspeth shook her head. 'Of course not. Actually they were Baptists, though I'm not.' She grinned. 'They really wanted six children.'

'I see. . . . That's all right,' I said, though I was not sure I hoped Elspeth would want six children.

'We were very happy, really,' she said, 'though we had to go without lots of things that most children have.'

I saw the force of that.

'Do you know,' she said, 'that until I went to college I never had a dressing-gown.'

The fact she disclosed was poignant, but the portentous tone that came into her voice made me, I am sorry to say, want to laugh.

Elspeth was offended. I could see her saying to herself: 'I won't tell him anything else.' I realised that for me to say something even more poignant, such as 'Until I went up to Oxford, I never even had a pair of shoes,' would only make matters worse. And that would not have been in keeping with my parallel response to her remark, which was, 'I'll give you a wonderful dressing-gown. . . . You shall be warm, however chilly the night, for the rest of your life.' This was assuming, of course, that I did not lose my job as a civil servant and have all my manuscripts turned down by publishers.

'Here come your *marrons*,' I said.

Elspeth tried one and her expression melted. My absence of feeling had been shown to be only of the moment and possibly not characteristic. I ate some runny Camembert cheese and the meal ended in delicious harmony.

Afterwards, when we came out of the hotel, it was a dry night, and we walked up through Grosvenor Square to Bond Street Tube Station, where Elspeth went east and I west. On the station platform, before she got into the train, I took her hand again and kissed her goodnight.

Her train moved out. When I turned to go to the adjacent platform, I felt as if the image of her face, smiling as she waved to me through the window, were still lingering on my retinas. Sparkling eyes and a long mouth curled up at the corners: the right face for me. Was it, I asked myself in an effort to be detached about it, a beautiful face, the sort of face that could for instance launch a thousand ships? I supposed it was not. But that did not worry me. I had my doubts about such faces: I suspected that if I saw the face of Helen of Troy her nose would look to me as if it started out of the middle of her forehead. And furthermore I was not looking for a face that would launch a thousand ships. I was only looking for a face that would launch just my ship.

CHAPTER IV

MISCELLANEOUS CONVERSATIONS

I TOLD Robert I had spent an entirely satisfactory evening with Elspeth.

'Who on earth's Elspeth?'

Robert's attitude towards the existence of anyone whom he had not discovered for himself was incredulity.

'The girl I met at Harry's party on New Year's Eve,' I said. 'You saw her. I told you I was going to take her out to dinner at the Carlos.'

'Was it a good dinner?'

'Very good.' I began to describe the dishes we had eaten, in detail as boring as I could make it.

In retaliation Robert gave me what we nowadays referred to, *vide* W. H. Sheldon, as a mesomorphic glare. Mesomorph is the name for the square, all-muscle type of man, and the glare is the blank unchanging expression you see on his face. (The word 'glare' is chosen because the emotion in which mesomorphs most readily express themselves is rage. Undiluted men of action, they burst into rage when action does not produce the desired result. The glare gives intimations of this.) Most of our colleagues in the Civil Service, like men of action in all walks of life, were predominantly mesomorphic, and as a private parlour game Robert and I used to give them marks out of ten for the impenetrability of their glares. Robert's large F.D.R.-like face rather untypically did not score more than about seven out of ten. And my own score was so much less that, in order to keep up in my Civil Service career, I practised my glare regularly in the mirror after shaving.

I said to Robert:

'You ought to pay attention when I mention Elspeth. Because I think it's possible I may marry her.'

Robert's glare disappeared instantly. He said with emotion:

'I hope you do.'

And while he said that his face fell into an expression which I readily identified — it was the expression into which both our faces fell when, for example, somebody whom we loved who had no literary talent announced that he or she was going to write a novel.

'You must meet her,' I said.

'I should like to,' he replied — in a tone with which we accepted the prospect of reading the first 10,000 words of manuscript.

I gave up.

In fact it turned out immediately afterwards in our conversation that Robert was preoccupied about something else. He had been called over to see Murray-Hamilton. One of the senior people at the research establishment at which I had done my staff-review had complained to Murray-Hamilton about something I had said.

'The snitch!' I cried, finding just the word I wanted from the vocabulary of my pupils when I was a schoolmaster.

Robert looked grave.

I asked who the man was.

Robert shrugged his shoulders. 'I don't know. As it was some deputy superintendent or other . . .'

I asked what I was supposed to have said.

'History in this case doesn't relate that.'

I was about to comment angrily when Robert went on: '*I* don't know what you're supposed to have said. I suppose Murray-Hamilton does, but that's not what concerns him. As he sees it, whether you said it or not, even whether you were provoked to it or not, you *offended* somebody.

88

Introduced friction into the machine. . . . That's something he takes seriously. He's bound to take it seriously.'

'Oh, blast!' I said. 'Why can't he take no notice for once?'

'He's not the sort of man who could, even if he approved of you in the first place. . . .'

That remark shut me up for quite a while.

I had a picture of Murray-Hamilton sitting in his office brooding and reflecting. A new thought crossed my mind. Could it be that what he was interminably brooding and reflecting upon was the awesome difference between Right and Wrong? A book, a large ledger, lay open in front of him. Then I saw Spinks, 'Stinker Spinks', come in — at that I discontinued thought in favour of speech — and I said to Robert:

'I wonder what I really did say.'

Robert had got up and gone to look glumly through the window. He said:

'Probably something sharp and bright.' He paused. 'But that's immaterial. . . . The fact of the matter is that you say things that set these people's teeth on edge. You make them feel you're getting at them.'

'Oh,' I said.

'Even your quips are not the sort they're used to — or even take to be quips, for that matter.' He turned on me. 'I've heard you, myself, invite people to think mesomorphic glares are funny, when they have mesomorphic glares themselves!'

'Oh,' I said again.

Robert turned away from me. 'You may have to pay for it, that's all.'

'What do you mean by that?' I asked quickly.

'I don't know,' he said.

That remark shut me up altogether.

Robert went on glumly staring out of the window. He had nothing else to say on the matter, either then, it appeared, or later.

During the next few weeks I had other, different things to think about.

The time came for me to invite Robert and Annette to meet Elspeth. I invited them to dinner with us at my flat. I bought some very expensive *pâté* and spent an additional ten shillings a bottle on the claret. The flat was central-heated and warm, and three hyacinths growing in a pot gave my living-room — I had two rooms — an agreeable smell. It was the first time Elspeth had been to my flat: I should have thought it quite improper to invite her alone. Robert and Annette seemed to me, though they might not have seemed to everyone, to constitute proper chaperonage.

After dinner Robert and Annette sat on the sofa and held hands, at least they began by holding hands. I thought it was a good thing for Elspeth to observe that a man as eminent and as lofty in general purpose as Robert, and a girl as high-minded in the philosophical sense as Annette, made no bones about liking — well, you had only to see them together to see what they liked.

And I must say that Robert knew how to play his part. He instructed both girls on how good a novelist I was. By this time Elspeth had read the proofs of my new novel and declared that she liked it. This, of course, was not enough for Robert. I listened to him with pleasure and satisfaction. Girls do not, more's the pity, want to sleep with a man because he writes good novels; but if they are not averse to the idea of sleeping with him in the first place, then hearing that he writes good novels sometimes appears to help things along. (For this reason the artist's life is not entirely composed of suffering and rejection.)

Robert did me proud. None of us were left in any doubt that my new book was a small masterpiece. Small? You may think that was not doing me as proud as all that. I recommend you to concentrate on the important thing. It is masterpieces that live, whatever the size. Better a tiny masterpiece than the most massive of potboilers. Robert said:

'He may even make a bit of money with it.'

I glanced at Elspeth. She was looking radiantly pretty, in the dark green dress which made her eyes look so blue. The same dark green dress — she probably had not got any other dress. . . . Money. I thought of making a bit of money in an entirely new light. How could two live on the income of one? By the earner taking a cut.

'How much?' I asked Robert, poignantly.

He mentioned a sum. Not enough. Nothing like enough!

Elspeth's expression of general enthusiasm and amusement did not falter. No more did it need to. Nor did Annette's falter. No more did hers need to, either. Robert earned much more than me, and Annette never wore anything but the same jumper and skirt.

'Of course,' Robert was saying loftily about my novel, 'it's probably the most original book to come out since the war. And it may well be the progenitor of a whole series of similar books.'

'But the money?' I interrupted. 'What about the money?'

Robert shrugged his shoulders, as one does when a man of talent reveals a petty obsession — which happens to be pretty often, if it comes to that. Of course I wanted my book to be a masterpiece and a progenitor and all the rest of it. I wanted that first of all. But *after* that . . .

The following morning at the office, Robert came in and said:

'I think Elspeth's a nice girl. A very nice girl. Intelligent . . . and comparatively relaxed.' He nodded his head in agreement with his own description.

I nodded mine. I said:

'I need someone who's pretty relaxed. Someone to cushion my . . . fluctuations.'

Robert nodded his head again, probably not so much in agreement with my description of myself as in censure of what I was describing.

91

'Yes,' he said gravely. 'I think she'll do that for you.'

I was satisfied. In fact I was happy.

Annette, too, was approving, though on different grounds. Next time we met, she said to me:

'I knew I should like Elspeth. I admire her.'

I said: 'She admires you.' I thought that actually Elspeth admired above all Annette's First in Modern Greats.

Annette went on: 'I think I envy her really.'

I said with astonishment: 'What do you envy her for?'

'Her profession, of course.' Annette looked at me, smiling. 'It's a very useful one.'

I had forgotten for the moment that Elspeth was a school-teacher — possibly I was thinking chiefly about the time when she would cease to be one. And I had also forgotten that Annette was still doing nothing, apart from turning her D.Phil. thesis into the form of a publishable monograph and writing occasional reviews for professional journals.

'Oh,' I said. 'I didn't know you'd been talking to her about it.' Nor did I see why, with marriage imminent, Annette had been talking to Elspeth about it.

Annette laughed. 'I haven't.' She looked away and her hair swung girlishly. 'But I think I will,' she said, in a firm clear voice. And then she added, even more clearly and firmly: 'I must.'

CHAPTER V

APPROACH TO MARRIAGE

MY NOVEL came out in April. I have observed that it was a book on the same lines as this one you are now reading, so you can judge its quality by inference. Masterly? Oh well, have it your own way! Though I can tell you that *some* people said it was masterly. And what is more, they were paid for *their* critical efforts.

Robert and I followed the reviews with the sort of excitement with which one follows the results of a General Election. I had made a list of the days of the week on which novel reviews appeared, so I duly arrived at the office on any particular morning with a copy of the right paper. Robert, of course, had one as well. We hurried out of the office at lunch-times to buy the appropriate mid-day editions of the London evening papers, and after we came out of work in the afternoons we went up to our club and furled through magazines like *The Sphere* and *The Tatler*, for which, since they were inclined to lag behind in reviewing, we were not prepared to risk the outlay of ready money. And I had a press-cutting agency, which I used to telephone for reviews that Robert and I had missed but which watchful friends had seen in, say, *The Farmers' And Stockbreeders' Gazette*.

It was a thrilling time, more thrilling in my opinion than watching election results come out — though it would presumably not be so in the opinion of a political party leader.

'I think it's going to be all right,' Robert announced when the most important reviews were in.

So I settled back for 'the bit of money' to come in. My

publishers appeared to be settling back too, because the book went out of print three weeks after publication. Several weeks elapsed before it came into print again, but everybody said it did not affect my sales; at least, my publishers said that. I trusted the bit of money would come in.

While I was waiting and trusting, the time for Robert's marriage to Annette came near. Now that I was buoyed up by thinking I might manage to get married myself, I was freed from my disfiguring envy of Robert's good fortune. In fact I began to think he might envy me, who foresaw no trouble of any kind with my loved one. For signs of trouble, as far as Robert was concerned, were beginning to appear. They were trivial, of course. Signs of trouble always are to start with.

I sympathised with Annette. The first difference of opinion arose over whether the wedding was to be grand or not. I first heard of it one Sunday afternoon when Annette invited Elspeth and me to tea with her and Robert at her father's flat.

We were eating slices of bread and butter and marmalade. Annette gave Robert a clear-eyed look and said:

'Must I dress up?'

She was awaiting an answer Yes or No. Love and devotion for the person to whom she addressed the question seemed to shine from her face. At the time she asked it she was wearing the usual polo-necked jumper and some wrinkled navy-blue trousers — as it was getting towards summer I presumed it was a thinner jumper, but it looked the same. Her complexion had its delicious cleanly sheen and her bell of hair glistened as if she had just washed it.

'Dress up in what?' said Robert.

'In bridal white,' said Annette. 'You know I don't want to, darling.' She gave him an amused smile. 'I don't see myself as the central figure in a fertility rite.'

Robert burst into a laugh. 'That's just what you'll be, my girl!'

Annette smiled back at him, simply, without inhibition. I was reminded of Robert's observation, when he first got to know Annette and her philosopher friends, that they believed in their new brand of high-mindedness being accompanied by plenty of copulation. To Robert and me, who happened to have been brought up on a brand of high-mindedness that was accompanied by continence, this new combination was surprising. It made us ready to re-consider our former unfavourable judgement on high-mindedness.

'I'm on Annette's side,' I said. 'After all, neither of you have any religious beliefs.' And they had been sleeping with each other for months.

Elspeth said: 'Oh, I'm on Robert's side. It's something that only happens to one once in one's life.' She suddenly faltered and blushed. 'At least I hope it does. . . .' She looked down — I realised that I had not breathed a word about marriage to her.

'Exactly,' said Robert, and rewarded her with a dazzling look of friendship. He went on: 'Elspeth is right, you know. At certain points in one's life, the maximum ceremony may well be desirable.'

Annette said to Robert: 'I find ceremony embarrassing.' She looked at him. 'It really is embarrassing to me, you know. Can't we do without it?'

'If you can't bear it, of course we'll do without it,' he said, and gave her a quick, faintly mechanical smile.

Annette's father came into the room.

We had not heard him come into the flat and we were all surprised to see him. He did not usually come back from his house in the country till later on Sunday night. He looked round to see whom Annette was entertaining. It was a characteristic gesture, such as I had often seen grand people make — he was weighing up whether to stay with us or not. He said:

'I should like some tea if there's any left.' He spoke with a mixture of politeness and carelessness that amused me.

Annette's father was different from the Civil Service bosses
in our part of the world. Our department had none of the
social advantages of being, say, antique, like the Home Office,
or chic, like the Foreign Office. In fact I had once caused
a bit of trouble by remarking, innocently and truthfully, in
what had turned out to be the wrong company, that our
department, as far as cachet went, was one of the slums of
the Civil Service. (You may ask how there can be such a
thing as the wrong company for Innocence and Truth.
Kindly address your question to Murray-Hamilton and
Spinks!)

In the first place, Annette's father looked different from
our bosses. He was tall and slender, whereas they were
mainly of medium height and broad: he looked as if he
might once have played badminton, whereas they looked as
if they might have excelled, in fact most of them had excelled,
at games where you run about all the time, knocking other
people over. And of course his manner was different.
Murray-Hamilton and Spinks, for instance, had a manner
that was affable and jocular and rather commonplace,
though in their different ways neither were commonplace
men. Not so Annette's father — scholarly and *dégagé* were
the words that sprang to my mind as I watched him.

Annette said to him: 'I'll make some fresh tea for you.'
From the way she looked at him it was obvious that she was
very fond of him.

He sat down, folding his long legs gracefully. He said:
'Don't, if it's any trouble to you.'

Somehow it made me think of the way he conducted his
public life, of the cultivatedly diffuse sort of minute he wrote
to his peers — 'Do you think X is a good name?' he would
write of some Vice-Chancellor of a university. 'I met him
in the Club and thought he might do for us, but you may
think differently.' Annette's father, I thought, showed you
how the power-game after all really flowered at the top;
though I never quite understood, being convinced that in

general it was active, opaque, heavily-muscled men who got to the top, what phenomenon was responsible for Annette's father flowering there. I used to speculate on two questions. One was, had the upper reaches of the Civil Service in the previous generation been more sheltered, more university-like? The other was, was Annette's father only about one-third as *dégagé* as he seemed?

Annette went out to make some fresh tea and her father said to Robert:

'Really I shall have to give up this house in the country. It's an extravagance I can't afford any more.'

He gave a brief circular glance at Elspeth and me, to make sure that we were taking it in. His eyes were somewhere between grey and hazel in colour, very bright without being specially humorous.

Robert nodded his head in statesmanlike agreement.

'On the other hand,' Annette's father went on, 'going down there is my only chance of getting away from the Civil Service. And doing some of the things I really want to do. . . .'

He was writing a book on Hellenistic art between two dates of wonderfully esoteric significance.

'But of course,' he went on again to Robert, 'I know I'm not telling you anything you don't know already.' He was referring to Robert's writing novels.

Robert was beginning to say something about senior civil servants having to work too hard when Annette came back with the tea. 'I'm sorry we've only got marmalade,' she said to her father. 'I forgot to go out and buy some jam.'

Her father began to eat a slice of bread and butter, without marmalade. 'I was talking to Robert about giving up the house.' Then he turned to Robert as if the idea had just struck him. 'I suppose you and Annette wouldn't care to live there, or perhaps it's too far out of London?'

Robert's cheeks went slightly pink. 'Clearly, we should have to think about it,' he said. 'I think we probably——'

Annette interrupted: 'Oh no, Father. I don't want a house at all.'

We all looked at her. I cannot say Annette looked in the least perturbed as a consequence. I glanced at Robert: he did.

Annette said: 'I don't want to have servants. It would embarrass me to have servants . . . I don't think we *ought* to have them.'

Suddenly Elspeth spoke for the first time since Annette's father had come in. 'All we ever had was a woman who came in once a week to do the washing.'

'What's that got to do with it?' I said to her.

Elspeth replied: 'I was just telling you.'

Annette said: 'I'm not laying down a principle for other people. It's a personal choice that I shouldn't think of presuming to impose on other people.' She smiled. 'Though I should try to convince them of it if they came to me for advice.'

Her father said: '*Do* they come to you for advice?'

Robert said: 'Yes, that's a good question.'

Annette just went on smiling. The result of that round — Two Civil Servants *v.* Annette — seemed to me a draw.

Robert said: 'It's going to be increasingly difficult to get servants anyway. So I suppose Annette's views may be regarded as bringing her into line with the times.' He said it humorously but he sounded distinctly huffy all the same.

Annette's father said: 'I can only hope the times won't move too fast for me. I shall have to have some servants to look after me when Annette leaves me.' He helped himself to another piece of bread and butter, without marmalade.

Annette said nothing. Nor did anybody else.

In the social class to which I, like Elspeth, had been born, the question of whether one had a woman in to do the washing was decided by whether one had the money to pay her or not.

Annette and the others remained silent for a long time. I had a distinct feeling that a moral choice was floating over our heads.

Moral choices, I thought, are a pain in the neck.

CHAPTER VI

APPROACH TO BED

I SHOULD have prophesied that Annette and Robert would be married in a registry office and then live in a big house. They were married in church and then lived in a smallish flat.

The flat where Annette and Robert went to live was the one which had formerly been occupied by Annette's father. He had sold the house in Berkshire and set up in a big flat at the back of Gorringe's, where he employed two servants. Annette employed none.

Robert said to me: 'We've been rather fortunate, as a matter of fact. This arrangement will mean we shall have a good deal more money in hand for entertaining.' He paused.

'Who's going to do all the cooking and so on?' I asked, feeling very unimaginative.

'Annette will do some. And we shall get people in, professionals, to do the rest.'

I said: 'I see.' I thought I did see. I suspected that Annette and her father were turning out to be distinctly richer than I — or Robert — had thought. And why not? I liked the idea of big dinner-parties, and of anybody I knew being richer than we had thought. The bigger the better. The richer the better!

At this point I have to say that I was not getting any richer myself. As far as making a fortune out of my new novel was concerned, I was still trusting. I had written a book, the most original novel since the war, the probable progenitor of many others like it — I had Robert's word for all this — and yet . . . Furthermore some people who were so revered as to be paid for writing their opinion had said it was masterly, and yet . . . A dent must have been made on the public's mind: what about that dent on the public's pocket?

My desires, my expectations, were modest. For instance, I was not expecting the traffic in Piccadilly Circus to come to a standstill. All I desired was that a fraction of the total public, a small fraction — just a few tens of thousands of them — should go into their booksellers, even into their Free Public Lending Libraries, and utter the title of my work. But how many had done? I have been advised not, for my own sake, to tell you.

'I have kept your book out of your father's way,' my mother wrote to me, 'but I have read it. Shall I send it back to you?'

I judged from his silence that my literary agent must be in America, even though it was the season of the year when American publishers streamed over to London, looking for books. One morning Harry joined me as I strode down Putney Hill to the bus-stop.

'I was having a drink with your agent last night,' he said. 'He'd got an American publisher with him. I asked him if he'd read your book. Nice chap. He said he had.'

'What did he think of it?'

'Actually he said it was the funniest book he'd read in years.'

'Is he going to buy it?' I looked at Harry.

Harry shook his head. 'I'm afraid not. He said it was too British.'

We went on walking.

I considered the verdict. I looked at it from many angles. First angle: how could it be too British when I *was* British, when all my forbears, as far back as any records went, had been British? What did he *expect* it to be? Second angle: the implication seemed to be that Americans would not understand my book, would not understand what it was about. This puzzled me even more. Were Americans unable to comprehend the situation of a young man who sleeps with his girl and does not want to marry her? I should have thought not. Certainly I should have thought not, when I recalled the situation of some of the young Americans whom I had got to know in London during the war. Too British, indeed. I liked that! Third angle: no, two are enough. . . .

By the end of the summer I thought it was time to start writing another book. Another book? Yes, another book.

I went to Norway for a holiday, thinking that if I could bring a Norwegian scene into this new book, I could get my holiday expenses off income tax. While I was away I wrote a long letter to Elspeth. I was delighted with the result. She wrote a long letter back. She said she had an idea that she wanted to discuss with me when I got back. I have to admit that the first thought, the first, imbecile, groundless thought that crossed my mind was that it might be marriage.

We met in a public-house in Soho, near to a restaurant where I was going to take her for dinner. With the possibility in view of two having to live on the income of one, I was beginning to consider the Carlos a hasty choice of rendezvous. As Elspeth was a bit shy of going into a public-house by herself, I got there early. It was an unusually hot September evening, sultry and airless. The doors of the public-house were wide open, and the resident smell of spirits was tinged with a visiting aroma of garlic and French cigarettes. On the opposite corner of the street there was a collection of swarthy little men wearing black suits and shirts without ties: they seemed to be doing nothing, as if perhaps they might be dreaming blankly about the eastern shores of the Mediterranean; but I had been told they were engaged with the machinery of betting. They turned slowly to gaze in the direction of my pub. Elspeth came in.

She was wearing a thin summer frock, prettily draped over her small breasts, swirling out across her not so small pelvis.

'Goodness, you're sunburnt,' I said, and kissed her enthusiastically.

She laughed. 'So are you.' There were small dots of perspiration on her upper lip — apart from using lipstick, she appeared to be copying Annette in going without make-up.

'I'm glad you asked me out straight away,' she said, 'before my sunburn fades.'

'Didn't you think I should?'

For an instant she looked me in the eye, and then the corners of her mouth went up. 'How was I to know?'

'You might have,' I said humourlessly, in fact slightly shaken. Marriage, indeed!

We sat down at a table by the door and she said she would like to drink some iced lager. When she took off her short pair of white gloves I noticed the trace of dark gleaming down, all the way up her arms. I wondered how soon I could ask what her idea was.

We drank some lager and put the tall glasses on the table. A huge bluebottle made a buzzing circuit of them and went its way towards some sandwiches under a glass dome on the counter.

'I liked your letter,' I said.

'Yours was very funny,' she said. 'It nearly scared me off replying at all.'

'That's ridiculous,' I said. 'Now yours even incorporated suspense.'

She looked astonished.

'I'm dying to know,' I said, 'what the idea was you were going to talk to me about.'

To my surprise she blushed. 'Oh, it was nothing. I mean, it was only just an idea. *You* know . . . I mean, well, I wondered if it might be a good idea if I changed my digs. I'm always coming up to Putney nowadays, to see you, and Barbara . . .' She broke off, and then suddenly she said: 'After all, you never come down to the Green.'

'You mean you're going to come and live in Putney?' I cried.

'If you think it's a good idea . . .'

With an effort I said: 'I think it's a marvellous idea.'

Elspeth drank some more iced lager. The colour remained rosily in her cheeks.

A marvellous idea. Marvellous or menacing? It transpired that she had already found somewhere suitable and was only waiting to give her new landlady the word that she was ready to move in.

I told Robert about it first thing next morning.

He said: 'It's an encircling movement, old boy.'

'You only say that because you've been caught yourself!'

'I don't think so, you know. I see no evidence for that presumption.' He paused in a dignified way. 'I should have said it was entirely my own doing.' From dignity he passed to moral initiative. 'Anyway,' he said, 'you've been encircled before, haven't you, and got away with ease?'

I regarded this comment as unhelpful.

Robert looked at me. 'And anyway,' he said, 'I thought you wanted to be caught this time, don't you?'

'Yes. I mean, no,' I said. 'Yes. No.'

Robert shrugged his shoulders.

Was it yes, or was it no? Or both? I tried to forget about it. Elspeth came to live in digs in Putney, and the immediate results were happy to say the least of it.

'You reproached me with not coming down to the Green,' I said to her one evening when we were out for a stroll after dinner. 'But it's rather nice to be up on the Heath.' We had an arm round each other's waist.

'You should see Victoria Park on a summer's evening.'

I asked myself what that could mean.

I thought things over. From the beginning I had felt that Elspeth was going along the same lines as me. And what did those lines lead to? An act of will. An act of *my* will.

I decided to ask Elspeth to go to bed with me. No, do

not misunderstand me! Above all, do not misunderstand me! I argued that going to bed with her would make my act of will easier. Do you see? In a way, I should be half-way there.

I recalled an event of my young manhood that must have impressed itself on me. One of my friends, son of a high-minded, free-thinking, upper middle-class family, had been sent away for a week-end with his fiancée by his mother — to make sure everything was all right before they married. As I recalled it now, I thought how, in spite of everything, I was a child of my time, of those far-off early 'thirties when any reasonable couple made sure that everything was all right before they married. I was comforted by the thought of myself as a child of my time.

However, when it came to the point, I felt very nervous. How I envied that chap who had his mother to organise it for him!

I broached the subject with Elspeth one evening when we were lying on the sofa together.

'I've been thinking about us,' I said, trying to make it sound as if 'us' were spelt with a capital U.

She lay still, with her head resting on my arm.

'If we're thinking of going on . . .' Shades of girls who had used that phrase to *me* when they meant getting married, as I did now! 'I mean,' I said, 'if we're thinking of getting married . . .' I practically had palpitation at using that word.

'M'm,' said Elspeth, still lying very still.

'Well,' I said, 'don't you think perhaps we ought to make sure everything's all right, first of all.'

I waited.

Quietly Elspeth turned her head and kissed my cheek.

'Do you?' I said, joyously, getting up to look at her.

She whispered something that I could not hear.

I swore to myself there and then that if everything was all right I would let nothing stop me asking her to marry

105

me. I lay down again, putting my arms round her more tightly.

'When?'

She whispered: 'Not now . . . Not to-night.'

'Oh, no, no,' I said. 'We don't want to rush it. Perhaps you ought to come and stay here. At the week-end?'

I thought she nodded her head.

So I found myself with four days to wait. In four days I should be half-way towards having my act of will made for me.

The following Friday evening Elspeth arrived at my flat. I had made it look neat and pleasant, flowers in both rooms, clean sheets on the bed — it was a double bed — all kinds of drink in the cupboard. She was wearing a dress I had not seen before, dark blue with a light blue pattern on it. Her hair smelt delicious when I kissed her.

'I'm sure the hall-porter saw my case,' she said, as she opened it to take out her sponge bag and dressing-gown.

'I don't see that that matters.'

We went and had dinner in the somewhat indifferent restaurant in the basement of the building. I doubt if we noticed what we were eating.

At last we got to bed, hugging each other closely because the clean sheets felt cold. We kissed each other prolongedly.

I said: 'I'm a bit nervous.'

'So am I,' she whispered, though I thought that hardly mattered so much.

This went on for some time.

'I'm very nervous,' I said.

She whispered: 'Never mind . . .'

I began to get very worried. 'This is bad,' I said.

Elspeth hugged me and caressed me.

Everything was not all right. It was not all right at all. My act of will! I was not half-way towards it — I was making a grotesque progress in the opposite direction! What can I do now? I thought. If everything is *not* all right, there is no point in asking her to marry me, even if my will would stand up to it. I turned away from her and looked at the light of the bedside lamp shining on the ceiling.

I waited. No sign. No sign. . . . I saw my hopes crumbling, my dreams come to nothing, my life recurring in the same empty pattern for ever. I turned back to her and buried my face in the curve between her ear and her shoulder.

'I'm no use,' I cried. 'I'm no use to you.'

'*You must never say that again!*'

Her voice rang out resonantly, firmly. As my lips were against her throat I could feel the resonance through them. I was startled. I was more than startled.

Looking back on it now, I know exactly how I felt. I felt as if I had suddenly thought: Why, there's somebody *else* in bed with me!

Until this moment I had been so preoccupied with myself, or rather with my self, that I had not really thought of Elspeth as a separate, independent person at all. She was the person at the other end of *my* problem, only seen by me so far as she affected *me* . . .

With one fine resonant speech, Elspeth had ended all that. I had got somebody else in bed with me, a living, whole, human person. I was too startled even to say 'Good gracious!' I felt that it was the biggest surprise in my life.

Well, one of the things about a surprise or a shock is that it is said to take one out of one's self. I lay there with my face against Elspeth's throat. The vibration of this shock went on tingling in my lips.

After a few seconds, I really did say: 'Good gracious!' I felt the blood beginning to bump in my pulses. I had been taken right out of my self, without a doubt — I was a different man!

'Darling,' I said.

Elspeth took her hand away and turned *her* face into the curve between *my* ear and *my* shoulder.

'Darling!' I said. I could not even hear what she replied.

I moved over.

So there it was. Everything was more or less all right. Not the performance of a lifetime, I admit, but you can tell whether everything is all right or not. It was.

After we had had a rest I got out of bed and said:

'I suppose you could do with a nice cup of tea, now?'

Elspeth, deliciously pink in the face, looked up at me — I could not think why she seemed surprised.

The fact was that I was feeling as if I could do with a nice cup of tea myself.

CHAPTER VII

A DECISION AND A CELEBRATION

Y ou may wonder if I immediately asked Elspeth to marry me. Well, no, as a matter of fact, I did not. I had sworn to myself that if everything were all right I would make my act of will. But then, I asked myself, could I say yet that everything was all right? I mean, definitely? One swallow did not make a summer, though I conceded that most people would think it meant they could reasonably look forward to a spell of warm weather.

Elspeth came to stay with me every week-end.

'I miss you in the middle of the week,' she said, 'darling.'

The discussion which followed was about which night of the week was more nearly equidistant from the week-ends.

The weather, in my metaphorical sense, was getting pretty warm; and had my act of will not been hanging over my head all the time, I should have basked in it without restraint. Even as it was, I basked quite a lot.

In our leisure moments, Elspeth and I indulged ourselves in true lovers' speculations and reflections. 'Wouldn't it be dreadful,' she said one day, 'if one of us didn't like it?'

'Dreadful,' I said.

Her imagination took a Gothic turn. 'Wouldn't it be dreadful,' she said, 'if one got married and then found the other person didn't like it?'

'Horrible,' I said impetuously. 'Appalling!'

And then I came to. Married. . . . Had somebody said something about getting married?

I realised that Elspeth now saw no reason whatever why we should not get married. This exemplified to me one of the characteristics that most markedly differentiated women from men. Confronted with the prospect of being tied, of being trapped for life, women showed neither reluctance nor caution. How different from men! I thought. Or, to be precise, how different from me! Women's nature seemed to make them ready for the trap. Men had to steel themselves to it. I felt that in my nature the steely element was . . . well not very steely.

One evening when Elspeth arrived, she said: 'I'm sure the hall-porter knows why I come here.'

This seemed probable. He never did much work, but he kept a very efficient eye on everyone who came in and out. I said: 'Oh.' We had agreed not to tell our friends — in particular we wanted to tease Harry by keeping it from him — but I did not see that it mattered if the porter knew.

'He says "Good evening" in a particularly insolent tone.'

I was surprised. He was a tall, lounging fellow, with a full-cheeked, oval face that made me think of a rabbit's. I had never had any trouble with him.

'I don't see what I can do about it,' I said. 'I can't very well tick him off.'

'No,' said Elspeth, thoughtfully.

I could, of course, put her in such a position that she did not have to suffer this kind of thing. But could I? Could I?

As the weeks passed I had found that I was getting no nearer to my act of will. Half-way there, I had told myself when I asked Elspeth to put our relationship on a somewhat marital footing. I was certain now that Elspeth was the one for me, and I must say she gave me little basis for arguing that I was not the one for her — on the contrary. So why could I not bring myself to the point of asking her to marry me? As I did not like putting the question to myself, I decided to try putting it to Robert.

I told Robert one dull wintry afternoon when we were coming out of the tea-shop after lunch. I felt it was a crucial occasion in my life, a day I should always remember: the only thing I can remember now, apart from what we said, is that a little way ahead of us on the pavement there was a woman in a red coat exactly the same shade as the pillar-box she was just passing. Robert said: 'Annette and I thought you probably were.' He looked at me affection-ately. 'I'm glad. You've been looking much better these last few weeks.'

'Better?' I said. 'Was I looking worse before?'

'A more regular life seems to suit you.'

We walked in silence for a few moments, threading our way between people walking two or three abreast. Robert bought a newspaper. I was reflecting on the favourable effect on me of a regular life. Marriage was a regular life.

'The question is,' I said, 'what to do next?'

'Are you going to ask her to marry you?'

'What do you think?'

'You could do worse, much worse.' Robert glanced at me. 'Come to think of it, you *have* done in the past.'

'Considering that was on *your* advice, too,' I said, 'I——'

Robert said: 'I think Elspeth's a very nice girl. Very suitable.' He paused. 'You're very lucky.'

I laughed. 'You make it sound as if my deserts were a broken-down hag aged fifty!'

'I meant you're lucky in the sense that I'd say I was lucky to have found Annette.' A tone of strong feeling came into his voice. 'Someone odd enough to interest you, and equable enough to make you a good wife.'

Actually I did not think Elspeth was at all odd.

We came to Trafalgar Square and waited for the traffic lights to let us cross the road.

'Are you going to marry her?' Robert asked, as buses whizzed past the ends of our noses.

'That's what I can't make up my mind about.'

'Do you want to?'

'Yes. I suppose I do.'

'Then why don't you? I'm sure she'd marry you.'

The lights changed and the buses lined up their radiators across the road. We went in front of them and walked along the south side of the square, dodging the pigeons.

We came to the next road-crossing. Robert said:

'Of course there's the possibility that *she*'ll settle it by marrying *you*.'

'She's much too young and too shy.'

Robert laughed. 'I shouldn't rely on that.'

I was shocked by his cynical tone. He did not seem to realise that I was in love with Elspeth. I sincerely did think that — sweet girl! — she was too young and too shy.

This was a crossing without lights: we got safely as far as the island.

Robert said, on a different tack: 'Well, I suppose you can go on as you are.'

'Don't you see, that would mean I've fallen into my recurring pattern again?'

'I do see that.'

There was a lull in the buses and taxis. 'Come on, jump for it!' I said. We got to the other pavement. Though we had not discussed our objective, I judged that we must be making for the London Library. We went on walking in silence.

Suddenly, 'I really *will* marry her!' I said loudly.

'Good,' said Robert. 'I hope you will.'

We had to cross another road.

'I take it you're going to the London Library?' said Robert.

'I thought you were.'

'I hadn't thought of it.'

'Nor had I. Apart from thinking that's where you were going.'

'I'm perfectly willing to go, if you want to.'

'So am I, if you are.'

'Let's go, then!'

We crossed the road and continued on our way.

My will had hardened. I am not pretending it was steely yet, but somehow I felt sure that from this point I was not going to slip back any more.

I felt so sure that I stopped dead in the middle of the pavement, making Robert stop to look at me with the maximum attention, and said to him again:

'I really *will* marry her.'

This time his expression was quite different. 'Good!' he said, and his large grey eyes shone with pleasure and belief.

As we started to walk on again, he said: 'We ought to have a drink to-night.'

'To celebrate my decision?' I said, grinning.

Robert grinned too, but looked away in order to avoid answering my question. He said: 'Why don't you drop into the club late-ish to-night and join me for a drink? I shall be there with Annette's father and Harold Johnson.'

I recognised this instantly as a real treat for me. Sir Harold Johnson, another high civil servant, had only recently come Robert's way and had made the greatest of impressions upon him. As I gathered it from Robert, Annette's father and Sir Harold Johnson were, as far as exercising power in the outward direction went, among the top half-dozen or so men in the Service. As far as having influence in the inward direction, among those top half-dozen or so men themselves, Sir Harold Johnson had the edge over Annette's father, hands down. The fullness of time was going to bring Sir Harold Johnson to even greater boss-hood.

But this was not all. As far as Robert and I had observed, there was something in the opinion of the general public that senior civil servants, able and admirable though they might be in their jobs, were in their personalities not very exciting. But when it came to the highest bosses of all, public opinion had got it quite wrong. Among the highest of bosses, with Sir Harold Johnson as a case in point, personality could proliferate to a degree that, in the eyes of Robert and me, qualified as grand eccentricity.

To be allowed to meet Sir Harold Johnson was a great treat for me. 'Why not?' I said, enthusiastically.

Dutifully following Robert's instructions I entered our club at half past ten that night. I made my way through its Piazza San Marco, where there were a few cheerful, but comparatively quiescent members, drinking and chatting. From the doorway of the bar, however, came trumpeting, hallooing noises. I went into the bar.

In the semi-darkness I saw about three groups of noisy men. The noisiest, standing beside the bar itself, consisted of Robert, Annette's father, Sir Harold Johnson and a couple more members of the club. Robert waved to me as I came up. 'Come and join us, Joe!' He and Annette's father and Sir Harold Johnson and the other two men were happily and obviously drunk. They were hallooing with drink — at least Robert and Sir Harold Johnson were.

Robert said, with a don't-careish effort at formality: 'I don't think you've met Sir Harold Johnson.'

Sir Harold Johnson shook hands with me. He was a tall, strong man, like an ex-rowing Blue.

As I looked at him for the first time closely, I was reminded of another public misconception about high bosses in the Civil Service, i.e., that they all look as if they have come from Eton and Balliol. Annette's father did, as a matter of fact. Sir Harold Johnson, I saw, did not. Definitely not. His face, long-jawed with fleshy-lidded bright blue eyes, could not have sprung from one of our oldest families. Though one might have seen its characteristic expression at a racecourse — the expression, with lids momentarily half-dropped and mouth drawn knowingly down at the corners, of a man just about to take a trick — it would not have been *inside* the Royal Enclosure. I took to him immediately.

Robert had obviously taken to him. Handing me a large glass of port that I had never asked for, Robert looked at him and said to me:

'You ought to know he's read all our novels. In fact he's read practically *all* novels.'

I looked at Sir Harold Johnson, staggered, and remained standing beside him.

He looked at Robert steadily.

'Very remarkable, very remarkable,' said Robert, having some trouble with his r's.

I drank some of my port.

Robert glanced at everybody else's glasses and turned to the bar to order some refills.

Sir Harold Johnson now looked steadily at me.

'I'm not going to talk to you about novels,' he said. 'I've talked enough about novels this evening.'

I nodded my head.

'I'm interested in your job,' he said. He nodded his head in the direction of Robert. 'You chaps must have a very interesting job. People! Seeing people.'

I began to nod again.

Suddenly his eyelids half-dropped and his mouth drew down at the corners. 'Seeing them as ectomorphs and mesomorphs!'

Robert's voice came over my shoulder. 'It's all right — he's picked *that* up from Huxley's *Perennial Philosophy*!'

Sir Harold Johnson was watching me as if he were waiting to see if I knew he had got endomorphs up his sleeve. I said: 'Yes.'

'Well?'

Another nod was out of the question. I said: 'I think there's something in it.'

His eyes remained steady for a moment, and then a smile seemed to spread slowly round his long jaw. 'What do you think of this?' he said, and, looking up in the air, recited:

> 'Let me have men about me who are thin,
>   Rough-headed men and such as wake o'nights.
>   Yond Cassius has a fat and well-fed look.
>   He thinks too much — such men are dangerous.'

Everyone standing round laughed.

Triumphantly Sir Harold Johnson finished his port and handed his glass to Robert for some more. He swayed.

Annette's father, on whom drink appeared to have had a silencing effect, proposed that we should all sit down. He and the others moved towards some chairs. Sir Harold Johnson stayed waiting for his next drink. Looking down at me, with the cheerful expression of a man who has just taken a trick, he said:

'Was that quotation up your street?'

I said it was.

He did not move. Robert handed another glass of port to him — and another to me. Sir Harold Johnson went on staring down at me. At last he said:

'You know what *you* want to do?'

I shook my head, waiting . . .

'Get rid of your inhibitions!'

CHAPTER VIII

A SILVER RUPEE

I DID not say anything to Elspeth immediately about getting married, but I felt that she must sense my new internal stability. We spent a most enjoyable week-end. I had told her I was going to tell Robert about us, and she asked me what he said.

'He was very pleased,' I said. 'He told me I was lucky . . .'

Elspeth said, out of the blue as far as I was concerned: '*I* told Joan.'

Joan was Elspeth's friend on the staff of her school. I said: 'And what did *she* say?'

'Oh, I think *she* seemed pleased . . .'

The following evening I did a thing that I very rarely did. Instead of walking straight up the hill from the bus-stop, I dropped in at a public-house for a drink on my own. The saloon bar was large but at that time of day it was likely to be deserted. I was prepared to see a workman chatting over a pint of beer with a barmaid, or a couple munching pork pie and potato salad, and to hear the wireless playing what sounded unremittingly like the Light Programme. I glanced round — and saw Harry. He was sitting at a small table, opposite a man who had his back to me.

'Joe!' he called, in his high sweet voice. 'Come and join us!'

I went.

'This is a surprise for you,' said Harry, as I got to the table and his companion turned towards me.

His companion was our hall-porter.

'You know Jamie Gordon,' Harry went on with cheerful

effrontery. 'Jamie used to be a lab-attendant at the first anatomy lab I ever attended.'

I looked at Gordon — I had not recognised him at first because he was not in his uniform.

'It's my day off, sir,' he said, grinning. In ordinary clothes he looked slightly less like a big cheeky rabbit, but that was not saying much.

I pulled up a chair to the table. I looked at Harry, and then at our hall-porter. So much for Elspeth and me trying to keep Harry from knowing what we were up to!

'I ran into Jamie,' Harry explained, 'just outside the pub.'

I did not know what I was expected to say to that.

The wireless said: 'This is the Light Programme,' as if it were necessary.

However, when Harry went to the bar to buy a round of drinks, I could have sworn he set up slightly less whirling disturbance in the air.

And when I stood up to leave after we had finished the drinks, he said: 'Come in and see us soon,' in a slightly lower voice than usual.

I could not help smiling. I had caught a glimpse in Harry's small, inquisitive, brown eyes of something I had rarely seen there before — shame.

The next day I told Robert about the incident. Robert had for some time shown a peculiar passion for hearing about Harry's manoeuvres — I could only suspect he was thinking of someone like Harry as a character for his next novel. On this occasion, however, Robert's passion seemed to be less. He scarcely waited for me to finish before he said:

'Did you know that Elspeth had been talking to Annette about her career?'

'No,' I said. 'And I don't see what help Annette could be, anyway.'

'The situation, old boy, is the other way about. Elspeth has been seeing fit to give Annette help, if that's what you choose to call it.' He paused. 'Elspeth has been asking Annette why she, Annette, doesn't become a teacher.'

'What sort of a teacher?'

'The same sort of teacher,' Robert said crossly, 'as she, Elspeth, is.'

You will remember the emotion with which I first perceived that Elspeth was a person who existed in her own right outside the bounds of my egocentric cosmos, that she was a living, whole, human person — and what a delightful one, at that! — separate, independent, and so on. . . . Well, it is one thing to perceive that the girl at the other end of one's problem is a living, whole, human person, separate, independent, and so on: it is another to contemplate her taking separate, independent action in one's friends' affairs.

Robert had been taking it as settled, now that Annette was married to him, that she would give up exercising moral choice over careers and occupy herself with social duties on his behalf. His projected series of grand dinner-parties, I was happy to note, had already begun. Elspeth and I had been to one of them — wonderful food from Fortnum's and the men all in dinner-jackets. (Annette, somewhat startlingly, had worn her wedding-dress.)

'What are you going to do about it?' I asked him.

Robert shrugged his shoulders. 'I don't know.' He looked away. 'I think perhaps you might have a word with Elspeth.'

I thought perhaps I should have to.

In general I was convinced that 'speaking' to people was liable to do more harm than good. In this particular case, it suddenly occurred to me after I had left Robert, it might also bring worse things to light. Suppose that in their state of admiring and envying each other, these two girls had *exchanged* suggestions — suppose that in return for Elspeth's suggesting Annette should become a school-teacher, Annette had suggested that Elspeth should take a degree in philosophy. I saw myself married to a wife who kept going out every evening to lectures at a Polytechnic. What a thought!

What a marriage! I decided not to 'speak' to Elspeth. Undesirable ideas are best left unwatered by discussion.

And so Elspeth and I came to Christmas, nearly a year since we first met. We were each going to spend the holiday with our families — should I ask her before or after? I had not made up my mind. It was to be one or the other, anyway. I was now so certain that I was going to marry her that I had been to my tailor's and ordered a new overcoat and new evening-clothes, on the grounds that if I did not get them before I was married, I should never be able to afford them after.

On the last evening before we went away, Elspeth came to stay at my flat. She was just thinking it was time to start cooking the dinner when, to our embarrassment, the door-bell rang. We straightened ourselves up and went to the door. It was Harry.

We were surprised. Since the occasion when I had found him drinking with Gordon, the hall-porter, Harry had kept out of my way. Elspeth had seen Barbara from time to time down at Bethnal Green, but we had not been invited to their house.

'Can I come in?' Harry said.

'Of course.'

Harry's face looked less pink than usual. 'I've got something for you,' he said nervously. 'I expected I'd find Elspeth here too.' He was carrying a parcel. 'Just some Christmas presents for you both.'

The presents were a bottle of whisky for me and a bottle of scent for Elspeth. It was the brand of whisky I liked best and the most chic and expensive kind of scent. Both Elspeth and I were touched.

'Let's open the whisky!' I cried.

Elspeth laughed at me. 'Let's open the scent!'

While Elspeth took the scent into my bedroom, I poured out some large drinks. Harry was satisfied. He sat down fatly on the sofa, his face as pink again as ever.

'Barbara was sorry she couldn't come,' he said. 'She's gone to listen to somebody giving a paper at the P.M.A.'

If I knew anything about it, Barbara had never been consulted. 'M'm,' I said.

Elspeth came in and we smelt the scent. 'I'll sit by you,' she said to Harry. He sprang up politely, and a whirling gust of air set up.

We started to drink. Harry, in high spirits now, seemed determined to show us how affectionate and uninquisitive he was. I have to say that he succeeded. You see, for the present he really was affectionate and uninquisitive.

We invited him to stay for supper. He accepted. We had a huge dish of eggs and bacon. By the time we were drinking our coffee our rapprochement was complete, in fact perfect.

In a gust of boundless, selfless, uninquisitive concern for our happiness, Harry said to us:

'*When are you two going to get married?*'

I saw Elspeth blush, and my confusion was so unbearable that I looked down at the table and could scarcely form an intelligible reply. In fact I cannot remember what I did reply. Somehow we managed to pass the hiatus over. But I swore to myself that I would ask Elspeth to marry me *immediately* I got back from the holiday. 'I really can't let that happen again,' I kept saying to myself, not only that night but every time during the following week at home when I remembered it.

Actually Harry, when he left us that night, said to me while he was putting on his overcoat:

'I'm glad you didn't take it amiss when I said that.' He wagged his globe-shaped head with boyish satisfaction. 'I thought I'd chance my arm.'

At home my mother, though occasionally permitting herself an oblique reference to 'your Elspeth', made it clear that nothing would persuade her — not that she had any need to fear persuasion from me — to mention my marrying

Elspeth. With my father I had no private discussions. His clerical duties, i.e. preparing his sermons, delivering them and visiting his parishioners, resulted, as always, in his being either *incommunicado* or not.

I had resolved to ask Elspeth to marry me immediately I got back. I did.

Elspeth came round to my flat on the evening of our return to London. I still kept remembering Harry's kindly, hopeful, selfless, uninquisitive question. . . . We were washing up after dinner, or rather Elspeth was washing up while I changed the living-room back from dining-room to sitting-room. We were conversing while Elspeth stood at the sink and I moved to and fro. The emotion I was feeling!

We were supposed to be talking about our plans for the week-end. Above the rattle of crockery in the sink, Elspeth was shouting to me:

'I think we ought to stay in, just by ourselves, this week-end.'

'I think,' I shouted back, 'we ought to get married as quickly as possible, don't you?'

'*What?*' Something splashed into the water. She sounded amazed.

I felt amazed.

I went into the kitchen — it was a very small kitchen. 'I think,' I said, 'we ought to get married as quickly as possible, don't you?'

She had turned from the sink to look at me. Her pale complexion was suffused with carmine, her sparkling blue eyes seemed to have gone smaller. Looking at me she saw the truth of my generalisation, that when somebody says something and you cannot believe your ears, they certainly have said it.

Her lips were moving, the lines at the corners of her mouth flashed in and out. 'Well, yes . . .' I rushed to embrace her.

There was a flap, which came down from a cupboard to

form a table, that served as an obstacle between the door and the sink. 'My darling!' I cried, putting one hand on her waist and rubbing my hip with the other.

We kissed each other.

'My darling!' 'My darling!' We kissed each other again. She was fumbling to take off her rubber washing-up gloves.

'Darling, I love you,' I cried. 'I want us to be married as quickly as possible.'

She looked at me. Tears were coming into her eyes.

'For ever,' I said.

'Oh yes, that's what I want, too . . .'

I lifted the flap so that we could get past. 'Let's go and sit down!'

She managed to get the gloves off and left them on top of the refrigerator.

We went and sat on the sofa and kissed each other many times. 'Isn't it wonderful?' I said.

Elspeth nodded her head.

'I love you,' I said.

She touched my lips with the tip of her middle finger.

'I do so want us to be married.'

'Yes . . .' she whispered.

After a while she looked down at her lap. 'But you didn't ask me,' she said.

'Didn't ask you what?'

'Well, if I'd marry you.'

'Oh dear! I wanted to come to the point as quickly as possible.'

She looked back at me. The corners of her mouth showed a fleeting grin.

'I thought,' I said, 'you *would* marry me . . .'

She was smiling.

'Didn't you think I'd marry *you*?' I asked.

She stopped smiling. 'Yes, I did to begin with, but I began to wonder . . .'

'But I always meant to.' I took hold of her hand.

'Darling.'

This kind of conversation went on for some time, but gradually it became less romantic and more practical. I wanted to settle where and when we were to get married. I wanted to be married by a registrar.

'The alternative,' I said, 'if we were to be married in a church, would be to be married by my father. We should have to tell him, and he'd volunteer to do it. I really couldn't face that.'

Both Elspeth and I were unbelievers. If we asked my father to marry us, I knew he would conclude that somewhere in us lay the seed of belief. I did not like the idea of unbelievers taking advantage of believers any more than I liked the idea of believers taking advantage of unbelievers.

'At a registry office,' I said, squeezing Elspeth's hand, 'we can get married sooner.'

Elspeth squeezed my hand in return.

In the end we decided to get married at a registry office without telling anyone but the witnesses. An exciting, romantic atmosphere came back into the conversation. (Perhaps I ought to say that in our romantic excitement we innocently overlooked the construction that some people — I will not say what sort of people — put on marriages that take place in a hurry.)

Next morning I set about making arrangements to marry Elspeth. I had some surprises. When I asked the registrar how soon we could get married, I learnt that for £3 6s. 9d. I could get married in two days' time.

And then I took Elspeth to buy a wedding ring. Robert and I had a habit of looking in the windows of jewellers' shops. (I thought we were odd until I did a day's count of the relative numbers of men and women who were doing the same as us.) Robert had a particular taste for sapphires. I chose diamonds that were not pure white, especially pinkish ones. The rings we were used to staring at often cost thousands of pounds, though of course I knew there were presentable rings to be had for hundreds or even tens of pounds. I had no idea that wedding rings were to be had for units of pounds.

'It's incredible,' I said to Robert, 'you can get married in no time at all, for next to no money!'

'Society sees to it that getting married is made easy.'

'I'll say it does.' We used to entertain ourselves with the concept of The Pressure of Society. As far as getting married was concerned, it seemed to me now that you had only got to make the smallest first move, and the pressure of society rushed you through the next before you knew what you were doing. No wonder some bridegrooms looked white as a sheet on their wedding-day — finding themselves at the ceremony perhaps a good six months, perhaps a good six years, before they meant to.

Four days later Elspeth and I got married. I did not look specially white in the face nor did Elspeth. But Robert and Annette did.

Elspeth and I arrived at the registry office about ten minutes late, because we had begun our preparations by spending too long over titivating my flat for the reception. It was decorated with large branches of mimosa which we had been keeping cool in the bathroom till the last moment. There was a bottle of champagne and a luscious cake from a French shop in Soho. The guests, our witnesses, were Robert, Annette and Elspeth's schoolteacher friend, Joan.

Anyway, we arrived at the registry office, and there in the waiting-room we found Robert, Annette and Joan. I had never seen Joan before, and expecting her to be the plain partner in the alliance, was surprised to find her quite as pretty as Elspeth. We were ten minutes late. Annette looked pale. Robert looked chalky.

The ceremony seemed to be over in no time, and Elspeth and I were delighted with the result. The thin gold ring was on her finger — never, on any account, to be taken off, I told her. We got into a taxi and embraced each other all the way home. Married! Married for good! I got out of the taxi first, and while I was paying the driver saw Elspeth pause, before she got out, to pick something off the floor.

'Look what I've found!' she cried, holding out her palm for me to see what was in it.

It was a small coin, silver, stamped 1 *Rupee*.

The taxi drove away leaving us standing there, smiling with delight. It was an omen. It was too fantastic to be anything but an omen.

'Darling, keep it!'

'Of course I shall,' Elspeth said, putting it in her bag.

Hand in hand we went quickly to the lift, so as to get up to the flat before the others arrived. When we opened the door the smell of the mimosa was overpowering.

The reception was a success. The guests ate some of the cake and drank all the champagne, and then did not go away. It is difficult to know what to drink after champagne at five in the afternoon, if your host has not got more champagne: they all said they would like some tea. I did not hurry them, I was so happy. I was triumphant, if it comes to that. They had all said I could not get married, but I could. I had done it.

Suddenly, looking at Robert, I realised why he had looked chalky. When we were ten minutes late he must have thought I was not going to turn up. Silly fellow!

As soon as they were gone, Elspeth carried the telephone into the room and we began sending telegrams to our families and ringing up our friends. While Elspeth was talking on the telephone, I was drafting the notice of marriage for *The Times* and the *Daily Telegraph*. I felt in this case it ought to appear surrounded by a special border like that on a greetings telegram. Or possibly just encircled by a wreath of laurels. They had said that I could not get married, that I had missed the boat. Not a bit of it. I was on the boat. I looked at Elspeth. What a boat! My boat. . . .

Elspeth was ringing Harry and Barbara.

'It's Barbara,' she said, handing the receiver to me. 'She wants to congratulate you.'

'Well she may!' I whispered to Elspeth. Then I said: 'Hello, Barbara. What do you think of the news? Isn't it wonderful.'

'It really is. Congratulations, Joe.'

'I've pulled it off. What do you think of that?'

'Splendid,' she said.

'I've got married after all.'

At that I heard Barbara laugh. 'Yes, you have, Joe,' she said. 'But you have to remember *getting* married is very different from *being* married.'

'What!' I cried. And then added: 'Well, of course it is. I can see that all right.'

'You have my congratulations, all the same,' she said.

I handed the receiver back to Elspeth. 'It's your turn to talk to her now,' I said with my hand over the mouthpiece.

I did not listen to what Elspeth was saying to her. Of course there was a difference between *getting* married and *being* married. Or was there? What the hell did Barbara mean?

PART III

CHAPTER I

NEWLY-WED

W E AWOKE next morning before the alarm went off, and I stretched out to find the catch on top of the clock which prevented the bell from ringing. There was scarcely any light coming through the gap in the curtains. The air in the room seemed close and scented. I rolled quietly back into my place.

Elspeth was stirring. As it were in sleep, her hand came on to my waist and her breasts brushed across my chest. I kissed her on the eyelids.

'Darling,' she murmured.

'My wife.'

She stretched a little, away from me, and then came back. 'I feel so sleepy. . . .'

I whispered 'So do I', more not to disturb the warm drowsy atmosphere than to express the whole truth. In one way I felt sleepy: in another I was obviously not. Our first morning married. My thoughts drifted round the idea for a few moments, and then began to circle round another idea. I put my hand on the small of her back and pressed.

Everything was so quiet that I could hear the clock ticking. We stayed for a while, just touching each other. I kissed her again.

'I feel so sleepy,' she murmured in a different way.

I whispered: 'I'll go very, very gently. So that it won't wake you up.'

I felt her kiss my shoulder.

With Elspeth lying drowsily, I acted according to my stated intention; but of course the fallacy in it began to assert itself, and soon she could no longer seem to be asleep. As I did not suppose either of us had ever thought she could, I was not specially conscience-stricken — after all, what nicer way was there, I asked myself on her behalf, of coming awake.

In due course we both came fully awake. Our first morning married. . . . I had time now to consider it at leisure. When I thought I must be getting a bit heavy, I raised myself on my elbows and looked at Elspeth. She smiled at me. Her dark hair was strewn across her forehead and I caught a glimmer of light from her eyes. I thought of a quotation, something about on such a morning it being bliss to be alive, and kissed her enthusiastically under the chin from one ear to the other. Having read physics at Oxford and not English Literature, I was never able to lay my hands quickly and accurately on quotations; yet I never felt it held me back.

'Goodness, it's warm in here,' I said, pushing off the bedclothes. I switched the light on.

Elspeth said: 'We forgot to take the flowers out of the room last night.'

This explained why the air smelt so scented to me when I woke up. I smelt it now. 'A good job, too,' I said.

Elspeth laughed and put her arm round my neck. 'I don't mind, darling,' she said. 'You can't be having baths all the time.'

All the time. I made no comment on the implications of that. 'Just think!' I said, looking into her eyes, 'you're here to stay. . . .'

Although I was looking into her eyes, I noticed she was yawning.

I exclaimed.

Elspeth blushed. 'It wasn't a yawn, really.'

'I'd like to know what else it was.'

She glanced away with an expression so melting, as if I had touched some secret she was keeping, that I kissed her again.

After that I said: 'Now I really must get up and have a bath. Do you realise what time it is?'

Though it was our first morning married, we had both got to go to work as usual. The alarm clock, with its bell put out of action, had given a frustrated click a quarter of an hour ago. I jumped out of bed, gave Elspeth a parting slap, and went to the bathroom. We were already late.

I was late getting to the office. I sent for Froggatt, in order to put the news of my changed status into the official grapevine. To my mind it was worthy of an office notice, being much more piquant than the records of transfer and promotion which formed the typical content of Froggatt's communications. Anyway, *I* was transferred, *I* was promoted. Transferred to respectability, promoted to the ranks of decent ordinary men. Married!

Froggatt looked at me with his drooping, bloodhound eyes and permitted his long face a momentary gleam of amusement.

'May I be the first person here to congratulate you?' he said, in the musical lugubrious tone wherein he combined to perfection that mixture of superficial deference and underlying opposite which characterises the Executive Class.

'You may,' I said. I was delighted to see his feeling for his status — 'the first person here' — peeping through his genuine congratulation. 'Thank you.'

'I take it you'll inform Accounts.'

'Accounts,' I said.

'You'll have a different code number for tax purposes now,' he said. 'As I'm sure you know.'

I tried to look as if I did know.

'In fact you'll get a rebate for the whole of the present tax-year, won't you? As from last April.'

I had often been irritated by Froggatt's getting at loggerheads with the inhabitants of the snake-pit, but at moments such as this I forgave him. This kind of support was just what an S.E.O. was for.

'If you like,' he said, 'I'll notify Accounts. Then they can get in touch with you.'

'Excellent.' In the past Accounts' getting into touch with me had usually meant they were going to try and disallow the taxi-fares on my claims for travel expenses.

When Froggatt had gone, I reflected on how my absence of interest in money had been shown up. Robert was always telling me that I did not think enough about money; and for Robert to tell was for Robert to reproach. Apropos income tax, I did know that the possibility of claiming a full year's rebate brought the national marriage rate to its peak in March, but I had never thought of taking advantage of it myself.

I felt deflated, even chastened. I saw that one of my many moral defects was now going to have greater significance. I liked money very much when it came to me. The trouble was that I never thought hard about how to make it come to me. With a wife to keep I had clearly got to think about how to make it come to me. How many times as cheaply could two live as one? I asked myself. Just under half was my estimate.

I rang up Accounts instead of waiting for them to ring me.

After that I deliberately sat for five minutes trying to think hard about money. I wished it did not happen to be the day when Robert had seen fit to stay at home to correct the proofs of his new novel, because I could have done with his advice, despite its reproachful tone, on how to make money come to me. I reflected on the hastiness with which I had persuaded Elspeth to give up being a schoolteacher, not that she needed much persuasion or that I felt the least inclined to change my mind. I wanted no more of being roused by an alarm clock so that she could set out for Bethnal Green; and I wanted to come home in the evening certain of finding her there already, possibly already cooking something delicious for dinner. You may think it had not taken me long to accept the decent, ordinary man's idea of married life. That is what I thought.

It was clear to me that as a civil servant I could never make money come to me. Robert and I used to comment with surprise on the fact that we had never been offered any bribes, even during the war when we had in our gift, so to speak, civilian jobs for people who were liable for military service. The nearest we came to it was when Air Marshals came to see us about jobs for their sons which would, in the national interest of course, keep the boys away from flying. What was the bribe there? The mateyness of an Air Marshal's manner, the glances, as between equals, from his glaring *beaux yeux*. Not, as Robert would say, a bribe and a half, that.

I supposed there was promotion to be thought of. With Murray-Hamilton and Spinks in the saddle, not, as Eliza Doolittle said, likely. Anyway, I could not be promoted without doing a different job.

Which left me with my art as a source of money. I thought of the excellent press my last novel had got; and then I thought of my publisher's most recent half-yearly statement of royalties. Robert still insisted that the book was a minor masterpiece. My publisher's half-yearly statement of royalties insisted on a minor balance. Of course I consoled myself again with the fact that it is masterpieces, minor or not, that last. The difficulty, as I saw it now, was how was *I* to last? I was nearly at the end of another novel, in the same vein as the previous one. I was pretty happy about it. I had written just what I wanted to write, and I had hit off exactly what I wanted to say — that, in case anybody would like to know, is how original works are written. Robert had identified it as yet another minor masterpiece.

Now, what was to be done? I had been told often enough. I had plenty of friends who were willing to tell me, friends who were in a position, were I to do what they told me, to help produce the result I desired. By that I mean friends in the film industry and the magazine industry. They admired my talent. While having to say that my minor masterpieces were not the slightest use to them, they had not the slightest doubt that I had the talent to provide just what they were looking for. Now you see what I am getting at. What I was required to write was not just what *I* wanted to write, but just what *they* wanted me to write. In other words, crude words, I was required to prostitute my art.

With only the slightest change in tone, in attitude, in subject, I could provide just what was wanted — so ran the argument. With only the slightest change, I could be a prostitute. I was not surprised by the argument, since one of the underlying themes of women's magazine stories, and obviously one of the dearest themes to their readers, was that all women, with only the slightest change, could be prostitutes. Let them try it! was all I could say, speaking as their artistic counterpart.

Speaking as their artistic counterpart, I can only say I believe it is nothing like as easy as it sounds to prostitute oneself. One has to have the talent for it, and if one is born without that talent, one had better stick, so to speak, to monogamy. One's talent, be it for communicating truth or untruth, is nothing like so flexible as people think. I could not decide which people struck me as the more unrealistic, writers who were not born with the talent for pleasing all men planning to write best-sellers, or writers of best-sellers planning to go somewhere, such as a purifying island in the South Seas, to write a serious work of art. If only one could be born all things! I thought. I knew it was no use my setting out to prostitute my talent because my talent would not stretch that far. No, I repeat, it is not as easy to be a prostitute as everyone thinks. In fact, it is jolly difficult. When I saw those girls on the streets, I took off my hat to them. They were doing something I could not do.

My meditations on how to make money come to me were at an end. Robert was wrong in thinking I was incapable of thinking hard enough about it. What I was incapable of, to my regret, was thinking on the right lines. I felt very discouraged. I pressed the bell for my P.A. to bring in my morning's work. While I was waiting for her to come, I wrote on my scribbling pad: 'Go to bank.'

I needed some cash with which to take Harry and Barbara out to dinner. We had invited them earlier in the week, without telling them that by then we should be married. Our reasons were sentiment. We could never forget that it was under their roof that we had met for the first time — tenderest recollections moved us, of dancing at their New Year's Eve Party, of 'The Dark Town Strutters' Ball' in which I hauled Elspeth up from the floor and first looked into her eyes — 'This is the one for me!' And then later, supreme cause for our gratitude, Harry's crucial question, asked out of selfless, uninquisitive affection for us: ' *When are you two going to get married?* ' There was no argument between Elspeth and me about whom we should take out to dinner on our first day married. Thank goodness for Harry and Barbara! was how we expressed our feelings towards them in anticipation of seeing them.

It happened that before they arrived, Elspeth and I expressed our feelings towards each other. We mixed ourselves some martinis and then set about bathing and changing — a procedure fraught with the likelihood of expressing marital feeling. I was standing in my vest and shorts, getting a clean shirt out of a drawer, when Elspeth came from the bathroom, holding a towel in front of her. The towel gave her a delightful air of modesty and unconcern.

'That looks nice,' I said as she went past.

She pretended not to hear.

'It would be wonderful just to see a bit more,' I said, and kissed her on the shoulder.

She turned to look at me. Without make-up her complexion had a glossy sheen: there were damp curls of hair on her temples.

'Darling!' I put my arms round her.

'The towel's damp.'

I took it away.

Her cheeks went pink. 'Darling, you know what time it is?'

'Indeed I do.'

I pushed her quietly backwards to the bed. 'You're wonderful!' I whispered, leaning over her.

'Harry and Barbara'll be at the door at any moment.'

'I'm practically at it, now.'

'Darling!'

We had to be quick. At any moment the doorbell might ring and we could not pretend we were out. I began to sweat. A race against time. A race against time.

We won it.

'Oh!' I said.

Elspeth was quiet.

'Well . . .' I murmured. For a few moments we were both quiet.

I glanced at Elspeth — just at the moment to catch her yawning.

We burst into laughter.

'Good Heavens! Just look at the time!' On the chest of drawers I saw the remainder of the drink I had been carrying round with me while I got dressed. I drank it. I handed Elspeth hers and she sat up and drank it. We kissed each other; and then we began to rush into our clothes.

'They'll be here any minute.'

We saw each other in a mirror, looking pink in the face. I was knotting my tie.

The doorbell rang.

'There they are.' I put on my jacket, kissed Elspeth's bare arm, and ran to let in Barbara and Harry.

Harry and Barbara stared at me briefly: I suppose I stared briefly at them — after all, there was no reason why I should not. 'Come in!' I cried. 'You wonderful pair. . . .' I was still thinking Thank goodness for Harry and Barbara! I kissed

Barbara on the cheek and shook Harry's hand. They followed me into the living-room. They congratulated me again on my new status.

I was just pouring some drinks for them when Elspeth came in. All three of us now stared briefly at her. She looked sparkling — in my eyes her whole outline seemed to shimmer — and the moment I caught her glance I knew that our expression of marital feeling, in combination with a couple of martinis, had produced one of those bursts of hilarity-cum-elation that are impossible to hide.

'I'm afraid we've had a drink already,' I said, as I handed glasses to Harry and Barbara.

'So I see,' said Barbara with a smile.

Elspeth came and stood beside me and I felt her elbow brush against mine. Barbara saw it and went on smiling. There was nothing wrong with Barbara's smile, and yet somehow it contrasted with Elspeth's and mine. I looked at Harry, to see how he was reacting.

'Is that some of your new manuscript?' he said, with an artlessly innocent glance sideways at a sheaf of papers on the table.

'Yes,' I said.

Harry turned his head to look at it steadily and longingly. He was wearing a new very dark grey suit, and his great girth, encased in almost black and momentarily unrotating, seemed to have a faintly sinister quality that was missing when it was light and on the move.

'Yes,' I repeated, in a disinterested tone. 'That's the first draft of Part I.'

Harry waited. He waited for me to ask him if he would like to read it. I let him go on waiting. I had no intention of letting him read a word of it before publication.

'You do work hard,' said Barbara.

'Have to,' I said. 'If I don't work, I don't eat.'

Barbara finished her martini. Smiling, she handed me her glass.

'I suppose now I'm married,' I said, 'I can still go on eating if Elspeth works — happy thought. . . .'

'Is Elspeth going to go on working?'

Though my back was turned to her, I could tell this must be a key question in Barbara's catechism — I recognised the 'I-know-you-better-than-you-know-yourself' sort of tone. I swished the stirring rod vigorously in the jug so that the ice cubes clinked and clattered.

I turned back with Barbara's drink. With her left hand she was fingering her big topaz and diamond brooch. With her handsome topaz-and-diamond-coloured eyes she was giving Elspeth a look of friendly interest. As she took the drink from me she switched the look to me.

'I'm delighted that you've got married,' she began, 'and I hope you'll both be very happy — I'm sure you will — but I'm still not sure I quite understand. . . . Tell me, Joe, what did you get married *for*?'

I gave the contents of the jug a splendid swish and said: 'Whadda ya think?'

Barbara's expression did not change. On the other hand, Harry's did. I just happened to notice him give her an odd glance — he looked momentarily hunted . . . I thought I knew why. I guessed it. My answer did not go for his marriage. Poor old Harry!

Barbara tasted her drink. 'You've made this very dry.'

'You've got to catch up with us.' I glanced at Elspeth's complexion, which was now radiantly pink.

Barbara laughed. 'I doubt if we shall!'

We took them to a restaurant where we could dance. Elspeth and I danced together.

'I'm afraid we're in disgrace,' I said. 'They're rather cross with us.'

Elspeth giggled.

'I know we've not behaved in good taste, but between friends it oughtn't to matter. Look at the times when we've called on Robert and Annette, and they'd practically only just——'

Elspeth giggled again.

I went on — 'And we didn't take umbrage like this.' I thought about Robert and Annette. 'In fact I envied them. I wished it were us.'

Elspeth rubbed her cheek against mine. 'Never mind, darling, *I* don't think you've done the wrong thing.'

I laughed and looked at her. 'With a bit of luck I'll do it again before the night's out.'

Elspeth moved slightly away from me. 'Oh no . . .!'

'Poor old Harry and Barbara,' I said.

'"Tell me, Joe,"' said Elspeth, '"what did you get married *for*?"'

The music stopped and we returned to our places. I ordered another round of brandies. I was beginning to feel tired, and I noticed that shadows were beginning to appear under Elspeth's eyes. Harry and Barbara did not look tired.

Elspeth and Barbara began to talk to each other, and Harry talked to me. First of all he gave me a quick, bright glance, and then said:

'You must be thinking about your future, now.'

His baggy eyes were sparkling, I thought, as if he were in possession of some peculiarly private information. Looking inordinately shrewd, he said: 'Your long-term future.'

'Oh, I suppose you mean children . . .'

Harry grinned. 'I think some of your father's congregation think you've thought of that *already*. . . . So your mother tells me.'

'Really!' I said. 'Oh, oh, oh!'

Harry said, slightly unconcernedly now: 'I meant you must be deciding whether you're going to stay on with Robert or not.'

Just to lead him on, I said: 'Yes.'

Harry looked away, diffidently. I waited. He looked back. 'Are you going to move away?'

I said: 'I don't think so.'

Harry drank some brandy. I noticed that Elspeth and Barbara seemed to be getting on very well together. I said to Harry:

'Why do you ask?'

'I was just wondering.' He paused. 'It must be very difficult for you.'

'Why difficult?'

'Difficult to see what there is for you, if you stay on.'

I was just on the point of drinking some more brandy myself. I halted, angrily. And then I saw that Harry's expression was unreservedly friendly and thoughtful.

I did not reply. How in God's name, I asked myself, did he know about my relations with Murray-Hamilton and Spinks? Had he managed to get to know Spinks? And if he had heard something about my future, what?

Harry was waiting for me to comment. I said:

'As long as Robert stays on, everything remains static, and that suits me.'

'And if he goes?'

I did not say anything.

Harry nodded his head as if I had.

I glanced at Elspeth. My wife — another mouth to feed in the future. And children, we were hoping to have children. In the long-term future more and more mouths to feed. That was what the phrase long-term future meant to me.

Harry looked at me. 'Anyway, you've got plenty of friends to make useful suggestions.'

I was touched.

At that moment the band stopped. Harry looked at Barbara, and said it was time for them to go home.

Our celebratory party was at an end. At the last moment, when we saw them into a taxi, there was a recrudescence of our sentimental regard for them. Thank goodness for Harry and Barbara! A little later, when we called a taxi for ourselves, we suddenly felt the evening had been a success.

'Goodness, I'm tired,' said Elspeth, leaning her head on my shoulder.

'So am I.'

She giggled. 'I'm a bit drunk, too.'

We embraced.

'What a pity,' I said, thoughtfully. 'Too tired and too drunk. . . .'

Elspeth laughed.

When we got home we went straight to bed. We lay in each other's arms. My faintly regretful mood persisted. 'Too tired and too drunk. . . .'

'We'd better go to sleep,' Elspeth murmured.

I waited a little while and then I whispered: 'I don't think I *am* too tired and too drunk. . . .'

'I know. . . .'

My regretful mood dispersed in no time. 'Darling!' I said.

I was not too tired and too drunk. I was just at the point when fatigue and the effects of alcohol counterbalance each other in such a way that one can go on and on, as it seems, indefinitely. There is a tide in the affairs of a man, I kept thinking as I went on and on, which, if taken at just the right point, like this, leads to a remarkable fortune. I felt uplifted by it, exalted. I got more than a bit above myself.

'This,' I said to Elspeth, 'this, this is what I married you for.'

'Oh,' she said. 'Oh.'

At last, at long last, I had opportunity to think over what I had said. I felt that I had taken advantage of Elspeth's ignorance about the tide in the affairs of a man. And not a bad thing, at that, I decided.

Elspeth was asleep.

CHAPTER II

OIL-CLOTH ON THE TABLES

A<small>T THE</small> beginning of March I thought Robert was looking more pre-occupied than usual. It was always on the cards that Robert's looking pre-occupied in my presence was the result of further sniping from Spinks and Murray-Hamilton, but this time I judged that it could not be so. During the last few weeks I had not been to a meeting of any kind and had conducted no interviews.

Often when Robert was troubled by something he was provoked to confide it through being stirred by something else. In this case I happened to stir him by reporting a conversation between Elspeth and me. It was a conversation I thought Robert ought to know about. It had taken place the previous Sunday morning.

Elspeth and I had had an enjoyable breakfast in bed. We were lying side by side. I was thinking that I ought to be reading the Sunday newspapers. Elspeth yawned.

I raised myself on one elbow to look at her.

'Tired?' I said.

A look of amusement shone in her eyes.

'What?' I asked.

'You've got black circles.'

'They'll go when I get up.' I smiled at her.

'What are you smiling about?'

'I was just remembering the first book about Married Life that I managed to get hold of when I was a boy. It said one of the most important problems that faced a newly married couple was: "How often?"' I laughed.

Elspeth laughed.

144

'Ridiculous,' I said.

'M'm,' said Elspeth.

I went on laughing. 'As if you arrive at that sort of thing by argument!'

Elspeth went on laughing.

Then she said: 'How often did it say?'

I was still laughing till that moment.

'How often did it say?' she said again.

'I don't remember. I don't think it said. It couldn't, anyway.'

'Oh.' Elspeth looked up at the ceiling. 'I read something like that that did say. You know, what a bride ought to expect . . .'

'Good gracious!' I was so surprised as to be gormless enough to add: 'How many was it?'

Elspeth said: 'Once a night for the first year, twice for the first six months, and three times a night for . . . you know, just the beginning.'

'Oh! Oh!' I cried.

'What's the matter?'

'What's the matter? Why, it's mad. *What* a programme! It'd be killing!'

Elspeth was silent.

I looked at her. 'Is this what you were expecting from *me*?'

Elspeth blushed.

'Oh!' I cried again, and lay down.

Then I said: 'You must have read it in a woman's magazine.'

Elspeth said: 'I don't think I did . . .'

'Well, it must have been written by a woman. No man could possibly have written it.'

Elspeth had nothing to say.

For a little while I too had nothing to say.

I jumped out of bed. 'I know how to settle this.'

'What are you going to do?' Elspeth asked suspiciously.

'Look it up.'

'You can't,' I heard Elspeth saying, as I went to a book-shelf in the living-room. I took down a book which was the record of a statistical enquiry that had recently been published and that, at the time, was being much talked about. *Sexual Behaviour in the Adult Human Male.* To my mind it was a pretty satisfactory enquiry, since it disclosed principles that had always been obvious to me, namely that people's range of possible sexual behaviour was much wider than it was officially supposed to be, and that people did not do what they publicly said they did. I furled over the pages now for an equally truthful disclosure of detail.

'Here it is,' I said, taking it to show Elspeth. 'Total outlet, active population — age forty, that's me; average 2.3 times per week.' I was delighted with the information: I even felt I might claim a small pat on the back. I repeated loudly: '2.3 times a week!'

Elspeth looked nettled, and tried not to see the graph at which I was pointing.

'Now, let's see,' I went on. 'Robert's forty-five. 1.8. Think of that! Poor Annette. . . . Just think of one point eight per week!'

'I'm not going to,' said Elspeth. 'And I think you ought to stop thinking about it.'

I was sitting on the bed beside her, with the book in my lap. She raised herself and turned over a wad of pages before I could stop her.

'Thought-control,' I said.

She was not listening. She had caught sight of what was on the new page. 'I don't remember this bit,' she said, in a tone that was different.

'Two point three,' I said, slipping my arm round her back.

She pretended not to hear me. My attention was caught by the lobe of her ear, peeping between two dark curls. The hand with which she was holding the book was touching me.

Of course, deliberately, I only reported to Robert the first part of the conversation to begin with, up to 'once a night for the first year, twice for the first six months, and three times at the beginning'.

'Good God,' he said.

He was standing between the top corner of my desk and the window, where the leads from my telephone and buzzer dropped to the skirting.

'I thought you ought to know,' I said. 'I didn't want you to be living in a fool's paradise.'

'That's the most daunting piece of news I've heard for a long time,' he said, and moved heavily towards my easy chair, catching his feet in the wires and bringing the telephone and buzzer crashing to the floor. I picked them up and stood by the window while he sat down. I let him suffer for a little while.

'Extraordinarily daunting,' he muttered. And then: 'What did you say?'

'Oh,' I said, putting on the tone of loftiness and confidence in which he normally addressed me, 'I saw my way through it quite rapidly.'

'What did you do?' he asked, for once in the tone in which I normally addressed him.

'I checked it in the standard work of reference.'

'What in God's name is that?'

I went on with the account of my conversation with Elspeth. Robert agreed with me that it must have been written by a woman. 'Or a man who ought to be a woman,' he said, impatiently waiting for me to come to the figures.

I watched him when I came to the 1.8. Instantly his eyes flickered with a recognisable glint, secretive, prudish and triumphant.

I laughed without saying anything.

Robert laughed without saying anything.

We were both silent for a while. Our laughter died away, as did our feeling of being daunted. It was at this moment that Robert's mood changed over unpredictably. He suddenly came out with what had been troubling him.

'Annette's going on with this idea of taking Elspeth's job when Elspeth gives it up.'

I stared at him. Elspeth had been keeping it dark from me.

'You poor old thing,' I said.

Robert shook his head gloomily. 'It's a moral choice,' he said. 'She sees it as a moral choice.'

'You poor old thing,' I repeated.

When I got home that evening, I reproached Elspeth. She said:

'I did tell you once and it upset you. Anyway, nothing very much has happened. I shall have to finish out my term's notice — we couldn't work an exchange in the middle of term. Whether Annette will get my job isn't decided.' Elspeth paused. 'She still wants it. She's been going ahead to try to get it.'

I asked how far she had gone ahead.

'She's got on to the L.C.C. about it, and she's having an interview with the headmistress. There's a terrific shortage. They'll let her come "on supply", if not as a permanent member of the staff. She's having her interview with the headmistress next week.'

I decided to talk to Annette.

Elspeth arranged a meeting that she considered would look un-arranged. Sometimes when I had a light afternoon at the office I left early and met Elspeth out of school. I met her the afternoon Annette had an interview with the headmistress.

I arrived at the school gates just before Elspeth and Annette came out. It was a cold blustery afternoon with patches of icy drizzle carried in the wind. The darkness of the sky made the hour of the day seem later than it was. A few yards further down the road stood a man in white overalls holding a pole with a circular sign on top of it to stop the traffic while children crossed the road. The children, as far as I could see, were well-fed and warmly dressed; and the prams that some of their mothers were pushing looked as new and grand as anything one saw in Hyde Park.

Suddenly a burst of emotion took me unawares. The impetus to make the change from what I remembered from my boyhood, when my father worked in a working-class place where underfed mothers pushed their babies about in little carts made from orange-boxes mounted on broken wire-spoked wheels, had come from Socialists: and I *was* a Socialist. I had always felt that I was a Socialist by birth, by social origin. My burst of emotion — I may say it was as unusual to me as it was unexpected — came from feeling that I was *right* to be a Socialist. At the thought of feeling I was right to be anything whatsoever, I exclaimed 'Good gracious!'

I saw Elspeth and Annette come through the gates. I kissed Elspeth. And then I kissed Annette.

'Tea now,' I asked them, 'or when we get back?'

They glanced at the dark sky and hugged their overcoats round them. 'Now,' said Elspeth. 'Now,' said Annette.

I said: 'We'll go to a Lyons or an A.B.C.'

Elspeth said: 'We won't, darling. We don't have Lyonses or A.B.C's down here.'

I felt ashamed of my ignorance and Annette burst into laughter. 'Lead us somewhere!' I said to Elspeth.

As we walked along I said to Annette: 'How did things go with the headmistress?'

'Very well.'

'Do you mean she'll have you?'

Annette smiled. 'If I decide I want to go.'

So she had not decided? I advised myself to hold back from argument.

Elspeth led us to a café behind a large window that was too steamed-up for us to see what was inside. It turned out to be a big place, the inner half a step lower than the outer, filled with tables covered in old-fashioned oil-cloth. All the tables were made to take six persons at least.

The girls settled down and I went up to a counter with its back to the large window. There was a burly man in a white apron behind the counter: on a shelf to one side of him was a small wireless set, playing popular jazz. The tea cost twopence a cup less than the lowest price at which I had previously been led to believe it could be profitably served in a café. I thought the burly man in the white apron must be a good chap. I bought some solid-looking buns.

The girls, like all the girls I had ever known, ate heartily. 'What a nice place!' said Annette. 'If I come to work down here I shall come here for tea every day.'

'What on earth for?' I asked.

'I feel at home here.'

I said: 'It can't be very like any home *you*'ve been used to.'

Annette laughed. 'Not in the material sense. The material sense isn't important to me.'

'It would be to most of the people sitting at these other tables, if they were offered the chance of having their tea every day in the sort of surroundings you're used to.'

'Exactly. One makes one's choice for one's self.' Her tone was light but firm. I noticed, now that she had loosened her overcoat, that she had gone back to the dark knitted jumper she used to wear all the time before she married Robert. 'One makes it for one's self, not for anyone else. If I go on having my tea every day in the sort of surrounding I'm used to, I shall still be choosing to do it.' She bit a piece of bun.

'I see,' I said. I also saw that we were discussing a great deal more than choice of locale for tea-eating. 'And what about these people?' There were a couple of elderly men, dressed very shabbily, sitting at separate tables nearby. 'Don't you think they'd think they were lucky if they found themselves in a position to have any choice?'

'Yes.'

'In fact, if we get down to talking about things that really matter, isn't the kind of choice, in particular the moral choice, that pre-occupies you and your friends, one of the perks of the leisured classes?'

Before she could answer, I went on. 'In fact, really getting down to business and talking about the pattern of one's career, for example — do you think that I've ever felt I had much choice about what I was going to do next? Because I certainly haven't.' I glanced at Elspeth, rallyingly. 'Do you think Elspeth has, either? You may argue that I actually have done, but all I can say is that it's never seemed like that to me. The only option I have had was to take the one thing that was offered me or to starve. You may say, of course, that I had a choice there.'

Annette smiled: 'I suppose I should.'

'Well, I can tell you, that isn't how it seemed to me.'

We stopped arguing for a moment. The tea was good as well as cheap. The sound of the jazz was cheering.

'I wonder why those two poor old chaps are having their tea here, all by themselves,' I said.

Elspeth looked at them. 'I suppose their families have migrated to one of the new estates up the line, Hainault or Woodford, or somewhere. They're probably too old to move. . . . And yet I'd have thought somebody would have asked them in for a cup of tea.' She answered my question: 'I don't know.'

'The school seems crowded,' Annette said to her.

'Do you really think of coming to teach here?' I asked.

Annette looked at me. 'If I do I shall cease to be a member of the leisured classes, shan't I?' She laughed. 'At least I shall have no leisure.'

I did not like the sound of that. Poor old Robert! Poor old thing! Out of the corner of my eye, I saw Elspeth become more attentive. I said:

'You'll have made your choice, anyway.'

'And I shall feel, as a consequence, that I'm really doing something useful.'

'And that will satisfy you?'

'I shouldn't have put it that way — but yes . . .'

'At the expense of poor old Robert's feeling homeless?'

Annette was not piqued. 'At the expense of Robert's being a bit put out,' she said in her light firm tone.

'Sometimes when you talk about moral choice,' I said, 'you make me feel it's something I've missed. More than that, as if it's something I lack. As if my moral nature were coarse, and insensitive, or even as if I were in some way morally blind. At other times' — I paused — 'I feel it's something I'm just as well without. Exercise of moral choice is one of the perks of the leisured classes, for one thing. For another thing, it often seems, to people who aren't pre-occupied with it, to come pretty close to self-indulgence.'

Annette suddenly blushed. I went on. 'You mean your statement "One chooses for one's self" to be a scientific observation of what happens. But it often rings with a note of *approbation*, which makes it sound like the statement of someone who is exclusively pre-occupied with his or her *self*.' I shook my head. 'You see what I mean.'

'I do. And if it did, I should agree with you.'

'Are you sure,' I said, 'that you don't want to come and work down here in order to avoid what, for some reason I don't understand, would be the greater effort of running a house and home for Robert?'

'I don't think it's right to have servants,' Annette cried. 'And I don't want to have to do myself the things they do — I can do more valuable things.' She raised her voice a little. 'And some things *are* more valuable than others. Some ways of living are more valuable than others.' She paused. 'And value,' she went on, 'if it means anything means value here and now.'

I drew back. I had been lectured before on the super-significance of 'here and now'.

'The value of our way of living, here and now, arises from the personal choice we make, here and now,' Annette said.

'Ergo, the succession of here-and-nows,' said I sarcastically, 'is a succession of personal choices.' Which made the future, I thought, a poor look-out for Robert.

'I was not going to say that at all,' said Annette. 'I was going to say, ergo — if you commit me to ergo — our way of living is just as valuable as we succeed in making it. Our lives are what we put into them.'

'Cor!' I said, but it sounded unconvincing — which was no surprise to me, because I agreed with what she said. The concept of moral effort was as dear to me as it had been to my non-conformist forbears.

There was another pause. Elspeth was the first to speak. 'I suppose I'm going to do the opposite thing to Annette,' she said. 'It seems funny, doesn't it?' She glanced at me. 'It isn't going to make *me* feel immoral, darling, to live on your moral earnings.'

Annette laughed. I gave Elspeth a look of praise. That's the sort of girl you want to marry! I thought.

After a moment, Annette said: 'Perhaps I shall let Robert choose for me.'

I smiled at her. 'Perhaps . . .'

Annette moved her head suddenly, so that her bell of hair swung to and fro.

'I don't think I shall,' she said. 'Let's talk about something else!' She took off her overcoat, letting it fall across the back of her chair.

Elspeth said to me: 'I should like some more tea.'

I picked up our empty cups and went to the counter. As I walked away, Annette set her elbows on the oil-cloth and said animatedly to Elspeth: 'When you come here alone, do you talk to people sitting at the same table?'

Suddenly an idea that had been lurking at the back of my mind came to the front. I could have said: That's broken my dream! Annette, twenty years ago, would have become a Communist.

As I waited while the burly man in the white apron poured the tea, I gazed through the steamy window in the direction of the street; but I was back in the thirties, at Oxford . . . thinking of intelligent, upper-class girls, choosing to join The Party.

Those days had gone, and I was confronted with the difference. Annette was a Socialist of sorts. She had little use for the Labour Party, which she regarded as worn out. 'They've got no theory for *now*,' she had once informed me. 'They had a theory fifty years ago, but it's no use for now and they know it. They're just hoping to muddle through without.' And she had less use for the Communist Party: she was completely disillusioned with revolution.

'Oh dear!' I said to myself, as I carried the cups of tea back to them. I was confronted by the fact that I was a generation older than they were. Was that difference the root of my feeling irritated by Annette? When I remembered that I had been equally irritated by intelligent upper-class girls, especially pretty ones, choosing to join The Party, I thought not.

What irritated me was something that had irritated me throughout the whole of my life — the peculiar kind of self-concern that always seemed to go with the deliberate making of moral choices. I had never liked it. I never should. I thought of Robert, who liked it as little as I did.

'Poor old Robert,' I said to myself. 'He's had it.'

CHAPTER III

AN OFFICIAL VISITOR FROM AMERICA

ONE afternoon my P.A. rang me.
'I've got someone to speak to you, Mr. Lunn, who says he knows you. I think he's an American. Do you know a Mr. Thomas Malone? He says he met you in Washington. I've got him on the line now.'

I could not remember anyone named Thomas Malone, not anyone special, that is. It sounded the sort of name that a lot of people might have. I said:

'If he says he knows me, I suppose he must. Put him through to me.'

I heard her say 'Here's Mr. Lunn for you, Mr. Malone', and then a loud, exuberant, American voice said to me:

'Hello there! Is that Mr. Lunn? This is Tom Malone here. How are you?'

I said I was very well.

'Remember me?' he said. And then he announced the name of his office.

At that I remembered who he must be. Three years earlier I had been over to America on an official trip, and for one of the jobs I had to do he was my opposite number. Without being able to recall what he looked like, I did remember that we had got on well.

'Remember that night at the Statler?' he asked, even more exuberantly.

We must have got on very well. I had a weakness for hearty evenings, for being a man among men.

'Wish I could!' I said facetiously, while trying to think which one it was.

'That's the boy! I can hear you haven't changed.'

What is commonly called a warning instinct made me say quickly:

'Oh, but I have. Wait till you see me!' I thought I had better put him wise to my change of status as soon as possible. 'Since you last saw me I've got married.'

'Then you look better than ever, I guess.' He laughed. 'Am I going to have the pleasure of meeting Mrs. Lunn?'

'Certainly you are,' I said, recalling that on the evening of the party at the Statler I had not had the pleasure of meeting Mrs. Malone, very definitely not. I had gathered that Mrs. Malone was at home looking after their five children. I said: 'How long are you staying?'

He said he was planning on staying through Wednesday — to-day was Monday — when he was going to Paris. 'I've got to drop in on NATO and SHAPE.' He had also got his plans for London, these including an evening with me, and a morning looking round what he chose to call our 'outfit'. He wanted to meet our bosses — I may say that after his fashion he was quite a big shot, himself. 'I may even tell them how good you are at your job!'

To my chagrin Robert was not in London. It was just my luck, I thought, for Robert to be hearing about people with whom I had made a negative hit and then to be missing when I could produce somebody with whom I had made a positive one. Positive, I thought, and not afraid to say so!

Tom — I had to call him Tom, since Americans give one no alternative between calling them by their Christian names and calling them Mr. — had already got hold of Robert's name. Also of the name of Murray-Hamilton. He had not previously met either of them.

I was free to fit in with his plans. Elspeth and I would take him out to dinner that evening. The next day he could have a look round our outfit and meet Murray-Hamilton. I put down the telephone receiver and pressed the buzzer for my P.A. to come in so that I could tell her about it. I felt excited. The telephone seemed to have transmitted to me a gust of euphoria.

When Elspeth and I met Tom Malone that evening his state was clearly euphoric. I could not say whether I should have recognised him or not. He was short and stocky, about the same height as me and a stone and a half heavier — that stone and a half being composed of muscle, powerful active muscle — and he had the sort of square, snub-nosed, grinning Irish-American face that seems to be made for expressing a mixture of blarney and ruthlessness. It was obvious, from the moment we met, that he liked me. I could not for the life of me think why.

It was obvious that he liked Elspeth, too. Every glance he gave her was so filled with life and energy that I felt ashamed of lapsing from my duty as a host — the trouble was that since getting married my list of girls, from whom I might have rustled up one for an occasion such as this, seemed to have dispersed. So soon, I thought, so soon. . . . How sad I felt to have lost them! And yet, how cosy I felt to be just with Elspeth!

'You didn't tell me your wife was so young and pretty,' he said to me, while we were drinking some preliminary whiskies.

'Did I have to?'

'Well' — he gave Elspeth and me a vigorous, blarneying look — 'no!'

Elspeth blushed. I was delighted.

When we had settled at our table in the restaurant and were looking at the list of things to eat, Tom said:

'If you won't raise any objections, I'm going to buy the champagne.' He glanced at us to make sure he was carrying us. 'O.K.?'

'Champagne!' we cried enthusiastically, meaning that it was O.K. — actually it usually gave Elspeth and me stomach-ache.

I was amused. We had brought him to an expensive restaurant. Up to now I have omitted to tell you that Tom

Malone was both clever and quick in the uptake. I may also take this opening to observe that in my experience there is nobody like an American for summing up on the spot exactly how expensive a restaurant is. 'Lots of champagne!' he said.

I decided he should have caviare if he wanted it. He chose smoked salmon.

The evening was a great success, and I was pleased for more reasons than one. Honesty compels me to admit that in the first place I had felt relief at having Elspeth to get me out of spending another evening like the one at the Statler. Much as I had enjoyed it — it really was one of those nights when one cannot remember next morning what happened — I just did not want another. Not here. Not now.

'You take him out to-night on your own, darling,' Elspeth had said when I had first told her Tom Malone was here.

Let me explain why she said it. A few months earlier, just after we got married, I had happened to make, in passing and yet not unaware that she would pick it up, one of my favourite generalisations, that married men had a tamed look. Elspeth took it amiss. She took it touchily, I thought.

I did not start an argument with her about the truth of the generalisation: it stood up to the test of experiment to the extent of enabling me, when I was interviewing our scientists and engineers, to judge whether they were married or not and get the answer right eight times out of ten. I could never understand why people took it amiss. They would not have expected a man with a full belly to have the same look as one who did not know where his next meal was coming from.

In my opinion, based on observation, when a man was satisfactorily married a certain look went out of his eye. A certain, identifiable look. (Its disappearance had enabled me, only a few weeks earlier, to guess that a candidate who came up before an annual promotion board had got married since we saw him the previous year. When he asked me how

I guessed and I innocently told him, he said with a furious glare: 'I happen to be rather tired at the moment because we've just been moving house!') That tamed look. . . .

It was women who took the generalisation the most touchily.

'I suppose you think you'll look tamed?' Elspeth said.

'Why not?'

'You'll think it's my fault.'

'I shan't *notice* it. That's the point.'

'I don't like to think other people will.'

'*They* notice next to nothing.' I changed my tone. 'And anyway, darling, *I* think it's worth it. . . .'

At that Elspeth's tone changed. But not her intention. From then on she encouraged me to have hearty evenings out with my friends, to keep up my minor taste for games-playing, and so on.

So you can see how it came about that Elspeth asked me if I would like to take Tom Malone out for an evening on my own. And I am afraid you will also be able to see why I declined.

While we were eating some particularly succulent fillet steaks, I looked at Tom and wondered if he regretted the kind of evening we were having. Sybil! — I suddenly thought of Sybil. She would have been just the girl for this evening. She would have liked Tom Malone and Tom Malone would have liked her. I wondered where she was, and I felt glum. And ashamed of myself. . . . However cool and remote she was, I had no excuse for just quietly letting her go, with hardly a word, when I decided to get married. Dear Sybil, who had never done me a scrap of harm, in fact had always done me a power of good.

However, Tom Malone did not appear to be regretting the kind of evening. On the contrary.

Incidentally, just to finish off my case about being tamed, let me add that all men who are satisfactorily married — and most men are: I was astonished by the number of letters

I got from men from whom I would never have expected it, writing to congratulate me on my marriage, who said with obvious truthfulness: 'I can only hope you and Elspeth will be as happy as we have been' — all such men have a recognisable, tamed look; but this does not mean that they all do not have an eye for a pretty woman, far from it. A certain look, which identifies an unmarried man, goes out of their eyes. But other looks can come in. I would not have needed to glance twice at Tom Malone to know that he was a married man. I did not need to glance at him twice to know that, were I out of the way, he would have made a pass at Elspeth.

I thought Elspeth was looking remarkably pretty. She was pressing her knee against mine.

Tom said to me:

'Next time you come to Washington, you must bring your wife with you.' To Elspeth: 'Have you ever been to the States?'

Elspeth shook her head. As scarcely ever having been out of the country caused Elspeth exaggerated feelings of inferiority, I intervened quickly.

'I'm afraid the Civil Service don't pay for wives to go to Washington with their husbands.'

'Why shouldn't *we*, if we invite you? Why don't we do that? You did us a lot of good last time you came. It would be worth it to our outfit just as much as to yours.' Tom looked at us with blarney and ruthlessness in his bright blue, slightly bloodshot eyes. 'Come on, let's say we're gonna do it! O.K.?'

'O.K.!' we both cried, caught up by the spirit of the moment.

'As soon as I get back to Washington, I'll have us send an official invitation. Who do we send it to — Mr. Murray-Hamilton?'

'That would be correct,' I said. I could not subdue a wish that for once Murray-Hamilton should hear good of me, even though I knew — Robert had told me often enough — that I stood the best chance of survival in my job if Murray-Hamilton heard nothing of me, neither ill nor good. (Why, I asked myself, should people who think ill of one become even worse disposed to one if they hear a good report?)

'Then that's as good as settled,' said Tom. 'Here's to Mrs. Lunn in Washington!' And he finished his glass of champagne.

I did not see it ever happening, but that did not stop me finishing my glass.

'We need another bottle,' said Tom and beckoned the wine waiter.

Elspeth now appeared to be blushing all the time.

By the time we left the restaurant it was nearly midnight. We were all floating in euphoria. Tom and I went and stood out in Jermyn Street while Elspeth got her coat: we needed air.

'It's been a very, very swell evening,' he said. 'London's a wonderful town. Wonderful people.'

'Glad you liked it.' I glanced up the street, thinking about taxis and home. 'Which way do you go from here?'

'Got 'ny ideas?'

He was giving me a knowing, encouraging grin. How could I possibly pretend to misunderstand him? I looked round quickly for Elspeth to save me — she did.

'Ready?' she said, coming down the steps to us.

Tom burst into laughter. So did I. Elspeth said to him:

'Are you coming back to have a drink with us?'

Tom said: 'Well, no, I'll stroll back to my hotel. It's only just down Piccadilly.'

We said our goodnights, and then Elspeth and I got into a taxi. I put my arm round her.

'What an extraordinary man!' Elspeth said. 'What do you think he's going to do now?'

'I hate to think.'

I felt Elspeth kiss my cheek and I heard her whisper: '*I* don't. . . .'

She kissed my cheek again.

'Good gracious!' I whispered. 'Surely you don't mean in a taxi?' I knew that was just what she did mean; but I thought it well, now that I was married, to start being a bit stuffy about such matters.

'It's quite a long way to Putney,' she whispered.

On the following morning neither Elspeth nor I had stomach-ache from the champagne. 'You look very well,' she said to me. I was relieved. I did not want to take Tom Malone over to see Murray-Hamilton looking as if some of the things I was supposed to be accused of were true.

My P.A. had arranged for us to see Murray-Hamilton at eleven o'clock, and at a few minutes to eleven I got a telephone call from the policeman on the front door to say that Tom had arrived. I said I would go down to meet him, to save him coming up to my office first.

'Hello there!' The exuberant call rang through our foyer. Tom and I shook hands vigorously. He looked spruce and freshly shaven. 'All set?' he said.

We began to climb the staircase — Murray-Hamilton's office was on the first floor.

'Did you get home safely last night?' I asked.

'Fine,' he said. 'London's a wonderful town. Wonderful people.'

I glanced at him. He glanced at me, with his Irish grin — and caught his toe on the edge of the stair. 'Since I last saw you I haven't missed a minute of it.'

I glanced at him more closely. 'You don't mean,' I said, 'that you haven't been to bed?'

'Not to sleep,' he said. 'How do I look?'

I laughed. 'No different.' It was true. His blue, slightly bloodshot eyes looked bright and clear. His step was powerful and energetic. Looking at me, he laughed with satisfaction. A great gust of his breath came across to me. Brandy. Pure brandy. He was drunk.

'I'm looking forward to meeting your Mr. Murray-Hamilton,' he said.

I could well imagine that he was.

It embarrasses me to describe the meeting of Tom Malone and Murray-Hamilton. In fact I seem, presumably for the sake of my own peace of mind, to have forgotten a good deal of it. I remember crossing Murray-Hamilton's large room and seeing Murray-Hamilton sitting brooding and reflecting behind his huge mahogany desk. A particularly handsome Ministry of Works picture glowed from the wall behind him. Our feet made no sound on the carpet.

'It certainly is a pleasure to meet you, Mr. Murray-Hamilton,' said Tom, striding forward to shake his hand. 'And I certainly consider myself fortunate to have Mr. Lunn here to introduce me to you.'

'Sit ye down,' said Murray-Hamilton, banishing his brooding look in favour of an affable smile. He handed Tom a cigarette, and then lit it for him — I wondered if the match would ignite Tom's breath.

They began to talk. They began to talk about Tom's work, and about ours. Tom talked loudly and forcefully and with sustained emotion. I tried to keep out of the conversation. Things could hardly be worse, I thought. The brooding, reflective look was creeping back into Murray-Hamilton's eyes.

In due course Tom referred to my last official trip to Washington. At that I realised things could be worse.

Loudly, forcefully, and with sustained emotion, Tom Malone told Murray-Hamilton how wonderfully I had represented our department, how wonderfully I had represented *him*, Murray-Hamilton. Do you wonder my memory begins to give out?

Tom paused — I wondered if I had ever seen a man so drunk.

Tom went on. He told Murray-Hamilton what a grasp I had of my job, and what a technique I had with which to do it. And he ended up by telling Murray-Hamilton I was the best interviewer of scientists and engineers in the United Kingdom.

I really do not remember anything else till I had got Tom Malone out of the room. I do not want to remember anything else.

When Tom and I got outside we went steadily down the staircase. At the turn we met Spinks, Stinker Spinks, going up. Spinks and Tom Malone turned to eye each other; Tom missed his footing, and with a succession of bursting laughs bumped down to the bottom of the staircase on his backside.

He was a damned good chap, Tom Malone.

CHAPTER IV

ROBERT'S TROUBLES

I DID not give Robert an account of Tom Malone's visit
— for once I thought he might be allowed to preserve
his disbelief in the existence of anyone whom he had not
found for himself. I was haunted by my picture of Murray-
Hamilton sitting at his desk, the ledger open before him . . .
on opposite pages he recorded Right and Wrong.

Robert had a new novel coming out. Also he had Annette
to cope with. In case you have not had the opportunity to
study the artistic temperament, perhaps I ought to say that
it was the former which occupied him the more.

Robert had a fit of gloom. He was always in a hyper-
sensitive state just before a book came out — a state from
which he was readily thrown into apprehension if not gloom.
And this essential state appeared not to be seriously altered
when, as the centre-piece of his excellent press, he had the
middle page to himself in the *Times Literary Supplement*. Very
useful, indeed. People do not appear to read it, but they do
appear to know it is *there*. For instance, the *T.L.S.* circulates
officially, along with *Nature*, *The Economist* and others,
through the offices of the upper echelons of the Civil Service.
Within a fortnight of Robert's getting the middle page, he
had been invited out to lunch by first Murray-Hamilton
and then Spinks.

'What did Stinker Spinks say to you?' I asked.

Robert was markedly offhand. 'Actually he was rather
interesting, when off his normal beat. It appears that he's
got quite an important collection of Roman coins. I didn't
know about it. He talked quite interestingly about them.'

'Do you think he'll invite *me* out to lunch when *I* get a middle in the *T.L.S.*?'

Robert said: 'I think he might, you know. Murray-Hamilton definitely won't, I can tell you that. But Stinker might. There are moments when his desire to be near to success, even somebody else's, is even greater than his envy of it. I think he might ask you.' He paused. 'If you have this ambition, peculiar as it is, you ought to be warned that his club gives you a very poor lunch. An execrable lunch.'

When we went to our own club it was obvious that Robert in their opinion was doing well. No body of men responds more quickly to a change in the barometer of one's prestige than one's club, especially to an easily visible movement in the upward direction. Members who have not spoken to one before, speak to one: members who have spoken to one before, offer one a drink: members who have offered one drinks before, suggest one goes up to dinner with them: and members with whom one has dined for years say they are going to buy one's book. It is difficult not to let it go to one's head.

The first weeks after publication passed. And once again gloom, this time a different kind of gloom, supervened. The reviewers who had put Robert's book at the head of their columns were now, with equal hebdomadal panache, putting somebody else's book there. Robert came into my office and sat heavily on the corner of my table.

'I feel,' he said, 'as if I might just as well have dropped it into the sea.'

I understood how he was feeling.

Why worry? you may ask. How right you are — please go on! Why be a writer? Why be Robert or me? Why not be two other chaps? Robert and I sometimes considered your last suggestion as the one, true way out of our dilemma.

'I might just as well have dropped it into the sea,' Robert said again.

The poignance of the concept kept me silent. Attention,

attention . . . all artists are endlessly craving attention. A neurotic lot — not like everybody else.

Robert found little to console him in his domestic situation. Annette was still holding to her moral choice. Speculating on what he might do, I took it into my head that he might get Annette's father to take his side.

Then one day I happened to meet Annette's father. I called at Robert's flat on my way home from the office, to collect some of my manuscript which Annette had been reading. To my surprise, the door was opened by Annette's father.

'Come in,' he said cordially. 'I'm here on my own.' Tall and stork-like, he walked ahead of me down the corridor. 'I'm staying here while my flat is being re-decorated. It's rather more agreeable than getting a room at the Club.'

I was touched by his unusual cordiality. Tall and stork-like, he preceded me down the corridor — to the kitchen.

'I was just going to have a whisky,' he said, 'to save myself trouble, though I should prefer to have some tea. Perhaps as you're here we might make some tea?'

In the kitchen he turned to look at me with a sparkling, encouraging look in his eye. It was the most intimate sign of recognition he had ever given me. I felt that he was almost offering me his friendship. Actually, I realised, he was inviting me to make tea for him.

'The first step,' I said, 'is to put on the kettle.'

'I believe that is so,' he said, with an amused glance round the kitchen which indicated little intention of doing it himself. I filled the kettle and lit the stove.

'At least it is,' I said, 'for people of our class.' I did not see why he should not get something of what he was asking for. 'In schools for the lower classes,' I said, having picked up the information from Elspeth, 'the child's first instruction is, "First empty the pot!"' In case he did not follow, I added: 'The implication being that the pot has not been emptied after being used.'

To my surprise he bestirred himself to the extent of looking for Annette's tea-pot. It was on the window-ledge. He picked it up, weighing it, and then with a negligent gesture handed it to me.

It was full.

I burst into laughter. I could not help admiring him. I had demonstrated that I did not give a damn. No more did he. He smiled with sub-fusc satisfaction.

'I wonder where Annette empties it,' I said.

He stroked his moustache and gave me a swift glance from under his eyebrows — he had long eyebrows that curled outwards. 'She used to empty it in the lavatory — after we'd once suffered a slight contretemps after emptying it down the sink.' He took the tea-pot from me and went out of the room.

When he came back the kettle was boiling and I had got cups and saucers for us.

'Shall we have tea in here?' he said. 'It will save us trouble, won't it?'

'I think Annette and Robert have their tea in here,' I said.

'Very sensible of them.' He got a bottle of milk and some butter out of the refrigerator. 'There doesn't seem to be very much to eat,' he observed as he shut the door. 'We must be going out for dinner.'

I opened a bread bin and took out half a sliced loaf wrapped in waxed paper. We sat down at a small table and began our tea.

'I wonder where we're going for dinner,' he said. 'I know Annette's first choice of place to go out to for dinner is a coffee-stall in the Fulham Road.'

'I didn't know there was a coffee-stall in the Fulham Road.'

'They're getting harder to find,' he said, with a touch of gloom. 'We're always having to go a long way . . .'

I tried to find a happier topic.

'This is superior tea they have,' I said.

'Very good.'

He got up and looked in some of the cupboards.

When Annette and Robert moved into the flat they had had the kitchen completely done up by one of the classy kitchen firms that had made their appearance since the end of the war. The tops of the stove and sink and the benches of drawers were all on the same level, while the hanging cupboards also were perfectly aligned. Some of the cupboard doors and drawers were painted bright yellow, the rest white, while the benches and our table were covered with the latest thing in plastic surface materials. The kitchen was much envied by Elspeth.

Annette's father opened a hanging cupboard which, as far as I could see, was empty except for a small jar on the lower shelf. He brought the jar out.

'Marmite,' he said. 'Annette used to eat a lot of it when she was up at Oxford. She believes it to be highly nutritious.' He spread some on a slice of bread and butter, and then passed the jar to me. 'I don't know if you know it? I rather like it.'

I said: 'You'll need something pretty nutritious if you're going out to a coffee-stall for your evening meal.' I thought of the pork chops which Elspeth had ordered for us. What a satisfactory marriage mine was!

'That's what I thought,' he said.

I waited a moment and then said directly:

'What line are you taking over Annette's becoming a schoolteacher in Bethnal Green?'

'I would have thought she might find a teaching-post nearer home.'

We stared at each other.

After a pause he said: 'Of course, she's changing, you know. I mean, since her marriage.' He could see that I was expecting some revelatory comment. 'She dresses better, don't you think?'

'I suppose I do.' It occurred to me that at dinner-parties which succeeded the first one, when she had appeared in her wedding-dress, Annette had worn a black frock which Robert had chosen — Elspeth thought it was cut too low at the front, but I thought it was all right.

'I always thought when she was at Oxford,' her father said, 'she looked as if she had just landed by parachute.' He could not resist glancing at me slyly.

I laughed.

'Oh yes,' he said, pretending not to have heard me, 'I can see Robert's influence.' He gave me the same glance again; and this time I saw a gleam, light and clear, of malice.

I stopped laughing. The full measure of his detachment had for the first time really struck home to me. He was clever, cultivated, cordial and humane; he was unusually free from envy and stuffiness. He was also free, I thought, from serious concern with anyone but himself, dazzlingly free. . . .

And I had taken it into my head that Robert might be hoping for his intervention! I had made a frightful ass of myself. I knew Robert could not possibly have hoped for such a thing.

Annette's father spread some Marmite on a second slice of bread and butter. 'I do recommend this,' he said.

Out of sheer moral disadvantage I took some. A look of amusement was glimmering in his eyes.

'What do you think of Robert's new novel?' he said. 'You and he write very different kinds of novel, don't you?' He paused. 'I think it's very interesting that you should have such a high opinion of each other's books. It does you both credit.' He leaned forward a little. 'And it *interests* me.'

We engaged in literary conversation.

Meanwhile I was reflecting on a matter that had not occurred to me before. I knew that every shrewd man considered it was a good idea to marry his boss's daughter. To a really shrewd man it is so self-evident as not to require consideration — he just does it automatically. What I had not reflected on before was what the boss thought about it.

I kept thinking of the gleam of malice, light and clear, that Annette's father had let out of the corner of his eye.

CHAPTER V

SEVERAL POINTS ILLUMINATED

ANNETTE moved into Elspeth's job.

One day when I happened to see Barbara — it was a day when I was going to the office by Tube and we met on the station platform — I asked her how Annette was getting on at the school.

Barbara was going down to her Bethnal Green clinic. 'I suppose you see Annette quite often now,' I said.

'Yes, we're getting to be quite friends.'

'How's she doing?'

'Very well indeed.' Barbara looked down the railway line. It was a cold June morning and there was a drift of mist in the cutting. 'I think she's made an excellent adjustment.'

'That's fine,' I said. 'What has she adjusted?'

Barbara smiled. 'You know what I mean.'

'You mean she's adjusted herself to the children,' I said, modelling my tone on that employed by Robert on such an occasion — the tone of a bright boy successfully taking part in a guessing competition.

Barbara said: 'She's made an excellent *overall* adjustment.'

'Over all what?' I burst into laughter. 'All right. I won't go on. You mean that you think her "moral choice" has made her feel cheerful.'

'I do.'

'And what about poor old Robert?'

Barbara began to say something, but I did not hear it because the train came into the station. We got in and sat down side by side. After a while I could not resist teasing her.

'I suppose it was "adjustment" you had in mind when you warned me that it was easier to get married than to be married.'

She nodded her head.

'What does it mean,' I shouted, 'actually?'

She thought for a moment. We were crossing the river: it looked pretty in the morning light.

'Learning to live with each other. Making allowances for each other's different desires.'

'Most of the time we seem to have the same desires.'

Barbara looked at me. The train stopped in the next station.

'Do you really find that?' she said.

I thought about it. It was true. I said:

'I suppose we must be easy-going, that's all.'

Barbara was smoothing a crease in her skirt — she was wearing an expensive-looking dark grey suit. Just before the train started again she said:

'And you have no feeling that you're *missing* something?'

'Well, no. . . .' What could we be missing? Children? There was not time yet for us to have had any. I was at a loss. I said: 'Missing what?'

Barbara leaned towards me.

'Have you had many quarrels?'

'No.'

Instantly I knew that I had failed to recognise a key question, and as a consequence, worse still, had truthfully given the wrong answer.

'You mean,' I shouted, 'we ought to quarrel?'

'It's very unusual not to.'

'Why ought we to quarrel?' I put my ear close to her mouth to be sure of hearing her answer.

'It's one of the commonest ways of relieving the tensions of marriage.'

I was confronted with the possibility that my marriage had no proper tensions.

I was silent. I got out my newspaper. It was *The Times*. Since getting married I had started to take *The Times* and to wear a bowler hat. I felt that such a radical change in status as getting married ought to be marked in my case by an appropriate change in outward habit. Elspeth did not mind my taking *The Times*, but she hated the bowler hat, on the explicit grounds that it did not suit me. I suspected that implicitly she considered it was a symbol of tamedness. Actually I thought I looked ridiculous in it. (Come to that, I thought all other men looked ridiculous in bowler hats. Just think detachedly of a human face, and then of a bowler hat on top of it!)

Throughout the day I considered the fact that Elspeth and I did not quarrel. If there were tensions in our marriage we were not releasing them. And if there were no tensions there must be something seriously lacking. I meant to discuss it with Elspeth when I got home.

When I got home — delightful experience!... Elspeth was there — Elspeth opened the door for me. A delicious smell of cooking came out. I realised exactly, now, what it meant in romantic novels when it said 'He kissed her hungrily.' Elspeth, by a marvellous combination of instinct and intelligence, was turning herself into a first-rate cook. The time was just long enough after the war for food to be getting varied and plentiful again, even though some of it was still rationed. Publishers were racing each other to bring out new cookery-books: I used to give them to Elspeth as presents.

After dinner we sat on the sofa, enjoying the pleasures of digestion before we did the washing-up. I was holding her hand.

'Men are carnal,' I said, as a more highbrow way of expressing the fact that the way to a man's heart was through his belly.

Elspeth stroked my hand consolingly.

'I must say it's wonderful being married,' I said.

Elspeth gave me a quick look.

'It's specially wonderful being married to you.' Luck had come my way after all, and all at once.

Elspeth said: 'You never asked me.'

I was caught. I could not think what on earth she meant.

'You never asked me to marry you.'

'No more I did.'

She looked at me closely. 'Don't say you don't remember!'

I frequently got into trouble for not being able to remember cardinal events in our married life. 'Of course I do,' I said. 'You were washing-up, and I was in this room.'

She relaxed. 'Near enough. . . .'

I touched the wedding-ring on her finger. 'Ought I to have asked you?'

'Yes.'

'Didn't you know I was going to ask you?'

'I wasn't sure . . .' She faltered. And then she picked up. 'I thought it was getting time.'

I laughed and then kissed her.

I touched her wedding-ring again. 'Poor baby, you didn't get an engagement ring, either.'

She blushed.

'When I get the Book of The Month in America, I'll buy you a great big diamond.'

'I don't want a great big diamond.'

We were silent. Suddenly she laughed. I asked what was the matter.

'I just thought of you buying yourself all those new clothes before you got married.'

I thought the best thing I could do was to laugh.

And then *I* picked up. I kissed her cheek. 'You're not doing so badly.'

She turned quickly and kissed me.

We were silent again. 'It *is* wonderful . . .' she said.

175

At that moment I recalled my conversation with Barbara. *Was* it wonderful? *Was* it?

I said: 'Darling, do you think we ought to quarrel?'

Elspeth looked at me in some stupefaction. 'What for?'

I then reported my conversation with Barbara. Elspeth listened with attention, and at the end said:

'I don't agree.'

I was relieved. In fact I was pleased, terribly pleased. I confided:

'I don't like quarrelling.'

'Nor do I,' said Elspeth.

I said: 'I don't quarrel easily, and when I do, I mean it. Unfortunately I can't make up and forget it. I remember it.'

'I've hardly ever quarrelled with anyone. And when I did it upset me for months.'

I said: 'In that case, I think we'd better go on as we are. It seems all right to me.'

'I don't want to quarrel with you, darling, ever.'

I said: 'Then, don't let's!' I was very happy about this outcome.

Elspeth sat quietly, thinking about it. After a little while I became discursive. I explained to Elspeth a fact which had first occurred to me several years ago, that some people seem to need to quarrel. 'It seems to provide the friction, the stimulus,' I said, 'which makes them feel they've really been brought to life.' I recalled one of Robert's former loves — the one who hit him with the whisky bottle.

'In fact,' I wound up, 'it seems as if, for some people, a clash of wills is inseparable from sexual excitement.' I paused. 'I should have thought it must be very tiresome for them. And tiring. . . .'

We were silent. I was thinking that my generalisation was profound and that the tone in which I had stated it was admirable.

Elspeth said: 'I've remembered — I think that book was by an Indian . . .'

I was caught again. I simply could not work it out: I had
to say 'Which book?'

Elspeth said: 'That one that gave you and Robert such a
shock. What did he call it? Daunting?'

'An Indian!' I said. I suddenly thought of millions of bright-
eyed, birdlike little Bengalis, perpetually on the boil. But I
was not willing to give an inch. 'An Indian *woman*,' I said.

Elspeth laughed. She looked at me sideways. Her eyes
were sparkling.

I jumped up. 'Come on!' I said. 'It's time to wash up.'

Elspeth got up. 'I've been waiting for you all this time.'

We went into the kitchen and did the washing-up. If our
marriage was missing something, we still had plenty to keep
us satisfied.

The following morning, whom should I meet, as if by
chance, but Harry. I was sure he had been lying in wait for
me somewhere on the route to my usual bus-stop. He fell
into step with me.

'Lovely morning, Joe,' he said.

I agreed that it was. The lilacs and laburnums were in
flower in people's gardens. It was some time since it had
rained, and the dust on the road gave out a faint familiar
scent — it reminded me of being somewhere abroad, where
roads were always dry — the South of France on a dazzling
spring morning, in the days long before the war. . . . Some
little girls in purple blazers passed us.

Harry said: 'It's nice to see you again.'

I nodded my head.

It was difficult to say whose fault it was, that we had seen
so little of each other recently.

Somehow Elspeth's and my getting married had estranged
us from Harry and Barbara. 'You could scarcely think it
really could be that, when it was they who brought us
together,' Elspeth had said.

'The movements of the soul,' said I, 'are not necessarily
to be explained mechanically.'

177

As this speech had a somewhat dowsing effect on Elspeth, I added: 'Actually, it's one thing to bring people together, and another to know how you're going to take the outcome.'

The light had come back into Elspeth's eyes.

So, when Harry said it was nice to see me again, I felt it as unintended reproach, and yet there was nothing I could do about it.

'Why don't we have lunch together?' I said, doubting if it would do any good. Harry and Barbara, in their married state, had looked at Elspeth and me in ours, and something had — well, made them turn their heads away.

'Yes, we will,' said Harry.

He swung along beside me — he walked with short steps, seeming, compared with me, to be balancing forwards on his toes.

'I hear you saw Barbara yesterday morning,' he said.

I smiled. 'Yes.' I wondered if it was to discuss this that he had waylaid me, and decided not. Harry was too innately wily to come straight to the point, even when there was not the slightest reason for not doing so.

'She's a strange girl,' he said, looking in front of him.

I was touched.

'I'm very attached to her,' he said.

I was touched again.

He turned his head — I was aware of an odd glance coming round his snub nose — and said: 'She has a good deal to put up with from me.'

I said mildly: 'Yes.' It seemed fair enough.

'Even if I didn't see myself as others see me, I should realise that,' he said. He seemed to be laughing.

'Yes,' I said again, now completely mystified.

Harry said nothing else. In a little while we came to the bus-stop.

We climbed to the upper deck of the bus and settled ourselves in two seats at the front.

'Well,' said Harry, speaking now in his high, fluent,

conversational tone. 'What do you think of Robert's new novel? I've scarcely seen you since it came out.'

The scales of mystification fell from my eyes. Though there had been a break in our conversation, and though Harry's tone was different, the subject was still the same. Before I could answer, he said:

'I enjoyed it tremendously.'

I knew what he had waylaid me for.

You may remember that although Robert did not see much of Harry — in my belief because he had not found Harry for himself — he used to question me about Harry with such interest that I suspected he must be thinking of someone like him as a character for a novel. Well, there was a character in Robert's new novel who resembled Harry in some important respects, in particular being globe-shaped, whirling, and impelled by curiosity — while differing in others, such as social origins, profession and so on.

'I enjoyed it tremendously,' Harry repeated, just to make sure the point had gone home.

I said nothing. I should have loved to question him about what he thought of Robert's character — it would have taught me a lot about Harry and a lot about literary art. For Robert's vision of Harry, as far as it actually was of Harry, was different from mine. I tended to see Harry as a sort of non-sexual voyeur, whose ferretting out of details about everybody's lives somehow fed his sense of power. Robert saw his own Harry-like character in a more Dostoievskian light, as wildly whirling in the flesh and pretty wildly whirling in the soul as well, held in control only by a strong will — a will stronger than I would at first sight have given Harry credit for. Yet every so often the will of Robert's character failed him, and an act of a most peculiar kind so to speak escaped him. It was an act of what Robert chose to name 'motiveless malice'.

The vision fascinated me, partly because I had seen nothing of such acts in Harry's conduct of recent years, partly because it evoked an extraordinary recollection from my boyhood. Harry had told a schoolgirl whom I was going out with that I was writing love-letters to another girl. It was untrue: there was no basis for it: Harry had absolutely nothing to gain. The girl dropped me, refusing to tell me why, and I was unhappy for weeks — during which time Harry had listened to my confidences and gone to great lengths to console me!

Such an act of 'motiveless malice' provided Robert with a dramatic turn — completely invented, of course, since in life his own path and Harry's scarcely ever crossed — in the central plot of his novel.

Suddenly I heard, to my stupefaction, Harry saying:

'I enjoyed it most of all for the portrait of that young economist.' This was the character I was thinking of.

'It was splendidly done,' Harry said. 'I know what it's like to be that sort of man.'

I turned to look at him and in his expression saw strong emotion. His eyes were shining. 'Yes,' he said. 'Robert understands us very well. . . .'

Then, just as suddenly, his mood changed. His shining glance shifted obliquely and his tone of voice went up.

'I think,' he said, 'Robert understands me better than you do, Joe.'

I looked through the bus window as if I had noticed something specially interesting about the traffic.

'Don't you?' he asked triumphantly.

'I think that's for you to say.' I went on looking through the window.

For a little while Harry looked through the window, too.

'Yes, Joe,' he said. 'Let's have lunch together — let's make it soon!'

CHAPTER VI

A SURPRISE AND A SHOCK

THROUGHOUT the next months I worked hard on my new novel. I was beginning to have the highest hopes of it. I had made a dent in the public's consciousness with my previous book. It seemed reasonable to believe that another small masterpiece, banging on the identical spot, would make the dent deeper. Why not? The public's consciousness is not like a tennis-ball.

'You're bound to make a bit of money sometime,' said Robert. 'I rather fancy it may well be this time.'

I was not, of course, expecting to make a similar impression in America. My sense of humour had not become the least bit un-British, as far as I could see, during the last year. When I read through my manuscript, it made me laugh. When Robert read through my manuscript, it made him laugh. But what was the good of that? *We* were British.

'One thing's certain,' Robert said, still in his optimistic mood. 'Courtenay will be delighted with it.'

Courtenay Chamberlain was my publisher.

I said: 'I think he will.'

This encouraged Robert still further. 'If you don't get an excellent press for this, I shall be very surprised. Very surprised indeed. And, well . . . you may well make a bit of money.' He grinned. 'And so will Courtenay.'

I grinned, but not quite so much.

Anyway, in October, having given the manuscript its last cuts and titivations, I sent it on its way to Courtenay. Another small masterpiece. (Actually, by now, I was getting a bit sick of reading it, but that did not make me feel any less inclined to accept Robert's opinion of its quality.) I registered the parcel.

Then Robert and I sat back to wait. In these days Robert seemed to be enjoying a remission from his gloomy, apprehensive, pre-occupied state of the last few months. For one thing my affairs were clearly going much better. For another his own affairs, I judged, were troubling him less. All the same, I was completely unprepared for what he said to me one morning when he came into my office.

Robert was sitting on the corner of my table, stirring a cup of tea which our P.A. had just brought in. We had been talking about a visit we were going to make to one of our research establishments, and he had lapsed into gazing idly through the window.

'By the way,' he said, turning to me, 'it looks as if Annette's going to have a baby.'

For a moment I was too surprised to think, and then, I am ashamed to say, I thought something unworthy about him.

'Good gracious!' I said. 'That's wonderful news.'

'It's not a hundred per cent certain yet, but I shall be very surprised if she isn't.'

I began: 'Did you — ?'

Robert gave me an authoritative look. 'It's unintentional as far as both of us are concerned.' He paused.

I paused. 'What does Annette think about it?'

'She seems very happy about it.'

'What about her doing a job? It will affect that.'

'I realise that.' Robert thought about it. 'In some ways it's a little awkward, happening at this particular point in time.' He glanced at me sideways. 'But she's quite certain that she wants to have it . . . And I don't need to tell you that I want her to have it.' He looked at me full face. 'I want it very much.'

I was moved by his emotion. 'Then I'm very, very glad indeed.'

'I think it will be all right.'

I laughed with relief. 'All women want to have babies, anyway.'

'Some less than others.'

We were thoughtful.

I told Elspeth that evening. 'You must admit it's a surprise,' I said.

She glanced at me oddly. 'Yes, darling.'

'What's the matter?'

She began to smile. 'It's a bit alarming, isn't it?' she said. 'Think about us . . .'

That point had not struck me. 'We shall be all right.' I hugged her. 'You're a wonderful wife.'

We were silent for a little while.

'It makes all the fuss about whether she ought or ought not to become a school-teacher look rather academic,' I said.

Elspeth said: 'Why?'

I said: 'Well, she won't be able to, now.'

'Not at all. She can have time off to have the baby and then go back again. Time off,' she repeated emphatically, 'with pay!'

I did not argue. That was as might be.

And then I thought: Suppose I made a bit of money with my new book, should Elspeth and I think about having some children? I began to long for that bit of money.

And that reminded me that it was time I heard from my publisher about my new small masterpiece.

Another fortnight elapsed, and then one morning I had a telephone call from my literary agent. Robert was in my office at the time, sitting on the corner of my table.

My agent was ringing me with news from Courtenay.

'What is it?' said Robert, beginning to turn pale.

I tried to listen to both him and my agent.

'Doesn't he like it?' Robert asked incredulously.

I put my hand over the mouthpiece. 'He thinks it's wonderful. But he can't publish it.'

'Why on earth not?'
My agent rang off.
I turned to Robert.
'He thinks it's too improper.'
Robert went on turning pale.

PART IV

CHAPTER I

LEARNING THE LAW

Two days later I had lunch with Courtenay.

Courtenay was an excellent publisher. The discouraging thing about him was that there was a startling physical resemblance between him and me — discouraging to me because, though we looked startlingly alike, I was an artist and he was a businessman.

Let me give you an example. The first time we met, Courtenay asked me to have lunch with him at his club. Being young in those days and unused to clubs, I was pleased and impressed. We sat down at a table and ordered what we were going to eat.

'What would you like to drink?' Courtenay asked. 'A glass of beer or something?'

'Thank you,' I said shyly, 'I should like a glass of beer.'

Courtenay called the wine waiter and ordered a glass of beer for me and a bottle of wine for himself.

You see what I mean about being a businessman? And yet he was not insensitive, far from it. Later in the meal, when I was finishing my glass of beer and he his glass of wine, a rueful look came into his eyes, large, light-coloured eyes that Robert, with a more romantic vision than mine, used to refer to as sad and lemur-like. Courtenay put down his glass not quite empty and said to me consolingly:

'It was only cat-piss, really.'

We looked, I can tell you, surprisingly alike. He was the same size and shape as me; he had the same large rounded forehead as me and the same sort of curly hair, now turning grey like mine. He looked very lively and, worse still, he

looked — painful though it is to say it, artistic integrity
compels me — dapper . . . I looked at him and I thought of
myself. I was an artist and he was a businessman. I wore a
bow-tie; he wore a bow-tie and a carnation. One day, when
we were washing our hands in a club lavatory, he suddenly
looked intently into the mirror above his wash-basin, and said
in a rueful tone:

'Joe, why do I look such a cad?'

Far was it from me to give him an answer.

He was an excellent publisher. To be an excellent
publisher you have to be a businessman. I had no intention
of leaving Courtenay.

On the other hand, the morning I met Courtenay for lunch
I was not what my Civil Service colleagues might have
called happy in my relationship with him. I felt amazed
and injured. My small masterpiece *improper*? (Or, more
accurately, perhaps too improper to be published.) It
seemed to me incredible. It was no more improper — if you
want to be able to judge for yourself — than this book you
are now reading! (To be accurate, just about the same.)
I went to Courtenay's club looking pale, I have no doubt,
but feeling proud.

I was early and had to wait in the foyer. I meant to
reproach Courtenay as soon as he came in, not to wait until
after lunch. Businessmen, I had learnt, went in for lunch
first, business afterwards, a form of etiquette that I, as an
artist, found intolerably digestion-destroying. In the past
I had put up with going through the whole lunch, with
wine, waiting for Courtenay to say what he thought of my
new manuscript. Nowadays I used to ask him before he got
his overcoat off. Lunch first, business afterwards — O.K.
But Art before either!

Through the glass doors I saw Courtenay coming vigorously up the steps. He was not wearing an overcoat. A
carnation glowed in his smartly-cut lapel. He shook my
hand.

'It's a very good book, Joe,' he said, warmly. 'Very good.'

I stared at him.

'But I can't risk publishing it.'

Before I could say anything he got me moving up the staircase to the bar.

Courtenay got some drinks and we settled down in a corner by ourselves.

'So you think it's improper?' I said.

Courtenay gave me a shrewd glance. 'Who said I said that?' Though his eyes might normally, according to Robert, look sad and lemur-like, they could give a shrewd glance that was positively levantine.

I told him my agent said he said that.

Courtenay then did look sad. 'How you both misunderstand me,' he said. He looked at me straight. 'Do you think I'm a prude, Joe? Do you honestly think I'm a prude?'

I said I did not think so.

'You, Joe, can write anything you like,' he said, 'and I should like it.' He began to smile. 'In fact, in this book you have . . .' He went on smiling. Then suddenly he stopped smiling. 'But if I print it, I shall have the Home Office down on me like a ton of bricks. It won't do, Joe. . . . Publishing's a business, you know. Something you artists sometimes don't fully understand. The firm's got to make money, not lose it. If I brought this book out I'd risk losing a hell of a lot of money.' Then he added. 'And it's not *my* money . . . It's the firm's money.'

I cannot say my heart was wrung as much as his by that thought. I said: 'But surely it's not as improper as all that? I've read books much *more* improper.'

'So you may have. So have I. They've been published and nothing has happened to them because the Home Office hasn't been interested in them.' He drank some of his gin-and-tonic and then gave me his levantinely shrewd look. 'But we've just heard that the Home Office is going to start getting interested.' He glanced round as if he might be making sure that nobody was eavesdropping. 'Apparently they're just about to open a new drive . . .' He paused. 'In case you should be thinking that some other publisher might be ready to publish your book, I'm afraid that won't be so. The word's going round . . .' He drank some more gin-and-tonic and said modestly: 'I just happened to be the first one to hear.'

This left me for some time with nothing to say.

'I suppose,' I said at last, 'I shall have to alter the book?'

'I sincerely hope you will,' he replied.

I remarked. 'You sound doubtful . . .'

'I am, Joe, I am. I don't know how much you'd have to alter it to make it pass.'

'There must be some standard of reference,' said I.

Courtenay shook his head. 'The Home Office, or the Director of Public Prosecutions, can set the standard more or less where they like. Since the war everybody's noticed that it's been going down. Now they're going to put it up. We shan't know how high they're going to put it' — he made a gesture with his hand — 'till they put it.' He rested his hand on my arm. 'It's got us publishers worried, Joe. Definitely worried.'

'No more worried than it's got one of us writers,' I observed.

'For instance,' said Courtenay, 'they could take *The Decameron* out of circulation tomorrow if they felt like it.'

'But you don't publish *The Decameron*.'

'No.'

'And I,' said I, 'am nothing like as improper as Boccaccio.'

'I know.' He patted my arm. 'Have another drink, Joe. I wish I could help you, old boy.'

With a lively step he went to the bar. When he came back with two more drinks, he said:

'Of course I'm not entirely without any suggestions for you, Joe. Don't think that! I want to publish that book, Joe. I believe in it.' He looked at me. 'My suggestion is that you should talk to our solicitor about it. I rely on him. Will you do that, Joe? He'll explain the law to you, and then even make some suggestions about how to . . . tone the thing down so as to get by with it. You just twist the book a bit' — he grinned — 'and we'll twist the Home Office.'

I said all right, I would see the firm's solicitor.

We drank the rest of our drinks without making any further headway. And I must say I did not feel very much like eating any lunch afterwards.

In his businesslike way, Courtenay arranged for me to see the solicitor on the next afternoon.

The solicitor had his chambers in an old rabbit-warrenish sort of building. However, the room in which he himself worked when I finally got to it reminded me agreeably of a tutor's room in a college. It was a square room with a tall sash-window that looked out on to a green stretch of grass. The walls were panelled and painted white — as in college rooms, they looked fairly dirty — and they were ornamented with old county maps in Hogarth frames. An electric fire was glowing in the fireplace.

When I entered the room the solicitor got up from his desk — I saw my manuscript on it — and smiled at me in a pleasantly composed way. He was tall, slender, nicely filled-out. I judged him to be about fifty. His neck was long and cylindrical, and he had a smooth oval face. His hair appeared to have gone white prematurely. Altogether he was a nice-looking man. Beautiful teeth, I noticed, when he smiled. Nice grey eyes.

'Ah,' he said, shaking my hand and speaking in a warm unaffected voice. 'I want to tell you how much I've enjoyed and admired your book.'

I must have looked startled.

'You see,' he said, giving me his pleasantly composed smile again, 'I want you to see right from the start, that I'm not pi.'

π? For a moment I was startled again. Then the language I had never spoken at a prep. school came back to me. 'Oh, pi,' I said, nodding my head. 'Yes, not pi . . .'

'H'm — h'm.' He sat down again.

Actually I would not have thought at first sight that he *was* pi — or not pi, for that matter.

I sat down in a big leather armchair beside his desk.

He clasped his hands beneath his chin and began.

'The first thing I have to explain to you, Mr. Lunn, is that the law relating to Obscene Libel is——'

'*Obscene Libel!*' I cried.

He smiled. 'Libel, in this case, does not mean what you think it means. The word derives from *libellus*, meaning "little book".'

Little book! That was just what I had written. A charming, attractive little book, a masterly little book!

'But obscene!' I still cried. 'That means repulsive, repellent. There's nothing repulsive or repellent about what I've written.'

'Not to you, clearly. Not to many people, I dare say.' He spoke slowly and evenly all the time. 'But that is not relevant, I'm sorry to say. One of the questions we have to ask ourselves in the first instance is: Might it seem repulsive, repellent, to the Director of Public Prosecutions?'

'How am I to know? I've never met him. Anyway, there's always *somebody* to whom *something* is repellent.'

'I was referring to the D.P.P. in his official role.' He smiled a little.

'What's that?'

'That of advising the police whether or not to take action over a particular book.' He paused. 'Though I must tell you the police are not bound to take his advice.'

'I see,' said I.

'Not,' he went on, 'that it need necessarily be the police who set the Act in motion in the first place. Any person, any private person, can set the Act in motion.' He paused again. 'But we are straying away from the point. I have to explain to you that in connection with the Act there is no definition of what is obscene.'

'Oh,' I said.

'Nor is the punishment for "publishing an obscene libel" anywhere defined or limited.'

'Oh,' I said again.

'Of course,' he went on, 'there are, as it were, *some* sign-posts.' He smiled at me.

'M'm?' I said.

'In the absence of a definition of obscenity, we have a test for obscenity. You probably know it? That of Chief Justice Cockburn in 1868.'

I shook my head. He nodded his.

'In any case, I should have felt bound to remind you of it,' he said. 'It goes thus: "The test of obscenity is whether the tendency of the matter charged as obscenity is to deprave and corrupt those whose minds are open to such immoral influences and into whose hands a publication of this sort may fall" . . . Let me anticipate' — he held up his hand in a pleasantly composed way — 'a claim that I'm sure you must be going to make, that you, as the author, had no intention to deprave and corrupt any of your readers.' He smiled at me, shaking his head. 'In the court, this is ignored. The intention is judged entirely from the book itself . . . I can go further. In the court the author has no *locus standi*, as we call it. He may neither give nor call evidence.'

It dawned on me that he must be the most composed person I had ever met.

'And lastly,' he went on, 'two final points, before we get down to work on your book, in which, I'm afraid, we shall have to make radical alterations if we are to meet the Home Office in its new mood — in what we have reason to believe will be its new mood — two final points. With reference to Chief Justice Cockburn's test. There is no certainty in *theory* as to the meaning of the words "deprave and corrupt" nor to which class of persons they apply.' He paused. 'Nor is there any certainty in *practice* either.'

There was a short silence.

'Well, thank you,' I said. 'It sounds to me as if you've covered the lot.'

'Thank you for saying so.' He turned slowly to look out of the window. The light glimmered on his beautiful teeth. The contrast between his white hair and smooth uniformly brownish complexion was striking. He turned back to me.

'In our work we shall have two signposts on which we can rely,' he said. 'The one, my knowledge of previous indictments. The other' — his voice became more resonant — 'our own good feelings.' He nodded his head. 'It is the latter which in the long run will make the more important signpost. Incomparably the more important. I'm confident that if we rely on our own good feelings, all will be well.'

Something made me feel inclined to reserve my judgment.

'Now,' he said, beginning to turn over the pages of my typescript. 'To begin with I think we'd better look for isolated passages that might cause us trouble.' He glanced up and smiled. 'I can reassure you. They are fewer than might be expected. If I may say so, that is a tribute to your talent.'

As he appeared to mean it, I smiled back.

'Here is the first point. I see here a word consisting of the letter "f" and three asterisks.'

'Good gracious,' I said. 'That word's printed in full, about ten times a page, in ——' I named an American war-novel that everybody had read.

'In that work,' he said, 'you will recall that the word was *mis-spelt* ... I'm afraid your device leaves it open to the correct spelling, when no doubt might be left in the mind of the Home Office.' He held up his hand. 'Now, please don't

think I'm being pi! I'm not suggesting you should remove it.
Indeed, I'm not. We all know the word is sometimes used,
even if we do not use it ourselves. What I'm suggesting is
that you may keep the letter "f" and add four, or perhaps
five asterisks.'

'That might certainly leave some doubt in the mind of
the Home Office,' I said.

'With five asterisks we might have no trouble at all. And
our good feelings would be spared.'

I said: 'I think I'll cut the whole remark out.'

'That would be meeting the Home Office more than half-
way. I'm glad, Mr. Lunn.'

He went on turning over pages. 'And now,' he said,
looking down, 'I have to notice that here you've mentioned a
member . . .'

'Member?' I said, startled. 'Member of what?'

His head remained down. 'I was hoping you'd take my
meaning without further explanation. I was using the word
"member" in the sense of . . . "organ".'

'Oh dear,' I said. I felt as if I were going to blush. Then
I said: 'Where have I mentioned it?' I went and looked
over his shoulder at the manuscript. 'But I *haven't* mentioned
it,' I said. 'Show me where!'

'Ah, that is merely a tribute to your literary skill. It
is not mentioned by word, but I have no doubt that the
Home Office would feel it was *there*.'

'If two people are making love,' I said, 'it's bound to be
there! Home Office or no Home Office.'

'H'm, h'm,' he said thoughtfully. Then: 'Making love . . .'
He looked up from the manuscript. 'I wonder if your good
feelings tell you that kissing might serve your purpose just
as well?'

'I can tell you,' I said, tapping the manuscript, 'it
wouldn't serve *theirs*!'

There was a long pause.

I said: 'I suppose that scene will have to go out.'

'That's excellent, Mr. Lunn. I'm very glad indeed to hear you say that. I can see that ours is going to be a very fruitful partnership.'

There was a pause. He quietly turned back the pages of my manuscript, so that the book was closed.

'I see that I can now safely leave isolated passages to you, Mr. Lunn.' He smiled. 'I wish that were the end of our troubles. If the law were concerned only with isolated passages, I can assure you it would be. However, the law is so framed that there is no certainty as to whether the test of obscenity is an isolated passage or the book's dominant effect. We now have to consider the book's dominant effect.'

'The dominant effect,' I said with authority, 'is that of a work of art.'

He said: 'In declaring a book "obscene" according to the law, it is very doubtful if a judge or jury may take that into consideration.'

'Oh,' said I.

He smiled. 'I hope I'm not tiring you with so many explanations. I think I can make quite shortly the statements in the light of which we have to consider your book for the purpose of judging its dominant effect. Obscenity, as you know, has always been confined to matters related to sex or' — he completed the sentence hurriedly — 'the excremental functions. Furthermore, we say something is obscene, we know it to be obscene, if it arouses in us a feeling of shock, of outrage.'

I was really irritated.

'In your book there is a good deal about matters related to sex,' he went on. He smiled friendlily. 'Now didn't your good feelings tell you that the dominant effect of the way you had presented them might arouse a feeling of shock, of outrage, in some persons who might read it?'

'Not till there was some question of the book not being published.'

He shook his head in a way that signified composed disappointment in me. 'I'm afraid it may arouse that feeling. It well may. The characters in your book make love to each other. There appears to be no likelihood of their generating children thereby — in fact you go to no lengths to conceal from the reader that they are not married. What is the dominant effect of the passages in which these actions are recounted?' He answered the question himself, after first posing another one. 'Do we see them in a light of immodesty, of shame? . . . Undeniably we don't.' He paused. 'The dominant effect of these scenes is of pleasure.' His lips formed the word as if it were spelt with a capital P. 'Of undivided Pleasure! Of complete Enjoyment!'

'That was what I had in mind,' I conceded honestly.

He said: 'Suppose, then, a jury were directed to imagine a typical young person — tempted to sexual activity, and asking desperately "How do I stand?" and "Where do I go from here?" — searching for an answer to his problem in your book.' He paused. 'What answer do you think he'd find in your book?'

I did not say anything. He was making me feel shy again.

'The answer he'd find would be Yes, a thousand times Yes, wouldn't it?'

I said: 'I think a thousand's a bit much.'

'You may be right . . . But twice would be enough.' There was almost a tremor in his composure. 'Or even once, more's the pity!'

I looked out through the tall sash-window. The grass looked very green, the daylight very limpid. Not like his imagination, I thought.

'You now see what I mean by the dominant effect, Mr. Lunn.'

'Indeed I do,' I replied.

He smiled very composedly, very friendlily now. 'I'm glad you've been so understanding,' he said. 'Obscenity is a very difficult thing to make clear to authors. And the task of making it clear is specially difficult for anyone like myself, who, as you now see, is not in the least pi.'

I nodded my head.

He picked up my book to give it back to me. 'This is an excellent book, Mr. Lunn. When you are re-writing it, just let *good* feelings be your guide. Then the Home Office will let it go by. In affairs relating to sex, remember modesty, concern for the conventions, awareness of sin; above all don't give us a dominant effect of undivided pleasure, complete enjoyment, as you have done!' He smiled. 'Think of that typical young person whom the jury might be directed to imagine! . . . Keep him *clean*!'

He stood up, and I stood up. As he shook my hand he said:

'When I look into your face, Mr. Lunn, I can see that you *can*!'

CHAPTER II

WAS IT A HELP?

WHEN I bore the news back to Robert he was very distressed. By that time I was beginning to feel more than distressed.

'Altering isolated passages is child's play,' he said.

I nodded, thinking of the infallible device, i.e. excision, that I had already hit upon.

'But the dominant effect . . .' Robert shook his head.

'I don't see,' I said, 'how I can produce a different dominant effect with those characters and that story.'

At the thought of them Robert bowed his head. He was no doubt dwelling on undivided Pleasure, complete Enjoyment.

'The trouble is,' he said, 'that the dominant effect is . . . *you*.'

I did not quite like the sound of that.

'It's you,' he said, 'who shine through the whole book.'

Shine! That was better.

'If only,' I said, 'I could shine a bit more *cleanly*!'

'That,' said Robert, 'is the disability we've got to get round, somehow — the disability, I may say, *vis-à-vis* the Home Office. I personally don't agree with either Courtenay or his solicitor that the book is obscene, and I doubt if anybody we know would.' He paused. 'But it isn't anybody we know who's going to set the Act in motion; or anybody we know who's going to decide whether the Act shall take its course.'

'In some ways it would be a help in these circumstances,

I said, 'if you did think it was obscene, and then I could alter it so that you didn't.'

Robert glanced at me. 'Yes. I see that.'

'Or,' I said, 'if the dominant effect is *me*, I could ask *you* to re-write the book.'

'I think you can take it,' said Robert, in a slightly sharper, loftier tone, 'I should treat the subject rather differently.'

I had nothing to say to that. We remained silent. I was concentrating on how *I* might re-write the book so that, in the circumstances of there being no definition of what was obscene, it could in no circumstances be pronounced obscene.

Robert interrupted me.

'I wonder how this business started,' he said. 'I bet you when Courtenay first read this book he didn't think it was anything worse than mildly improper, in an amusing, amiable, acceptable way.'

'I didn't even think it was improper!' I cried. 'I just thought it was natural.'

Robert went on: 'Granted that, when he put it to this egregious solicitor you saw, he got the answer he did get, I still don't see why he sent it to the solicitor in the first place.'

'He heard the Home Office were going to start a new drive.'

'That's as may be. But I wonder what made him associate a prospective Home Office drive with your book . . .'

I shrugged my shoulders. I was too preoccupied with my own actual problems to be drawn into Robert's speculations. I was trying to think of the typical young person whom I was to try not to deprave and corrupt — remembering that nobody really knew, least of all cared to say, what being depraved and corrupted entailed.

'And I wonder how it's done, anyway,' Robert was saying. 'I suppose people at the Home Office get together with people in the Department of the Director of Public

Prosecutions, and then they tip off Chief Constables to start reading books.'

'*My* book!' I said, thinking of my innocent, natural, small masterpiece in the hands of a Chief Constable.

Robert said: 'I think I'll make it my business to have lunch with Courtenay. It can't do any harm to find out how he got the word from the Home Office, and it might do some good.'

There were occasions, it seemed to me, when Robert sounded more like a civil servant than an artist. However, I did not say anything.

Two days later Robert had lunch with Courtenay. When he got back, he came straight into my office. Without taking off his overcoat he sat on the corner of my table and said:

'I've found out how Courtenay heard the Home Office were going to start a new drive against books. He didn't hear direct. He was told by an intermediate person. And your book was specifically mentioned at the time . . . Who do you think that intermediate person was?'

I looked at him. Having declared our thoughts to each other continually over the last twenty years, there were occasions now when we just read them. I said instantly:

'Harry.'

Robert nodded.

'Good God!' I said.

Robert went on nodding.

'But why?' I said. 'And how?'

Robert paused and then said with heavy detachment — and very faint knowingness:

'I suppose "motiveless malice" . . .'

I pondered this.

'Incidentally,' said Robert, 'have you let Harry read the manuscript?'

'I have not.'

'How could he have read it?'

'He has a drink sometimes with my agent. I suppose he got a few pointers out of him, harmlessly enough, and then' — I thought of one of Harry's favourite phrases — 'pieced it together. . . . Nobody has more skill, or more practice, at piecing things together than Harry.'

We paused. Suddenly I had a new idea. I said:

'I suppose Harry didn't fabricate the rumour about the Home Office?'

Robert shook his head. 'That would be carrying motiveless malice to inconceivable lengths. No. I should think he did pick up something, probably from some bird in the Home Office who belongs to his club. It's very much a place for senior civil servants, especially youngish ones who're on the way up.' He continued my education by naming some of them.

I brought him back to Art. I said:

'But it doesn't follow that because Courtenay heard the Home Office were going to start a new drive that it was going to be directed against me for one.'

Robert shook his head.

There was a pause.

Robert said: 'I'm afraid the result of my researches isn't relevant to the immediate literary problem that confronts you.'

Now I shook my head. The result of his researches was not relevant to what I proposed to write; but it was relevant to what I proposed to do. I meant to see Harry without delay. I told my P.A. to ring him up.

Harry invited me to lunch at his club. It was not a club I liked at the best of times — like most men I cared only for my own. And this was far from the best of times.

In outward appearance Harry's club seemed to me to combine gloom with stodginess, its most imposing feature being a huge staircase of considerable grandeur and practically no illumination. And somehow my invariable recollection of the club was of having coffee, after a poor meal, in an alcove on this staircase. In fact there were no alcoves on the staircase itself, but that did not affect my invariable recollection. This was the club, as Robert observed, where senior civil servants had seen fit to swarm, as for instance bishops and vice-chancellors swarmed at the Athenæum, or men of unusual talent and exceptional good-will swarmed at mine.

When I arrived Harry and I went straight up to lunch — partly because we were late and partly because his club, like several others which prided themselves in not moving in an ungentlemanly way with the times, had no bar. (My invariable recollection of another club, much superior socially to Harry's, was of having to have drinks before meals standing up, more or less *under* the stairs.)

I dodged the club's soup by asking for potted shrimps, which were imported in blue cartons from a reliable contractor.

'I'm afraid,' said Harry, 'I don't belong to this club for its food.'

Not feeling called upon to express an opinion on that, I said:

'On the whole civil servants don't notice what they're eating. They're too busy thinking.'

Harry's eyes brightened. 'What are they thinking about?'

'What Action they ought to Take, of course.' I could never understand how the idea had got into circulation among the general public that civil servants were characterised by their capacity for doing nothing. The lower orders of the Civil Service may not get much of a chance, but the bosses are indomitable men of action. Confronted with a new fact, the first response of any moderately senior civil servant is to say 'What Action ought we to Take?' or of a boss as grand as Annette's father to ask 'Is there anything we ought to do about it?'

Harry laughed — a high-pitched, fluent laugh.

'By the way,' I said, 'did *you* tell Courtenay Chamberlain you had reason to believe the Home Office would object to my novel?'

'Yes,' Harry said immediately.

I looked at him. His small brown eyes looked at me unwaveringly. And yet he blushed. The whole of his face — which was quite a lot, I can tell you — was suffused with bright carmine. I do not think I had ever seen him blush so deeply before.

'Why?' I said.

'Because I did have reason to believe it,' said Harry. The blush was fading upwards into where the scalp showed through his thinning dark mouse-coloured hair.

'Will you explain to me how?'

'With pleasure, Joe.' He was trying to recover himself. 'You have a right to know.'

I gave him my mesomorphic glare.

'The Home Office are going to switch their policy,' he said, 'in the direction of cleaning things up. That's definite. I heard it from someone in this club who's in the Home Office. He didn't actually tell me in so many words, but I pieced it together.'

'I see no reason why he should not have told you in so many words.'

Harry jumped. 'I wanted to be discreeter than that,' he said.

'Discreeter?' said I.

The wine-waiter belatedly put two glasses of sherry in front of us. I drank some. Harry drank some — he had apparently given up abstention for this occasion.

'I immediately saw the danger to you,' he said.

'Danger?' I said. 'What danger?'

Harry drank a little more sherry to wet his lips.

'I knew this chap had read your previous books.' Harry tried to smile. 'He enjoyed the last one very much, thought it was very funny — *and* true.'

'Yes?'

'I wanted to find out what line the Home Office might take if you brought out another book that was . . . more so.'

'More what?'

Harry drank some more sherry.

I said: 'What reason have you to believe my next novel is what you choose to call "more so"?'

Harry looked at me brightly and blandly. 'Well, *isn't* it?'

'That,' I said, 'is a matter of opinion.'

'Exactly!' said Harry. 'Of course *I* haven't read it, so *I* don't know. . . . But why do you think your agent's so enthusiastic about it?'

'Because it's an excellent book.'

There was a pause while we finished our shrimps.

Then I said: 'So you wanted to find out what line the Home Office might take if I brought out another book that was more so?'

Harry looked menaced. 'I thought it would be interesting to know.'

'And what was the outcome?'

'He thought yours might well be the sort of book that a Chief Constable might pick on.'

I have to admit that my confidence fell.

'So you see, Joe . . .'

I said nothing for a moment. Harry looked round for the wine-waiter. He had ordered one of the best bottles the club stocked: there was no sign of it.

A waitress brought us some veal croquettes.

We began to eat. I said:

'So instead of telling me all this, you went and told Courtenay?'

Harry said: 'I happened to *see* Courtenay!' He gave me an unhappy look. 'I've seen so little of you recently. We don't seem to see as much of each other as we used.'

I glared at him.

'I can see you're angry with me,' he said.

'You weren't expecting me to be pleased with you, were you?'

'I *was*!' Harry cried. 'You've misjudged me!'

My glare changed, against my will, to a look of amazement.

'I thought I'd chance my arm for your sake,' Harry said. 'Suppose the book had come out and you'd been prosecuted.'

The wine-waiter poured out two glasses of claret at last. We waited for him to go away.

'I'd have told you if I'd seen you,' Harry went on. 'I can see you think I was trying to make trouble. You don't know how difficult things are for me.' He paused, his face bright with emotion. 'I know I've sometimes chanced my arm in the past and it's caused trouble. But this time it wasn't like that, Joe. If you're thinking it was what Robert calls motiveless malice, you're mistaken! I *had* a motive ... And it was to *help* you!'

I felt as if my head were beginning to spin a little.

I proceeded to eat some more veal croquette with an unusually wet-looking brussel sprout.

'I'm not the sort of man you think I am,' said Harry.

I had never before felt so closely confronted with what is referred to as the mystery of personality. What for certain was at the core of spinning Harry? And how could I for certain tell, bearing in mind relativistic notions, if he set me spinning myself?

'Not quite, anyway,' he said. 'Not always.'

Something made me want to laugh.

Instantly there was a gleam in Harry's eye.

'Isn't this food awful?' he said. 'But the wine's good.' And he drank some wine.

I said: 'I'm in a hell of a mess over the book, Harry. I just don't know how to alter it. Courtenay's solicitor's opinion makes it simply impossible — and Courtenay won't publish unless his solicitor is satisfied.'

Harry nodded his head sympathetically. 'How's Elspeth taking it?'

'She's very upset.'

There was a pause while we finished our veal croquettes.

'Yes,' said Harry. 'That's a pity.' A look of special unconcern came into his face. 'Last time we saw her we thought how well she was looking.' He had picked up the menu card and was looking at the list of puddings.

He handed the card to me.

'She isn't going to have a baby, is she?'

I said: 'No,' with what I meant to be equal unconcern.

Harry smiled sweetly. 'It's all right, we were just wondering.'

I said: 'Give us a chance! We've only been married a year.'

'Yes,' said Harry, pacifyingly. 'That's just what I said to your mother.'

'To my mother!'

I thought it would probably be difficult to estimate, now, which of our heads was spinning the faster.

'Now don't get me wrong, Joe!' Harry smiled shrewdly at me round his snub nose. 'Your mother doesn't necessarily think you ought to have started one yet. I think she's being got-at by members of your father's congregation.'

'Those old tabby-cats!' I said. 'When we got married they suspected Elspeth was going to have a baby and thought she ought *not* to. Now we've been married a year without having one, they think she *ought* to.'

Harry smiled. 'It's the way of the world.'

'Too damned symmetrical,' said I.

And yet I was wondering too. *Ought* we to be going to have a baby? I had not thought of it in that light before. Could it be that the pressure of society was getting me mobilised for the next step?

In due course Harry and I finished our meal and then, it seems to me in recollection, we drank some tepid black coffee in an alcove on the staircase.

Somehow Harry had composed our quarrel. There was

207

no doubt about it. I did not know if I could possibly believe
what he had told me, and I was suddenly feeling more
hideously got-down than ever by the prospect of changing
my novel. Yet I was glad he was there.

In my reflections I heard him saying again:

'You don't know how difficult things are for me.'

CHAPTER III

DARK DAYS

I COMPLETED my work on the isolated passages — I found what I thought might be mistaken for several more. This kind of work was what Robert and I called literary carpentry, and we both enjoyed it. For example, it never failed to give me pleasure to see how, if one began using one's blue pencil at any point on the page of a manuscript and stopped at almost any other point, the thing still read on. (Would that more novelists, especially American naturalistic writers who produce 900 pages of 'total recall', would discover this innocent professional pleasure!) My pleasure in this case was mixed with a good deal of regret for some pleasing, natural scenes. And when I happened in my spare time to read a Deep South novel in which, as you might expect, there was printed a lavish description of a rape, my pleasure was mixed with a lot of bad temper.

However, I thought it wise to show my manuscript with its first alterations to Courtenay's solicitor. In the first place I felt that a pat on the head from him would be encouraging: in the second I had hopes that somehow the excision of isolated passages might have reduced the dominant effect.

Courtenay's solicitor was indeed pleased. I went to see him to collect the manuscript from him.

'This is a step in the right direction, Mr. Lunn. Surely a step in the right direction.' His smiling grey eyes and his shapely lips remained steady. 'I see that you've removed several major isolated passages that must surely have given the Home Office cause to think . . .'

'Cause to think? As if they didn't know!'

And then, thinking of the pleasing, natural, isolated passages that had gone, I thought of the passage in the Deep South novel that, in contrast, had been allowed to remain. My bad temper got the better of me. I pointed out the contrast to Courtenay's solicitor.

He nodded his white-haired head smoothly.

'But, Mr. Lunn, I don't think there'd be any harm in your writing about rape.'

At this my bad temper broke out. 'Thank you for nothing!' I cried. 'I don't want to write about rape. I couldn't anyway — I've no experience of it!'

I saw him looking faintly perturbed by my anger, so I changed my tone.

'Actually,' I said, 'I don't think I could get any experience of it. I'm rather shy, by nature. I like to be encouraged. . . .'

'I wasn't suggesting you should write about rape. I was only illustrating the major contention that you'll remember my putting to you last time we discussed this matter.'

'I see what you mean,' I said. 'I'm allowed to describe sexual activity if it's a crime. What I'm not allowed to describe is a simple, natural f***** that both parties enjoy.'

He nodded his head slowly, as if, for instance, I had at last seen that a straight line is the shortest distance between two points.

'Exactly. That is what I have been trying to put to you in essence. Though of course it's a question of degree. No one, not even the Home Office in its strictest mood, would expect an author not to refer to the phenomenon you mentioned. Refer to it, of course. But in describing it there must be limits to how far an author may go.'

I was reminded — I am sorry to say I was reminded — of a favourite recollection that Robert and I shared, of overhearing two office-girls sitting in front of us in a bus.

'I'm not going out with *him* any more. He wants to go too far,' said one.

To this the other said: 'I agree with you, I really do. If you let them go as far as they want, where would they stop?'

The concept of far-ness had exercised Robert's imagination ever since. What was too far? Or not far enough? And finally what was the farthest you could go?

'I think,' said Courtenay's solicitor, 'we should all agree that in this first draft you go a good deal too far for the Home Office.'

I said: 'I see.'

'That is what governs the dominant effect.' He handed me back my manuscript for the second time. 'I now look forward to reading this excellent book again when good feeling has kept you from going a fraction of an inch further than is absolutely necessary.'

I was dismissed. My alterations had clearly not altered the dominant effect at all. Far from feeling that I had been patted on the head, I felt that I had been kicked in the b**.

It took me some time to realise what the total effect of this interview had been. 'I just can't alter the dominant effect,' I said to Robert.

'I have to admit,' he said, 'that I can't see how the concept of far-ness can be applied to it in any way that would help you.'

'The only thing I can see for it is to scrap the book altogether.'

'I think that would be very foolish of you,' he said sharply.

I said nothing. I felt that Courtenay's solicitor, the Home Office, the Director of Public Prosecutions, and the typical young person into whose hands my book might fall, had between them got me down altogether.

I put the book aside.

'I'll come back to it in a little while,' I said to Elspeth, 'when I feel less persecuted.'

But I did not believe I could ever come back to it.

In the weeks that followed I concealed from Robert that I was not working on the book any more. I could not conceal it from Elspeth. She said nothing to me about it. I could see that she was taking it to heart in a way I had never bargained for. After all, was it not she who was the stable, relaxed person whom everybody had said would cushion my fluctuations of feeling?

I started to wake up in the middle of the night. In the first moment I would feel as if I had awakened naturally, and then suddenly, like a shutter dropping, the cause would come to me. My masterpiece, my small masterpiece . . . dropped into the sea, before it had ever been out in the air and light. I can't see how to alter it, I thought, I *can't* alter it.

One night I realised that Elspeth was awake too. I turned my head on the pillow, and I felt her hand take hold of mine.

'What is it?' I whispered.

Her fingers gripped mine.

'Tell me . . .!' I said.

'I'm worried for you. I know what it means' — she meant my book — 'to you.'

I squeezed her fingers in return. 'Please don't worry, darling. . . .'

There was a pause.

'It can't be helped,' I said.

Suddenly her whisper carried strong emotion. **'If only I could *help* you!'**

I smiled in the darkness. 'Darling, that isn't a thing to worry about. You couldn't be expected to re-write the damned thing.'

'If only I could!'

I whispered lightly, 'One novelist in the family's enough.'

She did not reply.

212

'Cheer up . . .!' I whispered, and to show that I was being playful I began to stroke her face.

I felt tears rolling down her cheeks.

I thought: Oh dear!

I went on stroking her face and then I began to kiss her. It suddenly struck me that it was difficult to know who was trying to comfort whom.

Those were indeed dark days. I simply did not see my way out of them. And my sufferings as an artist were not alleviated, I remember, by my current activities as a civil servant. Not only did I have to go to the office and behave as if there were nothing the matter: I had to put up with one of the chores I would most gladly have let Robert in for if I could. It was interviewing, for some temporary jobs in one of our explosives research establishments, a string of organic chemists.

Organic chemists had come to be my *bêtes noires* — they seemed to me to be characterised by a peculiar combination of narrowness and complacency, having changed neither their techniques nor their opinion of themselves since the days of World War I. Organic chemistry had seen some truly glorious days at the beginning of the century, and the 1914–18 war, with everybody thinking mostly about explosives and poison gas, had been a chemists' war. But after that had come the glorious days of atomic physics; and World War II, with everybody thinking mostly about first radar and then atomic bombs, was a physicists' war. To the sort of young men I had to see the point had not gone home. On they went, sticking together parts of molecules, by their crossword-puzzley techniques, to make big molecules: then, by more crossword-puzzley techniques, they verified that they had made what they thought they had made: and then they started all over again.

When asked if they used techniques nowadays invented and used by physicists, they said to me rebukefully:

'I rely on classical methods.'

And when invited to discuss the way their parts of molecules behaved in terms of electronic structure, they said very rebukefully indeed:

'I'm afraid I'm not a theoretician.'

Some of them, it seemed to me when I got particularly desperate, might never have heard the electron had been discovered.

(In fairness I have to say that since then — I am writing about 1951 and it is now 1960 — my opinion has changed. Young organic chemists have changed, to the extent of whipping at least one 'modern technique', nuclear magnetic resonance, smartly out of the hands of the physicists.)

Anyway, it was in 1951 when I had to see a string of rebukeful, classical, non-theoreticians, in a dark February when I felt more like hiding in a corner and seeing nobody. However, the chore at last came to an end.

One weekday morning I found myself, instead of interviewing anybody whatsoever, looking into the window of an antique shop in Sloane Street. I had already stopped to look into the window of several others, but I should have been hard put to to say exactly what I had looked at. I was wandering. There was nothing I wanted to do or, for that matter, to look at. Elspeth had gone to stay for a few days with her mother, who was ill, and I had taken a day off from the office. I found it a consolation to be walking instead of sitting still, and I had calculated that I could rely on the contents of antique shops to have a slight but certain fascination for me — it was not often, I thought, you came across a work of art that seduced you with its colour, symmetry and balance, and at the same time offered you the opportunity to sit on it, eat off it, or keep things in it.

I lingered in front of the windows, hunched in my overcoat, though for February the morning was unusually sunny. When there was too much reflection from the plate glass, I put my face close to the pane and cupped my hands on either side of my eyes; so that I could peer into the calm, uninhabited depths of the shops, calm with the sheen of lamplight on velvet and brocade, uninhabited because all the things for sale were so expensive that nobody was inside buying anything.

On a small table at the side of one window there was a marquetry box that caught my eye. The door of the box was left open to reveal that it was a miniature chest of drawers. 'It couldn't be prettier,' I said half-aloud. I thought it would do for Elspeth to keep her jewellery in.

Suddenly I was pierced by superstition. If I bought Elspeth the box, we should both come out of our desolation. The gods would be placated. The Home Office would be placated. Elspeth would be happy again. I stared at the box. I pushed open the door of the shop.

The owner of the shop quietly but expeditiously brought the chest out of the window and set it down for me to see. I asked how much it was. Oh, oh, oh!

'It couldn't be prettier,' I heard myself saying. I should not have been surprised to hear myself telling him the whole of my story. I went on staring while he pulled out the drawers one by one, to show me that the bottoms were made of oak and had no worm-holes.

'As far as we know,' he said, courteously giving me what I took to be the old malarkey, 'it was made between 1750 and 1780. You might say it was a copy of the kind of cabinet that came in in the latter part of the seventeenth century.'

I managed to get out of the shop without buying it.

In the street again I was dazzled by the sunshine, and I stood still for a moment, recovering from the price.

I was startled when I heard someone say: 'Joe, what are *you* doing here?'

It was Annette. There she stood, in a tent-like overcoat.

'If it comes to that,' said I, 'what are *you*?'

'The school's shut for scarlet fever. I've just been shopping

215

at MacFisheries.' There was one a few yards further down the street.

I said: 'Surely there's one nearer to where you live.' It seemed incredible that she had taken to shopping at all.

'I prefer this one.' Her tone was so indisputably that of a connoisseur of fish-shops that I did not argue.

I tried to raise a smile. 'I must say London's comforting. One's always running into people one knows.'

'When I first saw you, you were looking as if you were lost.'

I took hold of her elbow. 'Let's go and have some coffee!' I knew where there was a Kenya café. When we were settled over our coffee and chocolate biscuits, I told her what I had just been doing when she met me.

'I think you ought to buy it,' she said.

I was not surprised by one woman's advising me to buy a present for another woman, as this was the recognised policy of what Robert and I usually referred to as the Trades Union of Women. I said:

'But it's sheer superstition! You can't act on superstition.'

'That's just what you can do,' said Annette. 'One doesn't take the gods seriously, but one does take mental states seriously.' She took off the head-scarf she was wearing and shook out her bell of hair.

I watched her, slightly mesmerised. Her clear light brown eyes seemed to shine with amusement. 'All choices aren't necessarily moral ones, you know.'

I was suddenly reminded of a conversation I had had with her and Elspeth in a steamy café in Bethnal Green. 'Oh, aren't they?' I said — was she taking the mickey out of me?

Annette said: 'I wish Robert's superstitious feelings could be bought off in a similar way.' Her light-eyed smile disappeared. 'He's terribly apprehensive lest anything should go wrong with me or the baby.' She looked at me earnestly.

'He's so persistent with his apprehensions that they become catching.'

'Don't I know that!' I calculated that her baby must be due in about four or five months.

'I hope Robert will get over it,' Annette went on. 'After all, I want to have at least three more.'

'Three more what?' I said. I could scarcely believe she meant babies.

She did mean babies.

'Good gracious!' I said. 'How you've changed!'

'I don't think so.'

I thought for a little while and then enquired with some diffidence: 'How have you fixed on four?'

'That isn't so interesting,' she said, 'as *why* we've fixed on four.'

'All right,' I said, willing to please. 'Tell me *why* have you fixed on four?'

'We think the degree of possessiveness we feel about each other will be less in a family of six than in a family of two.'

'I should think it couldn't help but be,' said I. But then I asked: 'What about your degree of love, though? In particular that of you and Robert for each other?'

In my opinion, loving people takes energy, takes time. If you start to love more people, those you already love have got to accept a cut.

Annette said: 'One has to make up one's mind whether it's worth it or not. I think it is.' She paused and then her tone suddenly changed. It became tender, almost shy — it reminded me of some other occasion, when she had seemed much younger. She said:

'I was never sure Robert wanted me, until he married me. And now I'm terribly possessive about him.'

I was touched. Then I asked:

'What about teaching? Do you intend to go on teaching as well?'

'Naturally.'

This really did give me something to think about. I guessed it must have given Robert something to think about, too.

Our waitress, seeing me apparently inactive, came over and asked me if we would like more biscuits or coffee.

Annette said to me: 'Of course, Barbara thinks I ought to go on teaching.' And she laughed to herself.

I laughed to myself.

'You know,' said Annette, 'that she's pregnant too?'

I did not know. 'Good gracious!' I said again. 'I thought they'd finished procreating.' Their youngest child, as far as I recalled, must be about seven.

'She and Harry thought they'd like to start again.'

I said nothing.

'I don't know if it was our example,' Annette said with a sort of comfortable amusement.

'I have a theory,' I said, 'that people's marriages interact when they come up against each other.'

Annette laughed. 'Everybody will be having babies!' She finished her coffee.

I suddenly thought: What about Elspeth and me? I felt, I have to admit it, that we were being left out of something. So much for that old Pressure of Society, dammit! I felt envious of Robert and Annette, envious of Harry and Barbara, envious of everybody who was going to have a baby.

Annette put on her head-scarf and then picked up a string bag in which there was a parcel of what I presumed to be fish. I noticed that her face looked thinner, as if the flesh were drawn down from her chin. She said thoughtfully:

'I shall have to get a taxi.'

We went out into the street. The morning was still calm and sunny, and there was a faint smell of wood-smoke diffusing from where a gardener must have been burning leaves in Cadogan Place.

'It's like spring,' Annette murmured. I thought of my book, unprinted; of Elspeth, unable to help. . . .

Two stringy superior-looking women who were passing glanced with distaste at Annette's head-scarf — they were hatless, their grey hair being beautifully arranged and dyed, in one case purple and in the other steely blue. They got into a large Rolls. I stopped a taxi for Annette.

'You go and buy that chest for Elspeth!' she said happily, and drove away.

I stood alone again on the pavement.

I went back to the shop. You may think I was in the grip of neurosis. Maybe — but not quite so far in the grip of neurosis as not to reflect that, if I were going to try and buy off the gods, I was not necessarily bound to pay Sloane Street prices.

The box was back in the window. Compulsively I pushed open the shop door. Courteously the owner made his appearance from the depths of the shop, and, when he saw that it was me, got the box out of the window again and placed it in front of me. I stared at it.

I admired it, said how much I should like to have it, and observed how costly I thought it was. Then I uttered the formula:

'Is that the lowest you'll let it go for?'

'Let it go' was a dealer's expression. What an expression! I thought as I waited to hear this dealer reply. Two things might now happen. He might say Yes. Or he might say — you think he might say No? Then you have not bothered to learn the ritual. The alternative to Yes is the antiphonal formula: 'I'll go and look in my book, and see what I gave for it.'

With a thrill I heard him utter the antiphonal formula. While he retired to wherever he kept his book, I waited patiently, quietly opening and shutting the drawers of the chest.

He was willing to 'let it go' for £8 10s. 0d. less than he had originally asked. I bought it.

Afterwards I stood outside the shop, holding the chest in

my arms while I waited for a taxi, and feeling a peculiar emotion. The price I had paid for it was enough to make anyone feel peculiar, yet it was not the price that caused me to feel so peculiar.

In my arms I was holding a present. A present for Elspeth, a present for the gods, a present for the Home Office...? I scarcely knew which. I only knew that somehow the dark days had reached a turning-point. Whether they were going to turn lighter or even darker was a different matter.

CHAPTER IV

THE TURNING-POINT?

Elspeth was due to come home. The present was awaiting her. Now that I came to consider it with detachment, I was not sure whether I liked it or not.

And yet, as I moved round the flat, making everything
look tidy in readiness for her, I thought I did like it. With
a large gin-and-tonic in my hand I sat on the edge of the
bed and looked at it, on top of the chest-of-drawers. In the
shaded lighting from behind me the scrolly patterns of acan-
thus leaves, composed of golden-brown woods splashed with
malachite and mother-of-pearl, seemed to glisten with some
inner radiance of their own.

'It couldn't be prettier,' I said to myself. 'Elspeth will
love it.'

You can see from this that I was not certain about something. I was not certain that the gods would love it. I had
not seen my way yet through my literary difficulties. My
manuscript remained in the cupboard where I had put it on
its most recent return from Courtenay's solicitor.

Superstition, neurosis. . . . Not for nothing was I the son
of a nonconformist clergyman, I thought. Behind the words
superstition and neurosis, in my mind, lurked the word self-
indulgence.

'I shall be glad when Elspeth comes,' I said to the warm,
empty room.

Elspeth came. I told her about the present for her, but
not about the superstition and neurosis. I told her it was to
put her jewellery in.

'It's beautiful!' she cried. 'Oh darling . . .' She kissed
me and thanked me.

It did look beautiful.

We sat down side by side on the edge of the bed with our arms round each other. After a while she said:

'But I haven't got any jewellery to put in it.'

I smiled into her eyes. 'You shall have, my darling.'

I noticed that her eyes looked tired. At the same time they seemed to be searching in mine. I knew what she was thinking. The dark days. . . . The marquetry box had not diverted her.

'Buying it was a turning-point,' I said. 'I felt sure it marked a turning-point.'

She looked down at her lap.

I noticed the thin gold wedding-ring on her finger. I touched it.

She put her head on my shoulder.

We began to talk about other things. I tried to keep my spirits up and I could tell she was trying to do the same.

In the middle of the night I woke up. The shutter suddenly dropped. Nothing had changed.

I lay very still. Nothing had changed at all.

'Darling . . .' Elspeth whispered.

I did not reply.

Elspeth could tell I was awake. 'Darling,' she whispered, 'speak to me.'

I turned and put my arms round her but I could not speak.

'I wakened every night while I was away,' she said, 'wishing I could help you.'

'My darling,' I said. 'This is where we were the other night.'

'But it's *where I am*!' she cried.

I did not say anything.

'When two people are married to each other,' she said, 'they should be a help to each other. You're a help to me, but I'm not to you. . . .'

I held her more tightly. 'That's silly,' I said gently.

'We've been married a year and I'm no use to you.'

A sudden recollection came to me that was too poignant to be borne. *You must never say that again* — I heard her voice. Before I could manage to get any words out she said:

'You must wish you'd never married me!'

I was staggered by the incredibleness of the remark, of the *situation.* . . . It had never occurred to me that she might feel like this. My discoveries in our married life had been first that she was a living, independently existing person, and next that she was a living, independently acting person. Love, contrary to a lot of what is said about it, does not teach you to know everything about the loved-one. It makes you more sharply aware of some things, but it definitely makes you miss others. I ought not to have missed this. I was deeply ashamed of myself for not having seen it.

'My darling,' I said, 'I love you. I shall always love you. You're my wife. I wouldn't have it any different . . . I couldn't imagine it any different now. . . .'

I felt tears coming into my eyes.

I went on talking to her. I was speaking to her from the bottom of my heart. As the things that lie at the bottom of one's heart are few in number and very simple, I suppose I must have become somewhat repetitious. I would not have had my life any different: I could not imagine it any different now. I loved her. I wanted to give her confidence, unshakeable for the rest of our lives. And she listened to me.

Had things been such that the question could have been put to me at the time, I should have answered that I was thinking only of her soul and mine, that I was expressing truly spiritual love. I think I was. I was genuinely surprised, after a while, by being reminded that the soul and the body are one. I had not noticed the body, but it was clearly there.

When we next started to talk we had the light on.

I was looking at Elspeth's face. 'My darling . . .'

'Yes?' She did not smile at me.

There was a pause. I heard my watch ticking on the bed-side table.

'What are you going to do about your book?' She still wanted to know.

I looked at her. 'I've thought what to do,' I said. 'While I was in the bathroom.'

Her blue eyes looked at me steadily.

'My life,' I said, 'is obviously a series of acts of will. So I've just got to make another. Tomorrow I'll start writing the whole thing again, and then *not* send it to Courtenay's egregious solicitor. I'm going to ask Harry to get his Home Office friend to read it instead. With a bit of luck that could settle it.'

Her glance wavered, and suddenly, hesitantly, she smiled.

I remained bending over her, looking at her. The liberating idea actually had come to me in the bathroom.

But now I began to say something else to her — and until I had begun it I had no idea I was going to say it.

'My darling,' I whispered. 'I love you. . . . You're my wife. I shall always love you. I want us to have——' I did not finish the sentence. Instead I blurted out: 'I want you to make me a dad. As soon as possible!'

With a quick movement she turned her head away on the pillow. I heard her breath drawn in, and she burst into tears.

'What is it?' I cried, trying to see her face.

'Darling . . . *Yes* . . .'

At last she turned back to me. I got my handkerchief from under the pillow and dried her face.

'You'd better dry yours,' she said.

I stroked her hair for a long time while she looked up at me. Again I heard my watch ticking.

'Fancy all this happening in the middle of the night,' I said.

She appeared not to have heard me. Suddenly I noticed a faint flicker at the corners of her mouth.

'What are you thinking?' I said.

'I was thinking if only you'd said what you've just said half an hour ago . . .'

I burst into laughter.

We both laughed. And then went quiet again. Somehow we found ourselves staring at the marquetry cabinet, which seemed to be glistening radiantly at us.

'Like the flowers that bloom in the spring,' I said, 'it obviously had nothing to do with the case.'

'It's beautiful,' Elspeth said firmly. 'I shall always be fond of it. Thank you for it, darling.'

CHAPTER V

THE STREAM OF LIFE

WHEN I told Robert that Elspeth was pregnant, he was stirred, I could see, to strong emotion.

'I'm very, very glad,' he said. 'That's the best news we've had for a long time.' Startlingly he shook me by the hand.

'I think it's pretty good news too,' I said. (I must say it did strike me that fertility must be the predominant state in which the human race existed — hence, when you come to think about it, its history.)

Robert was also stirred to strong generalisation.

'There's no doubt that having children,' he said, 'does make one feel part of the Stream of Mankind, in a way that one wouldn't otherwise.' He nodded his head loftily in agreement with himself.

To one who was classed MISC/INEL for the Stream of Mankind this came as a most poignant, hope-giving thought.

I nodded my head vigorously in poignant hopeful agreement with him.

'It's a very good thing,' Robert went on in the same tone, 'for a writer.'

'Anything that's good for a writer will be good for me,' I said, trying to please.

Robert's eyes glinted. 'Though it's fair to say that the majority of writers have achieved it without its having done their books any noticeable good.'

The moment I laughed he switched to lofty seriousness again.

I said nothing. In fact, thinking of my own small master-piece no longer caused me such pain as it had in the days when I saw no way out of the dilemma presented to me by Courtenay's solicitor. I had spoken to Harry.

We had met again, for lunch yet again at Harry's club. Harry had insisted. There were not veal croquettes this time. There were chicken croquettes.

I put my proposition to Harry. I said: 'Presumably the chap who let you know the Home Office were going to start a fresh drive must be pretty close to the policy-making machine.' I saw a hunted look come into Harry's eyes. 'If you ask him to read my book, when I've re-written it, he ought to be able to let us have some sort of authoritative opinion.'

'I see that,' said Harry. The hunted look was disappearing.

'We could then tell Courtenay, and that would eliminate the necessity of having to get it approved of by his egreg-iously pi solicitor — which seems to me next door to impossible . . .'

Harry's small bright eyes became even brighter.

'You think I might,' he said, 'chance my arm . . .?'

I had never thought I should live to see the day when I would hear Harry refer to 'chancing his arm' with a frisson of pleasure.

'That's what I should like you to do, if you will, Harry.'

Harry gave me a look which indicated that he had a good idea what I was thinking. However, he was prevented from saying anything by an interruption. Two men were passing our table and we both happened to look up. One of them was Harry's boss.

Harry's boss stopped, gave us a shark-like smile, and then, glancing from me to Harry and back, said in his croaking voice:

'Hello, Lunn. I've just been reading your last book.'

And at that he moved on.

'A man of action,' I said to Harry, 'but not of comment.'

Harry grinned.

We went on with our chicken croquettes.

'Of course we know,' Harry said, 'my chap in the Home Office definitely did like your last book.'

I nodded my head.

'Joe, I *will* chance my arm! I'm sure I can manipulate it. I'll get him to read the manuscript and let us know if the Home Office would be likely to do anything about it or not. He wouldn't need to tell me in so many words.' A light came into his eyes. 'I could piece it together.'

'I'm sure he wouldn't,' I said.

'There's only one other thing . . .'

I looked at him, wondering what on earth that could be.

'There'd be no objection,' Harry said diffidently, 'to my reading it first?'

I burst into laughter. 'None at all, my dear Harry!'

I felt liberated. I knew I could get down to work again on the book with the prospect of getting a sensible opinion on it from an authoritative person. Thank goodness, I thought, for the Civil Service.

And so life had perked up again.

Soon after that Elspeth had told me her own liberating news.

As Robert remarked, there was reason for feeling part of the Stream of Mankind. Indeed calling it the Stream of Mankind seemed to me putting it in too abstract a form. I felt there was a sort of clubbiness in the air: Robert and Annette were due to have their baby in the late summer, Harry and Barbara in the autumn, and Elspeth and I at the end of the year. We were all in it together.

I happened to say to Barbara that as far as we were concerned, the Stream of Mankind was in no way to drying up.

'Parents,' she said firmly, 'have to have two children merely to replace themselves, and three to make a positive contribution.' She smiled. 'My dear Joe, you've got a long way to go yet . . .' All the same, her voice sounded softer. I noticed it was distinctly musical. I wondered why I had never noticed that before.

'Do you see me,' I said, 'having three children?'

'I don't see why not.'

I smiled at her without answering. And well I might! How things had changed!

Congratulating myself on my saintliness, in not pointing this out, I asked playfully:

'Or even four?'

'I expect Elspeth'll have some views on that,' she replied, smiling away the underlying Trades Union of Women tone.

'Naturally,' I said, like a well-trained member of the federation of employers.

After a few months the sort of clubbiness that had come into the air surrounding our close friends and us became even more clubby.

In the past I had been unequivocally in favour of the State running a free medical service, without considering whether I in particular stood to gain a great deal from it. If I, who happened to be well most of the time, helped to subsidise people who were ill, it seemed to me fair enough. Elspeth, a sterner Socialist than I, had come out even more strongly on this side of the argument: a free National Health Service was her idea of doing good; and given the opportunity of doing good or doing bad, she inevitably chose to do good.

One day, apropos of having the baby, she said to me:

'Of course I shall have it on the N.H.S.'

I said: 'Of course.'

And we discovered that she had been enrolled into one of the most gigantic, engulfing clubs in the country, that of mothers having babies on the N.H.S. At first Elspeth quailed, but conscience kept her to it, and soon she was overwhelmed. Month after month she had check-ups, did exercises, went to classes, and brought home vitamin pills and orange-juice. The effect of it all became so hypnotic that I began to feel like a co-opted member of the club myself. Elspeth told me some prospective fathers had sympathetic morning sickness. As I felt very well in the mornings, I offered to show willing by joining in the relaxation exercises.

At the time predicted, Annette had her baby. Robert, after going about for a few days so pale as to look green, turned up at the office looking as pink as if he had drunk half a bottle of brandy. The child was a boy, perfect in all respects, and Annette was extraordinarily well.

'Of course, having a child makes one feel part of the Stream of Mankind,' he said, too inflated to remember that he had said it to me before, 'in a way that one doesn't otherwise.'

Who was I to deflate him?

His speech sounded wonderfully lofty and detached, but I had intimations — and I was pretty sure he had intimations — that he was going to be an absurdly devoted father. Strongly affectionate and subtly power-loving, he was just cut out for it. Furthermore, if Annette's theories about the size of his family won the day, there was going to be plenty of scope for him.

It was a little while after this incident at the office that another, rather different one, occurred. I was chatting with my P.A. when she happened to say:

'I wonder if we're going to see you going to America later on in the year.'

'Oh?' I said.

She saw my surprise. 'I thought you knew . . .' She blushed at the thought of her indiscretion and explained: 'It's that Mr. Malone who came to see you that time, you remember him——'

'Indeed I do!'

'He's written to Mr. Murray-Hamilton about a conference they're going to have in Washington. And I *thought* he'd mentioned your name to go to represent the ministry.'

It was clear that she did more than think that Tom Malone

had mentioned my name — the grapevine must have told her. I did not press her for further indiscretion.

About three weeks later Robert was discussing our annual Staff Promotion Review.

'I'm afraid I may have to leave you to cope with the last part of it single-handed,' he said, and paused. 'I shall probably have to go to Washington.'

'*You?*'

He looked at me. I told him why I had said '*You?*'

Robert was apologetic. He admitted that Tom Malone actually had mentioned my name. 'As a possibility, but no more,' he said. 'He knows as well as you know that he can't formally ask for a particular individual to be sent.'

I saw that.

Robert said: 'Anyway, Murray-Hamilton couldn't be induced by me or anyone else to send *you*.' He paused and softened his tone. 'I didn't tell you all this because I thought there was no point in worrying you more than was necessary.'

So that was that. The incident, unlike the ledger for Right and Wrong, was closed.

I turned my mind to other things. The stream of life was carrying me on.

CHAPTER VI

STILL DARKER DAYS

AT the predicted time Barbara had her baby. Harry confided to me:

'You know, I adore very young babies.'

'Good gracious!' I said. I thought I should adore mine the more the older they got.

Harry looked knowing. 'There are quite a lot of men who do, you know.'

This had never occurred to me before. It seemed to me incredible that I must constantly be passing quite ordinary-looking men in the street, in Oxford Street for instance, whose natures were stirred to the depths by the sight of newly-born infants.

On the day of their child's christening Harry and Barbara gave a large party. Elspeth and I went.

'There'll be no jiving this time,' I said. She was getting quite large.

Elspeth grinned affectionately. 'I think it'll be all right, provided you don't throw me on to the floor again.'

I grinned affectionately back. *The Dark Town Strutters' Ball.* 'This is the right one for me! . . .' I remembered that statement which had expressed for me the poetic climax in human experience, falling in love. The fact of the matter was that, utterly flat as the statement was, I still had nothing whatsoever to add to it.

'Well, even so, we're not going to,' I said finally.

Elspeth smiled in a complacent way.

Everybody was of the opinion that her child was going to be a boy. Her doctor, her mother, the woman at the clinic, and even Barbara, committed themselves with a single practised glance to this opinion — the woman who came to clean our flat said: 'I can tell by where you carry it, dear. That's a boy, mark my words.' Talk about clubbiness! I, now thoroughly enclubbed, went along with the rest.

We enjoyed the party, even though we did not jive. I had just finished re-writing my novel, and that had brought me temporarily to a state of invulnerable high spirits. In the sense that the dominant effect was *me*, the book remained of course the same. In the sense that the dominant effect derived from specific expressions of feeling that might bring a blush to the cheek of a young policeman, it was toned down — rather skilfully, I thought. I handed the manuscript over to Harry on the day after the party. I then had to wait.

Immediately after that the Promotion Review began. Robert went to Washington.

The Promotion Review went on. Robert found official reasons for staying in America.

The Promotion Review ended. And then, late one afternoon, my P.A. came in and said:

'I've just heard from Mr. Murray-Hamilton's P.A. that there's a Parliamentary Question on the way over. Mr. Spinks has told her to mark it first to Mr. Froggatt, and then to you.'

I presumed it to be a question addressed by some Member of Parliament to our minister about something he thought was wrong. P.Q.s were a rare occurrence in our office. (Far be it from me to say that this was because we rarely did anything wrong. It was just that our work was not the sort that immediately evoked grievances among the public.) I regretted that Robert was not there to cope with it, and said:

'Tell Mr. Froggatt to bring it in as soon as it arrives.'

Actually this order was unnecessary, as everybody dropped whatever he was doing when a P.Q. came in — anyone who thinks civil servants are not sensitive to what is said about them in Parliament does not know anything about it.

It was next morning before Froggatt came in with the file.

'It's the usual thing,' he said lugubriously. 'If you don't get what you want, kick the civil servant whom you think's to blame.' He looked at me in a thoughtful way. 'I don't know what the public would do if they hadn't got us as scapegoats.'

Suddenly his long fiddle face and large slightly aggrieved-looking eyes struck me as exactly what you would expect to see actually on a scapegoat.

I nodded my head sympathetically.

'I think you'll find all the relevant papers are there,' he said.

The file began with a short letter from the Right Honour-able Mr. Adalbert Tiarks, M.P., to our minister, saying he would like our minister to advise him on the reply to a letter, which he enclosed, from one of his constituents. This is what the letter said:

Dear Mr. Tiarks,

I do not expect you will remember me though I re-member you, as I was the office-boy when you gained your first post with our firm as Assistant Sales Manager, North-West Sub-Region. In these circumstances I trust you will not think I am presuming to write to you. It is about my son Wilfred. I trust when you hear the facts that you will agree that it is a case of injustice as I do.

My son Wilfred has got his B.Sc. in chemistry with honours and has just taken his Doctor of Philosophy. Thus he is a highly-trained scientist. He read an advertisement for highly-trained scientists to work for the Government and applied for it. He got his letter for interview at the Ministry and went up with high hopes, as he is always reading in the newspapers that there is a grave shortage of highly-trained scientists. He told me when he came home that he thought he had failed. He had.

The reason my son thought he had failed was the unfairness of the chairman of his interview. The chairman told my son that he was not a chemist himself and asked in a manner which upset my son if my son knew something about electrons which Wilfred says do not come into his studies, as he has been making chemical substances that have never been made before. My son is convinced that if he had been interviewed by a highly-qualified chemist like his professor he would have got through with flying colours. Instead of that, because of the Ministry's chairman, he is debarred from working for his country and may have to have his call-up for the Army.

I trust you will pardon this letter for being so long, for I do feel it is a case of injustice that it is only right to write to you about it. It has been a great strain to his mother and me to keep Wilfred at college, and so it is a great blow to us when his hopes are shattered thus. Is it therefore the Government's intention that a boy like my son, who has got his Doctor of Philosophy, should be debarred from serving his country through the unfairness of a Civil Servant?

> Yours truly,
> R. T. Longstaff (Mr.)

P.S. I have not mentioned that I am writing this letter to Wilfred.

The letter was touching, but I have to admit that my predominant response to it was not sympathy for a father. It was a peculiarly unwelcome kind of concern for myself.

The file had been marked first to Froggatt so that he could attach all the relevant papers. There they were, attached. An application from W. Longstaff for a post as Temporary Scientific Officer; a couple of professional references, one from his professor and the other from his.

supervisor of research; a copy of a letter from us calling him for interview and another saying that we had no appointment to offer; and on top, the last object to be attached by my P.A. — a rectangular index-card covered with my own handwriting.

While I was checking them, there was a telephone call. It was from Spinks, Stinker Spinks.

'About that P.Q. you should have on your desk at the present moment——'

'Yes,' I said. 'I have it.'

'Murray-Hamilton will be in Glasgow till the end of the week. I've just telephoned him. He'll want a suggested draft reply from you on his desk without fail next Monday morning.'

I said: 'Yes.' *Suggested* . . . anybody but Spinks would just have said a draft reply. I put down the receiver and looked at the index-card. It was filled up with notes about W. Longstaff made by me during the course of his interview.

'Tallish stringy white-faced schizoid-looking individual with unusually handsome eyes. $2:3\frac{1}{2}:5$. Got a II(i) chem, took to organic "because it's more orderly". Ph.D. without a single fresh idea of his own but has given satisfn to his prof classical synthesis. Not the sort of soma for creative energy. Tight constrained meagre temperament. Thoroughly second-rate but will prob get on through nagging persistence. Passionately anxious to come to us thereby avoid military service. Proposing get married — "prefers cycling". Reads *Daily Tel* "because it's unbiassed". Cripes! P.T.O.'

I read it with sarcastic ill-humour. The aim of my notes was to recreate the man for me when I read them. Reading these notes I remembered W. Longstaff. He was awful.

I turned the card over.

'Board more unanimous not to have him at any price than I'd expected. P.H.S. wanted us to send protest to D.S.I.R. about his being given Ph.D. Grant in the first place. Cripes again.'

I must say I read that side with a diminution in ill-humour. W. Longstaff was awful, but it did not follow that my colleagues would inevitably see his awfulness. They had! And furthermore P.H.S. was one of our cleverest, toughest, youngish organic chemists.

The telephone rang again. It was Stinker again.

'A letter has just come in for Murray-Hamilton from W. Longstaff's professor. I'm sending it over by hand.'

'Thanks,' I said.

'Also I've just heard from the Minister's principal private secretary — the Minister's personally interested in this case.'

'Perhaps *he* remembers R. T. Longstaff as an office-boy.'

Stinker laughed. He at least had a sense of humour — but nothing, let me repeat, nothing else.

I sat waiting for the professor's letter, not surprised by the fact that, in the Civil Service, it never rains but it pours. The Civil Service is devised, rightly, to provide an elaborate system of cross-checks and cross-references: let there be a break at some point or other in the network and switches are tripped all over the place.

The professor's letter, I thought when I got it, was designed to trip me. It was from W. Longstaff's professor of organic chemistry to Murray-Hamilton, and it began characteristically 'Dear Sir, I am at a loss to understand why, etc. . . .'

I could have made his loss good in no time at all, I reflected. Unfortunately that was not what I was officially required to do. I was required to draft a reply from Murray-Hamilton to the Right Honourable Mr. Adalbert Tiarks, M.P. I wished Robert were at home to draft it instead of me.

I knew, of course, exactly what line the department should take — it was perfectly obvious, not to say laid down in the rubric anyway.

Justice to W. Longstaff had been done. Murray-Hamilton would accept that without much trouble. Justice to W.

Longstaff must now be seen to be done. W. Longstaff must be interviewed again by a board, (i) whose chairman did not ask him any unkind questions about the electronic structure of the molecules he synthesised and (ii) whose constitution was such that his professor was not at a loss to understand how it arrived at its verdict.

To settle (i) make Robert the chairman.

To settle (ii) co-opt the professor on the board, so that he would be a party to the decision.

It was perfectly simple, perfectly straightforward.

(And W. Longstaff, being awful, would be turned down again.)

Why, you may ask, did I find it so hard to draft a reply for Murray-Hamilton? Why did I wish Robert were at home to draft it instead of me? What inhibited me?

Every time I put my pen to paper I thought of Murray-Hamilton, brooding, reflecting. No matter what I wrote on my minute paper, I knew what was written on the great ledger . . . I had done Wrong.

Of course I managed to write something in the end. And I thought it wise to send Robert a letter by airmail, saying what was going on.

On the following Monday morning, when Murray-Hamilton must have been studying what I had finally managed to write, the door of my office suddenly opened and Robert came in.

His face was white. 'I got your letter and caught the over-night plane back,' he said.

His face was white but not white from fatigue.

'Gawd, do you think it's as bad as that?' My spirits were plunging so fast that I could not keep up with them.

Robert flopped down on my table.

'If I judge the situation aright,' he said, 'it's probably worse.'

I stared at him. He had fallen into one of those moods of heavy silence that always indicated despair.

At last he roused himself.

'Look,' he said, 'I shall have to tell you this. I haven't told you before because I didn't want to worry you unnecessarily. I thought you'd got enough on your hands, with your book sub judice and Elspeth pregnant. . . . For some time now Murray-Hamilton has been proposing to eliminate this directorate altogether, or rather "roll it up", as he calls it, with the establishments division. . . . They'll find something else for me to do, probably with wider scope, where they can give me my head a bit more. . . . But there was absolutely nothing I could do to make him change his mind about you. He wanted the changes to eliminate you altogether.'

I could not say anything.

Robert gave an odd wry smile to himself as he went on. 'He's a very pertinacious man. But so am I. Also he's a humane man — outside keeping you in the Civil Service he'd do anything to help you. But I told him his humaneness wasn't much use. . . . Anyway, before I went to Washington I thought I'd just about argued him into the position of letting you have some sort of rôle in the new organisation. . . .'

He stopped. He did not need to tell me anything else.

In the end he stood up and said, not looking at me:

'I suppose you've not had any news about your book yet?'

I shook my head.

He went towards the door. 'I'd better go over and tell Murray-Hamilton I'm back.'

CHAPTER VII

HELP

THAT evening I had to tell Elspeth. 'What is it, darling?' she said when I came into the flat.

'You'd better sit down while I tell you,' I said.

As she already knew about *l'affaire* Longstaff, there was not much more in quantity to be said.

We sat side by side on the sofa. The flat seemed absolutely silent. There was a faint smell in the air of the dinner cooking, possibly burning.

'So there it is,' I said.

Elspeth put her arm round me.

'Try not to worry, darling . . .' she said. 'We shall be all right. . . .'

I looked down at my hands. All right — you and I and the little one! I thought bitterly.

'We shall be all right,' she repeated. 'I can help you, darling.'

I looked at her.

'We can earn a living together,' she said. 'You can write. And I'll go back to teaching. I can work. I can help.'

I could not speak.

'So you see . . .' she said.

I put my arm round her and pressed my face against the side of her throat. 'My darling, my darling,' I kept on saying.

We remained like that for what seemed like hours. I cannot tell you if the smell of burning got stronger. I noticed nothing.

The telephone rang.

'What's that?' I said.

'The telephone,' said Elspeth.

I got up and staggered across the room to answer it.

A light, high voice said gaily:

'The coast's clear!'

'What?' said I.

There was a hiatus. The voice said: 'Is that you, Joe?'

'Yes, it is.'

'This is Harry. The coast's clear!'

'What coast?'

Harry laughed. 'Were you drunk, or fast asleep or something? I'm talking about your novel. The coast's clear. I've just heard . . . You can go ahead. Have it printed. It's O.K. by the Home Office.'

'Good God!' I said.

'And may I say,' said Harry, 'I think it's excellent, Joe. It's your best book.'

At last I understood. By this time Elspeth was trying to share the earpiece with me.

Harry said: 'I don't know what you and Elspeth are up to — you sound *non compos* to me . . . I'm going to ring off, and you can ring me back when you feel up to it.'

With an especially fluent, honeyed, triumphant Goodbye he rang off.

'Well!' I looked at Elspeth.

Her eyes were shining. 'Ring up Annette and Robert!' she said.

We rang up Annette and Robert.

And then we stood, facing each other. I put out my arms and Elspeth moved towards me.

'Whoops!' She put her hand on her stomach.

'What on earth?'

'It's all right. Just the baby moved.'

'The darling baby, the darling you!' I embraced both.

Then we noticed the smell of burning.

241

After we had eaten our dinner, we thought about Murray-Hamilton and the Civil Service again. We spent the night in each other's arms, not sleeping much because of the strange combination of misery and joy.

Next morning Robert came straight into my office to hear all over again such detail as I had heard from Harry.

'It couldn't be better,' he said. 'I wasn't able to do anything at all with Murray-Hamilton. Incidentally you'll be interested to know that in the new organisation there's going to be no place for your old enemy Stinker Spinks. He's a permanent, so he can't be sacked, but I think you'll find he's moved off into distinctly outer darkness.'

'Well, poor old Stinker!' I cried. Detestable though he was, at that moment I really did feel sorry for him.

Robert looked at me. 'I wasn't able to do anything with Murray-Hamilton; but it occurred to me, last night after your news had cheered me up, that we're not entirely without resources. You could appeal, of course; but as a temporary you wouldn't really stand a chance. No. I think we've got to try to circumvent Murray-Hamilton. There are higher bosses than him, and they haven't all consigned you to the wrong side of the ledger.' He paused. 'I'm going to talk to Harold Johnson about you. I know him better now. . . . In fact some little time ago, with you in mind, I got him on the subject of temporaries.' Robert's eyes sparkled momentarily. 'As usual with him, when you press the button you get a powerful — and possibly surprising — response. He took my point. And characteristically observed there's no reason why temporaries should be treated like dogs.' Robert paused again. 'I think I'm going to talk to him again. I don't know why I shouldn't tell him that *I* think you're doing good work and these people are trying to *get* you.'

I said: 'I shouldn't think he could reasonably intervene.'

'There you're wrong,' said Robert. 'Justice is an absolute fetish with all these people. If it struck him in that way, he could perfectly well, as a personal matter, have a look at the papers.'

In spite of my anxiety I could not help thinking of Sir Harold Johnson. 'You know what *you* want to do?' Pause. 'Get rid of your inhibitions!' Suppose, though, he did send for the papers and saw the record of what happened when my control over my inhibitions momentarily lapsed, what then?

Robert decided. 'I'm going to try it, anyway. Something tells me the tide has turned.'

Well, Robert tried it.

I am now at the stage in my story where you do not want another long scene in which Robert told me the result of his trying it. Sir Harold Johnson did not send for me, of course, so I did not have a scene with him. He sent, of course, for the papers.

We had some anxious days of waiting. And then Robert came into my office and I read the look on his face. I shall never forget it, because, just as he was about to speak, two men came into the room. Both were wearing raincoats, and one was wearing a bowler hat. The one who was not wearing the bowler hat was carrying a surveyor's tape-measure.

Neither of them said a word to us or to each other. I recognised them at once as from the Ministry of Works. They had a way of setting about their business, as if nobody else were in the room, at which I never ceased to marvel. It was utterly beyond reproach. I could only imagine that in training them for this kind of activity the Ministry of Works put them through a most rigorous assault-course from which only star recruits ever passed out. Dazzlingly oblivious of us, the one with the tape-measure measured my carpet, and the one without the tape-measure watched him. They went out again.

My fate. I was to be moved to another department, well away from Murray-Hamilton, to what was an Assistant Secretary's post. I was to hold this particular post in my present rank, with the prospect of taking on the rank of the job in a year's time.

'He's a fair-minded man,' said Robert magisterially, 'and used to doing as he sees fit to do.'

'I don't feel I can say anything impartial,' said I.

'What I don't understand,' said Robert simply archiepiscopally, 'is that somehow or other you must have made a favourable impression on him.'

'You * * * * * *!' I cried.

Robert only said: 'I'm inclined to think your troubles are now over.'

244

CHAPTER VIII

SCENE FROM MARRIED LIFE

I RANG up the hospital — it was just after midnight — and an Irish nurse told me the news.

'You've got a beautiful little durl.'

'Little what?'

'A beautiful little durl.'

I realised she must mean a beautiful little girl. A little *girl*? They had *all* said we were going to have a boy.

'Are you sure?' I asked. 'My wife's name is Lunn. Mrs. Lunn.'

'That's right, Mr. Lunn. You've got a beautiful little durl.' From her tone I could tell she was now thinking me as stupid as I was thinking her.

'How are they?' I said, playing for time.

'They're both fine.'

If I was going to ask her to make sure they had not made a mistake with the babies, I must do it now, I thought. I felt embarrassed.

'If you're quite sure . . .' I began.

'Sure, an' I'm sure. That's right, Mr. Lunn.' She wanted to get off the line. 'You can come and see them to-morrow night. Now you can have a good night's sleep, Mr. Lunn. Cheerio.'

I put down the receiver and burst into happy laughter. Of course we had got a beautiful little girl. I was delighted. I got back into bed again, but I was much too excited to begin a good night's sleep. For one thing I had to adjust myself to a new idea — as, in due course, would all those know-alls. Yet the new idea was entrancing. A beautiful little girl. . . . Fathers had made fools of themselves over daughters since the beginning of time, and I found myself ready to make a start.

The following morning I enjoyed sending telegrams to relations and advertisements to *The Times* and the *Daily Telegraph*. I thought of the people who would read them — how many of them would remember that as little as two years ago they had written me off as far as getting married was concerned? How many of them, now that they could be seen to have been wrong, would realise they had been wrong?

None.

Time had passed. Like Communists whom we had seen reverse their attitudes at regular intervals, they had never been wrong: what they had believed at any particular point in time was a historical necessity for that particular point in time — and therefore right. Happy persons! Fortunate human beings! However, do not think I bore them any ill-will. I felt too happy a person, too fortunate a human being myself — deserved though my fortune might be! In the New Year I was going to move to a better job, away from Murray-Hamilton and Spinks. And in the spring my second little masterpiece was going to come out after all.

That evening I went to see Elspeth and the baby. It was the first time I had visited a maternity ward. I, and all the other fathers, were collected in the hospital corridor till the clock struck seven, when we all charged along to the door of the maternity ward — and then slowed up. The floor was softly polished; the beds looked white and fresh; the air was warm; there were flowers on a big table in the middle of the room; and in all the beds round the walls were women looking radiant.

I found Elspeth and skidded across the floor to her.

'You look wonderful!' I cried. Her dark hair, which she had had cut specially short for the occasion, was brushed over her forehead; her eyes shone; the brackets at the corners of her mouth were flickering. I kissed her and the smell of lime flowers wafted into my nose. 'You really do look wonderful, darling.'

'Why not?'

I looked at her. 'Where's the baby?'

'There, all the time.' She pointed to a small box, which I had not noticed, hooked on the end of the bed.

I looked at my first-born child.

Then I looked at Elspeth. 'She looks like your mother,' I said.

'I,' said Elspeth, 'thought she looked like yours.'

I stood looking at the child for a long time. Her eyes were shut, and I thought she was breathing terribly fast — I did not know all babies breathe terribly fast. I touched her hand and she opened her eyes. I caught a glimpse of deep violet-blue. . . .

'Oh, she's going to be pretty!' I cried, and tears came into my eyes. I glanced at Elspeth and saw that she was smiling with some satisfaction.

I went and sat down beside Elspeth and held her hand. I stroked her wrist. I began to kiss her wrist.

'Is this allowed?' I whispered.

She glanced around the room and I did the same. In all the white beds were women looking radiant, and beside them dark-clothed men were sitting holding their hands, intently whispering to them. I heard Elspeth breathing.

'Good gracious!' I whispered.

She shook her head in a way that signified 'I know . . .'

I swallowed.

Elspeth put her hand on my hair. 'It's understandable.'

I looked up at her. 'Now I come to think of it, I suppose it is.' I glanced again at the dark-clothed men, intently whispering. 'All those poor bastards must be feeling the same.'

'Sh! . . . Don't use that word here!'

I began to laugh but was checked by one of the babies

247

beginning to cry. Elspeth said: 'It's all right. It's not ours.'

The first baby started off the others. A posse of nurses came and whisked the boxes containing the offenders out of the room. I went and had another look at ours.

She still had her eyes shut. She was still breathing terribly fast. After all, I thought, I am going to be able to feed this darling little mouth. I touched her again, and she opened her eyes.

I went back to Elspeth feeling very strange emotion. Elspeth said:

'While I think of it — will you leave me some small change before you go? I've got nothing to pay for my newspapers with.'

I got some money out of my pocket. She pointed to where her handbag was and asked me to put the money in her purse.

I opened the purse. Inside it was a bank-note and some-thing folded in tissue paper.

'What's this in the tissue paper?' I said.

'Can't you guess?' She smiled quietly. 'Open it!'

I undid the paper. It contained the silver rupee we had found in the taxi on our wedding-day.

I sat down beside her. 'Have you carried it about with you all the time?'

'Of course,' she whispered.

I held it in the open palm of my hand, so that the light shone on it.

'It was for luck,' I said.

I could only just hear her — 'That's what it's brought us, darling. . . .'

I looked at her. 'It *has*. . . .'

We went on looking at each other. Then I touched it to my lips and carefully folded it back again in its tissue paper. Very carefully.

In a little while it was time for me to go.

'Fathers,' enunciated a clear, authoritative, feminine voice from the doorway, 'not able to come in in the evening, may come in for a quarter of an hour at nine o'clock in the morning!'

When I got outside I started to walk instead of catching a bus. The night seemed very dark, but not exceptionally cold — like the night, I thought, of human ignorance. I was pleased with the concept as a simile, but could not see any special application for it at the moment. I felt illuminated, myself. I was in possession of the most important piece of knowledge, which seemed to energise my whole being with light and warmth. It sent my body striding along the twilit street, and my imagination circulating among the peaks of Art. I could have seen it written in stars across the night sky. . . .

You want to know what it was? It was:

MARRIED LIFE IS WONDERFUL

I dropped into an unfamiliar public-house for a glass of beer. A man standing beside me at the deserted bar said: 'You don't belong round here, do you?'

I told him what brought me there.

'Is it your first?' he asked.

I said it was.

He gave me a long look. 'Then *your* life is just beginning,' he said.

On the point of saying 'Then I can't think what I've been doing up to now', I said:

'I expect it is.'

At that moment, for no reason that I could find, I suddenly thought again of the official letter telling me I was MISC/INEL. What nobody knew, except me, was the effort I put into trying to be EL. That, I thought, was the theme of my life. MISC/INEL, trying to be EL. In this simple statement was embodied the poetry, the dynamism, the suffering of one man's existence.

I finished my beer and left the pub.

Next morning, in the lift on the way up to my office, I met Froggatt.

'I hear we have good reasons to congratulate you on a certain matter,' he said in his leisurely tempo. He was smiling.

I said he had.

He asked me if we were still living in a flat

I said we were.

'Ah,' said Froggatt, as the lift came to a stop, 'then you'll be looking for a house, now.'

Now I am not intending to make anything of this incident. But when I got to my office and thought about it, I saw it, as Froggatt might have said, in a certain light.

I had got a wife; I had got a baby; and now it appeared that I had got to get a house. . . .

I sat in my chair and expressed myself in a phrase everybody was using in those days. 'Can you *beat* it?'

Instead of ringing for my P.A. I meditated. The conclusion I reached was that this side the grave there is simply no end to anything. Simply no end.

Well, so be it.

SCENES FROM LATER LIFE

This Book
is Dedicated to
Jonathan

CONTENTS

PART I

PART II

PART III

PART IV

PART V

PART I

CHAPTER I

NOT TEMPERING THE WIND

My mother said: 'Tell me how old I am!'
I said: 'I'll tell you how old you are if you want me to. But you do know how old you are. And you know you know In fact ten minutes ago *you* told *me*.'

'Did I?'

'Yes, you did.'

'Well, you tell me now.'

'You're ninety-one. And when September comes you'll be ninety-two.'

'*Ridiculous!*' She spoke in a loud firm voice. Surprisingly loud and firm. I have to say that it always had been so. And the comment '*Ridiculous!*' was not out of character, either; in fact it was very much in character. I could never be sure that she was not going to apply it to me.

'Ridiculous,' she repeated.

I said quietly, 'That's for you to say.' I could tell she didn't hear me.

'I ought to have died ten years ago.'

What could I say to that, even quietly?

I was looking down at her, where she lay awkwardly in bed, half-propped up on a pillow and leaning to one side. If I asked the nurse to come and sit her more comfortably, she'd only slip back. On the other hand she was being kept warm, though there was a biting February wind outside.

She looked very old, very small, hollow-cheeked and frail. Her hair, scraped back from her forehead into a little knot, was very thin, yet it still gave signs, I don't quite know how, of having once been reddish brown – carroty, she saw fit to call it, herself.

She couldn't see me.

'It's no fun, being old,' she said. 'You ought to die when you're young and happy.'

I could see the point of her remark, yet I didn't feel it would persuade many people to act on it.

'Not,' she went on, 'when you're old and miserable, and lonely.'

And lonely. Nowadays I came down to the convalescent home to see her every fortnight. Once it had been every week. It was the Matron, who, taking me for a grand *affairé* Civil Servant, was concerned by my having to leave my office early in the afternoon to come down to the South Coast. Once upon a time it actually had been a bit tiresome to get away; but it happened now that my present job, this my last and final job as a quasi-Civil Servant, could scarcely be more gentlemanly. My fellow Board Members sympathised with my absenting myself, while our Chairman, if he was not using his official car at the time, would instruct his driver to take me to Victoria.

The Matron suggested the change. 'Your mother won't know the difference, Mr Lunn.' She was a youngish woman, rather coarse-fibred but very sensible. What she said was true.

My mother often said she couldn't tell one day from another. In fact she couldn't tell one year from another – she often seemed to think she'd only been in the convalescent home for a few months, sometimes even a few weeks; when it was getting on for eight years.

I looked round the room. It was always newly swept and dusted – there was no reason why it shouldn't be, as I always gave a few hours' warning of my visit. The wallpaper, patterned with sage green stripes, was fresh and unspotted; the curtains, patterned with a crisscross of pink and yellow, were clean; the blue of the frill round the edge of the bedcover was dazzlingly royal; and the carpet, patterned with huge fawn roses on a glowing turquoise background, looked – unfortunately – brand-new. My mother couldn't see the room. A room to be lonely in.

In former days my mother had tried living with my sister in America. That didn't do. Then she had come back and lived near to us. That didn't do. Then she lived *with* us, which manifestly was not doing; till, coming into her room time after time to find her fallen semiconscious on the floor, we'd had to give up.

Should we have given up? I wondered. (What we didn't know, what in the course of time the convalescent home discovered, was that a remarkable improvement was made by stopping her from being given a large gin-and-tonic before her evening meal and a couple of Tuinals at bedtime.) But living with us was *not* doing. Her effect on Elspeth, who had to be with her all the time, was alarming. It reached the pitch where I saw that I had to choose between my mother and my wife. There is only one choice a man can make.

When I explained it to Robert, that it was not doing, he said, with his usual insistence on comparative thought, 'What *would* do?' He knew my mother pretty well.

'There you have me,' I replied.

Yet now my mother was in this room, all day, every day. Old and miserable, and lonely.

'I only wish,' she said, 'I had a room of my own.'

'But you have a room of your own. There's another bed in this room, but it's unoccupied.' Over the years the Matron had alternated between trying her with company and without.

'Last night there were fifteen people in this room. You'd wonder how they could all get in. There were two men sat on this bed. Big, fat men, with beer-bellies.' She paused. 'I don't know what you think, but I think beer-bellies are positively disgusting.'

Though I hadn't got a beer-belly myself, I didn't want to be unfair to men who had. I merely said:

'I think you must have been dreaming it.'

'Dreaming it? I saw them with my own eyes. There were fifteen of them. If you had been here, you'd have seen them, yourself. There's none so blind as those who won't see.'

As I'd been brought up on this sort of adage, I was at something of a loss.

There was another pause, during which she was thoughtful. Then she said fair-mindedly:

'I suppose old people do dream sometimes.'

I thought it wisest now not to agree, least of all to agree with enthusiasm. She went back to what she'd been thinking before.

'The trouble is,' she went on, 'that you can't die when you want to. You have to wait till you're called.'

I remembered the Matron's warning: 'She might go at any moment, Mr Lunn.' She'd been saying 'At any moment' for the last three years.

I said quietly, 'Perhaps it's as well.'

This time my mother heard perfectly. 'Well or ill, it makes no odds. You've got no option.'

'No.'

I found that I didn't care for her saying You all the time, rather than I or One. I thought she might at least have said One – though knowing my mother I suppose I knew she definitely might not. It was not that she had no capacity for tempering the wind to the shorn lamb: she didn't seem to recognise that lambs existed in the shorn state.

'But I suppose if people had the option,' she went on, 'they'd not use it sensibly.' She paused. 'I used to wonder why they'd never make it legal for you to finish yourself off, when it got too much of a burden. Just take a dose one night and not wake up in the morning . . . But I suppose people would have done it for silly reasons. Taking the easy way out, for any little thing.'

I was silent.

'You don't say anything,' she said.

I was thinking, There speak generations of Wesleyan Methodism. I agreed with her. Of course I agreed – I was only one generation of Wesleyan Methodism later. What a thing to be faced with at one's mother's bedside!

'I agree,' I said.

'I thought you would.'

Suddenly something in *The History of Mr Polly* went through my mind – I'd just been re-reading it in the train. I loved it, enshrining Wells's message of optimism – 'If the world does not please you, you can change it.' I loved the book, yes; but I could never really stomach Mr Polly's solution to his troubles – *running away*. Oh dear! Generations of Methodism.

Trapped by my upbringing, that's what I was. Trying to escape from this thought, I glanced at my watch. Then I glanced round the room. As usual I noticed on the dressing-table, a cheap little wooden dressing-table, the small statue of an elephant, mysteriously made of what appeared to be white soap. I didn't know whose it was. There was another bed in the corner of the room, but there was nobody in it. Whose elephant? And why an elephant?

'You've got to wait till you're called,' my mother said again.

I thought about it again. It implied the existence of a Maker, to call one. I, myself, didn't believe there was such a thing as a Maker. My mother did at least appear to believe in one after a somewhat distant fashion; yet I was quite sure that awe for Him didn't overwhelm her, even though it was not going to be long before she was summoned by His call.

'How old are *you* now?' she said next.

'I'm sixty-seven.'

'Good Heavens!' She weighed it. 'You're not a chicken any more.'

I didn't say anything to that. Suddenly she said:

'Do you *mind*?'

'Mind what?'

'Not being young any more.'

'It's not much use minding, is it?'

'I thought you might.'

'Of course I mind slowly losing my powers, who wouldn't?'

'I mind not being able to see. If only I could read!'

'I know, I know,' I murmured. She had cataracts in both eyes, one of long standing, the other of recent development.

'The doctor says I'm too old for them to do anything about it.' She'd said this often enough before.

'That's true,' I said inaudibly.

'What about *your* cataract?'

'They'll perhaps be able to do something about that, fortunately.' I felt curiously ashamed of myself because I was hedging. It was now definite that some time during the next few months I was going into hospital to have mine operated on.

Trapped by my upbringing. And trapped by my genes. From my childhood I could remember two maternal great-grandparents in their nineties (my mother's family lived to great ages), both more or less blind; simple country people outside the reach of up-to-date doctoring for cataracts, let alone free doctoring. They crept round their little house, feeling their

way by catching hold of familiar objects. I had a sudden vision of
the great-grandmother, tiny, hollow-cheeked, frail, with her hair
scraped back into a little knot ... She was bent into a
half-stooping posture by arthritis. My mother had arthritis in
her hands, her knees, her feet. Arthritis had made its appearance
in my left hip-joint. My mother had suffered with arthritis
throughout the whole of her life; I not until the last couple of
years. So I was one up on the genes! *Sod* the genes!

Did I mind?

It would have been nice not to be forced by my mother at this
moment to think about such things. It would have been nice
throughout the whole of my life for the wind to have been
tempered just a little. Of course I minded. It was a bore not to be
able to see out of my right eye – I could just about tell, with that
eye, whether it was night or day. But I realised that there was
more to it, in this case, than that. I minded the pupil of my right
eye having turned milky in appearance – everyone could see it.
The fact of the matter is that I was vain. I didn't want people to
see that I was getting old.

Yet if vanity came to my aid in fighting off the sodding genes,
what was wrong with that?

'How's Robert?' said my mother.

When I first arrived she always asked, 'How's the family?'
When we were getting towards the end of my visit, when she
seemed to have a grasp at least of an hour's passing, to the
uncanny extent of guessing when I started to look at my watch,
she asked after Robert.

'He's all right. I saw him a week ago and we're going to have a
drink next Tuesday. He's very busy.'

'How's he getting on?'

'Well. Very well.'

'And how's Annette?'

'About the same.'

'Is she in or out? I can never remember which it is.'

'I think you'd be safest,' I said gently, 'to assume she's in.'

'I can remember, she first went in long before I ever came
here.'

'That's true.' Long before ...

'Poor girl. I'm sorry for her.'

264

I thought I was sorry for Robert, too. What a marriage! . .

'Tell me what they say's the matter with her!'

'A sort of schizophrenia.'

She didn't hear.

I bent down and said loudly, 'Schizophrenia.' It sounded terrible, exaggeratedly so through being shouted. Too technical and too meaningless to be launched on my poor old mother's ears, and too technical and too meaningless for describing Annette's agonising inability to cope with existence.

'I've heard you tell me that before, but I'm not much wiser.'

'I doubt if anybody is.'

She shook her head very slightly against her pillow. It was too late in the day, both actually and metaphorically, for explanations in psychiatry.

'I hope there'll be an improvement,' she said.

I said nothing, because it seemed to me that there couldn't be.

'Life's a funny thing. Nobody gets everything they want. Folk who don't know about *her* must think Robert's got everything.'

'I don't know about that.' I changed my mind. 'Yes, I suppose they must.'

'He's got money.'

'Yes, he's made a lot of that.'

Plainly thinking I'd made none, she said: 'I wish I'd more to leave you when I go.'

'Oh, don't worry about that! I'll get by, somehow.' What she had to leave was to be shared equally with my sister, anyway.

'I wish you'd got a pension coming.'

Now why had she to remind me of that? I said: 'Not half as much as I do.'

'Elspeth works.'

'Yes.'

She was silent for a little while. She was getting tired.

'I know I ought to know,' she said. 'How much younger is she than you?'

'Fifteen years.'

Silence again. I looked at my watch. In a few minutes a taxi was due to come and take me to the railway station.

'How's Robert's lumbago?'

'It comes and goes.'

'He's lucky not to have it all the time, like me.'

I thought perhaps he had got it all the time. My mother was stoical but her stoicism was noisy. Robert's stoicism was silent, very silent – in my opinion too damned silent, since he expected me to be equally silent about my arthritis.

I stood up and she heard me. 'It's time for you to go.'

'Yes, I'm afraid it is.'

'You mustn't miss your train.'

'No . . .'

'And the Matron will be waiting to see you.' She always told me Matron was waiting to see me.

With liberation in sight I felt I ought to be staying another hour.

She said:

'You're very good, to come.'

I muttered, 'I want to come. I like to come.' I thought, I have to come.

'It's what keeps me going. I think if it weren't for you coming, I should die.'

This, after telling me she ought to have died ten years ago!

I bent down and kissed her forehead – the complexion looked transparent. 'Oh, come on! . .'

She didn't repeat it. Perhaps, after all that talk about having to wait till she was called by a presumed Maker, it was as well. Though I didn't believe in Him, I didn't like to think I was holding Him up in the pursuit of His proper avocations. You have to be fair to everybody.

I said: 'I'll come again.'

Did she ask me *when* I'd come again, how *soon*? Or make *any* demand upon me? Out of the question. Pride and diffidence had ruled her life.

I collected my coat and my shoulder-bag from a nearby chair (naturally it was a commode.) Then I went back to the bed. The front-door bell rang downstairs. My taxi. I kissed her again –

'I'll be back soon.'

'You mustn't miss that train.'

'I said I'd be back soon.'

'Good.'

I touched her forehead. 'Goodbye, my dear.'

'Goodbye.'

A minute later I was sitting in a taxi, on my way to the station, on my way back to London, home, Elspeth – to the two latter after I'd restored myself with a pint of beer at Victoria.

CHAPTER II

OUR HOUSE

Elspeth and I were sitting indoors on either side of the french windows, having turned our chairs so that we could look out over the garden. It was early evening during a warm spell in April. The sun was shining on to the lawn and through the trees, and we'd opened the windows a little, letting in the busy noise of bird-song – sparrows, wood-pigeons, a blackbird – and the rattle now and then of an Underground train passing along the top of the embankment. Elspeth was reading a novel. I was supposedly thinking.

Everybody who came to see us said, What a beautiful garden you've got!

I didn't deny it. When we bought the house, nineteen years ago, we'd decided, unlike our neighbours, to keep the trees, trees growing there since the house was built a hundred years earlier – sycamores, holm oaks and hollies, trees deciduous and evergreen, one or the other shedding leaves gracefully on to the lawn all the year round. And we'd made a lawn, irregular in shape, surrounded by flowering plants and bushes. A natural look was what we said we aimed at, though whether Nature ever generated such a thing as a lawn seemed to me open to question. It was beautiful, anyway.

Elspeth was reading and I was supposed to be thinking. What I was doing was letting my glance wander round the little crowds of daffodils and narcissi beside the grass, with a break for a patch of deep blue where the grape hyacinths were; then over the yellow sprays of forsythia and up the poplar-like cherry, which was beginning to show pink and white clusters along its stem; and so into the trees and the sky . . .

'My darling.' Elspeth had noticed what I was doing. She

268

stretched out her hand towards me. I stretched out my hand towards her. They were a foot and a half away from touching.

'I'm hanged if I'll put up with that,' I said, and rolled my chair on its castors so that I could catch hold of her fingers.

She laughed. Her mouth went up at the corners in a way that had entranced me for more than twenty-five years. The little brackets, the lines enclosing it, had deepened. Who cares? I had not got any better looking, either.

'What are you looking at?' she asked.

'You.' I looked at her. 'I'm in favour of this short hair-cut. It suits you.'

'You should have seen the number of grey hairs when Corinne cut it.' Elspeth's hair was fair, her eyes grey.

'It's when I see Jane sweep mine off the floor,' I said. Jane might tell me it was silver – to me it looked white as Santa Claus's. By God's Providence I hadn't gone bald.

Elspeth shook my fingers. 'We can't go on doing this.'

'Why not? I like it.'

'You'll get cramp.'

I let go. We resumed our previous occupations. I noticed that from time to time she was glancing at me, but nothing was said. I was now thinking about the sort of things I was supposed to be thinking about, the sort of things I'd been avoiding – not that I hadn't been thinking about them off and on for several years. The compulsory end of my working-days in the official world. Retirement, as it was called. Money, the sudden absence of it. And I found it, always had found it, difficult to think about money, even when there was the prospect of its being alarmingly absent. There was something wrong with me. I mean, there were many things wrong with me, but this was, very possibly, the most serious one. Why, when I was supposed to think about money, did a curious sort of languor steal into my thoughts?

The sun was shining, the shadow of the trees coming up the lawn imperceptibly like the tide on a shore. What a pretty sight! We went in for small daffodils, with pale-coloured petals. I noticed the camellias, and the blackbird fluting its evening song.

There was a sound in the room behind us – Viola, the elder of our daughters, just come home from work. (She was twenty-four; her sister Virginia, twenty-two.) Looking lively and pretty in a black velvet blazer, she came and kissed us both. 'All right?' she enquired. And went out again.

The room was quiet, warm and nice-smelling.

When people came to see us they said, What a beautiful house you've got!

I won't embark on a description of the house, but I have to mention it. It wasn't merely that we had far too many rooms in it for three people – only Viola lived at home. It was that we were not going to have enough money, not nearly enough money after I stopped working in the official world, to heat them, light them, paint them, pay the mortgage on them, the rates on them and all the rest of it.

I'll put it bluntly – the beautiful house and the beautiful garden had got to be *sold*.

For the present we were all right, of course. I was earning about four-fifths of an Under Secretary's salary – I worked about four-fifths time. It came to some £12,000 a year altogether, the year being 1977. But when my present working-days came to an end, I was going to get £0 a year. I was not eligible for a Government Service pension.

Any of our friends who heard about my plight thought it was terrible, incredible after my lifetime since the War in Government Service. I myself thought it was terrible, but I knew it was definitely not incredible. Several Chief Establishment Officers, those men of utmost knowledge and goodwill, had exercised their knowledge and goodwill on my behalf. But who could know better than I exactly how far knowledge and goodwill can take you in the face of Regulations, in the face of the Law? To a blank wall in my case.

Like most of the disasters that befall one in this world, my plight seemed to me to spring from choices I'd made myself, choices grounded no doubt in my own eternal nature. And yet, again like many disasters, there was an extraordinary element of chance in it. I had chosen first to be a 'temporary' in the Government Service, and then a 'part-timer', because my eternal nature was fixed on being a novelist – dammit, I *was* a novelist! If only it had been fixed on Regulations! Acting for the Government Service as an employer, I'd come across all too many men whose first impulse, when we were offering them a good full-time job for life, was to start haggling over the pension. In men I didn't know I'd found it very unappealing; in men I did know, somewhat embarrassing. Unappealing or embarrassing – how I wished now that I'd been one of them!

But that isn't telling all. The Regulations about 'temporaries' and 'part-timers', which made the blank wall in my case, had since my time been dropped. I felt I was not short of material about which to reflect on Choice and Chance in this world.

I had not been *without* luck. The official world, though I had a deplorable knack of saying sharp, bright things that disqualified me permanently from being one of its favourite sons, had found me a number of miscellaneous jobs that had kept me going beyond sixty, then beyond sixty-five, the last two years' jobs being particularly fascinating. At sixty-seven, and now only just about to be brought to a full-stop, I had to admit that I had not done so badly – perhaps in view of my disqualifications, pretty well. Even now I had two jobs, one as Board Member of a quasi-Governmental organisation, the other as consultant to a company the organisation owned.

I'd done pretty well to keep going till I was in my sixty-eighth year. But what about the years to come? That's what I wanted to know. There might be rather a lot of them. I thought of my mother's ninety-one.

'Don't *worry*! . .' Elspeth must have glanced at me again. She spoke gently.

If you were me, you'd worry all right, I thought of saying; and realised that I couldn't. We'd been married so long that in a way we *were* each other. In this, anyway, she knew perfectly well what it was like to be me.

'You're worrying again about how we're going to live,' she said. She stretched out her arm and I took hold of her fingers again.

I nodded my head glumly, ashamedly.

'You mustn't. It's going to be all right. We shall manage somehow. You know that.'

I had some cause to nod my head ashamedly because she had gone out to work herself. She had taken a job that was bringing in about £3,000. And Viola, working too, paid us rent and keep.

'It isn't as if you won't have anything to do,' Elspeth said.

'Oh no! One can go on writing for ever – even if it doesn't bring in any money.'

'You're being unfair to yourself, my darling.'

I shrugged my shoulders, I'm sorry to say.

'And,' she said diffidently, 'unfair to me.'

That brought me down – or up, depending on which way you look at it. I crossed behind her chair and put my arms round her neck. The novel slipped off her lap onto the floor.

'Leave it!' I said, but she was already freeing herself to pick it up.

We stayed for a few moments.

'It does look pretty,' she said, meaning the garden.

'Yes.' This was one of the prettiest times of year.

'I do hope you're not going to go out and work in it again tomorrow.'

I laughed. 'What a woman!' I kissed the side of her cheek and went and sat down in my chair again.

The door behind us opened. 'Anything you'd like? A drink?' Brightly, Viola.

Elspeth shook her head.

I said, 'Not for the moment, thank you.'

The door shut again.

An Underground train passed along the embankment. Afterwards I said:

'The Blackwells' children are very quiet nowadays.'

The Blackwells lived in the house next door. Their children were extremely noisy, but not half as noisy as their mother and father, who respectively screamed and bellowed at them all the time.

Formerly we'd not seen very much of the Blackwells, nowadays even less; which was curious because we were united in a common purpose. The local Borough Council had put a Compulsory Purchase Order on our house and four others; we were united in a residents' organisation to contest the Order. The Council was controlled by the Labour Party, and all the residents, barring Elspeth and me, were True-Blue Conservatives.

Elspeth and I didn't think there was anything to be said for the Compulsory Purchase Order: the Council had a mania for buying up large houses in accordance with housing plans which they hadn't the money to carry out. The Borough was dotted with their purchases, most of them used for a while as temporary staging-posts for council tenants, and then boarded up indefinitely, inhabited by nobody and falling to pieces.

It was thought that the Council would give a lot of money to get the first of our houses, to break the tenants' front. But Elspeth and I had taken it as a matter of course that we should unite with our neighbours in their Appeal against the Order, even though we wanted to, we had to, put our own house on the market as soon as might be.

We duly joined the residents' organisation and contributed £150 to the Appeal Fund – to discover that our True-Blue neighbours had taken it as a matter of course that Elspeth and I, the local Reds, would sell out to the Labour Council. That was astonishing enough. What astonished us still more was that the general atmosphere we felt around us was what we might have expected if we actually had sold out to the Council.

The result of the Appeal was due in a month or so. I thought that we should lose it, Elspeth that perhaps we might not. If we lost we should have to take the 'fair' price laid down for the Council to offer in such circumstances: if we won we should get what we could on the open market. Before this hiatus an agent had told us he'd get us £60,000 for it – which I interpreted as meaning about £50,000. With that money we intended to buy a flat for some £20,000, spending, say, £5,000 on doing it up; leaving us with £25,000 with which to pay off our remaining £5,000 mortgage and then invest the remaining capital for income. An income for life.

Heigh ho, the way we live now!

Elspeth had taken on the detailed planning and estimating of our future finances. Washed to and fro by alternating anxiety and depression, I was not so lost to reason as to miss her skill and sense. She had run the house marvellously. She now made me understand the over-riding importance of Outgoings. ('Outgoings, the very word', I seemed to recall somebody saying, 'is like a knell.') Elspeth, although she must be washed to and fro by her own anxiety and depression, as well as by mine, demonstrated that our outgoings in a small, well-chosen flat could be halved.

Halved! I know it doesn't read like poetry, but it sounded like it to me.

I wondered how many other men in their sixties were listening to this sort of calculation. As the percentage of the aged in the population was going up, more and more of them, poor old sods.

'So you see,' said Elspeth.

'I do see.'

Actually if things went as we calculated, I was not in the least averse to the move. If only we had the money to buy a flat, the money to make it look pretty, and then the money to live in it! . . I could write novels in it, make love to Elspeth in it, and perhaps afford to have friends to supper with us in it.

'You won't have to do all the running up and down stairs,' Elspeth said.

'And *no gardening*!' said I. 'It kills my hip and my back and my knees.'

'Do try and take a rest from it this weekend, darling!'

'If we move into a flat I shall have a rest from it for ever.'

There was a slight pause. 'Perhaps,' said Elspeth, 'I can have some window-boxes.'

We both looked through the windows. The shadow of the trees had come further up the lawn, though the grass that was sunlit looked as brilliant as ever. Somehow there was a feeling of change in the air, exciting change. A strange antithesis to anxiety and depression.

Elspeth said: 'Let's go out in the garden before it begins to get cold!'

She held my elbow protectively while we went down the stone steps – being able to see with only one eye made it difficult for me to judge such distances. Then we walked down towards what the girls called The Dell. The buds on the silver birch we'd planted by the Blackwells' fence looked like spray. Beyond it, among the dark glossy leaves of a rhododendron, there were lots of flowers-to-be. Then, looking further into the depths, I spotted some fritillaries just coming into bloom. I left Elspeth and went to examine them – green hanging bells, some of them sinisterly checkerboarded. Snake's head lilies. Snakes in the grass . . .

'Joe!' Elspeth called me lightly.

I saw that she was looking over the fence. I thought she was looking at the Blackwells' garden, which they'd been neglecting of late.

'It looks to me,' she said, 'as if the Blackwells' house is empty.'

'It can't be.'

'I think it is.'

There was a moment of suspension. 'I'm going to see,' she said.

I said, 'You can't.'

She said, 'Yes, I can.' There was a gap in the fence up on the embankment. Swiftly Elspeth went up to it, through it, into the Blackwells' garden, and up to their house.

'It *is*!' I heard her with stupefaction. I went to the gap as she returned. We looked at each other.

'It's empty,' she said. 'They've gone.'

I still felt stupefaction. We knew nothing about it. We'd heard not a sound, seen nothing.

'It's incredible.'

'They must have sold out,' Elspeth said.

To the Council. To the Council secretly. For an inflated price. And then done a moonlight flit.

And then, then, the truth of our own situation hit us.

If we'd lost the Appeal, it wouldn't make any difference to what we were prepared for. The Blackwells would have got a jackpot, but we should still get our so-called 'fair price'.

But if we'd won the Appeal? If we'd won the Appeal the Council would pack that house with their tenants – and that would knock a good £5,000 off what we might have got for our house on the open market.

We went indoors.

A month after that we heard the result of the Appeal. Elspeth was right. We *had* won.

CHAPTER III

'IT'S THE BEST CLUB IN LONDON'

Robert was always very tactful about it. 'I know that *you* think we can't get any private conversation there,' he would begin, in the slightly hollow, emollient tone he had for such occasions – incidentally putting me on the wrong foot with the emphasised *you*. 'But it's the only time I can manage next week.' Truthfulness compelled him to add, 'With any sort of convenience.'

'Don't worry at all!' I'd reply with the magnanimity to be expected in a friendship of forty – no, well over forty – years' standing. (Yes, I really mean to be expected. Friendship doesn't stand for well over forty years without a show of magnanimity, at least sometimes, on both sides.)

Anyway, on this particular occasion I'd have met him for a drink in a public lavatory or a crematorium – assuming they sold drinks in those institutions. By the next week in question he'd have read the typescript of my latest novel. Is it to be wondered that I'd have met him for a drink in a public lavatory or a crematorium? After the moment when I finally and triumphantly got the book off my chest, it was the next peak in my literary year.

As I approached the neo-Gothic porch I made eye-contact with the policeman on duty outside. (Eye-contact – what an awful expression! It contrives to sound at once inhuman and indecent – perhaps that's why it has come into fashion.) Then I went into the large entrance-hall cum cloakroom, where I set down my shoulder-bag on the table in front of a majordomo with military ribbons across his chest.

I unzipped the bag. 'Do you want to inspect my bomb?'

'That's all right, sir,' he said, smiling with the bogus

sycophancy of his profession.

The bag contained my morning's copy of *The Times*, a couple of books I'd just got out of the London Library, and my swimming-kit. Judging by the way the bag was eyed by policemen and cloakroom attendants, I could only presume it must be one of the standard IRA bomb-sizes. (A very large bomb.)

At that moment I was aware of someone else's having come up to the table. It was a woman.

'Why, Veronica! Fancy seeing you here!'

I kissed her warmly on the cheek. She was a small woman, active and pretty, a Civil Servant of some distinction. It was she who for the last twelve months had been transforming Robert's desolate life. For that alone I'd have kissed her warmly. And her being active and pretty could only add to my warmth. She was what my mother would have called wiry, that is to say physically stronger than she looked. I'd never enquired her age, but I suspected that she must be a bit older than she seemed. She was thin-faced with a rather high forehead, sparkling eyes and a permanent bloomy colour in her cheeks. And she had a loud, firm voice.

She was just leaving.

'The Old Boy's up there, waiting for you,' she said. 'I've just been taking some manuscripts up to him.'

She had picked up my lifelong habit of referring to Robert, who in my eyes right from the time we first met was a Great Man, as the Old Boy.

At that moment someone else came up, also leaving. It was George Bantock. We saluted each other brightly and noisily.

'Joe!' he cried. 'How nice to see you, dear boy.'

I introduced him and Veronica to each other. She held out her hand and the bloomy colour in her cheeks deepened.

George asked me what I was doing here and I said I'd come to have a drink with Robert.

'I'll take you up to him, dear boy.'

His dear boy or not, I was about twenty years older than George. He was about the same size as me and he always reminded me of a lively small animal – he always seemed to be pointing his nose up a little in the air.

'There's no need, George. I know the way.'

'Oh, but I must.'

'George, you were obviously leaving. I know the way. One goes up that staircase, and then along a corridor that's too narrow and too lofty' – I was teasing him – 'with a crimson carpet down the middle of it, and grille-fronted bookshelves on either side made of rich, dark oak – exactly the colour my father used to stain the floorboards in our house when I was a boy.'

He burst into good-natured laughter.

I glanced round and realised that Veronica had gone. She was active and pretty, strong-willed, determined: I had forgotten that on some occasions she was shy.

George had capitulated. 'Give my love to Elspeth!'

'And mine to Liz!'

I made my way to the staircase and suddenly knew that I'd dropped my first brick of the evening. I was fond of George: he was lively, clever and fun. I hadn't the slightest desire to cause him chagrin. The place always struck me as astonishingly ugly, but that was my personal taste as an outsider: all the insiders I'd ever known simply loved it. George had recently been elevated to membership, so of course he wanted to show me, merely a visitor, the way. Oh dear!

Why did I have to try and be funny? It's never a good idea to tease anybody. And so on.

When I came to the institution's Piccadilly Circus or *Rundpunkt* or whatever they called it, I declared my intentions to one of a number of busy policemen and was duly appointed an escort to the visitors' bar, where Robert was sitting on the far side, waiting for me. It was at the beginning of the evening, so there were few people there – good!

I threaded my way between the tables. It was a large plain rectangular room, the floor-space crammed with square tables, each with four chairs to it – ineffably reminding me of a caff.

Robert was sitting in the corner of a high-backed, leather-upholstered bench, which occupied the space between two rows of neo-Gothic windows overlooking the river. I thought we got a little more privacy – what a thought! – by sitting side by side on this bench. Also I argued that the high-backed seat was better for his lumbagic back and my arthritic hip, though I never rehearsed the argument aloud to him as it would have offended against *his* stoicism and have called attention to *my* egocentricity.

We greeted each other. 'What would you like to drink?'

I heard the first call of the evening upon my magnanimity. We were looking across the room to where, between two doors at either end of the wall, was the bar – a sort of narrow cupboard behind which stood an elderly, nice-natured waitress ready to serve drinks.

The bar couldn't provide draught beer, only bottles of fizzy stuff. If I was willing to wait until six-thirty, or some such time, the waitress was willing to go across to another place and procure me a pint of draught beer. But I had to admit to myself, Robert's stoicism apart, that that was making too much of it. His own drink being whisky, Robert naturally thought I was being fussy.

I said graciously, 'I think I should like some whisky, please.'

Personally, I thought five-thirty was a bit early to start on the Scotch: but *autre locales, autre moeurs* . . . I watched him pottering across to the bar to order it.

In the high old days of 1945 it had struck me that Robert bore a physical resemblance to Franklyn D. Roosevelt. He was a big man, with the same sort of capacious cranium, the same sort of jaw that was not quite as heavy-boned as it looked, large bright grey eyes, a wide mouth with – a gift from the genes that I didn't then appreciate – smallish gap-teeth. (However odd gap-teeth may look when you're young, you're not half so likely to lose them when you're old.)

As F.D.R. had never reached the age of seventy-two, I couldn't have a recollection of his appearance at that age with which to compare Robert's appearance now. Robert looked years older now, yet I didn't find it easy to say exactly why, being foxed by his having always looked older than he was. He had always looked older: I had always looked younger. Naturally taking 'the passive attitude to reality', as he called it, he'd never made any bones about how old he looked. I, in my imperfect way, had spent my time up to forty trying to look older, in order to qualify for better jobs; and after that trying to look younger, for reasons we won't go into. (At forty I had married.)

I watched him come back from the bar. He sat down beside

me. I looked at him. In the air echoed my unspoken $64,000 question of the moment – What do you think of it?

'I've read your book,' he said. His voice had its slightly hollow, slightly lofty tone. 'I think it's one of your best. One of your very best.'

Slightly hollow, slightly lofty; very thoughtful, characteristically judgmatic, overwhelmingly convincing.

I didn't speak – I couldn't. I just breathed.

Given time I might have said, I think so, too.

'It's very, very good,' he said.

If there's an opposite to piling Pelion on Ossa – piling Ossa on Pelion? – that's what it was in my case. I thought, he must be right.

The elderly, nice-natured waitress brought our whisky. We lifted our glasses and drank. I said:

'Here's to the silly-billies seeing it!'

The generic term for literary reviewers was not my own. It was the invention of one of our friends, a young writer who'd artlessly spent time living among down-and-outs in order to get it right in the novel he was writing. He did get it right – when you read the book you could see so with half an eye – and was promptly taken to task by literary reviewers for 'political tub-thumping'.

'They'll see it,' said Robert. Slightly hollow and lofty, and entirely confident.

That's what you want from a friend, I thought – in like circumstances I'd do the same by him. And it wasn't a matter of our buttering each other up about our novels: we saw in each other's books things we most enjoyed, most valued – we saw the *best* in each other's books. And what's better than that?

'David was unlucky,' Robert said. 'In your case they'll see it.'

That's what I wanted, and naturally I wanted more of the same. Having got appreciation in principle, I was ready to move on to appreciation in detail.

I picked up my glass. 'Now I know your general verdict, there are lots of things I want to ask you.' I drank some whisky. Lots of things were crowding into my mind.

Robert drank some of his whisky. In the pause a very tall, thin man, whom I'd half-noticed crossing the room, arrived at our table.

280

'R-r-robert,' he began. 'I do hope you won't mind my interrupting your p-p-private conversation for a moment.' His delivery was a shade drawly and stylised – presumably to minimise his stammer. 'I m-m-merely wanted to ask you, Are you going to be here during the next hour or so?' He glanced up at the Visual Display Unit whose screen announced in flickering green letters the name of the person who was speaking at present.

Robert looked at me. 'Yes.' Then he glanced at the screen.

Our newcomer, intruder, smiled amusedly. 'He's emptied the place, don't you know. No surprise there, no surprise at all.'

Robert smiled. The newcomer, stooping stiffly in a way more elderly than he actually was, stood holding his glass. Robert introduced us. Mr Lunn: Lord Faux. Robert obviously had no choice but to ask him to join us.

'I never congratulated you, Robert, on that intervention of yours. Very p-p-pertinent.' He smiled at me as if I knew what the debate was – something about education, I thought. 'We've got to make the highest p-p-provision for the *ablest*. M-m-most important.'

My magnanimity was being called upon for the second time. And if my past experience of the place was anything to go by, the second time was probably not the last, either. I wanted to talk about my novel, just that and nothing else in the world. Lord Faux sat down in the chair beside Robert and addressed himself to me.

'I'm positively delighted by this. Your books have given me p-p-pleasure, Mr Lunn, a *deal* of pleasure.' He glanced at Robert, to make sure that Robert was not letting his attention wander. And then he went on, to me. 'I hope you don't object to p-p-praise?'

I muttered the inane sort of thing one does mutter in such circumstances. I think I said, 'It's music.'

'Very r-r-real praise. I was once in publishing, so' – he paused, mocking himself – 'I know what I l-l-like.' He gave me a very engaging smile. 'I'd been farming for twenty years and I thought I needed a change. Now or never. I went into p-p-publishing.'

Comment seemed otiose. Actually his firm of publishers was quite good.

'In a way it was a r-r-real blow when I was called back to farming.'

I thought that must have been when he inherited.

Robert said to him, 'Joe has just finished another novel.' In a super-weighty tone of voice, 'It's very good.'

Could I reasonably have said, What did you think of the opening scene? and Don't you think I hit it off perfectly?

I could *not* reasonably have said that.

Lord F said to me: 'I'm not surprised. Please let me get you another drink. What is it, whisky?'

Third call on my magnanimity. 'Thank you, yes.'

He tried to beckon the waitress, with no success; so he went away to the bar. I looked at Robert and began to speak. A miniature gale blew up beside us –

'I must come over and say Hello to you, Robert. I'm just out of hospital.'

A hefty, athletic-looking man was standing there. He went on. 'I read your intervention in Hansard – you really got him on the hop! If you do something special for music and dancing, why not for mathematics? I *like* that.'

Robert laughed as he stood up to shake hands with him. 'Nice to see you back, Tony.'

'It's splendid! I see you're having a party with Tolly. May I join you?'

'Of course.' Robert introduced us. Mr Lunn: Lord Balderstoke.

Lord B sat down on the chair beside me with a powerful crash.

'Sorry!' he said. 'I'm now missing a cartilage – but they tell me it's going to be all right. If it isn't, I shall soon be missing a coccyx.' He looked expectantly at me. Goodness knows what he was expecting – I'd got all my cartilages, and my coccyx, too.

Robert intervened. 'Joe is a novelist.'

'*That's* where I've heard your name!' Lord B said triumphantly. 'My wife reads novels.'

'He's just finished a new novel.' Slightly hollow, etc. 'It's very good.' That, I thought, is what you want a friend to be – persistent, pertinacious, persevering. (The only other word that came to mind on the spur of the moment was persiflageous, but that wouldn't do.)

Lord Faux was back in his place.

'Hello, Tolly!' Lord Balderstoke addressed all of us. 'We're talking about novels. While I was lying on my back, reading my way through *The Pallisers* – '

'They're very good,' said Robert, gravely, to no avail.

' – I realised that what I was missing, you won't believe it, was Order Papers.'

'I prefer *The P-p-pallisers*,' Lord F said across the table to me.

Lord Faux's round of drinks arrived, fresh whisky for Robert and me and himself; and a bit of argy-bargy ensued over a drink for Lord B, who, to tide him over, instantly and with enthusiasm accepted the gift of Lord Faux's whisky.

Lord Balderstoke looked directly at me as he raised his glass. 'Will you celebrate with me?' It wasn't a simple question at all. There was a sudden shrewd look in his eye – I was being scrutinised.

'Love to,' I said. It may have been the fourth call. I had no idea if I'd answered satisfactorily.

Surely this must be the end, I thought.

Lord Balderstoke turned away from us all. 'There's Bert!' he said. He beckoned. 'Bert, come and join us!'

He was beckoning to none other than Bert Smith, former boss of the —— Union. The times one had seen photographs of him going into No 10, coming out of No 10, haranguing the masses in Trafalgar Square, marching with them down Park Lane! For fifteen years he'd been the Marxist menace, bogy of the Tories – if he'd come on the scene nowadays, he'd indubitably be called Red Bert. (Present-day Trade Unionists appeared to have strictly two modes of appellation for their heroes, either Red or Big.)

Bert, small and sturdy, was walking towards us with an old man's short steps. His face was beaming. It struck me as an internal beaming, as if it were directed inwardly. Perhaps he was beaming at himself being a Lord.

Lord Faux stood up to his tall, stooping height to call the waitress. 'A drink, my dear B-b-bert?'

'Thank you. I'll take a bottle of Watney's, if she's got one.'

Lord Albert-Smith pulled up another chair, to sit between me and Lord Balderstoke – appropriately beside me, I thought; two men of the people together. He spoke rather slowly, as if it were cautiously, in the Redcar accent which through time and television had become mythological.

Lord F said: '*I* think Bert is looking rather pleased about something, don't you know.'

Lord Albert-Smith said: 'If you think I'm pleased about something, you know more about me than *I* know.'

Lord B said: 'Come on, Bert, there *is* something. Don't hold out on us!'

Robert had an amused, watchful expression.

'Well, if I've got to tell you, just among friends,' said Lord A-S, 'it's Lord Grimley as has asked me to go on his subcommittee.'

Lord Faux lifted his hands in playful horror. 'My dear Bert!'

'What did you say, Bert?' said Lord Balderstoke.

'I told him,' said Lord Albert-Smith, 'No Way.' He paused, savouring the literary flavour of his speech. 'No Way.'

'Good for you!' said Lord Faux. He looked up at the VDU, locally known as the Enunciator. We all looked up at the Enunciator.

'Aye,' said Lord A-S. 'I reckon it's 'im as has emptied the Chamber for this last twenty minutes.'

Everyone laughed. Lord A-S beamed some more. The waitress had brought his bottle of Watney's and she poured half of it into his glass.

How much longer would this sort of conversation go on? Indefinitely. The newspapers at the moment were full of high political argument about a 'Lib-Lab Pact' for the purpose of shoring up Mr Callaghan's Government. So much for the newspapers!

'At the present moment in time,' Lord A-S was telling us, 'I was fortunate enough to have a positive reason for telling him No Way.' He drank some of his Watney's. 'As you all know, I have an ongoing situation in another area.'

The times I'd seen him look straight into the television cameras and utter without a tremor these phrases. His political power had deserted him now, poor old chap, but not his egregious literary expression – that went marching on. All the same I had to give him credit for being a literary innovator of the highest order, once upon a time. It was Bert who had first launched that now immortal sentence – most perfect blend of Corn and Cant! – on the ending of a strike in which his Union, after the fashion for most Unions in recent years, had got more or less what it was striking for –

It isn't a victory for either side: it's a victory for commonsense

Nor, for that matter, had a guileful capacity for self-preservation deserted him. I couldn't help feeling drawn to him, though I wished him and the rest of them in Timbuctoo at the moment.

Lord Balderstoke said: 'You were right, Bert. Damn' right.'

Lord Albert-Smith said: 'I should like to have your view, Robert. You're keeping very quiet. Are you observing us all for your next book?'

I thought Robert was most likely being quiet because he was in pain.

Robert said: 'I suspect Grimley's is one of those committees that will never come to any conclusions; and if it did they would never be implemented.'

I was surprised by his acerbity. He usually kept a very firm check on his tongue in public. He must be in pain.

'There you are, Bert,' said Lord Balderstoke. 'Shows you know the ropes here, what?'

Lord Albert-Smith's rubicund face directed its inward beam upon me, the stranger present. 'The ropes are all the same, everywhere,' he told me.

I nodded my head in agreement. 'But this is a special place, all the same?'

I don't know what prompted me to say it. I couldn't have known it was going to provoke something which always caused me a particular happiness – the privilege of hearing somebody utter a judgement as if it were his very own, that one had been hearing from other lips as if it were *their* very own, time and again for thirty years.

'That's right,' he said. He turned his head slightly away, while still beaming. 'You know, this is the best club in London.'

Freshly-minted!

I didn't look at Robert. It was usual for him to enquire afterwards, in the cause of bringing comparative thought to bear, What other clubs would you say he's comparing it with? Pratts? Or Boodles? Or perhaps the RAC?

The others went on talking and I was beginning to feel desperate. I looked round the room, not that that was much consolation. We were sitting with our backs to the neo-Gothic windows: in front of the opposite wall was the drinks' cupboard with the nice, elderly waitress: and on each of the side-walls was a huge tapestry.

Suddenly, loudly, a bell rang. Division!

Everybody stood up, preparatory to moving off. 'We shan't be long!' As if that were good news to me!

I saw that Robert was hanging back, and then he returned. 'Aren't you going to vote?' I said.

'Yes, but I'll come straight out and meet you in the corridor, and we'll go to Vincent Square.' Vincent Square was where he lived.

CHAPTER IV

A HOUSE IN VINCENT SQUARE

'I'm sorry about that,' Robert said as he joined me again. 'I know you wanted to talk about your book.'

'I wanted to hear you talk about it.'

We made our way out of the building as fast as we could, and caught a taxi. The result was that in a surprisingly short time we were installed in Robert's sitting-room, in peace and quiet, with no likelihood of further calls upon my magnanimity. He handed me my typescript and went away to get water for our whiskies.

I made myself comfortable on a sofa, thinking At last! It was what could have been a comfortable room in a pleasant house. Yet it always struck me with sadness because Robert lived there alone and gave no thought whatsoever to keeping it comfortable and pleasant – such as by giving it a lick of fresh paint for a start.

I hadn't the nerve to tell my mother how many years Annette had been away, because they were so many; or how agonising it had been for Robert, too, while she was still here. He'd loved her deeply. That was readily understandable: she was intelligent and beautiful, with, in the early days, an appealing quaintness of 'living in a world of her own'. They married about six months before I married Elspeth – Elspeth had been very taken with her, Elspeth then being twenty-five and Annette twenty-nine. I realised at the time that Robert was allured by what I thought of as her quaintness, by the promise – dangerous – of a strange internal world to explore. I didn't realise that when her retirement into that world began to close in, he would be joined in a heart-rending struggle to draw her out of it. A fatal, useless struggle.

There was no question of divorce. Privately he seemed to have settled down to a sort of Thackeray-like existence – apart from

287

Thackeray's having had two daughters while Robert and Annette had two sons. (The sons had long since flown the nest: Arthur, the elder, was a surgeon in Toronto; while Harry, the younger, was in banking in New York.) Robert had a house-keeper, a Spanish woman who ran the house. And that appeared to be that.

Unlike Thackeray, though, Robert had not been without a string of young women who were prepared to console him – their offers were readily accepted. Veronica was the most recent of them. And although the earlier ones had come and gone, none of them had gone entirely. Although the present incumbent was usually unaware of it, Robert never lost touch with any of her predecessors. Open and friendly by nature, he was all the same a peculiarly secretive man.

'Here you are. Sorry I was so long.' My reverie was broken. I shifted my typescript in my lap. He sat down on the sofa facing the one I was sitting on.

So began the most delightful of literary interchanges, in which one gives the other person the opening to say what he thinks about one's work, and then says oneself why it is so good. There was a beautiful absence of let or hindrance to this interchange because, although he didn't necessarily think everything was so amazingly good as I thought it, he nevertheless thought it was pretty good. Is it to be wondered at, that before long I was getting well above myself? Oh Art, Art, what heights of vanity do we rise to in thy name! (Also what abysses of disaster do other people push us into later!)

We got over the opening scenes of the book, the introduction of the main characters, the beauties of this and that, the profundities of the other. I made notes in the margin of any improvements he suggested. Till we came to what I most of all wanted to know.

'What about the love-affair of the doctor and the girl?'

The doctor, the narrator and chief character, was a widower aged sixty-two; the girl, the youngest daughter of one of his friends, was twenty-two. It really was a love-affair, as much of a love-affair as any I'd ever known anything about, on both sides – if anything, she led him on more than he her. And the love-affair was the core of the novel.

'I thought it was very good,' he said.

'Did you believe it?'

For me that was the most important question of all. About this novel or about any other, it was, Do I believe it? If I didn't believe it, I really felt at the bottom of my heart that everything else about it, the author's intention, the author's language, the author's art, had been wasted.

'Yes.' Robert grinned wryly – 'I believed it all right.'

I was satisfied. In the burst of relief I embarked on fulsome talking.

'I had no idea, when I began the book, that it was going to take over the way it did. And then I didn't even know if I could do it, without its having actually happened to me now . . . I decided to work on the principle that what it's like to fall in love is the same at any age. What it's like to *make* love doesn't lose its edge.' (A private spark came and went in Robert's eye.) 'Therefore what it's like to *fall* in love doesn't.'

I secretly thought I'd made a discovery. As I couldn't announce it in the novel I wanted to boast about it to Robert.

'What it's like to fall in love at sixty-two,' I said, not worrying about re-iteration, intent on establishing my claim to the discovery and its proof by demonstration in my book, 'is really no different from what it's like to fall in love at twenty-two.'

Robert thought about it. We both drank some whisky, to encourage thought. It always seemed to me that Robert's capacious cranium was ideally designed for thought on the grandest scale. He gravely nodded his head.

Inflated beyond measure I suddenly saw my discovery taking its place alongside, say, Dostoievski's discovery of the double motive. What it's like is no different at twenty-two, forty-two, sixty-two, eighty-two. (Little did I know what Mr Auberon Waugh, the reviewer, was going to write!)

'Once I'd got over that,' I said, 'I enjoyed writing it. I had a marvellous time.'

'Yes,' said Robert. 'I think that shines through.'

Wanting to continue with How I did it, I was just about to embark on another confidence. While writing the love-scenes I'd resorted to artificial stimulants in the form of incessant playing on the gramophone of Rachmaninov symphonies. Yearning music, lush, romantic, twisting one's very soul between its fingers, I thought – just like being in love . . . I thought perhaps I'd better not tell Robert that. For one thing he was more or less tone-deaf. For another I was sure he would think it showed my typical incapacity for sustaining a serious attitude. And most risky of all – when he knew how I did it he might think less of what I'd done than he thought of it before.

'There is just one thing,' he said. 'I don't think it's a very good title.'

I'd called the book *Happier Days*. I didn't think it was a good title, myself, but I couldn't think of a better one. I tried to justify this one to myself by saying that the happier days were what the elderly doctor miraculously came to find ahead of him. Oh, happier days!

'Anyway, I suppose your publisher can change it,' Robert said. His American publisher had changed the title of his last novel from a title that we were agreed was not especially good to one that was both meaningless and excruciatingly flat.

'Sarcastic, aren't you?'

Robert did not reply.

We sat in silence for a little while, quietly finishing our whiskies. Robert was thinking about something. It suddenly crossed my mind – was he, by any chance, thinking about the next Division bell?

He said: 'The book itself, though, is quite certainly as good as anything you've ever written.'

'Or ever shall write?'

I think he took my question for a statement.

I put my typescript into its envelope. I said: 'As she thought you wouldn't be in, Dolores won't have put anything out for you to eat?'

He shook his head. Alas, he was incapable of boiling himself an egg. I thought Great Men were incapable of boiling themselves eggs – which was one of the reasons why I could only feel less than a Great Man, myself. *I* could boil an egg with anybody.

'Then you'd better go back,' I said. 'We'll get a taxi in the Square.'

He stood up. 'Yes, I think I'll do that.'

CHAPTER V

MENTION OF A LIFELINE

Although I saw Steve irregularly, I don't suppose a few months went by without my running into him. I knew the pub in Old Compton Street that he frequented; and sometimes, when I was 'taking an extended lunch-hour' from my office in order to go swimming at Marshall Street Public Baths, I dropped in at the pub after my exercise. I was a great believer in doing myself good, but determined not to let it get me down. The good of a half-mile swim could be mitigated by a drink afterwards, especially by a drink with Steve.

Steve's profession was that of stage-director. After the War he'd gone to a drama school and trained as an actor. To tell the truth, Steve was not a very good actor, but in fairness it has to be said that Steve didn't seem to mind telling the truth himself, not that particular truth, anyway.

In some plays he'd given a tolerable, perhaps a more than tolerable performance. In other plays – well, it was a different matter. When Elspeth and I went round to see him afterwards, sitting at his dressing-table with a half-finished bottle of Guinness beside him, he'd say, with a characteristic engagingly rueful smile, 'I'm afraid, Elspeth, I was' – spacing the words out – 'not . . . very . . . good.' What could one say to that?

Gradually Steve's career as an actor had petered out. However Steve was nothing if not an engaging cove. His rueful smile had a touch of pathos, it had many touches of intelligence and fun. He was an attractive man to have around, whether in the theatre or anywhere else. As his career in acting petered out, a career in directing petered in. To Elspeth and me he was wont to paraphrase George Bernard Shaw – If you can't act a play, direct it! (We doubted if he was wont to say it in the theatre.)

Steve's career as a director had petered in, but it still maintained a permanent petering quality. He seemed to spend a lot of time resting. And when he was working it was in 'fringe' theatre, very fringey theatre, very odd plays. The last production of his that Elspeth and I had been to see was performed in an upstairs room at a public-house in N11 of all places.

That performance had been devoted to improvisation. The actors were improvising as they went along – which was very apparent. Equally apparent was their enjoyment of their activities. They were getting a magnificent exercise in thespian art. Unfortunately we, the audience, couldn't help noticing that we weren't getting a play.

Steve was standing in the corner of the room, his chin resting on his fist while he listened intently. We were not surprised by his listening intently, since much of what was being said he couldn't have heard before. The evening set me meditating on how ineradicable is the conditioning of one's youthful days. Nothing now, I realised, could eradicate my expectation, when I came into a theatre, of seeing a play, of seeing some human beings conflicting with one another in a drama shaped and heightened by Art. I could readily see that in terms of current popular cant about *élitism* it was democratic to remove shaping and heightening by Art – artists are by definition an *élite*. But then I found that I didn't care for the performance in the same way, that is to say at all.

I dropped into the Old Compton Street pub one day, wondering if Steve would be there. The room had been decorated all round the ceiling with red, white and blue bunting for Jubilee Year. I saw that Steve actually was there. He was leaning against the bar, which had been permitted by some quirk in modernising brewery management to retain its Victorian row of swivelling little windows round the counters. He saw me.

'Joe!'

Obviously recalling the last performance, he went through a sort of shrinking gesture. It was a gesture he'd gone through ever since I first remembered him, when he was a youth of seventeen. The shrinking had not been due to any physical weakness – anyone could see that he was normally healthy and well set-up –

but had indicated his sensitive artistic nature and his consequent need to be taken care of. Such a need at that time had been met, shall we say (not taking too high a moral line) to the full, by an ebullient accountant ten years older than himself, patron and boss rolled into one, a friend of mine called Tom. All that happened in 1939.

Steve, still occasionally shrinking ruefully, must be in his mid-fifties now; and although not fat, he was at least a couple of stones heavier. He was tall and fair-haired and presentable. His fine-textured complexion had not stood up well over the years to alcohol; it looked pinker and shinier: and his nose, always inclined to be a bit shapeless, looked more shapeless – but persons under twenty-five ought not to take a high line about that: an ugly fate overtakes most of us. And in fact Steve, though obviously looking older with the years, surprisingly showed none of the more desperate signs of ageing, so I thought.

'Wasn't that play awful?' He was getting it over at the beginning.

I laughed and said nothing. Theatre people always delighted me with their capacity for finding the show in which they were currently performing Marvellous, Amazing, Fantastic! . . But of the previous show they now had no qualms whatsoever in coming out with the reasonable opinion that it was Awful.

'Let me buy you a drink,' he said, grinning. 'I think I ought to.'

He ordered a drink for me and I let him buy it, though my earnings, not yet reduced to £o per annum, were, if I was right in thinking Steve's earnings actually were £o per annum, an infinite number of times greater than his. (For the moment I had forgotten what he'd told me a year or so previously, that he'd inherited a little money – more than he expected – from his father.)

He handed me the drink, saying, 'You're looking terribly fit.'

'I've just been swimming.'

'You always look terribly fit.'

'Constant vigilance, my dear Steve.'

'How do you manage to go on looking so young?'

Not a question I could answer.

He looked at me speculatively. 'You dress young.'

'Nonsense.' I was at that moment wearing my suit for Board meetings, expensive black material with a chaste – yet interesting – fine stripe. 'This is what I call my banker's suit.'

'But you're not always wearing that suit, Joe.' He was dressed in ancient blue denim.

'That's true.' I thought about it.

I said: 'I can't resist telling you an incident that happened last Saturday afternoon. One of our Canadian friends brought his daughter to meet us. Afternoon tea on the terrace, and all that. I was wearing some whitish Levis I bought in San Francisco more than ten years ago. What do you think she said to her father when they got away? She said, "He wears trousers too tight for his age." '

Steve burst into laughter.

'For my age!' I repeated.

'Are they too tight?'

'No tighter than they were when I bought them. Close-fitting, perhaps. No different from what everybody else was wearing.'

Steve went on laughing.

'Censorious girl,' I muttered. Then I realised I was dangerously near to standing on my dignity. (When I was young I once wrote a poem that began, *Don't stand on your dignity / Till it's flat!*)

Steve said, 'I think she must have been attracted by you.'

'She was not.' I slammed my glass on the counter. 'Look, I was going to offer you another drink.'

'Was she attractive?' His eyes were brighter.

'I'm not prepared to tell you. Will you have the same again?'

He nodded his head, the brightness lingering reminiscently. Presumably he was thinking about some fresh girl he'd got his eye on.

Since his liberation, first by the War from the passionate attentions of Tom, and then by his initiation after the War in the *moeurs* of drama school, Steve had never ceased to have his eye on a fresh girl. After the drama school he married a girl who'd been there at the same time as himself, and they'd had two children. She'd become a very good actress. And she, it seemed, had never ceased to want Steve. I've already said that he was an attractive man. I don't know what his sexual powers were like, but they must have been satisfactory: I do know what his company was like – it was typically engaging, fluid, relaxing.

A little while after their second child was born his wife had become a Roman Catholic.

To Robert I observed, 'I should have thought for a girl who's married to Steve, becoming a Roman Catholic is the reverse of appropriate.'

Robert said immediately, 'It means he'll never be able to get away from her by divorce.'

(You see why I venerated Robert's capacity for perceiving the heart of the matter?)

Steve had never been divorced, but it was many years since he'd lived with his wife and family. He had lived with a succession of other ladies.

I have remarked that from his youth, Steve's manner, even when he was absorbed in entertaining, had continued to preserve something which indicated his sensitive artistic nature and his consequent need to be taken care of. In the psychological sense his need to be taken care of may have been illusory if not frankly bogus: in the financial sense, while his career in the theatre stayed permanently at the petering level, it was hard fact.

Such was Steve's charm that each of the ladies in succession appeared to have been happy to oblige in taking care of him. For a time. It was for that reason that I tended not to encourage his having his eye on a fresh girl. To put it crudely, I thought he ought to watch his step. (On the other hand, people who do watch their step all the time rarely endear themselves, alas! to other people.)

Refusing to indulge him by discussing that censorious girl, I handed his glass to him and said, 'Do you mind if we sit down?'

The outer walls of the room were pleasantly divided into compartments which offered a little privacy. Turning, we were confronted with a huge coloured photograph, on the wall above the compartments, of Her Majesty; under it, the legend in huge letters –

LIZ RULES OK?

Steve carried his glass across. 'I noticed you limping as you came in.'

'This bloody arthritic hip.'

'Can't anything be done for it?'

'It *is* being done. I'm going to the Westminster Hospital for physiotherapy twice a week.'

'And is it making it better?'

'If anything, worse.'

'Doctors!' (His elder son had become a doctor. A pleasing turn of fate, I thought it – conventional as any other doctor, the young man disapproved of his father.)

We sat down facing each other. He was looking at me directly.

'Joe, your eye!' His face, pinker and shinier than it used to be, was changed, almost distorted, by its look of youthful sympathy. 'The pupil's much whiter than it was last time I saw it.'

In the ordinary way I tried to pretend to myself that people didn't notice it. It was showing. Oh dear! I said:

'You don't have to worry about that so much. Last time I saw him, the eye-surgeon said it's ripe.'

'Ripe – how terrifying! What does it mean?'

'Ripe for excision.'

'I'm a terrible coward, Joe. What do they do?'

'They excise the eye-lens, which has gone opaque. And as you don't have that inside your eye afterwards, to focus with, you wear a contact lens on the outside.' Something, I don't know what, made me hear the tone of voice of my mother.

Steve looked puzzled by the science of it.

I said I was going into hospital sometime in August. Steve asked me if I was having it done privately.

I explained that I'd had a stroke of luck. For some years I'd gone to the surgeon as one of his private patients – he was one of the most distinguished in London – while the cataract 'ripened'. When the time for action had come we'd discussed how much it was going to cost, and he suddenly offered to do it on the NHS.

'He must be a nice man.'

'He's an excellent man. I think he's wonderful. And I'm sure *he* thinks he's wonderful. And he thinks *I'm* a bit out of the ordinary – being terrified neither by the operation nor by him.' I smiled at the thought of him. 'He's large and handsome, very efficient and very impressive. Getting on for sixty. Always wears a rose in his lapel. Very grand. He looks as if he used to play rugby football – he did.'

296

'How do you know?'

'I asked him, one day. There was a silver-framed photograph of two healthy-looking young men on the table beside where you sit. I guessed they were his sons, guessed they were rugby football-players, and asked him. One thing led to another, in a hearty sort of badinage. He doesn't play rugby football any more.' I couldn't resist adding, 'On the other hand he still leads a vigorous married life.'

'Joe, how on earth did you find out that?'

'I didn't find it out, it just sort of fell out. Let me see . . . I suppose it must have been when he was finding out how physically fit I am, my regular swimming and all that. I suppose there must have been a bit of fun in the air. After all, when you get down to bodily functions and think of their enjoyability, what else? I favoured him with my advice for the ageing – *The essential thing to do is to keep on doing what you've been doing*. He laughed at that, and gave me a look. Message exchanged – to the satisfaction and pleasure of both parties! He's a fine man. He's known to Elspeth and me as His Majesty.'

Steve was amused. 'So he's going to do you free of charge.'

'He probably feels it's taking the mickey out of the NHS at the same time.'

We sat for a moment, reflecting. The pub was not especially crowded or noisy. It was a fine day outside and the doors were wedged open. I glanced at my watch.

Steve looked at my glass.

I didn't think I had time for another. My personal assistant had his instructions, how to deal with importunate telephoners, but I thought I'd better give him a break.

Steve seemed to have changed in mood. I said:

'We've talked all the time about my affairs. How are things with you?'

He lifted his shoulders, another gesture I'd seen in the past. As if his shoulders were weighed down.

'What's the matter?'

'It's Marìa.'

'What's the matter?' Marìa was the latest lady in the succession, an Argentinian lady living in London. She'd been contributing to the fulfilment of Steve's need for some two years. He was installed in her flat in Regent's Park. I gathered that she was rich and interested in the theatre – the happiest of combinations for Steve. On the few occasions when Elspeth and I had met her we'd thought she was perhaps a shade predatory, but not unamiable. But how could Steve hope to be taken care of by someone who was not a shade predatory?

'I'm afraid that she's not as free as she used to be.'

'Free?' I said. 'What do you mean by free?'

Steve didn't reply, as if I'd merely been asking the question to tease.

Free?

'We've started to have quarrels,' he said. 'I mean serious quarrels. I mean not just love quarrels, where all you have to do is to get into bed.'

'I'm sorry.'

'She's started to find terrible fault with me, Joe.'

'Oh dear.'

'She says I'm lacking in seriousness.'

'Steve!'

'I mean seriousness as far as she's concerned.' A tone almost of anguish came into his voice. 'I *am* serious.' He looked at me with extraordinary sincerity. 'She's my *lifeline*, Joe.'

I could think of nothing to say.

At last Steve thought of something to say. He said:

'Do you think I shall find another?'

'I'm sure you will, Steve.'

Another lifeline.

After a pause he stood up and I did the same. It was time to part. He stayed beside me on the pavement while I waited for a taxi.

'By the way,' he said suddenly. 'Do you know Tom's coming to London?'

I looked at him, so surprised that I let a taxi pass.

'When?'

'Some time later in the year.'

'It must be the first time for ten years.'

'I know. Shall you see him?'

'I shall make no moves to do so.'

Passers-by were buffeting us. Steve said:

'He can't still be a menace to you, Joe.'

'I don't suppose he is, but why give him the chance?'

'You're much more strong-minded than me.'

Another taxi came up. 'We'll see,' I said. I got into the taxi and it drove off.

In Shaftesbury Avenue the taxi was held up by traffic and I was given time for thought.

So Tom was going to re-appear. Actually I didn't feel menaced, but I meant to keep him at a distance. In the past I'd been amused by his bounding, bombinating activity. No, that wasn't fair – there was a good deal more to it than that. There had been friendship between us. He'd always been ready with an unusual fund of human sympathy and, it seemed to me then, an unusual fund of human wisdom. Not that he was modest about possessing those unusual funds, especially the latter. 'I understand you better than you understand yourself,' was his line, even though he was a year younger than me. In those days I was shy of thinking I understood myself. His line was menacing yet it was comforting. Now I hope this hasn't made him sound pompous and over-bearing: he actually was pompous and over-bearing, yet he was also funny and frequently comical. He was a bit of a clown.

He was coming to England. If he'd been here during the last ten years I hadn't heard of it. And when I'd been in New York I'd made no effort to get in touch with him.

I had decided the most sensible thing I could do was let our friendship lapse. In this case distance had lent disenchantment. Thinking over the goings-on during the years of our close friendship, it seemed to me that in spite of his sympathy and his wisdom, in spite of his empathy, he was a destructive person. Only too often his clowning made trouble, did harm. On one occasion, when I really was in trouble already, it had made matters more troubling, more painful for me – and also for the young woman with whom I was having a love-affair that was coming to an end.

It was coming to an end because *she* wanted us to marry and *I* didn't. Tom, in the midst of pursuing Steve from pillar to post, conceived, in empathy for her, the idea of marrying her himself.

After the War he had resolved to make his future in the USA. In addition to bounding energy he had a great deal of ability, a great deal of shrewdness. He'd gone through the hoops of qualifying as an American accountant with distinguished success. After a few hard years, which he was helped through by marrying a rich American girl, his career had taken wing. He now lived in New York and was rich himself. His marriage had ended in divorce and he had not married again. When he travelled abroad nowadays it was invariably with an entourage of young men – some of them with wives – who were junior partners, personal assistants and so on, one of them clearly occupying a chosen rôle.

When Tom was young I'd made fun of his seeing himself as a great understander of human nature, a great writer – he wrote a couple of novels – a great connoisseur of the good things in life, and a great lover. He did not see himself as a great chartered accountant. Well, Destiny had lain in wait for him. It was a great chartered accountant that he'd become – a high bigwig in Boyce Peterhouse New York!

It had been part of Tom's tactics in America deliberately to loosen his ties with his native country. He must have been in the USA for five years before he came back to England, and he merely returned then to attend Robert's wedding to Annette.

It went without saying that Annette roused his empathy irresistibly.

'I've know Robert all his life, my dear. I'm sure you'll be very happy with him.' He smiled at her, his pop-eyes shining through his spectacles with understanding and wisdom, his arm warmly enclosing her waist. 'You'll have to be prepared for a string of petty infidelities, but I *know*, my dear, you'll be able to tide them over.'

I resolved to keep him out of Elspeth's way.

CHAPTER VI

GOODBYE TO A CATARACT

His Majesty had a ward of his own, His Kingdom, on the first floor of the hospital. It was a large handsome room with about seven beds ranged round three of its walls, the fourth being taken up by wide bay windows giving a splendid view of suburban countryside – a low valley, gleaming down below with half-hidden roof-tops and rising to a skyline of distant trees.

All but two of the beds were occupied when I arrived, occupied mostly but not entirely by men who were elderly, some of them with dressings fastened over an eye, others without. One of the two empty beds was mine: in the next was a tall Sikh, complete with beard and turban as well as a patch over the eye.

I was taken into a private office, Elspeth with me, and inducted with great tact into the whole plan of procedure – presumably on the principle that both of us would be less frightened if we knew exactly what was going to happen. At the same time it was clear that I had entered His Majesty's realm and was one of his subjects. Mr Harrison likes you to do this, and Mr Harrison will want you to do that. I didn't fancy the chances of anybody who didn't do them.

In due course Elspeth left and I enmeshed myself in the routine, a sequence of trips from one place to another for one test or another.

And then, 'Now, Mr Lunn, we shall want to cut off your eyelashes.'

'Oh!' I discovered I'd got a Samson complex.

The snipping felt very odd. I'd been used to imagining that I had long eyelashes. 'They'll grow again,' the nurse said. 'Yes, of course,' I replied, as if I believed her.

I was returned to the ward, where I observed the routine for those patients who had had the operation.

At lunchtime I had been given a decent meal. Now I was approached by a smiling, Chinesey little nurse with a basin and a spoon. 'I've come to feed you, Mr Runn. So you get used to it before the opelation.'

A delicious little creature with large, flat eyes and shining teeth. I prepared myself to be fed by her.

It was part of the procedure. After the operation you were placed in a sitting-up position, where you had to stay, sleeping in that position. Your head was not sandbagged down, but you had to keep it still. For a few days you had to be spoon-fed, and there was an absolute ban on brushing your teeth afterwards: if you had false teeth you were given the choice between not having them in at all for the four days, and having them in but on no account taking them out. Mr Harrison's orders.

I began to find spoon-feeding inordinately slow, and was suddenly visited, across twenty-odd years, by remorse – I'd done my younger daughter an injustice! When she was a baby, being spoon-fed, she'd given up eating after a while apparently out of boredom, and we'd been impatient with her. She was right. I'd been very unjust. Being spoon-fed really is boring and I felt inclined to give up. 'Some more, please, Mr Runn.'

Virginia hadn't had the encouragement I was getting. Slightly giggly and quite delicious. She told me she came from Malaysia, and her name was Marìa.

Marìa – I thought of Steve's lifeline! I'd had a drink with him before I came into hospital. He was not sanguine. Marìa's doubts about his seriousness had not diminished. I understood there had been no change in her being less 'free' than she used to be. If I hadn't been going into hospital he would have wanted me to see her, to help convince her of his seriousness. Poor old Steve, things were going to be serious for him if she wasn't convinced. So far he could still pay for his drinks. (In all the years I'd known him, throughout all his vicissitudes, he'd never proposed borrowing money from me and I'd never heard of his borrowing money from anyone else.)

Steve had no further news of Tom.

'Not much more now, Mr Runn.'

'A pity,' I said. 'I think you feed me very nicely, Marìa.'

Giggles and smiles. I wondered what it would be like to have a wife who was small and delicious and who came from Malaysia. Such wonderings were brought to an abrupt close. Maria – she must be a Roman Catholic! That wouldn't do for a Protestant atheist like me, Methodism coming with the genes. You can't giggle and smile away a great divide like that.

The meal ended, and in due course, rather early I must say, the day ended. With ablutions over, the ward composed itself for sleep. The Sikh in the next bed went to sleep – and began to snore like a steam locomotive. It was an incredible noise. Every so often one of the nurses would come and try to rouse him.

'Mr Singh, Mr Singh, stop *snoring*!'

It didn't have the slightest effect. Some of the other patients who were used to it managed to get off to sleep. Not I. In the early hours of the morning an Irish night nurse took pity on me. 'Will I be making you a nice cup of tea, Mr Lunn?' She brought it and chatted with me comfortably while I drank it. The Sikh, it transpired, had some kind of obstruction in his nose: there was no hope of a quiet night for the ward till he was discharged.

In the morning a visit from His Majesty, wearing a beautiful yellow rose: he was accompanied by the Sister.

'I expect you've met Sister Curtis,' he said.

I said Yes.

'Sister Curtis and I are old colleagues. She's been working with me for many years, more years than I'm going to tell you.'

I bowed politely. After all, I hadn't asked him.

'Sister Curtis knows as much about all this as I do. Probably more. Isn't that so, Sister?'

The Sister smiled – with a flick of her eyelids. 'Yes, Mr Harrison.'

His Majesty glanced at me. 'You see?' We laughed. The two of them looked briefly at my eye and then they swept on to the next bed. 'Good morning, Mr Singh.'

Poor Mr Singh, because of his nasal obstruction, had had to have his operation with a local, instead of a general, anaesthetic. He was somehow not made for hospital life – apart from his getting a good night's sleep. In bed he still wore the baggy trousers ordained by his religion: I saw them when he got out of bed to use his bottle. It was forbidden for him to get out of bed at present. Whether it was because of religious rules about cleanliness or because his baggy trousers made it impossible, he wouldn't use his bottle in bed. So he got out of bed – and immediately came up against his rules about exposing himself. Looking tall and proud he tried to use his bottle while hiding it behind the bed-curtains. Poor Mr Singh . . . How much better for everyone not to have *any* religion!

In the evening, though, Mr Singh had some compensations. He was visited by a wife and daughter, beautiful, dusky women dressed in beautiful, silk saris. Elspeth, sitting beside me, felt eclipsed. She concentrated on how far my own appearance fell short of what was desirable. This hinged on my pyjamas. After the War, when clothing required coupons, I'd ceased to wear pyjamas altogether. I absolutely refused to buy new ones now, solely to wear in hospital. Consequently I was dressed in a pair that had been hidden away in a drawer for thirty-five years.

'It's super silk,' I said to Elspeth, feeling my cuff. 'They' – I nodded towards the Sikh ladies – 'would agree.'

'They,' said Elspeth, 'can't see it's so thin that the jacket's already split down the back.'

'If they can't see, what does it matter?'

I took hold of her hand and squeezed it. One ought not to bicker with one's most loved person on the edge of general anaesthesia. You never know. I was to be operated on next morning.

His Majesty operated on me next morning and by the following evening I'd come out of the general anaesthesia and Elspeth was sitting beside me again. This time it was she who took hold of my hand. I was keeping still, pretty firmly held in position by the sheets. There was a dressing over my eye and I had no headache nor any pain at all. Now we had to wait and see – literally. Put your trust in His Majesty! The Sister came and chatted with us and reassured Elspeth. Four days to wait.

The four days passed, with spoon-feeding, drinking-cups, bottles and bedpans. I even began to sleep through Mr Singh's snoring. If I didn't sleep I had a job to get a cup of tea, as we now had an African night nurse who confounded the universally received idea that black people are indolent and ever ready to please. She was highly efficient and seemed intent, with success, on pleasing nobody. With Mr Singh her technique was to wake him up every hour. Poor Mr Singh, turbanned and bearded and handsome, proud and shy and not very sure of the language; I think she hated him. In my opinion he was lucky that she never saw his beautiful wife and beautiful daughter.

I began to get interested in the next lot of patients to come in. There were two old gentlemen put into adjoining beds, Mr Griffiths and Mr Davies. It was fortuitous not only that they were both Welsh but that they bore a physical resemblance to each other. They were small and wiry, wearing straggly little beards. In their brand-new Marks and Spencer's pyjamas they were constantly nipping in and out of bed, and they'd seen fit to bring in with them some bottles of Guinness which they surreptitiously stowed away in their lockers. Working on the inverse of another universally received idea, that to us pinko-greys all Orientals look alike, I thought our delicious little Malaysian nurses were going to have some difficulty in telling Mr Griffiths and Mr Davies from each other.

The previously empty bed, next to mine, was now occupied by a stocky fellow who looked about forty-five: he told me he was a Post Office engineer, name of Brian. He'd come in for the first of two cataract operations. I was astonished. Two cataracts by the age of forty-five. He explained that cataracts were common in his mother's family.

'The sodding genes!'

'That's right,' he said.

We were both taken aback by rapport.

I explained the concept of *Sod the genes*! I scarcely needed to. 'That's right,' he said as soon as I paused. 'That's how I feel.'

He stood beside my bed in a rather glorious dressing-gown – not M & S, possibly Austin Reed. 'Sod the genes!' he repeated. 'That's right.'

There was a pause.

'This man Harrison,' he said.

'What?'

'Is he OK?'

'Very.'

'S'what I thought.'

I felt I'd found a mate. I looked forward to the evening, to see

305

what his wife looked like. Alas! I was to be disappointed. He was working temporarily at Dollis Hill: his wife and children were up on Tyneside. He told me about them. I told him about Elspeth and the girls. I also told him that time was when my Civil Service job had taken me on visits to Dollis Hill.

'Did it really?' he said with wonderment and delight. He too had found a mate! He sat on the edge of his bed and we talked about Dollis Hill.

Then there was another pause. He looked round the ward.

'You ever been in hospital before?'

'No.'

'Me neither.' He went on. 'What's it like?'

'I've survived so far. I've had the operation and I'm still in possession of my faculties.'

He gave me a quick look. Shrewd brown eyes and a blunt nose – who did he remind me of?

'Such faculties,' I said, 'as I've had the opportunity to exercise.'

He grinned at me. I knew who it was whom he reminded me of – none other than the Noble Lord Balderstoke. I thought of Robert, then of *Happier Days* . . .

I shifted under the sheets. 'If you'll excuse me,' I said, 'there's a faculty I'll have to exercise pretty soon.' I began to fumble for my bottle.

'Let me get it for you!'

'Thank you, I must do it for myself, though I still find it a bloody nuisance, trying to find it without leaning over to look for it.'

He said, 'I suppost it's something I'll have to learn to do.'

'It's either this or bust.'

He politely looked away. 'I suppose there's nothing to it.'

'Not if you've set your heart on it.'

We both laughed.

I thought of Mr Singh's difficulties and decided not to mention them.

Poor Mr Singh, there was no longer any objection to his getting out of bed, but that was no help to his modesty: he was still trying to hide behind the curtains. But then I thought of his dusky wife and daughter in their saris – not poor Mr Singh, lucky Mr Singh!

Mr Griffiths and Mr Davies returned from having their operations. Then Brian. One felt the sort of bond men are supposed to feel who have gone through the same initiation ceremony.

The wives of Mr Griffiths and Mr Davies continued to make regular appearances in the afternoon. They were short, bustling women with the sort of unquenchable cheeriness that reminded me of our office-cleaning ladies. They brought with them, as instructed by the hospital, clean sets of pyjamas: they also brought more bottles of Guinness. They were extremely adept at stowing the bottles away when there was no nurse in sight.

Elspeth saw what was going on. 'Are they *allowed* to bring in all those bottles of drink?'

'I don't know. I've never asked.'

'It looks as if they're *not.*'

'They give that impression,' I agreed, 'but it may not be so.' I embarked on high psychological speculation. 'Isn't it just their instinctive behaviour? Confronted with a system, they instinctively set about circumventing it. Whereas if they only learnt to play the system, they could get what they want without circumventing it.' I paused. 'How about that?'

I wondered what Brian, lying unvisited in the next bed, thought about it. I knew perfectly well that you weren't allowed to say such things in democratic society. Elspeth frowned and I wasn't surprised. She said:

'Anyway, what about *you*? And your pyjamas?'

'I've brought some. I'm not instinctively circumventing the system, not being able to comprehend it.'

'They're indecent.'

'Only from the back.' Now that I was returned from the brink, there was no harm in a bit of marital bickering. I heard a slight snigger from the next bed and realised that I'd got the Trades Union of Men going.

'What about when you get out of bed?'

'I shall put on my dressing-gown. And that'll be a pity – my pyjamas are super silk. You can't buy silk like that, nowadays.'

Elspeth began to laugh. 'You're getting above yourself.'

I stopped. Tomorrow morning I was due to have my bandages off. I felt frightened.

Elspeth squeezed my hand. 'It's all right,' she whispered.

That night there was a rumpus in the ward. The African night nurse had come on duty and was making her first round. I'd begun to think less ill of her, though all the other men hated her. Her cool *de-haut-en-bas* manner struck me as explicable – I'd have been prepared to bet she came from the Nigerian aristocracy. Furthermore she really did know her job.

She was at the other end of the ward.

'Good evening, Mr Griffiths. How are you feeling this evening?'

'Very well, thank you, Nurse.' Earlier on one of the ambulant patients had surreptitiously poured him a night-cap of Guinness.

The nurse went through her routine. 'There you are, Mr Griffiths. Good night.'

As she was moving away, he called after her, 'Nurse!'

She turned.

'Can you pass me that, please, Nurse?'

I have to say that Mr Griffiths and Mr Davies had brought in with them receptacles for their false teeth, receptacles that looked like plastic butter-dishes with lids. It was at one of them, on top of his locker, that Mr Griffiths was pointing.

'What do you want that for, Mr Griffiths?'

'To put my teeth in, like, for the night.'

'Mr Griffiths, you know that if you chose to keep your teeth *in* you're not allowed to take them *out*. Not until Sister gives you permission.'

'I didn't choose to keep them in, Nurse, no indeed. I always have them out, like, to sleep in . . . '

'Well, you've got them *in* now.' She suddenly stopped as the significance of what he'd said struck her. 'Mr Griffiths,' she said, 'I'm going to look up in the records where your teeth ought to be.'

She turned and walked out. Horrors! There was silence in the ward. I felt my diaphragm shaking with suppressed laughter.

She came back. 'Mr Griffiths, you did choose to keep your teeth out after the operation. In that case you should never have had them *in*.'

'No, Nurse.'

She looked at him. 'I suppose the best thing we can do with you now is take them out, and keep them out, until you're given permission to put them in. Do you understand, Mr Griffiths?'

'Yes, Nurse.'

She passed him the plastic butter-dish and there was a rattling sound.

'Thank you. Now good night, Mr Griffiths.'

She moved on to the next bed. She was a tall, good-looking girl. I thought she was perhaps a chieftain's daughter, doing hospital training in this country: she spoke English like someone who had been educated here.

'And now, Mr Davies.'

Mr Davies said nothing. His straggly little beard was outside the sheet: his unoccluded eye was wide open.

'According to our records, Mr Davies, your teeth should be *out*. Are they?'

Mr Davies screwed up his mouth tight. Everyone else in the ward, and the night nurse as well by now, guessed where Mr Davies's teeth were.

'As you don't reply, Mr Davies, we can soon find out.' With a simple gesture she lifted the lid of his plastic butter-dish.

'Mr Davies, I think your teeth are *in*.' It suddenly occurred to me that she, too, was having a job not to laugh.

Mr Davies nodded his head without speaking.

She held out the butter-dish in front of him. 'Mr Davies, please – *out!*'

Mr Davies made a movement, and there was a second rattling sound.

'Thank you, Mr Davies. You understand? You're not to put them in again until you have permission.'

Mr Davies's one eye remained wide open, very bright. I wouldn't have trusted him for an instant.

She went on her way. It was one of the duties of the night nurse to rub baby-powder on the bottoms, as a precaution against bed-sores, of everybody who had had their operations a few days earlier. At length I saw the curtains being whisked round Mr Singh's bed, and a *sotto voce* conversation ensued as it did every night. From it I could overhear as usual, 'All right, Mr Singh. If

309

you'll promise to do it properly, I'll let you do it yourself.'

Poor Mr Singh, with those baggy pantaloons! How on earth could he do the job properly in those garments? As for allowing the nurse to see, let alone touch, his bottom! .. At length the curtains were whisked back and the night nurse finished her round without further trouble. Instead of going to her illuminated desk in the corner of the room, she went out.

Silence.

Then, 'Psst! .. Mr Thoroughgood! Psst! ..' It was Mr Davies, now capable of speech. Mr Thoroughgood was his next-door neighbour, an ambulant patient soon to be discharged.

'Yes,' Mr Thoroughgood answered.

'Mr Thoroughgood.' Mr Davies's voice was quavery. 'Mr Thoroughgood, I can't get to sleep. Can you pour me a little drop of my Guinness?'

There was the noise of Thoroughgood getting out of his bed and padding across to Mr Davies's locker. Clinking, a brief glug-glugging, and a pause.

'Mr Thoroughgood! .. ' It was Mr Griffiths now. 'Can you give *me* a drop of *mine*? Just to help me off, like. That's a friend.'

I heard Brian mutter from the next bed, 'They're like Tweedledum and Tweedledee.'

At last the diversions were over and everyone finally composed himself for sleep. The night nurse came back to her desk. Blessed silence.

Then Mr Singh began to snore.

I shouldn't have got off to sleep so very quickly, myself, that night. I was wondering how things would turn out in the morning.

I must have slept, because the day had dawned when I was awakened by the start of the morning's routine. In the grey light, a cup of tea. A farewell to the night nurse and a welcome to the day shift. We had to go through washing and breakfasting before the time for the crucial test would come.

At last the time did come. The Staff Nurse appeared, accompanied by one of the older, non-giggly, non-Chinesey nurses. They drew my curtains and gathered round me. Sister Curtis appeared.

'Now, Mr Lunn,' said the Staff Nurse, 'just lie quietly!'

I did as I was told. I felt them undo the bandage, then unwind it, and then gently loosen the sticky plaster that held the dressing. And then, with a smooth skilful stroke they took the dressing away –

I could *see*!

Where I'd only just been able to tell if it were night or day, now I could see, softly blurred, the pink shape of the nurse's cheek, and her nose, and the dark bit where her eye was, the white rectangle of her cap.

'It's amazing! I can *see* . . . '

'Yes, Mr Lunn. That's how it should be. Don't get too excited!' Pause. 'Mr Harrison will be coming to see you later this morning.'

His Majesty – the greatest king I'd ever met. How soon could I let Elspeth know? I lay patiently, gradually recovering, while they took it in turns to look into my eye and then collogue over me.

When they'd gone away Brian congratulated me.

'In a couple of days it'll be your turn,' I said. 'You'll be all right.'

'I hope so.'

In due course there was a stir outside the door, as of heralds trumpeting soundlessly. His Majesty came in, accompanied by Sister Curtis.

He reached me. 'It's amazing,' I said.

'I'd like to have a look at it.'

He examined it, leaning over my bed from one side while the Sister leaned over from the other. He said to her:

'His iris peaked, as you'll have noted.'

'Yes, Mr Harrison.'

'A nuisance, but it couldn't be helped.' He addressed himself to me. 'It's nothing to worry about, Mr Lunn. It sometimes happens. Instead of your pupil being circular you'll notice that at one point there's a little dark peak from it into the iris. It's my fault . . . It won't affect your being able to see.'

I made some acquiescent sound or other. If His Majesty said so, it must be so.

311

He stood up. 'You'll be able to see just as well.' He gave me an amused glance. 'But you just won't be quite as beautiful as you were before.'

In the nick of time I suppressed a facetious rejoinder – he'd said seriously that it was his fault . . .

I said: 'I expect I'll manage, somehow.'

'I expect you will.' He laughed. 'Somehow.'

Then he went on his way.

The eye was covered up again and I had permission to get out of bed. When the state visit was over I made a circuit of the ward and then went over to the window to stare at the sunlit vista of roofs and treetops stretching downwards and then up again into the distance. Though I was occluded again, I knew I could see. I thought of my poor old mother, too old for her cataracts to be operated on. Sometimes she said, 'It's a sunny day, isn't it?' How she could tell, I didn't know.

I thought about the peaking of my iris and felt a momentary, after-the-event qualm. Things *could* go wrong . . . But they hadn't.

I joined the group of ambulant patients who found themselves something to do by giving the nurses a hand with passing round meals and cups of tea, and generally by doing minor services for patients still confined to their beds.

The latter services in my case included attending Mr Griffiths and Mr Davies. They were irredeemably naughty. I interfered with them and needless to say they got the better of me. They sustained themselves with frequent nips of Guinness. They had been told that they were to sit up in bed and on no account lean over sideways. One day I saw each of them leaning out of bed to pick up a bottle of Guinness from the lowest shelf of the locker.

'Mr Griffiths! Mr Davies!' I expostulated. 'You know you're not supposed to lean out of bed like that.'

They looked at me mutely with one bright eye apiece. They reminded me terribly of a little long-haired dachshund we'd bought for the girls: *his* way of exerting his individuality on a system he was in the grip of, i.e. us, was exactly by this mixture of wilfulness and cunning.

'If you'd only asked me,' I said, 'I would have got your bottles of Guinness for you.' I proceeded to get the bottles. In my expostulations for one thing, and in my psycho-sociological reflections for another, I'd entirely forgotten that I was not supposed to stoop down to the ground, myself.

But just as wilfulness and cunning didn't always avail Silky against us – inexorably we would put him out in the garden even though he was convincingly pretending that he didn't need to go – so it didn't avail Mr Griffiths and Mr Davies every time.

It was an occasion for blanket-baths. The nurses usually began a fresh round of them at the window-end of the room, where Mr Griffiths's and Mr Davies's beds were. The nurses were always hard-pressed with work and they were frequently interrupted for long periods to do other jobs. On this particular day the beginning of the round was entrusted to the two delicious little Malaysian girls. Everyone was envious when they saw somebody's bed-curtains being drawn – there was something to look forward to.

The daily life of the ward had been rolling on, and nobody was paying much attention, when unusual sounds began to come from behind the curtains round Mr Davies's bed.

'Mr Davies, where are your crean pyjamas?' It was Marìa's voice. 'In your rocker?'

'I had them *on*, Nurse.'

'No. Your *crean* pyjamas, Mr Davies.'

'Yes indeed, Nurse. I had them on.'

'No. Those were your dirty pyjamas. We took them off. Now we put on your crean pyjamas. You have crean pyjamas? Where are they?'

The curtains opened at the corner near to Thoroughgood and the second little nurse threw out a pile of soiled sheets and a blue-striped pair of pyjamas. At the opposite corner, next to Mr Griffiths, there was already another pile, which had been lying there for some time, including an orange-striped pair of pyjamas.

'You've just taken them away, Nurse,' said Mr Davies.

'Mr Davies, you joking.' There were giggles.

'No indeed, I'm not.'

'Then where are your dirty pyjamas?'

'You took them away, the first time.'

'Mr Davies, you really joking.'

Silence from Mr Davies.

'What colour your crean pyjamas, Mr Davies?'

'Blue, Nurse.'

'What colour your dirty pyjamas?'

'Orange, Nurse.'

A delicious little Chinese head appeared out of either corner of the curtains. It was Maria's head nearer to Mr Griffiths's bed. She picked up the orange-striped pyjamas. (The whole ward were now listening with riveted attention. The truth had dawned to delirious effect.)

Maria picked up the orange-striped pyjamas. 'These Mr Gliffiths' pyjamas,' she said confidently.

Mr Griffiths joined in. 'No, Nurse. Those aren't *my* pyjamas. Mine are green, like. And purple.'

Maria began to giggle. She took the orange-striped pyjamas inside. 'Yes, Nurse,' came Mr Davies's voice. 'Those are my dirty pyjamas.'

Chu-Yin took the blue-striped pyjamas inside. 'And those are my clean ones.'

Now there were gales of giggles. Through them we could hear Mr Davies say:

'You've given me *two* blanket-baths, Nurse.'

While outside, his curtains still not drawn, Mr Davies said in a quavery voice:

'And I haven't had *one*.'

The sound of general hilarity brought in the Staff Nurse – Brian was commenting 'Lucky Mr Davies!' Instantly everyone piped down. I was thinking, Crafty Mr Davies.

After that incident any patient felt at liberty to invite Maria and Chu-Yin to give him a blanket-bath twice-over. Giggles and giggles.

The days rolled on further and discharge began to be a definite proposition, first for me and then for Brian. Mr Singh had already gone.

We heard His Majesty deliver a pre-discharge admonishment to Mr Singh –

'Remember, Mr Singh, *No violent exertion.*'

Brian and I had listened from our adjacent beds with great attention.

'Did you hear that?' Brian said to me afterwards.

'Of course I did.'

'Do you think he means? . .'

'I should think he does.'

A brief silence. 'That's a bugger, isn't it?'

'It is.'

'What are we going to do?'

I said brightly, to tease him: 'Do without.'

He groaned.

Smitten by pity, I said: 'It doesn't have to be violent, does it?'

'You mean if we go at it gently, it'll be all right?'

'More likely to be all right than if we go at it violently,' I said, thinking it was a good idea to inject a little comparative thought into the discussion.

He glanced at me with amusement. 'You're an educated chap, aren't you?'

'Up to a point.'

We both laughed. Then we lapsed into thought.

Two days later I had my penultimate inspection from His Majesty and Sister Curtis. He gave me his list of recommendations, instructions and injunctions.

'And remember, Mr Lunn, no violent exercise or exertion to begin with.'

I nodded my head. I have to admit I put one interpretation on the word 'exertion'.

After His Majesty had left the ward, Brian said:

'You got sentenced today. In a few days' time it will be my turn.'

'That seems very likely.'

He paused. 'We're in the shits, aren't we?'

'Well, remember, Brian, *we can see.*' I paused. 'Furthermore we've not got to go back to work for six weeks – that's nice.'

Brian grinned reluctantly. 'It'd be better if it weren't so vague. How long do you think we shall have to wait? Assuming, like you said, we go at it gently.'

'Like *I* said? It was your *immortal* phrase.'

'It's a reasonable phrase.'

'I thought it was an excellent phrase. An excellent idea.'

'Well, about how many nights would you think?'

'I haven't the faintest idea.'

Silence.

Suddenly I was inspired. 'I'll ask him!'

'You will?'

'Why not? I'm sure I can. He isn't God – he's only a man the same as us. He's human, he's fun . . .' I felt bold. Brian was impressed. I was impressed, myself.

So when the day came I was ready. I hadn't actually prepared my form of words. If one referred to it as 'intercourse' that removed from it any air of impropriety, but made it sound rather unlike what I was thinking of.

There was a good deal of scurrying round by the nurses that morning. They even took away dead flowers and put fresh water in the vases of the flowers that were still alive. Finally there was the stir as of a whole corps of heralds trumpeting soundlessly.

His Majesty swept in – at the head of a squadron of retinue, three baby doctors, the Sister, the Staff Nurse, three nurses including our African friend, and goodness knows who. He was wearing a glowing tangerine-coloured rose in his buttonhole and a glowing regal expression on his large handsome face.

I thought, *I shan't be able to do it*. In front of all those people. It was sheer ill luck.

His Majesty came and looked into my eye, talking to me in his usual un-stuffy way – I could have asked him easily had we been alone. Then he held forth to the audience. The baby doctors looked at my peak and learnt that it didn't affect my vision and so on. Finally when, this time from a distance, I received the well-known instructions and injunctions, I couldn't say a thing, other than Thank you, to him.

At last the grand visitation was over and the ward settled down to routine. I had to say something to Brian.

'I'm sorry, Brian. I let you down.'

'No problem, Joe.'

'I think my spirit was broken by sheer weight of numbers.'

'Mine would've been the same. That shower made it impossible.'

'So we're no forrarder, alas!'

There was a pause.

Brian said: 'We'll just have to play it by ear, Joe.'

I smiled at that. By *ear* . . . 'Don't we always?' I said to him.

Brian turned to look at me. 'Joe,' he said, 'I think you must be a good husband.'

'I don't know about that,' I said. 'I doubt it. What about you? I think you probably aren't so bad.'

'Maybe. Maybe not.'

The following day I was discharged. Kind friends came to take me back to London by car, so that I shouldn't be jolted by a train. Elspeth came with them, bringing presents for the nurses. Brian and I shook each other firmly by the hand. In a sudden outflow of emotion I kissed Sister Curtis on both cheeks. (Marìa and Chu-Yin were off-duty, unfortunately.)

So I came back again to our house and our garden – now up for sale. And to a special lunch that the girls had spent all morning preparing. It was like a celebration. The girls examined my peak and disagreed with His Majesty's opinion that I wasn't quite as beautiful as before – that's the sort of daughters to have!

After lunch Elspeth said: 'You'd better have a rest this afternoon. And go to bed early.'

'Go to bed early!' I cried enthusiastically.

'I've made up a bed for you in the other room.'

'I shan't have to go to it straight away?'

'You know what His Majesty said.'

'As if I could forget!'

'I'm not so sure of that . . .'

'Oh, all right.'

In the event I didn't go to it straight away, but we both behaved with utmost circumspection. Elspeth held my hands in a very firm grip. The minutes passed, bringing happiness. 'It's wonderful to be in bed again,' I said.

'Yes . . .'

A long pause.

'Wonderful.'

No reply. 'Isn't it? I said.

'I think you'd better be going. I don't want you to. But you know . . .'

'Not so soon.'

'Darling, you must be sensible.'

A call to my better nature. I had to answer.

'All right.' I got up, and after a lingering exchange of lesser civilities went to the other room.

So far so good.

The following night we were naturally a bit more easy-going about it.

'Isn't it wonderful to be in bed?'

'Yes . . .'

The minutes passed. Elspeth was not holding my hands firmly. She wasn't holding them at all.

'Wonderful . . .'

I listened for her to say 'No.' She breathed, 'Yes . . .'

One thing began to lead to another. I said:

'This is more than flesh and blood can bear.'

I listened again for her to say No. I could have sworn I heard her breathe, 'Yes . . .'

I said: 'If we go at it gently, very gently, I'm sure it will be all right.'

'Are you really sure? My darling?'

I said: 'I'll tell you what. I'll stay absolutely still, and keep my eyes shut. Then I'm sure it will be all right.'

Looking back on it I can see that it was sensible to stay absolutely still, but I don't know what good I thought keeping my eyes shut was going to do me.

I rolled carefully on to my non-operated side, and shut my eyes. 'There! . . .'

It was bliss, bliss every moment up to and including the last, especially the last. It was incredible.

And then, then I opened my eyes. 'Darling, I can *still see!*'

PART II

ABOUT PROPERTY

O ur house was up for sale.

The Blackwells actually had sold out to the Council. Our joint agent's professional discretion – or slyness – which had prevented his telling us what they were up to, and how much they were likely to get thereby, didn't stop him letting us know now that they had got an inflated price. Meanwhile, having originally encouraged us with the proposition that he would get us £60,000 for our house, he suggested, now that he'd got to prove his proposition, that we should put it on the market for £50,000. House-prices were falling everywhere, he said.

We learnt to speak the language of house-selling. We learnt to speak of Asking Price, which was an entirely false price, being neither what we hoped we might get nor what we'd be willing to take. It was a price from which one Came Down to the price one was forced to sell for. I'd always told Elspeth I thought house-agents were crooks: it came to us now that in house-selling and house-buying, the behaviour of all parties concerned could scarcely be called straight. We had our first intimations of that Great Truth –

Buying And Selling Property Brings Out The Worst In Human Nature

Our tenants' organisation held a party to celebrate its victory over the Council, the Labour Council. The Blackwells, now living miles away, were nevertheless present, large as life and universally received as true as blue. Elspeth and I, likely to drop £5,000 or more as a result of their manoeuvre – which was known to everybody present – were received as ever like the cads of the party, the local Reds. Knowing the ways of the world, what else could we expect? We were wondering, as the organisation had been awarded costs, if we should ever get our £150 back – fools that we still were! It was a jolly party.

With six weeks' convalescent leave under His Majesty's orders, I was conveniently at home to show prospective purchasers round. I was astonished by how many prospective purchasers turned up. I was not allowed by His Majesty to do much reading, so I'd resolved to spend my time listening to some of all those gramophone records I'd bought, played a few times, and then filed away. I'd decided to work my way through all the Beethoven quartets, then all the Bartók quartets, the Schubert song-cycles – not to mention whole operas, for instance *The Ring*. Did they give me a chance to do it? Not likely.

I have called the people who interrupted me prospective purchasers. I was coming to realise more clearly than ever how innocent I was. More than half of the people I showed round hadn't the faintest intention of buying the house, of buying our house or any other. For some of them it was purely a sight-seeing tour – why not charge them an entrance-fee, I wanted to know, for visiting an Unstately Home? There was another lot, though, who sounded more serious. They held most encouraging conversations among themselves – 'We should have to have that wall down, shouldn't we, dear?' or 'We could just fit the cocktail-cabinet in there, don't you think?' or 'It's so *light*, darling, we could paint the walls *blue*!' It was all fantasy. I've no doubt some of them went home and spent happy weeks decorating and furnishing our house – in imagination.

Occasionally there were what appeared to be bona fide prospective purchasers. After the grand tour they sat down in the sitting-room to talk to me, and in due course they asked politely:

'And who are your neighbours?'

The Blackwells' house was in full swing as a staging-post for Council tenants on their way to more permanent homes – or further staging-posts. There were usually about three families in the house at once. In fact they were quieter than the Blackwells, for the most part leading much more vocally-restrained lives. (One night somebody woke us all up by crashing through one of the huge plate-glass sliding doors that gave on to the Blackwells' terrace, but that was exceptional. The glass was not replaced for a long time, and we wondered if the tenants were counting on being moved on to their next port of call before the Council found out.)

'And who are your neighbours?' It was a little embarrassing if the prospective purchasers, while inspecting the garden, looked through the Blackwells' wire fence and saw the family of little Ghanaians at play.

The Ghanaian children didn't make a great deal of noise, but they had a habit of tearing off any of our plants that grew through the fence or that they could grab from their side of it. They seemed to have a special taste for shredding.

'They are rather destructive,' I said to our younger daughter, Annie, one day when we saw a lot of shredded rose-petals on the ground. Our roses flowered all the year.

(You may have noticed some time ago I said she was called Virginia. She was. When we decided on names for our children we knew that a time would come when they would reproach us for our choice. So we told them that when they were old enough they could choose fresh names for themselves and we would abide by their choice. At the ages of ten and eight, respectively, they got together and came to us with the information that they *both* wanted to be called Anne. Such confusion arose that in the end they agreed to give up. Viola remained Viola. But when Virginia went to a School of Art she moved into up-to-date circles – there's nothing so up-to-date as a School of Art – from which she emerged as Annie.)

'You must admit it's destructive,' I persisted.

'It's the result of deprivation,' she said, because they were black.

'Deprivation?' I cried. 'Look at their toys!'

Their garden was littered with expensive toys – a red plastic tricycle, a yellow plastic dolls' pram, a red and yellow and blue plastic roundabout or something that looked like a roundabout, and God knows what else in the way of broken plastic bits and pieces.

'If it's the result of anything,' I said, 'it's the result of indulgence!'

She turned away. Her current principles forbade her admitting it, but I could tell from the curving of her cheek, where it showed beside her hair, that she was trying not to laugh. (She was a pretty girl, with long silky fair hair that swayed when she walked.) I thought it was sweet of her to give up the argument, but of course I didn't say anything.

However it was no laughing matter when prospective purchasers of the house wanted to know who the neighbours were. The most we could do was to assure them that, whoever the neighbours were, they would not be in residence for long.

So the weeks passed and we began to get offers. A new phrase in the language – Offering Price. I was going to say it was neither more nor less false than Asking Price. But it could be, in its way, more imaginative. We discovered there were *soi-disant* purchasers who made offers without for a moment meaning it. They bought houses, in contrast merely to decorating and furnishing them, in imagination. I should have liked to put up a notice on the front gate –

NO FANTASISTS ADMITTED

In due course there were Offering Prices convincing enough for us to consider them, only to learn that they were contingent upon the offerers selling an unsaleable property elsewhere or raising a colossal mortgage on negligible security.

The weeks changed into months. I was back again for my final term at the office, and we had got nowhere, apart from devoting our Saturdays and Sundays to behaving like attendants at Madame Tussaud's. Then winter came along and our stream of visitors diminished because it was cold – and that was worse still.

'Never mind!' wiseacres who had been through the mill consoled us. 'Some day someone will come along who'll fall in love with the house.'

Fall in love with the house? In a long life I'd seen love take so many forms, mostly bizarre, that I supposed I couldn't profess to being surprised by this one.

In the meantime I refused absolutely to countenance our buying a flat before we'd sold the house. Robert had once been the not-so-proud owner of two monumental properties for over a year.

Elspeth nevertheless went out looking at flats – on 'a recce', as Field Marshal Montgomery might have called it. There was a dismaying recce after she had read in *The Daily Telegraph* that lots of smart people were going to live in Parson's Green. 'Peregrine

Worsthorne's gone to live there!'

'I know,' I said. 'He got into the Underground there, the other morning, in his scarlet socks.'

One Saturday afternoon she took me to look at a house there that *we* could afford. Street upon street of little red-brick petty bourgeois houses with bay-windows –

'Do you realise,' I said, 'this is the sort of house I spent my childhood in? It'd be going back to square one.' I was stirred to eloquence. *'Say the struggle nought availeth,'* I cried, 'if I've got to end my days in Parson's Green!'

That was that.

I had offended Elspeth. On the way home she sat beside me in the Underground, silently looking straight through the window on the opposite side. My offence dawned on me: after she'd gone to all the trouble of finding the house, I'd thoughtlessly dismissed it out of hand.

I leaned sideways towards her. 'Let's have something nice for supper this evening. Let's go out, shall we?'

'Why did you say that?'

'To try and cheer you up.'

No response.

'I'm sorry,' I said, 'that I turned it down so hastily.'

'Oh, that's all right . . .'

It looked as if tears had come into her eyes.

She had to locate houses and flats, arrange to go round and see them – all after she'd done a full week's work. It's something that doesn't seem to get mentioned in novels, I thought, how exhausted we all get with doing things.

At home Viola was waiting for us.

'Those people, the Poults, who came to see the house last Sunday, telephoned. They said they're going to make an offer – '

'Did they say how much?' I interrupted.

'Thirty-eight.'

We simply can't accept that, I thought. We had put £40,000 as our very lowest – whatever that might mean. I could have asked, Do you think they've fallen in love with the house? but I hadn't the heart. I remembered the Poults, nice people, and I fancied they might mean it.

I didn't doubt that the agent would advise us to take £38,000.

Or £36,000. Or any other number of thousands that constituted an offer which was likely to be honoured. He just wanted to take his 2% commission and clear out. The difference between 2% of £38,000 and 2% of £36,000 was £40 – who'd do a stroke of work for that?

'Are you going to tell those other people, the Eulers?' Viola asked. 'They were very enthusiastic.'

'They may have been enthusiastic but they didn't make an offer.'

'They said they were going to come and see it again.'

That was true.

Could the Eulers have fallen in love with the house? They were nice people, as well.

'If you tell them we've got a definite offer of 38,' said our darling offspring, 'they may come up with 40 to get it.'

The deplorable voice of experience came from her having worked, in her very first job after secretarial college, for a firm of property tycoons in its heyday. (In the five years since then they had of course progressed from boom to bust.)

For a moment I wished the voice of experience would be quiet. Elspeth and I had subsided on to a sofa: we were worn and depressed.

'We'll see,' I said.

Pause.

Brightly – 'Can I get you anything? A drink?'

There's a pitch of being worn and depressed at which one even refuses a drink. Fortunately we hadn't reached it. We said we'd like gin-and-tonics.

The effect of the drinks was faintly reviving. I began to feel that possibly all was not lost. What's £2,000? I asked myself. The answer was £2,000, of course. But the worth of £2,000 seemed to vary according to how one looked at it. I wished the way I was looking at it were not so dark.

I finished my drink. 'I'll start getting the supper,' I said masochistically, the idea of going out having been abandoned.

'Oh Daddy, *I*'ll do it!

Elspeth said: 'I think perhaps we *should* telephone the Eulers.' She scanned my expression. 'All right. I'll do it.'

It was not long before she came back from the telephone.

'Keep your fingers crossed! The Eulers were definitely thrown by the news. They're upset because they can't come and see the house again tomorrow afternoon. They can't manage it till Sunday week.' She paused. 'Since they saw *this* house, they've sold *theirs*.'

'Oh,' I said, not permitting myself to go any further. We'd concluded that the Eulers could raise the money. They had told us about their jobs: they both worked, and they were having a mother-in-law to live with them – it sounded as if she had money.

How could one think of fellow human-beings in those terms? As names, to which were attached sums of money, money that one was hoping to get *off* them.

We held our breath for a week. Will the Eulers or won't they?

Sunday week came, and so did the Eulers.

'We *love* this house!' said Mrs Euler as they came down the hall.

They offered our ultimate in Asking Price, £40,000.

It seemed unbelievable. The house was sold. Or as good as. We got our breath back.

60, 50, 40 – it scarcely bore thinking of in cold blood. Best not to think of it!

And would those nice people, the Poults, feel we'd Gazumped them? As indeed we had. Best not to think of that, either.

The Eulers, having sold their own house, wanted to move into ours as soon as they could get a survey done and the contracts exchanged. Everyone knew that exchange of contracts took weeks, if not months, since it involved lawyers. All the same we began to hold our breath again – *we* now had to find somewhere to live. We thought of all the places Elspeth had explored – mostly no longer for sale, of course. But we knew where to look: I'd said I thought I could live there. Mansion flats on the Embankment by the bridge. When you came out of them you had only to cross the road to find yourself beside a lovely curving stretch of the river. On the near side was a row of boat-houses leading to a long rural towpath; on the far side a long river-wall overhung by the trees of a park: in the foreground was a jetty and then a line of little boats moored in mid-stream; and far away the gleaming turrets of Harrods' Depository, sometimes flying Union Jacks –

'It's pure Monet,' said someone we knew who lived there.

We telephoned the place. Extraordinary. There was a flat going of the size we wanted. We arranged to go and see it, holding our breath still harder.

We were shown into the sitting-room. A small, stuffy room with a gas-fire burning . . . My spirits sank beyond recall, while Elspeth and Viola toured the other rooms. My hip began to be nastily painful.

Afterwards, when we were outside, Elspeth said: 'Why did you give up? Did you think it wouldn't do? Viola and I thought it might.'

'Really?' That little room, that gas-fire . . .

'It's got the right number of rooms. They're a fair size and well-disposed. And they're bigger than they look.' Elspeth paused emphatically. 'We could do all sorts of things with it.' She paused again. 'And at £18,000 for a 78-year lease, it's a snip.' She paused for the third time. 'The poor dears have got to sell in a hurry.'

At that I began to think again. £18,000, instead of the £20,000 we'd allowed for in our calculations. Could one profit by the disadvantage of fellow human beings who'd got to get out in a hurry? What about *Buying And Selling Property*? We could.

'Of course if *you* don't like it, we'll have to look for somewhere else.'

We could do all sorts of things with it . . . I began to think about it. We had joined the happy band of fantasists.

The flat was on the top floor and there was a lift – no more running up and down stairs for me. And one thing I had noticed was that the windows gave a splendid view of the sky. (At the house we'd kept the trees, at the cost of never having an unimpeded view of the sky, even from the attics.)

'I'm prepared to look at it again.'

So we made another appointment.

'And this time, darling, look at all the rooms properly! They're *not* small. And *think* about what we could do with them!'

We went. I looked. I thought.

We went again.

We were going to buy it; we were going to buy it . . . We did.

CHAPTER II
MY MOTHER AGAIN

I was in two minds about telling my mother we had sold our house and bought a flat. I always felt short of news to give her, but this particular news could easily revive an old row. After she'd been in the convalescent home for nearly three years, expensively keeping on her own flat nearby and a woman to look after it, it was quite apparent that she would never be able to leave a place where there was somebody on call night and day. Constantly she talked of going back to her flat – she still did – but there had been a brief spell during which she came near enough to recognising the truth to agree with a case for selling it. With my power of attorney I promptly sold it. And then she reverted to her fantasy of going back to it.

One day she said something to which I could only fail to disclose what I'd done by lying grossly: I couldn't do it. Hence the row. 'You've got rid of my home!'

The row was apparently forgotten, but I felt wary all the same.

I was let in to the convalescent home by one of the part-time helpers. I enquired how my mother was.

'Not quite so well today, Mr Lunn.' From the way she looked at me I suspected I was in for a bad time.

I went up to my mother's room. The door was propped open and there was a smell of wee. My mother was lying askew, as usual. Her mouth was in motion as if she were chewing. I pulled up a chair close to the bed.

'I'm glad to see you,' she said. 'But you shouldn't keep on coming here like this. You'll tire yourself.'

I went into my usual explanation. 'It's perfectly easy for me to leave the office early, and there's often a car to take me to Victoria.'

'Well, that's good. But I don't want you to tire yourself.'

'No, I won't do that.'

There was a pause. She said: 'So you're still going to the office.'

'Yes. But not much longer, I'm afraid.'

'How much longer?'

'Till the end of the year. I had a two-year contract and that's when it ends.' My spirits sank as I said it. That, I thought, is when my capacity for earning a living ends.

'And then you'll be pensioned-off?'

'You can't say pensioned-off when I don't get a pension.'

'I know that. What do *you* say?'

'I suppose you'd say I'm retiring, or being retired.'

She thought for a moment –

'You won't *like* it.'

I tried to laugh. I failed.

'You'll miss having an office to go to. And a secretary. And people to take orders from you. *And* a car to take you to Victoria.'

I thought, Oh God! I said:

'Those won't be the only things I shall miss.'

'You'll miss the money.'

'Well, if you must put it like that, yes.'

I don't think she heard me.

She said: 'I wish I had more to leave you.'

'I don't think about that. *You* shouldn't think about it, either.'

We were interrupted by the girl who'd let me in, bringing me a tray with a small pot of tea and a little cake. She went round the other side of the bed. 'Now, Mrs Lunn, let me help you to sit up a bit while your son's here!' She began hoisting my mother up, plumping the pillows and straightening the sheets.

I poured some tea, and glanced round. The elephant apparently made of white soap still decorated the dressing-table. Why on earth of white soap? Why on earth an elephant?

My mother said: 'Who was that? The Matron?'

'No. One of the girls who helps here.'

'That's funny – she wants to see you.'

'Who wants to see me?'

'The Matron, of course.'

I'd heard this story before and found there was no substance in it. It was my constant fear that the Matron really did want to see me – to ask me to find a place for my mother elsewhere. However I said:

'What for?'

'She's always wanting to see you. You can tell from the way she looks at you, she thinks the light of the sun shines out of *your* eyes.'

'Oh,' I said, rejecting the idea of asking how she could see the Matron's facial expression.

There was a pause, and I began to drink my tea and eat my cake.

'What did she bring you?'

I told her.

'I could do with a cup of tea, myself.'

'I expect you had your tea a little while before I came, and it will soon be time for your supper.'

'I don't see what that's got to do with me thinking I could do with a cup of tea now.'

'Well no,' I said patiently. Oh dear! This was a bad day. Something told me she was further round the bend than usual. Yet I was surprised by her energy, which seemed undiminished. I said: 'I'll put some of my tea in your drinking-cup, if you like.'

'No. I don't want to rob you of *your* tea. You need it.'

Saying Oh God! under my breath again, I poured some tea into her plastic cup with its serrated drinking-spout. I put it in her hand, and helped her to bring it to her mouth.

'Here you are!'

'Thank you.' She drank. 'You'd make a good nurse.'

There was a longish pause. I listened to the fluctuating sound of the traffic on the main road. There was somebody talking to a deaf patient in the next room. The tea was good, anyway.

'What were we talking about when the Matron came in?'

Taken by surprise I said like a fool: 'Money.'

'What I want to know is, How much longer am I going to be able to afford to live here?'

This was a topic I'd met before, and had no desire to meet again.

'Look here,' I said mildly, 'I've told you before not to worry about that.' I put my hand on hers.

331

'But I do worry about it. I've got nothing else to do – just lying here, all day and all night.'

'Well, don't worry about how you're to go on living here! You're managing all right. I've explained it to you before.'

'I suppose you have, but I can't remember it.'

'I'll explain it to you. You get your Old Age Pension. You get a Blind Person's Allowance. You get an allowance for Night and Day Attendance. And you have the income from your investments. If you add all those together, it's enough to keep you here.'

The place was no great shakes, I thought, but she conceded that the food was good and the bed comfortable. It happened that there was even a little money left over after her bills had been settled, and we were paying it into her Building Society account.

Suddenly I thought of all the old people who couldn't add up enough to keep them somewhere. My mother's investments were small, inherited from an old childless aunt. How fortunate she was! How fortunate *we* were! (Actually we should all have been more fortunate if she'd let our stockbroker advise her, but she refused to hear of it.)

'Have I got any money in the bank?'

'Yes.'

'How much?'

'I don't know. I'll tell you when the next statement comes in.'

I had no intention of doing so. She was now completely out of touch with the current value of money, which was decreasing at the rate of about 15% every year, and she hadn't had to buy anything for herself for eight years. She was appalled by the increasing charges of the convalescent home, which were perfectly justifiable; and when I told her the magnitude of the sums of money she held, she was too incredulous to take it in.

I leaned closer to her. 'Listen, my dear . . . You just mustn't worry. You're all right. Do you understand that? You're all right.'

Suddenly I heard the echo of Elspeth's saying exactly the same thing to me, trying to make *me* believe that *we* were all right.

'I suppose *you*'re worried about money?'

'We shall be all right, too. You mustn't worry about us.'

'I can't help it.'

I was in no position to make any comment. To shift the line of conversation I decided to risk uttering the word 'flat'. I said:

'I've got some news for you this week. We've sold the house at last. And we've bought a flat.'

'A flat?'

I thought, Here it comes – You've got rid of my flat and now I haven't got a home. I merely said, 'Yes.'

My mother said:

'I suppose it's for you and the Matron to live in.'

'*What!*'

'What I want to know is, what Elspeth thinks about the divorce.'

'What divorce?'

'Yours and hers. You're not going to set up with the Matron without marrying her, are you?'

To laugh or to cry, to scream or to shut up? I took hold of myself. I said:

'I think you've got everything mixed up again.'

'Have I?'

'You have,' I said. 'Now listen to this! Stop thinking about the Matron – I don't know anything about her; I'm not interested in her; I don't even see her every time I come here. Provided she runs this place properly, that's all that concerns me about her. Have you understood that?'

Silence.

'As for the flat,' I went on, 'we've bought that so that we can cut down our living expenses. It's quite a nice flat – at least it will be when we've done it up. And the people who are going to live in it are Elspeth and me and Viola –'

'What's become of Virginia, then?'

'Virginia doesn't live at home. She lives in a studio with some other artists.'

'Oh.'

'So the people who are going to live in the flat are Elspeth and me and Viola. Do you understand that? Elspeth and me. Elspeth and me . . . and we're very happy with each other.'

'I'm glad to hear it.'

'We're very happy.'

'I've always liked Elspeth.' My mother paused. 'Though when you married her I thought you were baby-snatching.'

'Baby-snatching? She was twenty-five!'

'Ar, but how old were *you*?'

Should I refuse to disclose my age at the time, or blushingly say Forty? While I was trying to make up my mind I realised that she wasn't waiting for an answer. She wasn't waiting for anything – apart from the one thing ... You have to wait till you're called.

I looked down at her in pity. And the question hovered over my mind, the question I was always trying not to hear when I went to see her – *Is this what's going to happen to me?*

I looked at my watch. When was the doorbell going to ring, to release me? It was nearly time.

'You mustn't miss your train,' she said.

'That's all right.' I stood up and began to collect my impedimenta.

The doorbell rang. I didn't know if she heard it. I said, 'There's the taxi now.'

I paused, and then bent down and kissed her goodbye.

'Thank you for coming,' she said.

'I'll be here again soon. I'll come and see you again.'

'I know you will. You're very good to me.'

To avoid saying anything I kissed her forehead again and then left.

In the train I tried to read, and at Victoria I made straight for the nearest public-house.

By the time I'd put down a pint of beer, I was feeling slightly better. Going over it all again I began to see that the fugue over the Matron had a comic side. In fact it was funny. I thought it was so funny that I began to rehearse telling it to Elspeth.

When I got home I told it to Elspeth. By that time it seemed to me extremely funny. I have to admit it didn't seem so to Elspeth. It's true, what they say – women are strange creatures.

CHAPTER III

TWO CONVERSATIONS AND A LETTER

The arrangement was that I should pick up Robert at his house in Vincent Square and we should then stroll round the corner and have a drink at his local pub. The period was during the Christmas Recess. I arrived punctually at five-fifteen. It was a dark, blowy evening and rather mild. There were wet leaves on the pavement, even at this time of year. In the humid air the streetlamps seemed dim.

To my surprise the door was opened not by Robert – it was Dolores's evening off – but by Veronica.

'Come in!' I kissed her on the cheek. 'The Old Boy's just gone out to buy the evening papers. You know what he's like about newspapers.' She led the way to the staircase. 'I'm to entertain you to a drink while you're waiting. That's if you'd like a drink. I expect you would.' She gave her loud characteristic laugh, nervous yet attractive, somewhere between a hoot and a giggle. '*I* should.'

We went upstairs to the sitting-room, and I sat down on a sofa while Veronica made two sizable whisky-and-sodas. I watched her. She had a remarkably trim, small figure – pretty legs, I thought. How *old* was she? Mid-forties? She was an Assistant Secretary in the Civil Service, wondering if she was going to make Under Secretary, so Robert told me. Her hair was dressed in a French pleat, with a few wisps allowed to stray over her ears. She turned and came to me. I stood up. Her narrow grey eyes were sparkling with amusement.

'I know *you* think that five-fifteen is too early for Scotch. The Old Boy told me.' She handed me my glass and I sat down. 'You needn't be alarmed. When he comes back he's going to take you out to the pub to drink some beer.' She looked at me a shade

335

wryly. 'So the two of you will have time together on your own.'

There was a pause. Over my glass I looked at her. Her cheeks were their usual bloomy pink, surprisingly unlined. Her tall forehead was rather pale. The pause felt odd to me. Suddenly she gave me a slightly nervous glance and said:

'Has he told you I'm now living here?' She gave her laugh again. 'Since yesterday.'

My face must have shown that I didn't know.

'He was going to tell you today.'

I grinned. 'He doesn't tell me everything.'

She was thoughtful. If I'd been given to thought-reading, I should have wondered if she was convincing herself that in future he *would* tell *her* everything. If so, then I thought she could be wrong.

I said in a friendly way, 'I'm very glad, anyway, that you've moved in.'

'He needs it.' Her glance moved round the room. 'Living here all these years on his own. It's not good for him.'

I said, 'No, it isn't,' thanking my lucky stars that she was not looking at me. The fact of the matter was that Robert had *not* been living here all these years on his own all the time. I had seen several women come, and go. Veronica appeared to be the strongest contender up to now for permanent residence, but she was far from being the first.

She drank some of her whisky-and-soda, and said:

'I'm glad I've got this chance to talk to you, Joe.'

I wondered what was coming now.

She said: 'I want to ask you something. Why does Robert carry this terrific burden of guilt about his marriage to Annette?'

I couldn't possibly have expected the question – nor have answered it. I said:

'I know what you're talking about, but I shouldn't put it to myself in quite that way.' Her phrase 'burden of guilt' was exactly the sort of phrase I could never have used, a phrase summing-up something that was to my mind un-summable. Though Veronica was not one of such people, the phrase satisfied those people who wanted, as Robert contemptuously put it, psychological explanations that could be expressed on the back of a postcard.

'What way would you put it in?' Her eyes were sharply bright.
(I suddenly had intimations of why Robert thought she might make Under Secretary.) I said:

'I should like to think it over for a moment.'

'Come on, Joe! You'll be telling me next that you want to sleep on it.'

'No, no,' I said easily.

'Well, don't! Because the Old Boy will be back in a few minutes.' She looked at me. 'I do want to know. And I do think you know more about it than anyone else.'

I said: 'In the first place you have to accept the idea that I believe some people are more given by nature to guilt than others. The strength of your predisposition probably comes with your genes.'

'That's what you and Robert think about everything that matters.'

'That doesn't prove we're wrong.'

She said nothing for a moment. 'Then Robert's predisposition must be stronger than anyone else's I've ever known.' She gave me a shrewd, amused glance. 'Stronger than yours.'

'How clever of you!' I cried. 'Do you know that Anthony Burgess once criticised one of my novels on the grounds that I, the writer, suffered from *insufficient sexual guilt?*'

Veronica gave a hooting laugh. 'Did he really? Oh, how killing!'

I didn't think it was quite so funny – nor literary criticism, if it came to that. Nor did I think she was right about Robert, generally speaking. But I wasn't prepared to argue. I set the conversation back on the rails by saying:

'I suppose you might say Robert feels some kind of guilt, among other things, you know, over his marriage to Annette.'

'Was she beautiful? He says she was.'

'Yes.'

'Was it obvious she was schizoid? Did he know?' She corrected herself. 'Of course he must have known.'

'Yes, of course. In a way, that was one of the attractions, I'm sad to say. Her inner world was quaint and remote, and fragmented . . . Robert spent years exploring it – he got drawn in.'

337

'Poor devil!' She went on: 'Do you think he did understand her? I'm sure he must have.'

I thought, He fell deeply in love with her, which may be a different matter, almost always is. But I said, 'Yes.' I went on. 'He got a pretty clear idea of how severe the split was – between living in the world of her own and living in the world other people were living in.'

'Did he think it was dangerous for her to marry?'

Now we were getting towards the sort of ground it was more usual for me to tread. I knew how deeply and how long Robert had pondered the question. And how uselessly. 'He thought it might be. Or it might not.'

'But he went ahead.'

Robert was in love with Annette. I could only say to Veronica, 'Yes.' What neither Robert nor I nor anyone knew was what difference it would have made to Annette's fate if he had left her to herself. I had a terrible feeling that, after all the suffering – and all the joy, which was not to be overlooked – for both of them, it had ultimately made none.

Veronica went on incisively: 'How did she get on? I mean as a wife.'

'Pretty bizarrely, as you might expect. Her ideas about running the *menage* were idiosyncratic, to put it mildly. For a start she had moral objections to employing servants. Coupled with a negative talent for house-keeping. In a house like this.'

'I suppose Robert wanted her to entertain. That's what they must have bought this house for.' She thought about it for a moment. 'I suppose it *might* have helped her to come out of her shell?'

I said nothing. I was suddenly grasped by memories, memories of this room and strange parties – of Annette dressed brilliantly, behaving like a duchess; and of Annette not appearing for hours, then, dressed in scruffy old jeans, passing wraithlike through the room as if there were nobody else there. That was in the days before she had drinking-spells.

'Was it Robert who persuaded her to have children?'

I could see the case Veronica was building up. I said:

'You know, for the first years after the children were born she was distinctly better, more able to cope with life. Don't forget she

338

was a highly intelligent woman.' I paused. 'But that spell was the last remission before the inner cold – '

'Clamped down.'

I couldn't bring myself to say anything.

There was a long pause. Our drinks stood beside us, for the time being untouched. Veronica said:

'I suppose she was treated for it?'

I said: 'You don't think Robert neglected anything, even if he didn't have any faith in it? Or still does neglect anything, for that matter? Psychiatry, chemotherapy, the lot ... In the Home, where she now is, it still goes on, so far as I know. He never talks about it.'

There was another long pause. This time it was not Veronica who spoke first. I said:

'I can see where you think the burden comes in.' I had dropped the word 'guilt' – who was I to single it out from regret, remorse, responsibility, love? . .

'We've got to get him out of it!'

I picked up my drink again.

'It's not *good* for him, Joe, going on like this for years.'

I had a suspicion that I was being at least half-accused, as his closest friend, for letting it go on. As if *I* were able to influence Robert!

'You do see that, don't you, Joe?'

'I do.'

She picked up her glass again. 'It's this terrific burden of guilt,' she said with fresh energy, 'that prevents him getting divorced.'

Ah! I thought.

I behaved as if I didn't know I was required to comment. I was not sure what I wanted to say in any case. I liked Veronica; I thought she was a good woman; I could see that she was determined to make Robert happier – I was prepared to give her every credit for doing her best for him. But was *her* best *his* best? . . Of course I'd thought about these things. I'd seen Robert's feelings about his marriage to Annette as a cause for his not getting a divorce. When, a moment ago, I had listed to myself guilt, regret, remorse, responsibility, love, I had momentarily forgotten conscience. Conscience came into it strongly.

But I'd also seen – and this I couldn't say to Veronica now – that the unattached, quasi-unmarried state was not without its appeal to him. (After all, he hadn't married, in the first place, till he was forty-five.) Disloyal to him though it might seem for me to say so, I admitted to myself that 'not without its appeal' could well be the understatement of the evening.

Veronica was drinking the last of her whisky-and-soda. I wished Robert would come back. I thought he was taking an extraordinarily long time to buy a *Star* and a *Standard*. She said:

'We've got to try and get him out of it. For his own sake.'

I drank some of my whisky.

'You do agree, don't you?'

'Yes.'

'Joe, I want you to back me up.'

So we'd reached the aim of the conversation. I said, 'All right.' I raised my glass to her, silently signifying that I was willing to be her ally. (It really was a tremendous difference – for the better – that she had made to Robert's life during the last year.)

'Good!'

Actually, while this had been going on, it had dawned on me that I was the victim of a put-up job. Robert had been sent out so that she could have this conversation with me. Oh well! . .

Veronica stood up, holding her glass. 'I won't offer you another one as Robert will be here at any moment to take you out.' She was having another one, herself.

As she came back to me she was looking critically round the room.

'Tell me – has this place ever been re-decorated since *her* time?'

I felt it would be disloyal to Robert to say No, but disloyal to Universal Truth to say Yes. She went on.

'Have you noticed the colour of the paint?' She suddenly gave her laugh. 'It's filthy dirty!'

'Dolores looks after him quite well,' I said peaceably.

At that moment I was relieved to hear the sound of Robert coming upstairs. The conversation was at an end.

'Hello, love!' Robert put his arm round her waist and kissed her. 'Everything all right?' he asked her – I thought it was a bit cool of him.

'I was just telling Joe it's time you had this place re-decorated.'

Years ago I'd told him many a time that the place needed re-decoration, and he'd looked so pained that I gave up.

'Good!' He hugged her. I thought, You old humbug!

'We'll get it done without disturbing you. I've got just the little man to do it.'

I thought, in view of the size of the place and the state it was in, that it would take a 'little man' the best part of three years. Robert was looking down into her eyes adoringly.

'It won't cost you half', Veronica was saying, 'of what it would cost to have an expensive firm of decorators.' (And probably wouldn't be done half so well, I thought.)

Robert was nodding his head in agreement. He could easily have afforded the best firm of decorators in London. It crossed my mind that in Veronica's Civil Servant's efficiency there might be a touch of parsimony.

Veronica disengaged herself from him. 'It's time for you and Joe to go to the pub.' She smiled up at him. 'I shall just sit down and finish my drink, and then I'll start cooking something for supper.'

What a transformation for him! Someone to cook his supper on Dolores's night off. Someone to be in the house when he came home. I thought of Elspeth and me – years and years of comforting happiness. And that made me think of Jonathan, who seemed to feel that comforting marital happiness of that sort stifled the spark of Divine Discontent which generates Art. Perhaps he was right. And perhaps he wasn't. Dickens didn't know comforting marital happiness: George Eliot and Trollope did. (Yes, I know George Eliot never knew the actual marriage ceremony with George Henry Lewes.)

'Come on!' Robert crammed on a shapeless hat. And we set off to the pub. When we were outside the house he stood still on the pavement. 'The pub hasn't opened. I passed it.'

I cursed. It was one of the signs of the times: some local pubs seemed to open when they felt like it. The upshot was that two elderly men, one of them an elderly man of considerable distinction, might be seen trailing round at five-thirty from one public-house to another, or else standing disconsolately still in

341

the doorway of one that wasn't going to open till six o'clock.

Actually on this occasion we were lucky with the second one we came to. It was neither small nor cosy nor free from juke-box music, but at this stage of the evening it was open; and the beer it served didn't offend what Robert regarded as my inexplicably pernickety taste for beer that was pumped by hand.

We settled down. First of all he asked, 'What about the house and the flat?' It was out of pure friendship: it was the sort of thing he had no interest in. I told him we'd triumphantly arranged to exchange contracts for sale of the house and purchase of the flat on the same day.

'We shall have to find somewhere temporary to live,' I said, 'for four or five weeks to begin with. While we have the flat done up – '

'What for?'

'You wouldn't understand.' I paused. 'But Veronica would.'

He grinned distantly in acknowledgement of my having made a minor score. We drank some of our beer.

'The flat's got to be re-wired for electricity; have central heating put in; have a fresh bathroom and cloakroom, and a fresh kitchen; and be re-decorated throughout.' I thought it served him right, to have to listen to all that.

He paused for a while, then said hollowly, 'Any news?'

I shook my head. 'I've now received my last monthly pay-cheque but one.'

He was silent, looking pained on my behalf.

I felt pained on my own behalf. Elspeth wanted me to ask our doctor for something to alleviate depression – retirement depression!

Robert said:

'Any news of *Happier Days*?'

I shook my head. Then I thought of something. 'Yes, there is.'

I asked if he remembered the American woman who'd published (with no success) my last novel but one – a very nice woman who liked my books and who understood what I thought of as my sort of novel. He did remember her. I said:

'Well, she read the typescript of *Happier Days* and wrote to my agent, saying she couldn't publish it – but "it's such an adorable book, do you think Joe would let me have a copy of it, when it comes out in England, to keep for myself?" Isn't that the best American publishing story you've ever heard?'

Robert smiled wintrily. 'It's explicable.'

'Entirely explicable.' I had a very fair idea of what I thought of as my sort of novel and what I thought of as the American sort of publishing industry – never the twain shall meet. I'd had a string of American publishers who'd tried me, not unlike many another English writer. Some of them had not *lost* money on me, but that was not the point of industry: profit was what was required – I could see that.

'I shall send her a copy,' I said. 'She's a good sort.' It wasn't her fault that large numbers of Americans didn't want to read my books. Come to that, were there large numbers of English who wanted to read them?

'It's a very good book,' Robert said. 'One of your very best.'

My spirits revived a little. Writers live for praise, I'm afraid. Afraid – fiddlesticks! It's perfectly natural and honourable.

I drank a fair amount of my beer – it was quite good. 'We'll see what happens in this country.'

'Have you thought what you're going to write next?'

'Give me a chance!' I then asked him a question I didn't usually ask him. 'Have *you* decided what *you*'re going to write next?'

As he'd got an American Book of the Month choice with his last book, he must have made a fair amount of money with it in the USA, but I wasn't by any means sure that it had done as well as he hoped in this country. Someone was being employed to turn some of his earlier novels into a television serial; but we'd had enough experience to know that you believed in a television serial when you actually saw it on the television screen, not before. (If you did see it on the television screen, though, that meant you stood to make a lot of money out of your novel as *The Book Of The TV Serial*.)

I said, 'What about another beer?'

'Yes . . . Will *you* get it?' He gave me a one pound note from his wallet. I thought his back must be painful.

I came back from the bar and put our two pints on the table, gave him his eighteen pence change, and noticed that he was looking unusually thoughtful.

'What are you thinking about now?'

'Books.'

'What, about books?'

He began his fresh beer.

'Oh, how publishing is changing. How books are changing. How people are changing.'

'How are people changing?'

'I was thinking about your books to begin with. One of the things you were original in, was not being especially prudish about sex.' He eyed me with an ironic look.

'That's as may be. I've been wildly overtaken since then.'

'Just so. Books, and people, have become steadily less prudish about sex.'

I interrupted. 'You'd sometimes think they were no longer prudish about sex at all.'

'Books and people,' he went on, 'have become less prudish about sex.' He paused. 'They've become *more* prudish about money. And *more* prudish about death.'

We thought about it.

'I'm taking as the standard for comparison,' he said, 'the degree to which people were prudish at the time of the classic Victorian novelists.'

True. The people around *us* were chary of talking about money in their private affairs, and of talking about death in their personal lives. It occurred to me that I didn't like the idea of making my will. And I thought of what happened if I asked people what their incomes were – the hunted look that came into their eyes!

As we drank our second pint – we never drank more than two – we talked on. Robert said:

'The Victorian novelists were much less prudish about money than we are. And much less prudish about death.'

'And somewhat more prudish about sex, you might say.'

'They wrote better books than we do.'

'Agreed.' What else could I say?

Towards the end of the conversation I said:

'This has given me an idea, for when I'm writing my next book.'

'What?'

'As I made a bit of headway in not being prudish about sex' – I paused – 'I might have a shot now at not being prudish about death and about money.'

Robert did not say anything. He never agreed over-hastily with my ideas.

I could see, myself, that there must be plenty of arguments against as well as for. One against money, that struck me there and then, sprang from my having just recently read in the *FT* or somewhere that 'with the annual rate of inflation running at 12%' the worth of money halved in six years. So £10,000 in a novel written this year would have to be equated, for worth, with £20,000 by a reader in 1984.

'Well,' I said, not letting Robert get away with silence, 'what do you think of that?'

He drank some of his beer. 'Your luck might hold,' he said distantly.

That set me thinking again. Perhaps I'd made a bit of headway over sex because I was swimming with a tide, even if I was unaware of it, or even if I was unconsciously helping to generate it. But – here was the worry! – might it be that that tide had set up, in the dialectical nature of things, counter-tides in people's attitudes to money and to death? (The question was simply asking for Freudians to give an answer, mechanical and jejune, no doubt.) If that were so, when I tried writing unprudishly about money and about death, I might find myself in trouble.

I realised that it was time for us to go. We drank up.

Robert seemed to be lingering. Suddenly he said:

'Look here, old boy – I want to talk to *you* about money.'

I couldn't think what was coming next. 'Yes?'

'I've just set up a Trust.' He looked away. 'And *you* are to be one of the beneficiaries.'

I tried breathlessly to intervene with Thank Yous, but he went on.

'It's a Discretionary Trust. The other beneficiaries are members of my family. Not Arthur and Harry, I've taken care of them already. But my brothers and sisters. Veronica, if her position doesn't change; and one or two other persons.'

I felt a fantastic mixture of happiness and embarrassment.

'It should relieve your anxieties and Elspeth's just a little.'

'It will. I couldn't be more grateful – it's wonderfully generous of you.' And so on!

I followed him out of the pub in a state of uplifted spirits. I left him to go to Vincent Square while I went towards the Underground. I walked along the dark windy streets, thinking, I shan't be entirely destitute in my old age – there'll be something to save me! The moon was up now, sailing through the clouds with its halo of rainbow colours.

When I let myself into our house, I found a letter lying on the hall-table. I picked it up. From George Bantock – on the front of the envelope it said *From The Vice-Chancellor*, and it had the crest on the back. I opened it.

Dear Joe,
For some years my Council and the Senate has been perturbed by the low level of literacy on the part of our students, predominantly scientists and engineers, as you know. We are taking steps to have them taught how to write their professional papers, but this does not affect their ignorance of literature. They are not lacking in intelligence or curiosity. Their need is for someone to make them read literature, and to talk to them about it as someone talks who knows how to write literature. I can think of no one better equipped to do this than you. Would you be interested? A single course per term, involving not more than 3 hours teaching per week, would not interfere seriously with your writing, would it? You could more or less please yourself in telling them what to read. I expect you would choose novels. Why not include one of your own?
I am off to Islamabad immediately after Christmas, so it would be a blessing if you could telephone me during the next few days. If you are willing to do it, we could agree terms, an honorarium in the region of £2,000 a year perhaps. I could then get a formal letter of invitation out to you before I leave.
I do hope you are willing.
    Yours ever
    George

346

By the time I got to the end of it I felt I was practically reeling with high spirits.

After the number of times I'd made fun of George Bantock for always being on the look-out for people to offer *him* jobs – that was why his nose pointed up in the air – he'd offered *me* one.

CHAPTER IV

GOODBYE TO A HOUSE

'We *must* start getting rid of things we don't want.'
'Yes, darling.'

I don't need to say which of us made which of those remarks. The exchange took place as soon as selling the house and buying the flat were settled. The house had been advertised as having 3 recep, 6/7 bdrm, 2 bthrm and so on: it was a 5-roomed flat we were moving into. (Why so many as five rooms? Because Annie, while saying she didn't mean to live with us again, insisted on there being a room for her to come home to. There's nothing one can do about one's children, especially when their behaviour is touching.) 10 into 5 won't go: we had an awful lot to get rid of.

'We can keep all the pictures,' I said helpfully. At that point I hadn't counted them – eighty odd, it turned out, two of them very large. 'And the big mirrors,' I went on. 'We shall need *them* to make the rooms in the flat look bigger.' I considered I was doing rather well. 'And the Eulers are buying all the curtains and carpets.'

'What,' said Elspeth, 'about all the furniture?'

'Can't everything we don't propose to keep go to auction? It's just the chance to get rid of that dining-table.' I'd never sat down at it without noticing it was really a reproduction. 'We'll use my Ma's old table in its place.' A plain eighteenth century breakfast-table my mother had thrown out because in her view it was rickety. I went on. 'And all those Victorian dining-chairs can go, in favour of the Regency ones.' I was becoming enthusiastic about getting rid of things.

'You,' said Elspeth, 'don't know the sort of things auction-rooms will take and won't take. They'll never take that bamboo bedroom furniture. And all those beds. Nobody wants second-hand beds.'

'Why not?'

'They'd rather buy new ones.'

I thought about it.

'And don't forget,' she went on more mildly, 'I want a decent new bed. You must have had that one for nearly thirty years.'

I thought of that bed over nearly thirty years . . . However I said:

'Won't that make one more to get rid of?'

Elspeth said: 'Sandra thinks she knows somebody who'll take it.' (Sandra came in to clean for us.)

'Then we'll have a new bed.' The present one must have cost about £50: the sort she had in mind, its present-day equivalent, would cost £200.

'I don't think you know how much *stuff* we've accumulated in this house.'

'Probably not.'

'And don't want to know.'

'What sensible man would?'

'Well, darling, you'll really have to. I can't do it all.'

'Of course I'll help.'

'Then I suggest you make a start by sorting out the stuff in the roof-space.'

The roof-space! It wasn't even mentioned in the house-agent's brochure. I wouldn't have mentioned it, either. It was crammed with an unspeakable amount of stuff. There were cases of wine in store; large parcels of remaindered copies of my novels (do you wonder I didn't want to go up there?); cabin trunks filled with blankets and sheets; boxes of plates and glasses we kept for parties; discarded pictures; toys the girls wouldn't part with, including a dolls' house; a camp-bed; and that was only the start of it.

Elspeth went on. 'And there's the garden furniture.'

'That's pretty,' I said defensively. It was painted white, of cast-iron designed on the lines of Chinese Chippendale.

'The only way I can see of getting rid of it is by advertising it.'

'Let's advertise it!'

'How about you putting an advertisement in the local paper?'

'Which local paper?'

'You know there's only one local paper.'

'I suppose I can do it by telephone. I'll draft an advertisement.'

Elspeth began to laugh. 'Do you have to have a draft?'

'Of course I do – how'm I to dictate something over the telephone if I haven't got anything to dictate it from?'

'What about from your head?'

We were both laughing. Elspeth said: 'We're wasting time, darling. You were going up to the roof-space.'

'All right. I'll need a notebook . . . ' I looked round hopefully.

'That's a good idea,' she said and walked away.

So we embarked on getting rid of things we didn't want. A man came round from Phillips's and told us what they would deign to auction. One or two local junk-dealers came round and offered to take everything else away, for sums of money appropriate to the occasion of their doing us a favour. Our advertisements and Elspeth's personal negotiations provided an incessant stream of telephone-calls followed by an incessant stream of people to the house. We decided it was best not to regard the price they offered us for things as in any way related to their intrinsic value.

The weeks passed by. The amount of stuff was getting less, but not less enough. My retirement depression, although I had not yet retired, got worse, much worse when I contemplated all the stuff.

'Please God,' I cried, 'take away this property from me!'

And addressing Elspeth I cried: 'Now I understand why people renounce possessions and become tramps and hippies. What did Jesus of Nazareth say? Lay not up for yourselves treasures on earth? *I* say, Lay not up for yourselves rubbish on earth, either! In fact, Lay not up for yourselves!'

She took my hand. 'It's all right . . . We've got rid of a tremendous amount. We're really doing quite well. And when we get to the flat you'll be glad of the possessions we've kept. You really will.'

'Just a sleeping-bag under the stars,' I said. 'That's all *I* want.'

She looked upset.

'With just you and me in it,' I said.

That was better.

And of course that made me think of the sleeping-bag scene in *For Whom The Bell Tolls*. I reminded Elspeth. 'I always think that bit, "and the earth moved", was rather overdoing it, don't you?'

After a moment Elspeth said, 'Perhaps.'

And that made both of us laugh.

Elspeth extended her getting-rid scope. People came to the house from the Red Cross, the St John Ambulance, Oxfam, the Salvation Army – we were now giving things away. The final stage lay before us, when, to get people to take things away, *we* should be having to pay *them*. Oh, lay not up for yourselves!

The last day was notable for the triumph of logistic skill on the part of Elspeth and of slapdash behaviour on that of the removal men. They came half an hour late, having been drinking tea at a caff on the main road. They were in possession of a pantechnicon with scraps of old carpet lying on the floor and containing a huge number of tea-chests partially filled with crumpled newspaper. There were four men; one, older than the others and smelling rather more strongly, appeared to be the foreman. He assured us that although they were starting half an hour late they would finish early. Early, if you please! It was immediately obvious how they were going to achieve that desirable end, when the house resounded with the noise of our chosen pieces of furniture crashing against the bannisters and banging into door-posts on their high-speed way to the pantechnicon.

'Don't you wrap the pieces of furniture in old sacking or something?' I asked, as I observed the purpose for which the token scraps of carpet were used.

'They'll be all right when they get into store, sir. They'll be unpacked straight away.'

'What about now?'

'That's all right, sir.'

I said to Elspeth: 'Is this what other people have to put up with?'

'Of course it is. Everybody will tell you that moving house is traumatic.'

'Traumatic, indeed – it's obviously one of the deepest human experiences. Doubting the existence of God is obviously nothing compared with it!'

When the men came to the pictures an altercation took place.

I'd ascertained that by special arrangement they'd brought wooden containers for the two very big pictures. The rest of the pictures they took off the walls and dumped straight into the tea-chests.

'Aren't you going to wrap the pictures in newspaper?' I said.

'No, sir.'

'Then what's the newspaper for?' I pointed to the crumpled balls of it lying on the floor.

'That's for your china, sir.'

'But you'll ruin the picture-frames by doing this.'

'That's the way we do it, sir.'

'Then you'd better stop doing it.'

He shook his head – possibly to induce thought, I hoped. Not so. He said: 'You'd have to speak to the Area Manager about that, sir. I can't instruct my men to do it no other way.'

'Then I'll telephone the Area Manager.'

I hastened to the telephone – *he* went on as before. It was Saturday morning and the Area Manager was not in his office of course.

Elspeth thought I'd better go out.

'Yes, Daddy,' said Viola. '*You* go out!'

'I won't go without you two. And somebody's got to stay.'

Elspeth was listening to something else. 'I think that's Sandra's friends come to collect the bed.'

Viola said: 'Daddy, why don't *you* make the elevenses?'

So the trauma took its course. The men finished half an hour early – thanks to the vast amount of preliminary stacking and packing we'd done ourselves – and promptly hinted at the consequent appropriateness of an augmented tip.

Desperate, we gave them an augmented tip. Catching the wing of the pantechnicon on one of the gateposts, they drove away. It said on the back of the pantechnicon –

A HOUSEHOLD NAME IN FURNITURE REMOVAL

We were left alone. The house was empty – apart from a small stack of baggage we were taking to sustain us through the four or five weeks we were going to spend living hugger-mugger in a very expensive two-roomed flat, on which my office had a lien, in Westminster – we'd had no time to look for anywhere else.

'Do you want to have a last look round?' I said to Elspeth.

She shook her head – she couldn't bear it.

I looked at Viola. 'I've been,' she said.

So I set off on a last tour, making my way first of all to the roof-space, now empty – believe it or not! Then to the attic bedrooms, Virginia's with paintings on the back of her door – a talented girl. Then through the present guest-room where first of all the four of us had slept in mid-winter, nineteen years ago, without furniture or carpets or curtains. (You'll never get the workmen out until you move in, wiseacres had told us.) The girls were very small, then, and very sweet, tucked up together in a single bed. The past, the past! . .

Nobody who has seen *The Cherry Orchard* can forget when the characters make their last tour of the house they're leaving. 'Goodbye, old home!' I could almost hear a pre-echo of some future owners chopping down the sycamores, the holm oaks and the hollies.

I heard Elspeth's – 'The taxi's come!'

I skipped the other rooms.

CHAPTER V

THE LAST LUNCHEON

Henry was sitting in the centre of the picture, at the head of the table, our Chairman – tall and good-looking as well! On either wing, down the two long sides of the table, were sitting the rest of us, his Board Members and his Directors, and at the far end of the table, opposite to him and separated from him by a fair distance, the Chief Executive of the Company we owned. (Lightning, one knows from experience, can leap any distance.)

The Members of the Board were a collection mostly of retired people, appointed by the Minister. Part-timers we were, who met once a month but sometimes oftener, to do as Boards do, that is to say, listen to what the Chairman had in mind, discuss it, criticise it if we had the nerve, veto it if we wanted to be out on our necks – not that Henry, throughout whatever we were saying or doing, didn't behave with the utmost suavity.

The Directors of this, that and the other, were the bosses who under Henry ran the place: they worked full-time, of course. And the Chief Executive of the Company we owned? Sebastian, always known as Baz. Henry was *his* Chairman, too; and *he* worked passionately, dementedly . . . full-time and a half. In our quasi-governmental organisation, Henry had the status of Permanent Secretary, Baz of Deputy Secretary, the rest of us of Under Secretary.

Henry was aged about fifty, Baz a few years older: they had both worked previously in the private sector, as they called it; now they were in the public sector, and the question always floated in the air, Would they or wouldn't they go back to the private sector? My fellow Board Members came mainly from the private sector – I was the exception – as one would expect in a Board properly constituted according to the current rules to run an organisation in the public sector. One of them was an elderly retired banker, a friendly chap but a bit of a dodo: another was an able lawyer of about Henry's age, who sometimes deputised for him: not one of us thought the Minister had chosen badly. And Henry appeared inclined to agree with us –

'I should like to have kept the same team,' he said.

He said it again *à propos* of today's monthly Board luncheon, which was the last one at which I and Alice Hargreaves, another Board Member, were going to be present, because our two-year contracts had run out. I was sitting on Henry's left, Alice on his right.

'I thought we'd have something nice to eat today,' he said with a consoling smile at Alice and me.

The waitresses had just served us with plates of smoked salmon. Being quasi, we didn't have to employ the Civil Service's corps of caterers.

'Delicious, Henry,' said Alice. (She was Dame Alice.) 'Can we afford it?' She was teasing him.

'I was thinking,' Henry said, 'of proposing that we should all contribute.' He had a way of saying something slyly amusing as if he were serious about it. 'Have you some views, Alice?'

He knew she had views, must have views, since she always had views on every conceivable subject. Alice was one of the only two Members of the Board whom I'd seen ruffle Henry's suavity. (The other one was our Trade Unionist.)

Current fashion decreed that every Royal Commission, every Governmental Board, every quasi-Governmental Board, should include a woman and a Trade Unionist. (I always presumed it must have something to do with the democratic representation of ethnic minorities.) When Henry and I were alone he referred to Alice as our Statutory Woman. Jock Williamson, our retired Trade Unionist, was unvociferous with his views, and so escaped being called our Statutory Trade Unionist – he ruffled Henry's suavity by seeming disinclined to produce any views at all.

'I meant,' Henry continued with his line of thought about our making contributions to the cost of the meal, 'according to our means.'

Alice was an old Socialist. Henry never made clear what *he* was.

355

'Very good idea,' said Alice. 'Lend me a pound, will you, Henry?'

I could see there was no need for me to intervene on either side.

In the Board Members' room, Alice and I usually got on with each other pretty well as two old Socialists together – she was about my age. She was a long-standing bigwig in Family Planning among other things, and was currently engaged in a battle for the recognition of pre-menstrual tension. And she was a magistrate, of course.

Alice and I sometimes got some fun in the Board Members' room, I'm ashamed to say, out of teasing Jock. (We often met in the Board Members' room because Henry found us all useful and interesting tasks.)

'We want your advice, Jock,' she said to him. 'Joe and I think we need a union of our own, here. To fight for better pay and working-conditions.'

'Eh?' said Jock.

'We think our pay of £1,000 a year could be improved.' She used the Trade Union term 'improved' which means 'increased'.

'Aye?' said Jock.

I didn't know how she dared mention working-conditions, since our Board Members' room was as palatial as the Board room itself.

'So,' said Alice, 'what do you think of it? Would you consider organising a little union for us, and leading it?'

Jock gave her a shrewd look. Though he was never going to be Lord Jock-Williamson, he was by no means daft.

'You won't get anywhere, nowadays, unless you join the big battalions.'

As Jock had skilfully carried his original Union – the Dry Cleaners' and Pressers' I think it was – first into the bigger Union, then into one of the big battalions, without loss of office for himself, he knew what he was talking about.

'Sorry, Dame Alice. Y'see – that's my advice.' And there was a look on his face that could well have been read as saying, That's settled *her* hash!

Alice began to talk about something else.

While we were eating the smoked salmon at this, our last,

356

Board luncheon, I was recalling other conversations in the Board Members' room, when Alice and I hadn't concealed from each other that we wanted our contracts to be renewed for another two years.

'I hope you'll like the next course,' Henry was saying to us. 'I don't know how good their *chicken kiev* is. I hope it's all right.' He poured some more wine into Alice's glass and mine, some more Perrier water into his own. He caught my eye on the Perrier water: he glanced down to the opposite end of the table and said to me *sotto voce*: 'I've got a meeting immediately after with Baz.'

I laughed, ruefully on his behalf, more ruefully on my own. For the last two years my four-fifths time job had been as personnel consultant to Baz's company, which meant to Baz. Now it happened that Baz was one of those men, passionate, energetic, given to paranoia, who don't want to consult anybody about anything. Characteristically he'd made a brave and dashing Army officer during the War: he'd been decorated with a medal – also with a wound across the cheek which looked dramatically like a duelling-scar.

I glanced down to the other end of the table, to see Baz with one of his own directors on each side of him, eating his smoked salmon perfectly undementedly.

Henry said to me: 'I know it must be a consolation for *you* not to have any more of them.'

He was smiling at me in a friendly way. He knew that it was the opposite of a consolation to me – I wanted to go on working: I didn't want to be retired: I'd gladly have gone on having meetings with Baz every day of the week. (Actually one of my secondary difficulties had been to get hold of Baz for any sort of meeting at all.)

Henry knew it was the opposite of a consolation – but he couldn't resist saying it. I smiled back at him, said nothing. Recurrently I reflected on what a strange man he was. I was fascinated, as well as admiring. There were so many things in his nature which one might have thought couldn't exist together, but which in Henry did exist together. He was ruthless, restless, ambitious, and very able: everybody recognised those. But as friendship between us came into the atmosphere, I recognised the degree to which he was sensitive, thin-skinned, fastidious.

Henry's rôle in affairs was to be sent for to put things right, in one organisation after another, that other people had got into an impossible mess. What more appropriate for a man who was ruthless, restless, ambitious and very able? So far, so explicable. Yet he struck me as sensitive in the way an artist is sensitive. (His younger son, like our younger daughter, had become a painter, and it would not surprise me if Henry were going to take, one day, to some form of art.) He was, I was sure, inherently thin-skinned. He made me think of Ian's dictum that a life in the Civil Service teaches you to be resilient, if not thick-skinned: under that tuition Henry's skin had thickened enough for survival, and yet . . . it sometimes blushed. And his fastidiousness? We all noticed his *frisson* when Alice got on to her campaign of the moment.

But what exercised me most was that he displayed flashes of innocence. (Actually Robert, that other Great Man in my life, did the same; always to my astonishment, because I thought of myself in the world of affairs as the most innocent of men while all other men around me were the least.)

It could only have been in a flash of innocence that Henry had arranged for me to be Baz's personnel consultant. Certainly Baz's personnel was in such a state of chaos that it was nothing if not sensible for him to have somebody to come in and do something about it. And it was not unreasonable for Henry to hope I'd succeed. I liked Baz, admired him in a way, wanted to try and sort things out for him, even to protect him; and to begin with Baz at least didn't dislike me. Where Henry had been innocent was in not taking account of Baz's streak of paranoia. That was now proven only too conclusively. The present situation, after my two years, was that Baz believed I'd been planted in his Company to spy on him for Henry.

'You've been unlucky,' Baz's chief lieutenant on his Board had once said to me, 'caught in the crossfire between those two.'

Those two! Where it came to firing, I didn't doubt which of them carried the bigger guns. But that was no help to me with Baz. Now that I'd come to the end of my two years, Henry might have wished to keep the same team: Baz couldn't wait for me to go. Relief tinged with triumph. (Triumph – yes, Baz had his flashes of innocence, too!)

One of the troubles with paranoia isn't only that it doesn't make you happy, but that it won't let you alone. Poor old Baz found himself constantly impelled to write drafts of the terms of reference of his job – in order to demarcate where Henry mightn't interfere. (I'd never heard of his showing his drafts to Henry, but I might have been wrong.) It seemed to give him a greater certainty of his job being preserved from Henry's interference if he saw its terms of reference written down in black and white.

Henry had said: 'I know it must be a consolation to *you* not to have any more.' Meetings with Baz.

Friendship in the atmosphere didn't preclude the occasional tiny cut. What a complex man! I said nothing.

Henry said: 'Now we shall see what the *chicken kiev* is like.' He drank some of his Perrier water.

I drank some of my wine. He'd chosen a very pleasant wine for the occasion. Alice, on the other side of him, was drinking it at a fine pace.

While the waitresses were moving between us I looked round the room, the palatial Board room, for the last time . . . Parallel to the long table was a wall taken up by tall windows with a splendid view; opposite to it a beam across the ceiling, supported by handsome pillars, marked out a kind of alcove – this was where a table for today's drinks had been placed. All the paint was a pale creamy colour, and on the floor was a very worn but still beautiful persian carpet. And to complete the room, but perhaps not to complete a palace, there were on the wall facing us, where we sat at the top of the table, what looked like two large school honours-boards: they bore the names of past Board Members and the dates of their reigns.

Henry noticed me looking up at the honours-boards.

'Next week,' he said, 'they'll be entering up your name and Alice's' – he turned his sly smile from me to Alice – 'in gold.'

I said nothing again, smiling to myself. He really couldn't resist it! I didn't think any the less of him for it.

'I shall insist,' said Alice, 'on coming in to see it.'

'I hope you'll come in to see us often,' said Henry.

Our *chicken kiev* had been served and we fell to. It was good. The hubbub of the party was reduced by everybody's falling to.

The sun shone upon us all through the tall windows.

The last luncheon. More wine. A rather superior fruit salad. Coffee.

'I don't propose,' Henry said to me, 'to make a formal speech of farewell. I know it would embarrass you.'

'It would.' All things considered, as one might say, it certainly would.

'It wouldn't embarrass me,' said Alice.

The men near to us laughed.

The occasion had come to an end. There was a moment when all of us at the table seemed to realise it. The hubbub faded into near-silence.

Henry spoke and everybody listened.

'I'm not going to make a formal speech,' he said. 'I know we shall all miss Dame Alice and Joe.'

There were assenting murmurs.

'We shall miss Dame Alice for the wisdom of her social conscience.'

He smiled at her. Could he mean it? More assenting murmurs.

'And we shall miss Joe for the wisdom of his experience with people.'

More assenting murmurs. I couldn't help glancing down the table. Baz's eyes were glowing, his duelling-scar looking deeper.

'I think everyone knows *I* should have liked to have kept the same team.' He paused. 'Ministers seem to like a change.' He paused again. 'Possibly because they get changed, themselves.'

Everybody smiled. (The incumbent Minister was different from the one who had appointed Alice and me, Jock and the other two.)

'I suppose,' Henry went on, 'this means we shall have two vacancies for some unspecified time. I'm afraid Dame Alice's activities will lapse.' He paused. 'So far as Joe's are concerned, I propose to interest *myself* more in personnel affairs.'

Interest *himself* – oh, oh, oh!

He'd said it blandly and seriously. There was no reason why he shouldn't interest himself more in personnel affairs: there was every reason to believe he'd do it as skilfully as everything else he did. But that wasn't the point.

Henry's glance moved smoothly round the table. Everybody

else's glance moved to one single place at it –

'Does *that* mean,' said Baz loudly, 'in *my* company?'

Blue eyes blazing with high tension.

Henry smiled imperturbably. 'It means, Baz, in the organisation of which I'm Chairman and in the company of which I'm Chairman.'

Lightning leapt the length of the table.

'I must see that *in writing*!'

Henry said, 'I think we could manage that.' His tone of voice was smooth and friendly as ever. But slowly the faintest of pinkening rose up the side of his neck.

Those two! Into the future together, I thought.

So ended my last luncheon in official life.

CHAPTER VI

HELLO TO A FLAT

We moved to our temporary quarters, Viola sleeping on a made-up bed in the living-room, Annie coming to see us and plainly thinking we ought to have made a more comfortable, less expensive arrangement.

Having now done my last day's work in an office, I had the opportunity to do other things. I had the opportunity, I discovered immediately, to take all my own telephone calls, make all my own telephone calls, answer all correspondence in my own hand or on my own typewriter, look up my own train-times, book my own table for lunch at my club.

There was nobody now whom I could tell or ask to do things *for* me.

'You won't *like* it.' It may have been the voice of senile dementia, but it was the voice of truth.

And suppose I'd been Henry, one of the people who had a car standing outside the door all day long . . . Most horrible fate of all – nobody now to *take* me anywhere.

It is not a laughing matter. Whatever you've been used to, you miss. Preach as you may, there are no absolutes.

I had accepted George Bantock's offer, but I was not due to start till the Summer term, which gave me time to prepare a course. Would I make his students read novels? Of course I would! Would I include one of my own novels? What a question! I sat in buses and Underground trains, having ideas.

Most of my sitting in buses and Underground trains was in the course of travelling to and from our new flat, where I was acting as a sort of self-appointed – and unpaid – site-manager.

I'd held a site meeting on the first Monday morning. One of the men I already knew, the electrician, who, after knowing us for fifteen years, counted as a member of the family. And I'd met the painter because he'd already started work on the previous Saturday, a 'little man' so devoted to the paintbrush that he'd be found painting henceforth on seven days to the week, painting everything white – which made sense to me when I discovered he'd been in the Navy. If it doesn't move, paint it!

The heating-engineer turned out to be superior, especially towards the two kitchen-fitters. We'd employed a classy firm of kitchen-designers, who, after satisfactorily designing us a kitchen, disclosed that they didn't have sub-contracted fitters: they could only suggest we made a contract of our own with these men whose work they had previously experienced – once. The plumbers didn't see fit to turn up. The carpenter put in a courteous if token appearance. I managed to collect all the different parties in one room, and then there didn't seem a great deal for anyone to say – other than what the electrician said.

We had got as far as the subject of wiring up the electrical machines in the kitchen.

'I'll do that,' the electrician said with a menacing glance to his left. 'I don't want any cowboys touching the electrics in this place.'

On his left were the two kitchen-fitters. The elder was Irish and had the sort of pasty, grimy complexion that I associated with its possessor's having sojourned rather long as Her Majesty's guest somewhere: the younger, born unusually pretty, seemed intent on living it down by a rabid display of low-grade *machismo*, being tattooed, of course.

I can't say I was surprised when, a few hours later, I was discussing the contract and the Irish senior one conveyed to me that the job would cost 30% less if I paid him in bank-notes; nor when, a few days later and Elspeth being with me, the younger one contrived to signify that he considered both of us were attracted to him but neither was acceptable.

I wondered whether the two of them objected to being thought of as cowboys; alternatively, whether the Irish one was too thick to worry and the pretty one too neurotic. In the kitchen the pair of them spent a lot of time poring over the plans provided by the kitchen-designers. They could be heard discussing technical points, such as That's the door that's got to be shifted, ay? (As the kitchen had only one door I was surprised by the implication of an alternative, but after more sustained thought I concluded they were perhaps giving vent to natural satisfaction upon recognising a door.)

A respite from troubles on the site, I'd discovered – just like everybody else – was in fantasies of interior decorating. Fresh curtains everywhere; all the furniture that was upholstered freshly covered; the walls and ceilings and woodwork all painted white; fresh carpet everywhere coloured greenish-blue for repose. Elspeth had chosen a classy individual firm of interior designers and decorators, where we paid many enjoyable visits, trying out pretty colours together and choosing sumptuous-looking inexpensive textiles. Dreams, dreams, everybody's dreams . . .

I didn't tell Robert what was going on, so as to avoid his giving me one of his characteristic looks which combined incomprehension with censoriousness.

'What for?' he would have said, in a slightly hollow, slightly lofty, slightly horrid tone.

He would find out What for? for himself, I thought, when Veronica got thoroughly under way with renovating Vincent Square. And then it occurred to me that Veronica would find out for *her*self that he was missing from Vincent Square, receiving honorary degrees in America, Russia, Australia . . .

Meanwhile at the new flat it began to seem to my innocent eye that my troubles were diminishing. But I distrusted innocence. Either you need to be trained as a site-manager, I thought, or you have to have an MBA. (I'd become a great believer in a Master's degree in Business Administration for teaching you how to run something you didn't understand – there were so many dazzling examples of it to be seen in all walks of life.)

The heating-engineer had practically finished. The electrician had gone as far as he could before the kitchen machines came in. The cowboys, having moved the door, had got on with building what they called the Breakfast-Bar, installing cupboards, and fitting the sink into what they called the Work-Top . . . The moment I heard those ghastly words, Breakfast-Bar, Work-Top, I realised that we should never get rid of them –
You Can't Stop The Progress Of Illiteracy

Then came the heating-engineer's final day. He came up to me and said:

'I think you ought to know the kitchen-fitters have boxed in my boiler, so that you can't even get at it to light the pilot-light.'

He must have stood superiorly by while they did it.

That evening the unfortunate kitchen-designers came whizzing round in their car after they'd finished work, and gave a rather impressive show of not looking appalled by what they saw. As a start they decided the cupboard that boxed in the central heating boiler should be mounted on castors – you could then get to the boiler to light the pilot-light by rolling the cupboard out. (A bit of resourcefulness that made one proud of being British.) Then they took out their tape-measures and measured how far from the wall the sink had been installed – four inches further than it should be, thus preventing the dish-washer from sliding next to it under the Work-Top.

'Would you mind going outside for a moment, Mr Lunn? While my colleague and I discuss this.'

I went out. I came back.

'They'll have to cut a new Work-Top and let in the sink at the correct place.'

'Who's going to pay for that?'

They gave a rather impressive show of not looking hunted.

'We shall have to consult our managing director, but we shall recommend that the firm pays for it.'

The following morning the cowboys were called to the designers' office. To be sacked, one might have hoped – until one realised that neither we nor the designers had anybody else on hand to replace them.

The cowboys returned to us. I was waiting for them. 'First of all we'll be finishing your hanging cupboards,' the Irish one announced on breath that was like a gale of Irish whiskey. 'Then we'll be putting the rollers under your lower cupboard, see? And then we'll be cutting you your new Work-Top.'

The butch pretty one said: 'Okeydoke?'

So we duly came to *their* last day. The day of the bank-notes. It was quite clear that they expected an additional percentage for themselves, though who the final recipient of the bank-notes was to be was not revealed.

Everything was ready for the arrival of the kitchen machines. The door actually had been moved the correct number of inches for the refrigerator-cum-freezer to stand beside it. The dishwasher actually slid into place without hitting the sink. The laundry machine fitted in. The cupboard rolled out on its castors so that one could light the boiler. The hanging cupboards were all lined up after a fashion.

Then the gas company delivered the cooker.

I was present when the engineers manoeuvred it into place. 'Good God!' I exclaimed facetiously. 'The top's actually flush with the Work-Top.'

The gas engineers weren't listening to me. Their eye was on something else. One of them took out a folding-measure and stood it on top of the stove. He looked at me.

'Your hanging cupboards have been hung five inches too low. It brings your cowling and your extractor-fan five inches too near to the cooker.' He put his hand on the cooker.

I said, 'And that means?'

'When you've got your cooker going full-on, your fan may seize up, and this acrylic hood may fracture.' He gave it further thought. 'Or it might possibly melt.'

A veil over what followed!

CHAPTER VII

MOVING IN

Another veil, more veils – please!

The removers delivered our property to us from store. A veil over the scratches and bashes in the furniture, over the scars and dents in the picture-frames! A veil over the vistas which opened before us of claims on insurance, of framers patching up gold leaf, of restorers appearing with bottles of glutinous french polish!

And the tea, yes, the tea . . . Anyone who thought those tea-chests had been emptied of tea was mistaken. A veil over the tea-leaves between the pages of the books, inside the sleeves of the gramophone records!

And above all a veil over the chaos that filled our new little home to the brim, in the name of that *Name In Furniture Removal* which will never be erased from our *Household*!

Is that all? It is not.

More veils in readiness for the arrival, a couple of weeks later, of our freshly-made curtains and newly-covered upholstery, especially for our wonderful made-to-measure, ceiling-to-floor curtains, which in two of the rooms mysteriously dangled a foot short of the floor, and for our two large sofas, to be covered in a wonderful soft corn-coloured material, which unwrapped were a dirty mustard yellow!

I'm afraid I hadn't got those veils in readiness, in fact I had simply run out of veils altogether by now.

I telephoned Elspeth at her office and insisted that we should go to a theatre that night, to see an Ayckbourn play. (There was always an Ayckbourn play on.) It would make us *laugh*.

So to the theatre we went, and a surprising coincidence happened. The house was not very full. As we went down one of the aisles, a man already in his seat looked up at us. It was Steve.

'Joe!' He stood up.

'Steve!'

He had a woman beside him. He turned to her with a fond smile, and then to us.

'Meet *ma petite amie*!' And he introduced her. Burke Loeb.

'Actually Burke's not French,' he said with self-deprecating amusement. 'She's American.'

We all smiled, arranged to meet in the interval, and then Elspeth and I found our seats and settled down in them. 'I wonder what's become of Marìa,' she whispered.

'So do I,' I whispered back. 'Do you think this is another lifeline?' 'I shouldn't be surprised.' I had never expected the previous lifeline to last – I believed that becoming less 'free' was one of love's irreversible processes.

The play began. It made us laugh.

At the interval Steve came across to us, alone. 'Instead of fighting for drinks in that awful bar,' he said, 'Burke wonders if you'd join us for a little supper after the show.' We said we'd love it.

The second act made us laugh.

On the way out our party collected together. 'Burke has her car,' Steve told us. We were driven out to a small Italian restaurant in Notting Hill.

'I like to go to some place I know,' Burke explained.

I'd been to the restaurant before: it was known as one of the best Italian restaurants in London. It became apparent that Burke lived somewhere in the vicinity. And that Steve now lived in the same place. (Later it turned out that the place was an attractive house in Campden Hill.)

Elspeth and I, sitting at the back of the car, exchanged glances. We had moved into our own flat: Steve had moved into Burke's. Moving in! . .

At the restaurant Burke was received with the sunniest of Italian smiles from the proprietor, and so began a delightful supper-party. Parma ham with melon, *scallopine alla Perugina*, and so on.

Burke was small, very lively and very attractive. She had dark

368

hair cut into short wisps, a pale complexion with almost no colour in the cheeks, and lustrous eyes so dark that they looked almost black. She was wearing a pretty black skirt that glimmered with lurex thread, a plain black sweater and a small collection of slender gold chains, and one ring only – but that was the largest square-cut emerald I'd ever seen.

The impression made by her personality was piquant. About her liveliness there was something nervous, almost jumpy; but it was overlaid by a slightly stylised relaxed manner. Very piquant. I watched her with interest: it suddenly came into my head that *au fond* she was a very self-conscious person – the sort of woman whose girlhood might have been made truly painful by self-consciousness. But now she had come to this stylised solution. Was I right? I didn't know. I continued to watch her with interest, and attraction . . . I liked her.

'I'm into children's theatre, in New York,' she was saying brightly. 'This is presently my main interest.'

'Very successful children's theatre,' Steve said. 'Peter Brook thinks it's terribly good.'

'Peter's a wonderful person,' Burke said, in the style of an actress, though I was sure she meant it.

'You remember, Joe,' said Steve, 'I've done some work in children's theatre.'

I will content myself with observing that this was the first I'd ever heard of it. I nodded my head acquiescently – after all, I was far from knowing everything Steve had worked in.

Burke said to us: 'I've done a lot of things – I *do* a lot of things. This is the most rewarding thing I ever did. You know?'

Elspeth said to her, 'I envy you.'

(I was not the only one who came from a long line of non-Conformists with a predilection for doing good: Elspeth's present job was with a charitable trust – where, like most people who do good by working for charitable trusts, her reward was to be underpaid.)

'I agree,' said Steve.

'My great joy,' said Burke, 'is audience participation. It's amazing, the things those kids can do.'

Something made me think of Steve's theatre of improvisation.

'I'm sure,' said Elspeth to Burke.

I thought the evening was going very nicely. We were finishing our Parma ham.

'The surprising thing is,' said Steve to Elspeth and me, 'that Burke knows *Tom*.'

'Good gracious!'

'My ex-husband and Tom,' said Burke, 'were Executive Vice-Presidents together at Boyce Peterhouse New York. Tom is still there.'

I thought that explained, and disposed of, Loeb.

'Isn't that amazing?' said Steve.

'Tom,' said Burke, 'gave me Steve's address.'

I could have said Good gracious! again.

'And that,' said Steve, looking at her fondly, 'was great good fortune for me.' I thought that was a very beautiful way of expressing it.

Burke smiled back at him, but said nothing.

The waiter took away our empty plates.

Steve said to me: 'Burke says Tom is rich.'

We all glanced at Burke. Did rich people, I wondered, talk in public about being rich, especially rich people who were *richer* than the rich person under discussion? Burke said blandly, rather as if she were somewhere else:

'I think Tom has a great talent for playing the stock-market. He always seems to know what's going to happen.' She was smiling. 'You know?'

I could only bow my head in agreement with that.

Steve went on. 'And Burke knows Robert, too.'

Burke laughed. 'Robert's often in New York. He loves it. In New York he rates very highly as a novelist. Very highly.' She paused and then looked me in the eye, sharply, amusedly, sceptically – 'How does he rate as a politician in your House of Lords?'

I blinked. A waiter moved between us, the waiter with fresh plates and the *scallopine*. I was saved from answering.

Now what had led her to ask that question? *Who* had led her to ask that question?

Tom.

I had absolutely no evidence that it came from Tom.

Our glasses were being re-filled. Steve spoke to me.

'I've heard again from Tom. He says he's definitely coming to London later this spring. He isn't going to cancel his trip again.'

As I was enjoying the food and the wine I received the news with equanimity, for the moment.

'But you know what Tom's like,' Steve concluded. 'Here, there, everywhere. I should know.' He laughed at me, probably referring to those days long ago when Tom harried him all over Europe. (It was for Tom that Robert coined the term *dromophilia*.) 'Steve has got to be educated', Tom was wont to tell the rest of us. We thought Education was a nice name for it.

'He's one of the most restless men,' Steve said, 'I've ever met.'

'Reminds me of a bluebottle.'

'Now, now . . .'

'What's he coming for?'

'A house. He's coming to find a house.'

'A house? What on earth for?'

'Oh, didn't you know? Robert knows . . . Tom's going to take a house over here for a month in the late summer. We're all going to be invited to go to it.'

I noticed that Elspeth was listening. Robert had *not* told me. I knew that Robert sometimes saw Tom when he was in New York. I always assumed it was because Robert felt safest if he knew what Tom was doing. Burke was listening, too.

'Tom has a beautiful house,' she said, 'on the Hudson River.'

I should have felt happier to know that he was going to it.

'That reminds me,' Steve said. He looked at Elspeth and me with sympathetic interest. 'You two have moved house.'

'Really,' said Burke. 'That's interesting. How was it?'

'Oh, oh, oh.'

'As bad as that?' said Steve.

I explained why we'd come to the theatre tonight.

Burke said: 'Then I'm so much happier we asked you to have supper with us. Isn't that lucky, Steve?'

Steve said to me: 'Do tell us about it – you've left us . . . all agog.'

'Go on!' said Elspeth to me. 'Tell them some of the things that happened!' I could see she thought it might have a therapeutic effect.

In fact it did have a therapeutic effect. I found myself telling my story as a subject for mirth instead of misery. By the time I'd covered the removal men and got to the cowboys they were all amused. Even I was beginning to think it was funny. Granted I was giving a theatrical performance – I thought that Steve and Burke, as theatre-people, could put up with it. It was being a help to me.

By the time I'd got to today's last straws we'd all finished our *scallopine*. The proprietor came and made up to Burke. We ordered coffee. Elspeth, having started me talking, now nudged me under the table to stop.

Steve said: 'I'm sorry, Joe. I really do sympathise.'

I said: 'I gather it's pretty universal – it's the way we live now. In this country, anyway.'

Burke said: 'It sounds unnecessary to me.'

Steve said mischievously: 'It's all experience, you know. The stuff of life.'

That was too much for me. 'That's exactly my point. That's just what I've learnt. And that's just what I complain of. For weeks this has really been *the stuff of MY life*. And I can tell you it's damned unnecessary. Worthless, wasteful stuff!'

Burke looked at me, her lustrous black eyes wide open.

'It's experience,' I said, 'that's of no value to man nor beast. I resent it.'

Burke said smoothly: 'You're going to have a beautiful apartment. I know it.' She looked at Elspeth.

'Of course we are,' said Elspeth.

Steve said: 'You can't have beauty without a price.'

The others laughed, but I didn't. Steve said:

'If it's been the stuff of your life, you can write a novel about it. That's what novels are supposed to be about, isn't it? The stuff of people's lives.'

'There's stuff and stuff!' I cried. 'And nobody wants this stuff.'

'I don't see why not,' said Steve.

'They want, they want . . . ' I realised that I didn't know what they wanted. 'They want,' I said furiously, 'profound spiritual experiences, profound psychic suffering, don't you see?' I paused. 'Not the worthless experience of being crucified on The Wheel of *Things*!'

Despite my agitation, I was pleased with the metaphor –

mixed *and* misconceived! (I'd recently been re-reading *Kim*, which was constantly going on about The Wheel of Things.)

'Have you had profound spiritual experiences?' Steve asked in evident surprise. 'Or profound psychic suffering? *I* wouldn't know what they are.'

'One man's common woe is another man's profound psychic suffering,' I said. 'It depends on how inflated a view you take of yourself.'

Burke intervened. 'Couldn't you use this experience in a novel? It's so valid.'

I thought Oh dear! And then I noticed the bright lustrous look she was giving me. I hoped Elspeth didn't notice it.

'There you are,' said Steve.

There was a pause.

'There you are,' I echoed.

It was the end of the party. Burke said they would give us a lift home. Steve and I went to the cloakroom. When we were alone he said:

'Joe, you're limping.'

'Yes.'

'Isn't it worse than it was last time I saw you?'

'You don't expect it to be better, do you?'

'Are you doing anything about it? You were having physiotherapy.'

'I gave it up. Physiotherapy made it worse faster.'

'Is it really painful? I'm a terrible coward about pain.'

'I can't say it isn't.' I laughed at him. 'The pain keeps waking me up during the night, and that's a bore.'

He didn't say anything.

I said to him: 'You can't have age without a price, either.'

He didn't laugh. 'Can't anything be done?'

'I suppose when it's thought to be bad enough, I can have the hip-joint replaced, by a stainless steel and plastic one, or something.'

'Another operation.'

'It can't be replaced *without* an operation.' I laughed again. 'Anyway, old age is a succession of operations.'

'*Don't!*'

I glanced sideways at him, struck by the tone of voice.

'Have you started to have to get up in the night to do this?' he asked.

'Yes.'

'Joe,' he cried, 'I don't like it!' And he looked at me.

In his face I saw a flicker of resentment, of fear.

So Steve was having his first desperate intimations of age. Oh dear!

We moved across to the washbasins. Steve said: 'What about your eye?' We looked at each other in the mirrors. 'I never asked you if that was all right.'

'I've got my contact lens. His Majesty says I can see like a hawk.'

'Thank God for that! I'm terribly glad.'

We dried our hands and moved out of the cloakroom. 'By the way,' he said in his more usual, amused, confidential tone of voice, 'Tom is very rich.'

I laughed at the idea, and we joined Elspeth and Burke. Burke said she, rather than Steve, would drive. Clearly an active sort of woman.

Elspeth and I let ourselves into the flat. Our evening out had really had a therapeutic effect. Even my hip was less painful. There, before us, we saw the origin of my crucifixion on The Wheel of Things, such Things as I'd run out of veils for — beastly-coloured sofas that had to be re-covered, dangling curtains that had to be lengthened. At the moment we didn't care. Our spirits were high. *Sod* The Wheel of Things!

'Well,' I said, glancing round while I took off my overcoat, 'if there's anything else that can go wrong, I'd like to know what it is.' And I flopped down on one of the sofas.

With a cracking noise the front sofa-leg nearest to me collapsed and I slid on the floor.

PART III

PART III

CHAPTER I

TOM

One bright morning in April Steve rang me up. 'Did you know Tom's actually here?'

I didn't know.

'I thought you mightn't.' Steve paused. 'Robert knows.'

We both paused, both reflecting on Robert's not having told me. I said:

'Have you seen him? Tom?'

'Not yet. We've had a long telephone conversation. Joe, he's got the American habit of holding long conversations on the telephone, as if he were in the room with you.'

'Had he got a lot to say to you?'

I heard Steve laughing. 'It took a long while for him to say it.'

In a lapse of taste I said: 'You can't pretend you're totally unused to being harangued by Tom.' I was thinking of those harangues in the long-distant past, as between patron and protégé, master and apprentice, corporal and private.

'That's true,' said Steve with alacrity.

'What was the gist of it?'

'That's what I couldn't really remember afterwards. I did so get the habit of not listening to Tom. You know. I had to.'

I laughed. I remembered the clarion-call with which such harangues began. *Now, Steve!* Obviously the signal for Steve to switch off. I said:

'You must remember *something*.'

'Well, yes, as a matter of fact I do. It's a bit embarrassing, Joe.'

'Come on, Steve, you've never been embarrassed in your life.'

'I have, Joe. I'm constantly embarrassed. You don't understand me.' He assumed a comically plaintive tone.

'All right,' I said. 'Tell me what Tom wanted, that embarrasses you to tell me. Stop! I know what it was. He wanted you to sound me out about whether I'd meet him. He wants to poke his nose into my affairs again, not miss anything.'

'Right.'

'What a nerve!'

'That's what I told him, but it didn't make any difference, Joe.'

I didn't believe that was what Steve had told him, but something else had occurred to me. That might be a reason why Robert kept it from me. If he had the nerve to ask Robert to sound me out, Robert would have turned loftily evasive. And not told me.

'That makes me sound terribly weak.'

'Not at all. Anyway, don't let's argue about it! You've delivered the message and I presume you want an answer.'

'Yes. He *is* going to go on telephoning me till he gets an answer, you can see that.'

'I can see it. Poor old Steve!'

'Yes.' There was a pause. 'Well? . .'

'I'll see what Elspeth says about it.'

'And you'll let me know? He *will* keep on at me. I can't take the 'phone off the hook all the time.'

'I'll let you know.'

'Thank you, Joe.'

'When are you seeing him, yourself?'

'Next Tuesday. He fixed it up with Burke – he talked to *her* for hours. We're invited to dinner with him at his hotel.'

I said, 'Which hotel's he staying at?'

'The Carlos.'

'Very nice, too.'

'Trust Tom, to stay at the best hotel.'

'I'd trust Tom to do *that*,' I said in such a tone of voice as to imply that my trust mightn't extend much further.

'It's terribly expensive. Do you know how much a night he's paying? £137!' (I imagined a malicious smile on Steve's face.) 'He couldn't resist telling me.'

'I'm sure he couldn't.'

'He loves having a lot of money.'

'I'm sure he does.' I thought about it. 'It'll give him another platform from which to chuck his weight about.'

'How right you are!'

'Never mind! You survived it in the past: you will in the future.'

'Hopefully . . .'

'You will. So let's have no nonsense, Steve!'

'Joe, you tear away my façade.'

I began to laugh. I heard him begin to laugh. It was the end of our conversation.

I broached the subject with Elspeth.

'What are you going to do?' she asked.

'Consult you. That's what I'm doing now.'

'Surely you're not expecting *me* . . .' Her voice trailed off.

'I'd like to know how you feel about it.'

'Darling, I haven't really got any basis on which to feel anything.' She paused. 'I scarcely know the man – I mean, personally. I only know him personally through you. I really do feel it's for you to decide – if you feel inclined to meet him again, I'll come with you; and if you don't, it doesn't matter to me in the least.'

That seemed clear enough. I was thoughtful. It struck me that she had not come out with a rousing No. I continued thoughtful. Was I making too much of it? Did Robert think I made too much of it? Did everybody?

I made an effort to make less of it. I said: 'I must say Steve was rather funny.'

Elspeth smiled. 'I expect he was.' In closer acquaintance with Steve her disapproval of his worthlessness seemed to have melted – it's not easy to keep up a high level of disapproval in the presence of somebody whose company constantly beguiles you in one way or another. Also I thought she liked Burke, a good woman who was going to make Steve a better man.

'He and Burke are going to have dinner with Tom at Tom's hotel. And where do you think Tom's staying? The Carlos!'

'Oh!'

I was touched to see the slight pinkening of her cheeks. Her eyes shone. It was to the Carlos that I had taken her out to dinner the very first time I ever took her out to dinner.

379

'My darling,' I said.

'Do you remember?'

'Of course I remember.'

'I was terrified.'

'Not terrified – just a bit shy.'

'That's what you think. I'd never been anywhere as grand as that before – '

'There isn't anywhere grander,' I interrupted.

'And I'd never been out with anyone – '

'As grand as me?'

She laughed. 'Well, you were trying to impress – admit it!'

'What man wouldn't?'

'You didn't have to work very hard to impress me.'

'Well, I didn't know that.'

'You ought to have.' She looked at me steadily, as a woman looks at a man she knows inside out. She was telling me what I knew, but knowing it seemed to make no difference at all, that perhaps I should not be unconfident about my powers.

We'd been over this conversation many a time before, but it never failed to give us pleasure. Elspeth began to smile with recollection.

'You were sitting in that chair opposite the revolving door,' she said.

That was in 1949. The Carlos entrance in those days had a fine mock-Tudor chair with square arms and a high back, simply inviting one to sit in it looking like Hamlet. I realise it must be obvious that my temperamental resemblance to Hamlet is nil. I have to disclose that my physical resemblance was nil also – Hamlet a pale, slender, intellectual-looking, melancholy fellow; I a short, healthy-looking, over-lively, dapper chap. Did that deter me, sitting in the chair, from trying to look like Hamlet while I was waiting for Elspeth? If we all had to *be* like Hamlet, to sit in a chair looking like him while we were waiting for our girl, none of us would stand much of a chance.

'And that delicious *lobster bisque* we began with,' I said.

'We didn't. We began with *hors d'oeuvres*.'

'I could have sworn it was *lobster bisque*.' I couldn't help laughing.

Elspeth laughed.

'It's the past, the past . . .' I said romantically.

'It would be if you got it right.'

I said sadly, 'We've scarcely been to the Carlos since.'

'You might have taken me sometimes.'

'Have you been holding that against me for all these years?'

Elspeth assumed an unconcerned tone of voice. 'Yes.'

There was a long pause.

I said, 'Oh, let's give in! Let's let Tom give us dinner there!'

'Do you really mean it?' Elspeth had stopped smiling. 'Are you sure that's what you want to do?'

She was giving me a chance to back out, alternatively making me recognise that it was my decision, not hers.

'Why not?' I said. 'I've probably been rather silly about it. It's time to stop.'

'What will you do?'

'I'll ring Steve and tell him to tell Tom we gracefully consent to dine with him.'

And that was what I did, there and then.

Steve was glad to be relieved of his task. He expected we should hear from Tom very soon. I expected that, too.

'And Joe,' Steve concluded, 'when you do see him, don't forget to ask him how he came here!'

'How he came here? Oh, you mean by what mode of transport. I can guess – the Concorde.' The flights had just started about six months ago: it was the height of chic – and expense – to travel on them.

'Right.'

We had a call from Tom that night. 'My dear Joe, I was so pleased to get your message.' For such social occasions Tom had a specially silky tone of voice – Tom, the diplomat. 'I was slightly diffident about asking you, but I thought, Why not? I'm delighted that you thought the same.'

How did Tom know I'd said to Elspeth, Why not? Ah! that empathy, that understanding, that second sight . . .

He went on. 'I called you straight away, but I'll have to call you again to make a date for our dinner, because my secretary's out for the evening. *He* keeps my schedule of appointments. I always travel with a secretary. *Invaluable* . . .'

Elspeth had her head close to mine so that she could hear what he was saying. At the word 'secretary' we exchanged ribald glances.

So that was that. Three days later Elspeth and I, dressed in our most up-to-date clothes, made our way to the Carlos. 'Don't dress!' Tom had told us. 'Old friends don't stand on ceremony.' We were going to find him in a very stately, gentlemanly mood, that was clear.

He was waiting for us at the entrance of the Carlos.

I thought that in appearance he'd aged less than I was expecting. He was about my height and sturdily built, with a somewhat plump, pneumatic look. I'd been expecting him to be much fatter – he loved food and drink. My first impression, though, was of his looking neither as much fatter nor as much older as I'd been expecting. He had never looked anything but Jewish when he was young, and he didn't look any less so now. However his rich, thick, carroty curls had turned grey and he was wearing them clipped very short – they had already begun to recede from his forehead when I first knew him, and they were distinctly sparse now. But his bulging greenish eyes were bulging as ever behind his spectacles.

'How nice to see you both!'

A silky smile lingered round his wide, pouting mouth. He was dressed in a dark, very gentlemanly suit, which looked as if it had been made for him in London. I'd been right: we were in for a very gentlemanly time – to begin with, anyway. That amused me. Tom's social origins, like mine, were petit bourgeois; and no one English could have mistaken his physiognomy for anything but petit bourgeois – a cause to him for more than fleeting misery when he was a young man, aspiring. But seeing him now, I concluded that it had not held him back after all.

He shook hands and he smiled with egregious silkiness at Elspeth.

'I thought perhaps you might come up to my suite for an *apéritif*? If that suits you?'

His *suite*! I liked the idea of that.

'Lovely,' said Elspeth.

Tom laughed at her. 'I thought you would.'

He began to lead us across the foyer towards the staircase. I was glancing briefly around me – the high-backed Tudor armchair in which I'd looked like Hamlet had been replaced by a high-backed Tudor chair without arms. You can't, I thought, look like Hamlet if your chair has no arms. Alas, alas!

Tom's sitting-room was decorated with flowers. We sat down. Tom rang for room-service. He said to Elspeth, 'Would you like a cocktail?'

Elspeth looked slightly flummoxed. Cocktails had come after sixty years into fashion again – for instance, a small hamburger restaurant in our High Street was now advertising a Cocktail Hour, when cocktails were a pound apiece – but she and I had not thought of drinking them. Tom was watching her. She asked for a gin-and-tonic. He looked at me.

'Oh,' I said, in as gentlemanly a tone as it was within my powers to muster, 'I think I should like a glass of sherry.' I guessed that was what he would choose for himself, so I'd got in first.

'I take it you'd like it dry but not too dry?'

'Exactly.'

Two men of perfect taste together I was very happy about that.

After the order had been given, we settled down to conversation, Tom addressing himself mainly to Elspeth. I noticed that despite his having lived in the United States for thirty-odd years he had not assumed an American accent. It didn't surprise me. When Tom wanted to please he knew how to please; but below the surface flummery he was a stiff-necked, obstinate little man. (He said he inherited his obstinacy from his mother, who had insisted on his being called Tom, though it was not a Jewish name.)

He and Elspeth were sitting on a sofa together. First of all he asked her about our daughters – all very nice, I thought. But it was not long – and I can't say I was surprised – before he was sounding her, his inquisitiveness having got the better of his gentlemanliness, about her job and how much she earned. When she told him she worked for a charity, he said with his friendly pouting smile:

'Then I expect you're underpaid, my dear.'

Elspeth said, 'Yes ..'

He'd made a score there. He said:

'Is yours a charity that's endowed, or one that lives from hand to mouth on subscriptions?'

Elspeth told him its name. 'Oh really?' he said. 'That must be more than comfortably endowed. Probably very comfortably indeed.'

'It is. Very comfortably indeed.'

He leaned closer to her. 'What *is* the endowment?'

Elspeth hesitated, bullied into telling him. 'About five millions.'

'Then they've no excuse for underpaying you.' His silky tone was entirely dissipated by the intrusion of irascibility. Tom's silkiness was beautiful but it was liable not to last. He leaned still closer to her, his eyes seeming to bulge with sympathy.

'How much *do* they pay you?'

Elspeth was surprised. I could have told her, being fair to Tom, that I would not have expected his becoming rich to have made him prudish about money – or prudish about anything for that matter. (After all, we had been close friends in that distant past.)

Elspeth said, '£5,000.'

'And what was their income surplus to expenditure last year?'

'About £60,000.'

Tom's complexion went purplish-red. 'Then it's disgraceful they don't pay you another £1,000!' His cheeks were swelling. 'At least!'

Elspeth was becoming roused. 'All charities are the same. They take advantage of their staff. It's like the way nurses are taken advantage of – they can safely be underpaid, because they have the reward of knowing they're doing good.'

'My dear, how wise you are!'

I wouldn't have thought he'd have the nerve to say it; but, having been said, it did him nothing but good. Rapport between them was visible. The times I'd seen him do it in the past!

We finished our drinks. Tom paused, while the simmering of his own and Elspeth's emotions subsided. I glanced idly round the room. The flowers were florist's roses and carnations. It was all very pleasant.

Tom, having cooled down, asked us if we would like another *apéritif*. We decided not, and chose to go down to dinner straight away.

In the doorway of the restaurant Tom and the *chef de restaurant* engaged in some typical flouncing. Meanwhile I noticed that the elderly man in charge of the booking-list was smiling at me – in recognition. I was stunned. After God knows how many years! Tom and the *chef de restaurant* were momentarily stopped – not with enormous signs of pleasure – in their flouncing. Then we passed on into the dining-room.

Elspeth and I looked round with pleasure, nostalgia, delight – the dining-room hadn't changed! The mahogany panelling was as ever, the chandeliers and the pink-shaded wall-lights . . . It had *not* been transmogrified by Time.

We settled down at our table with a flourish of table-napkins by the waiters and the subduedly enthusiastic receipt of the menus by us. We saw Tom, the *bon vivant*. (The nearer we got to the food, the more French everything became.)

Elspeth spotted *saumon coulibiac*, which instantly brought choosing to an end for her. As I too liked it very much, I chose it. Then Tom chose it. Our party was united. A little asparagus to precede the salmon –

'I have to be circumspect about my eating,' Tom said to Elspeth. 'I can see that *you* are.' Then he looked at me. 'And about my drinking, too. Gout, Joe. I'm having signs of gout. I hope you're avoiding it.'

I said I was, but that I was succumbing to arthritis.

'Ah yes,' he said sympathetically. 'When you came into the hotel I noticed you were lame.' He smiled. 'I hope it doesn't mean that you have to forgo wine?'

I said it didn't.

The wine waiter came up and Tom ordered. (When the bottle arrived I had to admit that he'd done us proud.)

We enjoyed the food. It was obvious that amity and reconciliation were prevailing. We all began to relax from our task of making them prevail. We became friendly and gossipy. When we were half-way through the salmon, the name of Robert came into the conversation.

Tom looked at me. 'Have you seen Robert during the last few days?'

I said I hadn't.

'Then you don't know?'

'Don't know what?'

Tom paused. 'I'm sure he'll tell you when he sees you, so there's no harm in my telling you now. It had better be in confidence, of course. A startling piece of news, a disastrous piece of news —'

'What on earth?' I interrupted.

'His accountant has not seen to it that his Income Tax was paid for the last two years.' He looked at me hot-eyedly. 'I discovered it. Thank God I did discover it!'

Elspeth and I were astounded.

'The Old Boy was going on,' Tom said, 'thinking he was all right, because his accountant didn't tell him about it.'

I said: 'He's been earning a lot of money in that last few years. He must owe the Inland Revenue a colossal amount.'

'By his standards, yes.' He smiled smoothly, and with an elegant gesture appropriate to a graceful turn of phrase, said: 'By *my* client's standards, chickenfeed.'

There was a pause. I recalled my determination not to be prudish about money. I managed to ask, 'How much?'

'That isn't completely worked out at the present moment. I'd say in the region of £50,000.'

'Good God!' To me that was truly a colossal amount. 'What happened?'

'The man who was handling his account appears to have been grossly incompetent – he's been sacked, of course – and dotty as well. I've never come across anything quite so dotty before. He wasn't being fraudulent in any specific sense.' Tom paused. 'If I hadn't discovered it, it's possible the state of affairs would have gone on longer. Not indefinitely – even in the most incompetent of firms there are checks and balances that come into operation in the end. Actually this particular firm was taken over last April by Pettinger's, who are pretty well organised.' (I'd heard of Pettinger's.) 'Pettinger's would have discovered it in some months.'

'That doesn't relieve Robert of finding he's in debt to the tune of £50,000. What can he do?'

'I'm acting for him.' Tom smiled blandly. 'In a purely personal way, of course. As an old friend . . . Pettinger's will pay the interest on the £50,000 he'll have to raise to pay the debt.' His silky smile came back. 'And I think I may be able to persuade them to contribute towards the capital sum.' Tom looked at Elspeth and me in turn. His pop-eyes shone with a fresh gleam through his spectacles, and his voice became quieter, liquider. 'You see, Sir Abe Pettinger, the head of the firm, wants to cultivate Robert's goodwill ... Sir Abe wants to get into the House of Lords, and he thinks Robert can help him.'

'But Robert couldn't!' I cried.

'Sir Abe doesn't seem to know that.' Tom shrugged his shoulders elegantly. 'It's astonishing how *naif* some of these City men are.' He was enjoying himself. 'You may assume, Joe, that I shall take no steps to reduce Sir Abe's *naiveté*. Least of all before he's made good his desire to help Robert.'

I couldn't resist laughing. 'Oh goodness!' Then I looked at Elspeth: she appeared not to be enjoying it quite so much – she might have been thinking about how many thousands Robert had still got to find after receiving Sir Abe Pettinger's help. (I rather liked its being called help.)

Our laughter subsided. I realised with regret that I'd finished my salmon almost without noticing it. Tom and Elspeth had finished theirs. Somehow the talk had been too dramatic – splendid meals should be eaten with the lightest of conversation.

Tom, the hero of the hour, turned his glance upon Elspeth again.

'What can I tempt you to have now, my dear? The puddings here are delectable. I remember Joe's weakness for them. Do you share it?'

'I simply couldn't, Tom.'

'Just a little sorbet? Just made with water and lemon juice.'

'Not to mention sugar,' I said, 'and white of egg.'

Tom said to Elspeth: 'You hear? Joe hasn't lost his touch.'

I said: '*I* will have a lemon sorbet, thank you, Tom.'

So we came to the end of the meal. I felt pleased and happy on the whole. We hadn't taken the bloom off a grand occasion by eating and drinking too much. As Tom had been wont to say when he was young, to the amusement of the rest of us – 'Everything was in perfect taste'. I was amused now: the exercising of our perfect taste was due to age.

We let Tom order brandy, which Elspeth liked after dinner.

'How nice it all is,' I said, glancing round the room at the other people.

Elspeth was still thinking about Robert. She said to Tom: 'How did you come to discover Robert's tax-position, Tom?'

'I suppose I have a nose for these things.' Smiling, he paused while the waiter poured coffee for us. Then he said to her seriously: 'And the fact that one has experience of handling, say, a Rockefeller account, doesn't mean that one isn't ready to cast an eye over the financial affairs of one's oldest friends.'

I thought I'd never heard bustling interference described in such poignant terms. On the other hand I had to ask myself, suppose Tom hadn't interfered? My ill-will towards him had simply been proved wrong.

A waiter poured Rémy Martin into our glasses – Elspeth's favourite among brandies.

'I should be happy, my dear,' Tom said to her, 'to be of any help whatsoever to you and Joe. I gather from Robert that you and Joe are staying afloat after Joe's retirement.'

'Oh, yes,' said Elspeth.

Tom looked at her admiringly. 'It must be entirely due to you,' he said.

'No, it isn't, you know.'

Tom gave her one of his I-understand-you-better-than-you-understand-yourself looks. 'I can imagine what it's like to be in your position, with Joe unfortunately having no pension, and your other resources limited. I take it that you have *some* investments?'

Elspeth reluctantly signified that such was the case.

'About how much are they worth? Robert didn't seem to know.'

Elspeth glanced at me and hesitated.

I drank some brandy.

'That's all right,' said Tom, not missing the glance. 'Don't let's go into the detail here and now! Some other time,' he went on, his eyes bulging again with sympathy, 'we'll study the figures together.' He explained to her: 'I've made a lot of money. You see, I can *think* about money.' And he glanced at *me*.

I said nothing.

Elspeth drank a little of her brandy. Tom drank a little of his. I drank some coffee.

Tom said to Elspeth: 'I expect *you* have to think about money for the two of you . . . I shall be very happy to think *for* you . . . if you'll allow me.' He added in a slightly different tone of voice, clearly intended for me: 'I haven't done so badly for Robert.'

Elspeth just smiled.

Tom said: 'Have you got a good stock-broker?'

Elspeth said: 'We had one who did quite well for us, but he died last year, and since then . . .'

'Ah,' said Tom. 'What you need is a financial adviser. There's been quite a development, in recent years, in financial advisory services, even for *small* investors . . . Sometimes coupled with brokerage services.' He paused. 'I know of one such that would suit you perfectly.'

I couldn't help listening to him. Had he come to London to save us all?

Tom went on addressing himself to Elspeth. 'I have in mind a youngish man I know in a very reputable firm . . . He'd be interested in you as people, not merely as investors. Able, thoroughly competent in his job. To be recommended. Will you think about it? And you, too, Joe?'

Elspeth and I looked at each other. I said:

'We *will* think about it.'

I admitted to myself a piercing sense of relief at the prospect. I knew that I couldn't really think about money and that Elspeth was forced to do it for both of us. Of course Tom was right. The prospect of his finding someone for us whose professional skill was in thinking about money was enhanced by Tom's gloss that the man would be interested in us as people. Tom would be right about that, too. I have to admit that a base thought crossed my mind – about how Tom had come to be struck by the young man. I dismissed it. Nobody's ear could be closer to the ground in this part of the financial world than Tom's, I didn't doubt. If only it weren't for the limitations of physiology, Tom would have *both* ears to the ground.

Tom saw that we had taken the bait. He said, 'Let's drink to this!'

We all drank a sip of brandy. I felt happier. I saw that Elspeth was feeling happier.

'I think some of your anxieties can be relieved, Joe,' Tom said. 'It's only a question of finding someone to think about money for you.'

I grinned wryly.

He turned to Elspeth again. 'I hope the future looks a shade easier, my dear. I'm sure it will be.' He paused. 'And that's pretty wonderful' – he paused again – 'when you think that once upon a time I should never have been surprised if Joe ended up on the breadline.'

'I THINK SHE'S LOVELY'

I rang up the convalescent home – before nine in the morning: we had to watch the telephone bills now – to say I proposed coming down to see my mother. I got the Matron at the other end of the line.

'Perfectly all right, Mr Lunn. Will you be coming at the usual time?'

I said I would.

'I should like to see you, just for a few minutes.'

Oh dear – what now? 'I'll look in at the kitchen on my way up to her. How is she?' I felt my recurrent fear that they were going to ask me to find somewhere else for her.

'That's what I want to see you about. She hasn't been so well, these last few days, and yesterday we had the doctor to see her.' She went on rapidly to lessen my anxiety. 'There hasn't been any sudden change but I think I should tell you what the doctor said.'

I took it that she was speaking from the telephone in the hall, where conversations were audible to some of the other patients. I said:

'I'll wait to hear it.'

I thought of travelling down by an earlier train, but decided against it. I arrived at the convalescent home just after tea-time and found the Matron in the kitchen, beginning the preparations for supper. For the moment there was no one else in the room. She said:

'We called the doctor in because we were having a bit of trouble over clearing up a sore place on your mother's back.'

I said nothing. Elspeth would have something to say about that. She considered there was no excuse for letting patients get bed-sores. (Suddenly I thought of the night nurse in the eye-ward, going the rounds rubbing baby-powder on everybody's rear-end – excepting the handsome Sikh's!)

'Your mother had been complaining about her back. And about her breast . . .'

I realised that I was being led up to the point. 'What's the matter with her breast?' I asked.

'He's afraid she has cancer.'

I knew it must be so. A cancer, at the age of ninety-two – no escape, even then . . .

'He's coming again, to give her a more thorough examination, but I thought I ought to tell you now, Mr Lunn.'

'Oh yes, of course.' I thought about it. I said, 'I suppose she's too old for very much to be done about it?'

'I'm afraid so.'

'At this age a cancer develops pretty slowly, doesn't it?'

'Usually.'

'Is it causing her pain?' As I said it I thought how she already suffered with aches and pains all over the place from arthritis.

There was silence. The young girl who'd let me in at the front-door came into the kitchen with a tray.

The Matron said: 'Would you like me to send up your usual cup of tea, Mr Lunn, and a cake?'

I said, 'Yes please.' I noticed on the dresser beside me a wire tray with freshly-baked little cakes on it – I could smell them.

I went up to my mother's room. The window was open and the sunlight was shining on the carpet, the huge fawn and brown roses on the dazzling turquoise ground.

My mother looked much the same, half-propped up in bed and lying as usual askew.(She sat out in a chair during the mornings and complained that it tired her.) I noticed that the movement of her mouth, as if she were chewing, had ceased – perhaps the doctor had changed the drugs she was being treated with.

'I'm glad to see you,' she said. 'If you'd come a few minutes earlier you'd have found the doctor here.'

'Oh,' I said. 'That's interesting.'

'I don't know what they sent for him for.'

'It's right that you should be seen by a doctor at regular

intervals.' I'd said it before I realised that Elspeth had told me it was necessary, for the issue of a normal death certificate – were my mother 'to go at any moment' – for her to have been seen by a doctor within the previous two weeks.

'I don't know about that,' my mother said. 'I could scarcely tell a word he was saying.'

Yet so far as I knew this was the first time they'd called in the doctor for many weeks. I said to my mother, 'Why not?'

'He mumbled. These doctors ought to be trained to speak properly.'

'Perhaps – ' I drew back, on the brink of casting aspersions on her hearing.

'Perhaps what?'

'Perhaps he was tired.'

'Possibly.'

I thought a change of conversational topic was to be recommended. I noticed a fresh air-letter from America – from my sister – on the dressing-table. I volunteered to read it to my mother.

'Yes,' she said, 'you can do that.'

I said, 'I suppose somebody here read it to you when it arrived.'

'Yes. But you can read it again. These people here can't read properly.'

'Oh dear.'

'You never heard such a mess as they make of it.' She paused. 'If they can't read better than that, they oughtn't to get the money.'

I began reading the letter. My mother seemed to find my reading and my sister's news relatively satisfactory. (Having a huge family to bring up in the USA, my sister never came to England; my mother followed reports of the children's activities with an affection that survived from the days when she had tried emigration to America.)

'You can read it again,' my mother said.

So I read it again.

Relief appeared – the young girl helper brought in my tea. I thought she seemed a nice girl. When she'd set the bedside table in place before me, she looked at my mother and said to me:

'I should like to make Mrs Lunn a bit more comfortable.'

'Yes – she always seems to lie askew.' A cause for the skewness now crossed my mind.

The girl bent over my mother. 'Mrs Lunn, I'm going to make you a bit more comfortable.' She lifted my mother with one arm – easily, because my mother was so shrunken and frail – and straightened the pillows with the other arm. Then she gently laid her back again.

'There you go,' she said.

'Thank you, my dear.'

The girl stood looking at my mother.

'It's very good of you,' I said to her.

Still looking at my mother, she said: 'Isn't she lovely?'

My mother, *lovely*?

'We all think she's lovely. She's very popular. She entertains us all.'

I felt stunned. Lovely, entertaining, popular! Could she really mean *my mother*?

'This morning,' said the girl, 'she was singing to us.'

'Singing?'

'Yes.' Pause. 'I think she's lovely.' She patted my mother on the head – 'There you go, Mrs Lunn' – and went away.

So I was left to join in private conversation with my mother, beginning with the usual catechism. 'How's Elspeth?' 'How's Viola?' 'How's Virginia?'

No sign, I'm happy to say, of senile dementia-born questions about the Matron and divorce. All that appeared to be totally forgotten.

There was a passing lapse in the catechism and I was wondering what to say next, when my mother asked earlier than usual –

'What about Robert?'

'What do you mean?' I said. She couldn't possibly know anything of Robert's financial tribulations. 'What about Robert?'

'About his lumbago, of course. I always want to know about his lumbago. I know what it's like, myself, to have lumbago. Year in, year out. If you haven't got it, you're lucky.'

I rejected the impulse to mention arthritis in the hip-joint. I said, 'About the same.'

Actually he seemed to me to be worse in health. Both Elspeth and I were worried about it, and Elspeth was suspicious – could it be only lumbago?

'And that poor girl? What's her name? My memory's suddenly gone.'

'Annette.' (That poor girl, I thought, must now be in her mid-fifties.)

'Yes, Annette.'

'I think she's about the same.'

'Don't you know?'

'Robert doesn't like to talk about it.'

'Does *he* go to see *her*?'

'Yes.'

'That's good. Regularly?'

'Yes.'

'How often?'

'I think about once a month.'

There was a pause. Then she said: 'Poor girl, I'm sorry for her.'

I realised that she genuinely was sorry for Annette. If only, I thought, she could make it sound like that!

There was another long pause. A cloud must have passed in front of the sun – the fearsome glow of the carpet was muted. The open window let in a loud zooming of cars and lorries going by. I was thinking about Robert.

I was sure that Robert went to see Annette regularly, but long ago he had quelled my asking him about it. Quite often he asked me, Had I been down to see my mother? and How was she? But I'd learnt that I wasn't to make similar enquiries of him. After always being told either About the same, or She's all right, in a tone of voice that, despite its friendliness, was brusque and dismissive, I'd given up. (It struck me now that her being in a private institution must be costing him a lot of money.)

Once he'd told me that they were trying a new treatment, but soon after that we were back again at About the same. Mere acquaintances, hearing the brusqueness and dismissiveness of his tone, might have thought that he didn't care about her, perhaps wanted to put her out of his mind. Yet the opposite was true. It was constantly painful and constantly hopeless – why should he be constantly asked about it? One lives with things without constantly examining them.

'You haven't got so much to say for yourself today,' said my mother.

'I'm sorry about that.'

'There's no need to be sorry. All that music, going on in the background, doesn't make it any easier to talk.'

'What music?'

'That choir singing. They're always singing. They can't get much work done. They're always at choir-practice.'

'*I* can't hear them.'

'*I* can. Listen!'

For a moment I listened; and then she began to sing, as if with them. Slowly, and for her age quite tunefully –

'*There . . . was . . . no . . . other . . . good . . . enough,*
To . . . pay . . . the . . . price . . . of . . . sin.
He . . . on-ly . . . could . . . un-lock . . . the . . . gates . . .
Of . . . Heav'n . . . and . . . let . . . us . . . in.'

There was, of course, no choir singing anywhere. She went on.

'*Oh . . . dear-ly . . . dear-ly . . . has . . . He . . . loved,*
And . . . we . . . must . . . love . . . Him . . . too . . .'

It was a tune I knew from my childhood.

'*And . . . trust . . . in . . . His . . . re-deem-ing . . . blood . . .*
And . . . try . . . His . . . works . . . to . . . do.'

Then silence. 'They've stopped now,' she said.

'I see,' said I.

'Do you still say you can't hear it?'

'I'm afraid so. I think you're dreaming it.'

She was not listening to me. She said:

'My eyesight's no good any more. But I can hear better than most folk.'

Most folk included me.

She recited now: '*Oh, dearly, dearly, has He loved, and we must love Him too . . .*' She paused. 'I was always fond of poetry when I was a girl.'

'I'm sure you were.'

'But nobody else was.' She was thinking of the stepmother's family, in which she was brought up alone, after her father had disappeared, her mother having died in giving birth to her. She went on.

'I was very fond of Wordsworth. I suppose nobody reads Wordsworth nowadays.'

'No, lots of people do.'

She was not listening to me. 'I wrote about Wordsworth in my scholarship examination, my scholarship to Owen's College.'

I was familiar with the story from its re-telling over a lifetime. She had won a scholarship to what was then Owen's College and later Manchester University. But her stepmother's family couldn't or wouldn't find the money wherewith she could take up the scholarship.

'If I'd been able to go to Owen's College I should have had a very different life.'

I couldn't bring myself to speak.

'But I was trapped.'

'Yes . . . '

'I suppose we're all trapped in one way or another.'

'You could say that.' Trapped by our genes: trapped by our circumstances . . . It was enough to make one weep – weep for one's genes, weep for one's circumstances!

'There they go again,' she said.

'Oh . . . dear-ly . . . dear-ly . . . has . . . He . . . loved,
And . . . we . . . must . . . love . . . Him . . . too.'

She went on singing but my thoughts drifted away to I don't know where.

Suddenly she said: 'How is your book getting on?'

'What do you mean?'

'Is it selling well?'

'It hasn't come out yet.'

'When does it come out?'

'Next month?'

'What month's that? Not that it makes any difference to me.'

'May.'

'What does Robert think about it?'

'He thinks it's one of my best.'

'That's good.' She paused. 'I've asked you all this before. haven't I?'

'I think so.'

And then I heard the doorbell ring. 'Oh!' I exclaimed.

'What's that?'

'My taxi.'

'Then you must go.'

I felt disinclined to go, I couldn't understand why. 'In a minute,' I said. 'There's no hurry.'

'You mustn't miss your train.'

'I suppose so.' I stood up and collected my impedimenta.

I went up to the bed. She was humming, *'Oh . . . dear-ly . . . dear-ly . . .'*

I bent down and kissed her forehead. 'I must go now. I'll come and see you again, soon.'

'It's good of you to come.'

'I have to come. I want to come.' Suddenly I said: 'Because I love you.'

She said: 'I love you, too.'

It struck me that this was the first time in my life that that exchange between us had taken place – it must have happened when I was a child but I couldn't remember it.

'Don't keep that taxi-man waiting!'

Half-laughing at her I said, 'Oh, all right.' And I went out of the room and down the stairs.

CHAPTER III

RUNNING LATE IN A PUB

I met Robert on the following Saturday evening, in a pub round the corner from his house – at six o'clock: for the time being we'd given up the struggle to find one open at five-thirty. It had been a fine day and he must have been sitting in the sun somewhere – I didn't know if there'd been any cricket for him to watch. His forehead was pink. I thought he looked altogether better in health.

I put our pints of beer on the table and sat down opposite him. We drank.

'Well, what have *you* been doing?' he asked.

'Nothing of note. A lot of domestic chores that wouldn't interest you. But that have to be done.' I expected him to say gloomily, *Why* do they have to be done? He said:

'Oh.' He drank some of his beer gloomily.

I decided to tease him by making him listen to what they were. 'Such as cleaning bathrooms, using the laundry-machine, shopping at Sainsbury's' – he hated shopping, and he had never been in a Sainsbury's – 'answering business correspondence, paying bills.'

They had to be done by me, I felt, because I went out to work, teaching for George Bantock, on only two days a week; whereas Elspeth and Viola went out to work on five. Oh, those happy years when I had an office to go to, every day! What man in his right mind, I asked myself, would choose to go to Sainsbury's? Pushing a trolley up and down aisle upon aisle of serried merchandise, and, having made his choice, queuing up for twenty minutes to pay for it. (Actually I'd discovered that supermarket shopping induced a sort of camaraderie among the shoppers, especially the middle-aged to elderly – the young never having known any different. I was always having sympathetic chats with women waiting next to me in the queue: it sometimes went as far as our guarding one another's place while we went back for something we'd forgotten. Suffering does indeed make fellows of us all. In Sainsbury's I was often reminded of the cameraderie of life in London during the Blitz.)

I drank some of my beer.

'I've discovered,' I said, 'what woman's work is like. And *I don't like it.*'

'No,' said Robert gloomily.

I said: 'I think our GP – she was a bit worried over my retiring – was afraid my having to do woman's work might upset my virility.'

Not for an instant gloomily now, Robert said, 'Did it?'

I laughed. 'That's for Elspeth to say. Hers is the opinion that matters.' (It was age, not woman's work, which caused me any lapses from what I regarded as my usual form.)

With an innocent, distant expression, Robert drank some more of his beer while looking away from me. 'Elspeth seems relatively cheerful.'

I was astonished. By the normal standard of Robert's prudishness in conversation, the present atmosphere was tinged, to say the least of it, with lubricity. I didn't miss an opening – I said:

'Veronica seems relatively cheerful, too.'

He nodded his head gravely, and said in a hollow, lofty tone of voice: 'She doesn't seem to have much trouble . . .' And then he drank some more beer.

I burst into laughter. Robert pretended not to notice.

We sat drinking for a little while. After all, we had something to think about.

Robert said, 'I think I should like another beer.'

'Going the pace, aren't you?'

He felt in his pocket for money, and gave it to me. I went up to the bar, which was as yet fairly deserted.

'How's the teaching?' he said when I came back.

'I'm enjoying it.' I sat down. 'And so are my pupils, apparently. They're quite a decent lot.'

'Wouldn't you expect them to be?'

'On second thoughts, yes.'

My first thoughts about them, when I took the job on, had been coloured by recollections of 1968 – the Sorbonne! Ten years had wrought a change.

'They're decent enough by nature,' I said, 'as you'd expect scientists and engineers to be. And they're very decent in behaviour.' I was reflecting on the riots of the Sixties having been in the province of 'Arts students'. (I thought of the 'Social Sciences' as 'Arts'.) 'They're not at loggerheads with post-industrial society. Nor with me.'

Robert laughed. I went on.

'They're prepared to read all the novels on my list, and to listen to me talking about them. What would you expect me to find more enjoyable than that, I should like to know?' I was laughing, myself.

'Nothing, I should say. Absolutely nothing.'

I paid no attention to his sarcasm. After all, I thought, the sort of things I told them seemed to me fun. To start off with –

There Is No Word Of God In Literary Criticism

(The fun of the aphorism was enhanced for me, I have to admit, by hearing in my imagination Leavisite screams.) And it wasn't my only aphorism, as a matter of fact. I'd never thought of aphorisms before; but finding myself in front of a class of young people seemed to provoke me to invent them one after another. Later on in the course –

Technique Is Like A Lady's Slip – It Must Be There, But It Should Never, Never Show

Or the same in shortened form –

It's Vulgar To Show Your Technique

(Let Henry James put that in his pipe and smoke it! I thought surreptitiously.)

And when I came down to the present-day academic priesthood of structuralists, post-structuralists, post-post-structuralists, their arcane and impenetrable writings seemed like a gift to me –

There's Nothing So Up-To-Date In EngLit As Ancient Alexandria

(The fact that in France, where it came from in the first place, structuralism was by now somewhat less than up-to-date, only added to the ironic beauty of the situation.)

I was having a high old time. Was I getting above myself? It was all very well to say these things to youthful scientists and engineers: if these things came to the ears of certain other less youthful persons, I might be rapidly precipitated below myself.

Robert went on grinning at me sarcastically. 'I'm glad you're enjoying yourself. And that your students are enjoying themselves.'

'How could I help it,' I said, 'reading a series of novels that begins with Jane Austen, Trollope and George Eliot, and ends with you and me?'

He drank some beer without saying anything.

I thought I'd better stop being playful. I said: 'It's possible that I'm at a bit of an advantage with my pupils, having gone through a scientific education myself. I suppose that was part of George Bantock's calculation.'

'Yes, it was.'

'How do *you* know?'

Robert pretended he was drinking some more beer. Keeping his head down, he said, 'I think he consulted me about it.'

'What do you mean, you think? You must know.'

Robert did not deign to reply.

'Really! The things that go on at the H of L! And anyway, why does everybody ask you about things, before they ask me?'

'I told him I thought it was a good idea. You approve of that, don't you?'

This time it was I who didn't deign to reply. I left a suitable pause and then said in more cosmic vein:

'It's a very pleasing turn of Fate, after all we used to say about EngLit. I mean for one of us, of all people, to end up teaching it.'

In our Oxford days, when Robert was a science don and I a science undergraduate (both of us intent on becoming novelists), we had gone about saying that EngLit ought to be abolished – because it stopped people writing.

Since then we had actually come across people whom reading EngLit had put off writing for three or four years, others, put off altogether. For one thing through making them feel that everything worth being written had been written already; for another through cluttering their minds and their time with stuff that had been fabricated in order to make something that was not properly an academic subject look as if it was.

However we had mellowed. We had gradually come to change our minds for an unforeseen reason. After decades of EngLit's being what was nowadays called 'a growth industry', there were so many dons in it that we couldn't face proposing its abolition because of the disastrous effect that would have on full-employment.

I was suddenly thrown out of my cosmic vein. A young man in jeans had come up behind us and put a coin in the juke-box. Music broke out. As he was passing us – we were the only people sitting at a table – on his way back to the bar, he gave us the most civil and unexpected of smiles and said:

'I hope you like Country-and-Western?'

Robert looked as if he'd been addressed in Swahili or Urdu.

The interruption brought us back again to conversation.

'What else has been going on at the H of L?' I asked, knowing that he wouldn't want to be bothered to tell me.

'Nothing of note . . . It's all pretty tiresome.' He paused. 'This Government hangs on.' He drank some of his beer as if to mark the conversation with a full-stop.

For months, now, the country had endured a 'hung Parliament', which couldn't be expected to make life less tiresome for anyone, apart from the Prime Minister and various colleagues who were hanging on to office.

'I wasn't thinking about government. I was thinking about people.'

Robert said nothing.

'What's my friend the Noble Lord Albert-Smith doing?'

'I told you about him.'

'You never did.'

'I'm sure I did. You've forgotten '

'Nothing of the kind. Tell me now – or tell me again, if that's the way you see it!'

Robert drank first, and then said:

'You remember that committee of Lord Grimley's he'd been asked to go on?'

' "No Way. No Way",' I quoted happily.

'After six months the wretched Grimley had got nowhere. So your friend Bert agreed to be "drafted" – as he inimitably expressed it – on to the committee.'

'And then?'

'Grimley was effectively elbowed out of "the driving-seat" and Bert installed in it.'

' "The ropes are the same everywhere",' I quoted even more happily.

'Grimley stays nominally the Chairman, but it's generally accepted as Bert's committee.'

'Excellent!' I said. 'That's just the kind of story I like to hear: it has a moral to it.'

Robert looked at his glass.

I looked at my glass.

Robert said: 'Look here, do you mind if we have another beer?'

I was astonished. We had already consumed our statutory two pints. 'You really are going the pace tonight.'

'Veronica won't have the supper ready quite so early.' He didn't tell me why.

I stood up to go and buy another round. I thought I'd better let Elspeth know I was going to be late, and that reminded me of one of the insoluble problems of married life. There was a case for saying that when I went out for a drink with one of my friends, I had two other courses that were to be preferred over the one I was taking. The first was to get home at whatever time I'd said I'd get home. How simple! If only Time didn't pass, *without one's noticing it,* twice as fast when one was out drinking with one of one's friends as in any other circumstances! The other was to say I didn't know what time I'd get home. I simply couldn't take that one: it seemed to me tantamount to admitting, before I ever set out, that I was going to put up no fight against *the temptation of drink.*

Coming away from the telephone I glanced at the clock on the wall and wondered if I'd been right to say another hour would see me home.

The pub was beginning to waken up. There were more people at the bar; the young man who spoke to us had gone – to be replaced by someone who chose music with a deafeningly invigorating THUD-THUD-THUD-THUD. I noticed that the daylight coming from the windows was beginning to lose its intensity. Night was on its way.

I bought our drinks and went back to Robert. He was looking

404

miserable, because of the deafening THUD-THUD-THUD-THUD. I said, 'I'll ask them to turn it down.'

'It's all right,' he said, stoic as ever. (Actually, while we were speaking, somebody else had it turned down.)

We drank for a little while. I realised that neither of us had mentioned Tom. I suspected that if I didn't mention Tom, Robert was not going to. I said:

'When you asked me what I'd been doing, I didn't tell you we'd been having a famous dinner at the Carlos with Tom. I suppose you knew?'

'Yes, he did say something about it.'

'You've seen him since then?'

'Yes.'

There was a pause. Robert looked up from his glass.

'You'll be pleased to know,' he said, 'that Tom expressed the highest approval of Elspeth.'

'That's nice of him, I must say.'

'He thinks she's sympathetic, and wise . . . '

Though Robert disclosed nothing from his tone of voice, I knew what he was up to. I said:

'By contrast with me.'

Robert ignored the remark and went on enjoying himself. The pinkness of his forehead seemed, either from the effects of earlier sunshine or present alcohol, to be spreading to his cheeks.

'He thinks that Elspeth could learn to think about money – under suitable tuition, of course.'

The provocation was so blatant that I forced myself to ignore it. I was being paid out for introducing the subject of Tom. All right – so be it. I said:

'That's all very satisfactory.'

'He enjoyed the evening.'

'He enjoyed having me there?'

'Oh yes. He thinks you've become much more sensible with the years. More ready to listen to reason.'

I couldn't contain myself. 'Insolent little bastard!'

'I think you must agree that he doesn't lose his touch.' Robert was laughing now.

'And *you* should agree that, too,' I said, preparing to take the war into the enemy's camp.

405

But Robert was much too cagey to ask what Tom said about him. He drank some beer and said mildly:

'He didn't say anything about you that wasn't more or less flattering.'

In that case Tom couldn't have reported that bit about my ending up 'On the breadline'. (Tasteful use of the English language, as well!) I said:

'Nor did he about you.'

That was true – if I excepted Tom's inference that if Robert had been more capable with his money, he'd have known whether or not his accountant was seeing to it that he paid his Income Tax for two years. A sum of about £50,000! (I bet Robert didn't know Tom had told us how much it was.)

Not, I may say perhaps unnecessarily, that my own knowledge of the state of our Income Tax payment, even though our accountant was neither fraudulent nor dotty, was much different from Robert's. The delays introduced by the machinery of the Board of Inland Revenue into dealing with Claims were, in my opinion, enough to ensure that any taxpayer could scarcely know whether he was coming or going. I regularly asked Elspeth, who read the letters from our accountant, where we stood. And when as a consequence of my income being reduced to goodness knows what, our accountant started to get money *back* for us from the Inland Revenue, I was stunned.

Robert was thoughtful. The music had stopped.

I said: 'Tom told us about the activities of your accountant.'

'Yes, of course.' His tone was dismissive. He'd asked Tom not to tell anybody, but he must have known that Tom would.

'I'm terribly sorry,' I said. 'It must be disastrous.'

'It's bad luck,' said Robert, with a short, hollow-sounding laugh.

I felt I was taking the plunge when I said: 'Elspeth and I were upset – to think this happened to you just after you'd laid out the money for the Trust, for me . . . and the rest of us.'

It was the first time I'd mentioned the Trust since the night Robert told me he'd set it up. I knew that he would never have mentioned it again, and I wondered if I'd done wrong by mentioning it, myself, now.

He said easily, 'You had the good luck, old boy.'

I felt relieved and pleased. I thought he was a wonderful man. I raised my glass to his health.

'Here's some good luck for you!'

He lifted his glass, and said in a tone of voice that I hadn't expected:

'And here's to more good luck for you!'

Suddenly I realised what he was thinking of. *Happier Days* was due out next month. I said:

'To *Happier Days*!'

He drank quietly and thoughtfully. I said:

'You still think it's one of my best books?'

'I do.'

'I think my publishers probably think so, too.'

'I think they do.' His tone of voice was still quiet, and curiously flat, as if he were worried.

'Do you actually know?'

He nodded his head to signify yes. I waited.

'I was talking to your publisher the other day. He does think it's one of your best books, just as he's told you. Probably one of your very best books . . .'

There was something else to come. He hesitated a moment. I waited. I felt I could see him make up his mind to tell me.

'The trouble, old boy, is that he doesn't think he can sell it.'

I can only say the night went dark immediately, the night of the soul.

I could understand why he'd been making up his mind whether to tell me. He could either prepare me for disaster or let me wait for it to strike me.

'That's the kiss of death for me.'

'I shouldn't be too hasty, if I were you.'

'It'll mean he'll print 3,000 copies at most, sell half of them at most; and write to me in a couple of years' time saying he's going to remainder the rest.'

'It may not happen . . .' He fiddled with his glass on the table.

I said: 'I've had it.'

'I don't agree.'

I wasn't going to argue with him. Just as we were in agreement that the nature and function of literature had changed during our lifetime, so were we agreed about the nature and function of publishing. In our New Age the fate of a book was more likely than not decided long before it was actually published. For one thing the sums of money involved were such that The Experts were bound to get in with a ruling say, The Experts being accountants, lawyers, MBAs, entrepreneurs of one sort or another – none of them, it scarcely needs to be said, knowing anything much about writing. In fact the writer was relegated.

In a recent speech I'd heard him making, Robert had come out to my astonishment with an aphorism of his own, delivered with great bitterness –

Writers Are The Serfs Of The Publishing Industry

There was no difficulty in seeing the sort of thing that happened. If a book was heading for making its author a fortune, all the things that brought in the money – serial rights, paperback rights, film rights, television rights – had been sold, possibly by auction, months before it reached the bookstalls, in some cases months before it had even been written. (Before the serf was set to work writing it!) And the more money that had been spent on its purchase, the more money was then laid out on its 'promotion' – in order to bring in a comparable return. You couldn't say all that didn't make sense, especially to accountants.

And what did I see happening to me? No book I'd ever written had ever seemed to be thought by anybody to be heading for making me a fortune – it must be that I hadn't written that sort of book. So I saw myself at the opposite end of the scale of fortune-making. And in our New Age of Publishing the two ends of the scale were getting further apart; and, more disturbingly, there was less and less in between. The tendency towards All-Or-Nothing. I saw myself heading for Nothing.

'You can never be certain,' Robert said. 'Odd things can happen.'

'Such as being run over by a bus.' I finished my glass of beer. Robert drank moodily.

'I'd like to know what else *can* happen,' I said.

Robert said nothing.

I was feeling terribly upset.

Robert said, 'Let me buy you another beer!'

'What – a fourth?' I cried. 'I can't go home to Elspeth after four pints. She'll tell me my eyes aren't focusing straight.'

Robert grinned briefly. 'Well?'

I glanced at the clock. My extension was practically up. I ought to go. I said, 'Suppose we just have halves?'

He felt in his pocket for the money.

While I was waiting at the bar I thought that over our last drink we'd better talk about something else. (I was feeling the effects of the drink.)

Robert must have thought the same thing. His face was now pink all over. He said in a friendly, matter-of-fact tone of voice:

'Been down to see your mother this week?'

I drank some of my half-pint. 'Yes.'

'How is she?'

I put down my glass. I said: 'You haven't done much better, alas! by the change of topic.'

He looked fleetingly hurt and then worried. 'Is she worse?'

I told him the latest news.

'I'm desperately sorry.' His voice was low.

I said: 'You have your troubles . . '

He said nothing.

Suddenly, in an access of courage and sympathy, I asked him something I hadn't asked him for ages. 'How's Annette? . .'

He drew in a breath. 'I'm afraid she's become diabetic. Apparently it's rather serious.'

I thought, Oh God! I said, 'How long ago?'

'Some months. I didn't tell you because I didn't want to distress you.'

'. . . There's nothing to say.'

He shook his head, looking down at the table.

'I'm afraid not.'

I glanced back at the clock again.

'We ought to be going,' he said.

'Yes,' said I. 'I'm afraid I'm going to be late home.'

CHAPTER IV

AFTERMATH OF A VISIT

W e had a telephone call from Veronica. 'Will you and Elspeth come and have supper with me at Vincent Square? Keep me company while the Old Boy's away.'

'While the Old Boy's away?'

'Yes. Didn't he tell you? He's gone to get an Honorary Degree in Minnesota.'

'He didn't tell me.'

'How extraordinary!'

'I suppose there's no reason why he should.' I realised that since I was in the habit of making fun of his appetite for honorary degrees, there was reason why he shouldn't.

'I want to ask your advice about various things.'

'What?' I said suspiciously. Was I going to be called on as an ally in the campaign for capturing Robert?

'Advice about alterations I'm having made to the kitchen, for one thing. Your kitchen is so super.'

'So super!' I cried agonisedly. The result of the cowboys' being sacked was that for our first two months nobody at all had been to raise the hanging-cupboards. Elspeth still had to cook only dishes that didn't require an oven-temperature above Mark 4, and even then she kept feeling the acrylic strip along the front of the hood to see if it appeared to be approaching melting-point. (Actually it didn't – we suspected the gas-engineers of exaggerating the cowboys' crimes.)

'I know, Joe. But it will be super. And the rest of the flat looks absolutely super already.'

'You don't know what you're saying!'

'Of course you're such a perfectionist.' Veronica was scoring off me: it was normally I who attacked her for being a perfectionist (which indeed she was.) Perfectionism I regarded as a manifestation of anxiety neurosis out of control.

'Nonsense! Don't you see? I want to get the place finished so that I can forget about it, and start *living* in it.'

Veronica laughed, and then had the effrontery to play, against me, one of Robert's favourite quotations from College history –

'If that's what you think, Joe, you have a right to say so.'

I'd often quoted it, myself, to great effect. A quotation to be recommended –

If That's What You Think, You Have A Right To Say It

We ended the telephone call, having arranged to meet the following evening at Vincent Square.

Elspeth and I speculated on whether the supper would be cooked by Veronica or Dolores. We thought it possible that Dolores was not accepting with any great equanimity the advent of a new mistress in the establishment, especially as galvanising and efficient a Civil Servant as Veronica. It was hard to imagine anyone less cut out for *mañana* than Veronica. In Veronica the interval between thinking of something and doing it was infinitesimally short.

We found the supper was being cooked by Dolores. Veronica gave us large whiskies, not necessarily to prepare us for it – Veronica didn't drink very much, any more than we did, but she did like a large whisky.

'What do you think of this room?'

We were sitting in the sitting-room which had been completely re-painted by her 'little man'.

'It's an extraordinary transformation,' I said, and Elspeth made sounds of agreement.

'The only trouble is,' said Veronica, 'it shows up the state of the loose covers. They're filthy dirty!' And she gave her laugh, 'Ho-ho-ho!'

I have to say that in her place I should not have laughed. The loose covers had previously looked dowdy: they now answered to her description vociferously.

'I shall cover them myself,' Veronica said. 'I've bought the material in a sale.'

Elspeth and I glanced at each other. In a sale!

I thought of Robert, gone to Minnesota. Next thing he'd be off to Novossibirsk or Tbilisi.

Then it occurred to me that he'd got to pay off £50,000 from somewhere; unless Tom managed to charm a slice of it out of Sir Abe Pettinger, by hinting that Robert might help him to get into the House of Lords – Tom knowing that Robert wouldn't be able to do much about it, even if the Prime Minister hadn't changed to someone whom Robert knew less well than the previous incumbent of No 10. (It was the previous incumbent who had sent Robert to the House of Lords in order to appoint him, without his having to go through being elected to Parliament, as a Junior Minister.)

'I suppose you've heard about the Old Boy's tax situation,' Veronica said.

'We have.'

'I don't know what would have happened if Tom hadn't arrived on the scene.'

I said: 'It would have been picked up when Pettingers' took over – so says Tom.'

'I wish I had that degree of faith. I'm jolly glad he came, that's all I can say. He saved us.'

'I see the force of that remark.'

'And I gather,' said Veronica, 'he's given you and Elspeth some helpful advice. Found somebody to help with your financial affairs.'

'He has. We now have a financial adviser.' I said it mockingly, but could only think of it with relief. I looked at Elspeth for encouragement.

'What's his name – Stewart Something-or-other?' Veronica said. 'Have you met him yet?'

'Yes, of course. We had lunch with him. He struck me as a very able young man; and also, as Tom promised, likely to be interested in us as people, not merely as clients.'

'He and his wife,' said Elspeth, 'do social work in their spare time. I don't understand how they manage it – they've got two children.'

I said: 'I'm very pleased with him. It really is a relief. I'm born with the twin gifts for not being able to think about money and for worrying about it.' I glanced, smiling, at Elspeth. 'So it's more than a relief for my loved one, here.'

'That's marvellous news,' Veronica said. 'All, thanks to Tom!'

I sensed a rebuke to me. Veronica knew my attitude to Tom, and it sounded as if she thought I was wrong. Time will tell, I thought. At the same time I knew my moral position had been temporarily weakened by finding that my base suspicion, about how Stewart had come to Tom's notice, was entirely misjudged.

'All thanks to Tom,' I said sarcastically. And then I corrected myself. 'That's not fair. So far as I can see, Tom's choice for us was extremely knowledgeable, unprejudiced, and sensible.' I couldn't help laughing at my own expense. 'Extremely knowledgeable, unprejudiced, and sensible. Who would ever have thought the day would come when I'd use those words to describe something Tom had done?'

Veronica laughed as well. 'It describes his intervention in the Old Boy's affairs.'

I went on with my own line of thought. 'One's always defeated in the end by the turns of human nature . . .'

There was a pause. Veronica said:

'Did you meet Jim, when you had dinner with Tom at the Carlos?'

'No.' Jim was the name of Tom's secretary. 'Did you?'

'Yes. He wasn't at all what I'd expected.'

'Oh, tell us about him!'

'You'll be meeting him – when we all go down to Tom's country house in August or September.' Veronica stood up. 'You know Tom's rented an eighteenth-century country house in Kent, complete with a chef to do the cooking and the chef's wife to keep house.' She looked at our glasses. 'Another whisky?'

At that moment Dolores came in to say supper was served, so we didn't have another whisky. We followed Veronica down to the dining-room, which presented a rather odd appearance as the 'little man' was half-way through painting it.

'We'll go and look at the kitchen later,' Veronica said, 'after Dolores has finished in it. I really do want your advice.'

I'd already seen enough of Robert's kitchen to know that my only advice to her could be to get rid of everything in it and start again from scratch. I said:

'We had someone to design our kitchen for us.'

We were sitting down at the dining-table.

'Yes,' said Veronica. 'But you and Elspeth have now learnt *so* much about it, I'm sure you could dispense with them if you were doing it again.' By that she meant if we were advising on the design of *her* kitchen.

I didn't risk glancing at Elspeth. We'd had a sort of bet on the subject. What were the odds against preventing Veronica from Doing-it-Herself? Infinite.

Dolores brought in pancakes stuffed with shrimps.

'Good gracious!' I exclaimed with pleasure. 'You don't need any advice on how to begin a supper-party.'

Veronica's cheeks were pink and her eyes were sparkling. 'I like them myself.'

I wondered whether I ought to retract my accusation against Veronica of having a touch of parsimony in her nature. And yet something made me hold back for a while. Mention of Jim had reminded me of how I was given to base suspicions. I had another base suspicion now. Veronica was doing us proud: I remembered that I was an ally in a campaign. Perhaps I ought to wait and see if anything was coming next.

It was quite a long time, however, before something did come next. We had a very good supper. Veronica, an excellent cook as one might expect, had supervised Dolores's preparation of beef *bourguignon*; then there was a delicious meringue-y gateau which Veronica had made herself. The evening began to pass very entertainingly and companionably. We went down and inspected the kitchen, gave our advice. Then we went up again to have a last whisky – 'for the road' said Veronica, although she was not going anywhere. And then we somehow found ourselves talking about Tom again.

'You know,' said Veronica, 'Tom gave his blessing to the Old Boy and me. I thought he'd got a bit of a cheek.'

I laughed. 'Tom wouldn't be Tom if he hadn't got a bit of a cheek. A lot of a cheek, as a matter of fact.' I glanced at Elspeth, who was smiling.

'Yes,' said Veronica. She paused. 'I think he thinks Robert ought to get a divorce.'

So there it was! I got her message.

I looked at Veronica with the expression of an ally. 'Let's

414

hope,' I said lightly, 'he doesn't tell the Old Boy that!'

Veronica got *my* message – which was that if Tom did tell him, Robert, labyrinthinely sensitive like an elephant, would immediately shy off in a different direction.

Veronica gave me a shrewd, clear-eyed look and said:

'He only said it to *me*, so far as I know.' She paused. 'I'm pretty sure he didn't say it to the Old Boy.' She paused again. 'I agree. Let's hope he didn't!'

All three of us drank some of our whisky – to occupy a rather strange few seconds of silence.

It was time for Elspeth and me to go home. Veronica called a taxi for us and five minutes later we were on our way.

In the taxi, Elspeth said:

'Well, what did you think of that?'

I said: 'You know, my darling, without my telling you.'

'What are you going to do?'

'Absolutely nothing. That is, I'm going to give no sign that I know anything about it. A thing I will not do, I will not do, is take part in manoeuvring.' She took hold of my hand. I went on: 'If I so much as mentioned the word "divorce" in the Old Boy's presence, he'd *know*, and he'd *remember* . . . for the rest of Time.'

CHAPTER V

MORE AFTERMATH OF A VISIT

I can't say I was surprised when I heard from Steve.

'Are you likely to be dropping in at the pub in Soho?'

'No, Steve. Now that my days in Whitehall are over I don't come up to Marshall Street Baths any more. They're shut, anyway.' They were shut supposedly for re-decoration, but in my opinion they were shut for ever. All over London public swimming-baths were being shut, because of the inflated cost of upkeep. Public swimming-baths were being shut; public lavatories were being removed; even public clocks were disappearing from the streets – anything that needed 'service' was destined to go. And the streets themselves were getting dirtier and dirtier.

'You can guess why I want to see you, Joe.'

'My guess is Tom.'

'That's right.'

'Nothing wrong?' I was thinking of Burke, of course.

'Oh, no . . .'

We agreed to meet in mid-afternoon, one day when I went shopping for Italian comestibles. A patisserie in Old Compton Street.

It was a sunny afternoon and the door of the café was wedged open. It was just a long room, dimly-lit, cheaply panelled, the minimum having been spent on meretricious (or any other) decoration. At the entrance was a counter, presided over by a big, rosy, business-like Italian and small, sallow, female members of his family: at the bottom end was a doorway opening into the kitchen. The point about it all was that the coffee was good, and the cakes, if not as good as they used to be, still acceptable.

Steve was already there when I arrived. He was wearing sun-spectacles.

'I've not been to this place for ages,' he said.

'I'm an infrequent sort of regular.'

We looked round the room, which in mid-afternoon was not crowded. The café was frequented by denizens of Wardour Street, talking about making films; by young persons who practised parasitic arts such as graphics, animation; by other young persons who sat sorting large photographs of themselves; and by a few quasi-intellectual old-stagers like me, refugees from a once-upon-a-time Viennese café in Gerrard Street, when the said café disappeared under an avalanche of Chinese non-citizens of the People's Republic, opening restaurants, emporia, and very busy centres of the heroin trade.

Steve and I ordered coffee from an Italian waitress whom I'd known for years; on the other hand there was a new waitress, a pretty girl who seemed to be German. Steve took off his sun-spectacles.

We made our choice of cakes from an old-fashioned, three-tiered cake-stand, such as stood ready on every table, the number of cakes having been previously counted. The coffee came.

'So,' I said, perhaps affected by recollection of the old Viennese café days.

'So,' said Steve.

'Tom?'

'Tom.'

We began to laugh.

'What's he been up to?' I asked.

'You're over-reacting, Joe.'

'Let's see you under-react, then!' I began to eat my cake. 'What was it you wanted to tell me, Steve?'

'Tom was in generous mood.'

I waited.

'He gave his blessing,' said Steve, 'to Burke and me.'

'Oh God!' I began laughing.

'What's the matter?'

'That's precisely what Veronica said. Literally the same words.'

'That's what Tom said to Veronica and Robert?'

'Just to Veronica, I think. Even he wouldn't have the cheek to say it to Robert.'

'He said it to us, Burke and me together, when he was giving us a very super dinner at the Carlos.'

I said: 'How did you and Burke receive the blessing, together?'

'I don't know how to put it.' Steve gave his rueful smile, then dropped it in favour of a shrewd laugh. 'Gratefully, Joe. Gratefully.'

'I'm very glad.'

'He knows Burke quite well, in New York.'

I didn't see what he meant by that. I said, 'One might say he knows you quite well.'

'Did know.' Steve corrected me.

I saw the aptness of the correction. 'Did know,' I repeated.

'You know' – Steve resumed his rueful expression – 'you'll scarcely believe it, but I can't remember a lot of it, you know . . . of the past.'

'I can't either. Perhaps it's as well.' I began to laugh. 'What I *can* remember is the clarion call, "*Now Steve!*" Can you?'

'Don't!' Steve began to laugh. Then he stopped. 'The trouble is, Joe, he hasn't changed.'.

'He didn't call "*Now Steve!*" clarionlike, at the Carlos, I hope.'

'No. But I'm not sure, you know, that he won't.'

I wasn't sure, either. I didn't say anything. We ate our cakes.

Steve said, 'These are nice. I've always liked cream cakes.'

I said: 'What's the basis for the blessing?'

'He told us we were good for each other. In those words, Joe.'

'How does he know?'

'How does Tom always know these things?' He was thoughtful. 'Actually he spent hours talking to Burke on the telephone.'

'Well, I don't know what you're worried about. By the way, what became of Marìa?'

'She went back to Buenos Aires.'

I said: 'Will Burke go back to New York?'

'That's just the point, Joe. She *will* go back to New York. It's not settled when. Possibly at the end of this summer. She's only taking what she calls a sabbatical half-year from her theatre and all the other things she does in New York.' He was looking at me with a rather soulful expression. 'She's a very busy lady.'

I said: 'As Tom gave you and Burke his blessing, as it were in conjunction, is he thinking of your remaining permanently in conjunction?'

'That's what I don't know.'

'Does Burke know?'

'She hasn't said.'

'Do you want to?'

'Well, yes . . .' He looked at me. 'I'm very devoted to her, Joe.'

One of the things that made Steve engaging was that he always sounded unconvincing: it was his misfortune that he could never sound anything but unconvincing when it was necessary that he should *not* sound so. He repeated –

'Tom thinks we're good for each other.'

'That may well be true.' I could think of a very simple way in which Burke was good for Steve.

Steve might have read my thoughts. 'I *am* good for *her*,' he said. 'She's had a bad time with men in the last few years. She doesn't find life as easy as you think. Being rich isn't everything.'

I couldn't have thought I'd ever live to hear Steve say anything as beautiful as 'Being rich isn't everything'. However I kept quiet about that, and I began to think how perhaps Steve might well be good for her, as Tom said. I could imagine there had been no shortage of men in the New York theatre and its environs who were trying to sleep with Burke to get money and influence out of her. I felt pretty sure that wouldn't be in her line of country at all. How very different a line of country was Steve's unobtrusive need – arising from his sensitive artistic nature – just to be looked after!

I continued to keep quiet. I finished my coffee.

Steve said: 'We get on very well together. Better than I got on with Marìa.'

It was time we came to the point. I said:

'Is there some thought, when Burke goes back to New York, of your going with her?'

'If you mean some thought of Tom's, I think there is.'

I suppressed the impulse to exclaim Good gracious! I remained thoughtful, as well I might.

'I think there is,' said Steve. 'But what I don't see, is – Where do *I* stand?'

As Tom had the gift for making anybody's head spin, I could well understand Steve's quandary. I said, in as cosy a tone of voice as I could muster:

'I think that will become apparent, as time goes by.'

'You think that?'

'I do.'

Steve's mood changed. 'I suppose,' he said, 'as time goes by when Tom's around, things do become apparent.' And then he gave me a grin of amusement. 'As if *I* didn't know that!'

CHAPTER VI

A SHORT CHAPTER ABOUT DISASTER

By the end of three weeks after the book was published, I'd had practically all my reviews. Some of my friends thought that was flattering. Perhaps it was. What they didn't realise was that one's publisher, if he thought the book was not going to sell, tended to regard the reviews as one's advertisement, as 'promotion' gratis; and that was the end of promotion. It was all right for the review-hounds, who didn't miss a review over those particular three weeks. But for the rest, it was silence – it was quite easy to be greeted, after another three weeks, by someone who'd say: 'Oh, Mr Lunn, when are we going to get another novel from you?'

Not that there weren't an encouraging number of review-hounds. I was continually meeting them, when they announced themselves with encouraging candour: 'I haven't read your *novel*, Joe, but I've read the *reviews*.' For myself I have to say that I'd given up reading my reviews several novels back. (It required some fortitude to stick them in a scrap-book for posterity without reading them now.) Reading my reviews, I'd learnt, roused in me little but exasperation. Exasperation is a sterile emotion. I decided not to lay myself open to it.

However I did read two reviews of *Happier Days*, more or less under duress. One evening in my Club a friendly fellow-member held the *Evening Standard* under my nose. 'Have you seen this, Joe?' And he held it there while I had to read it. It was the review I mentioned earlier.

In most reviews there is a sentence which leaps, as poets say, to the eye. You'll remember that the heart of the novel was a love-affair between a sixty-two year old doctor and the twenty-two year old daughter of one of his friends, a love-affair touching and poignant, but nonetheless full-blown. The sentence in this review that leapt to my eye was to the effect that after the age of forty-five all sex is disgusting.

I ask you!

I *ask* you!

While I was speechless with exasperation, my fellow-member said: 'Did you see your review in the TLS last Thursday?' Taking, I suppose, my speechless expression to signify No rather than the lack of presence of mind to say Yes, he went off to the morning-room to fetch it.

I didn't recognise the name of the reviewer and presumed him to be some minor provincial don. The sentence that leapt to my eye in this review was to the effect that after having completed the book I'd sprinkled it with cultural references in order to impress.

I said to my fellow-member: 'Thank you.'

So much for two of my reviews. Elspeth dutifully read them all, as the stuffed manilla envelopes came in from my publisher; and she tactfully withheld her own opinions. Now and then she offered one to me, on the assumption that it ought not to arouse exasperation; but I slid out of reading. On the other hand the information I'd have liked to get from her was whether my story of the love-affair had carried conviction with the reviewers: tact prevented my asking that. (Nor, of course, had I been able to ask her what was even more important to me, myself – if, when she read the book in typescript, it had carried conviction with *her*.)

One of the most serious vocational hazards for the wife of a novelist is having to read his stories about love-affairs that involve women obviously not herself (unless it be having to read those in which the woman obviously *is* herself.) Negotiating it requires great tact on both sides: Elspeth and I managed it by discreet silence on both sides. How could I ask her if my story of a love-affair between a man of my own age and a girl thirty years younger than herself, rang true, true to reality? I asked myself, of course I asked myself, if it embarrassed her. But a novel is a novel. I simply had to get on with it – which, in those terms, Elspeth understood perfectly. She knew that for me a novel had to ring true. If it doesn't ring true, as I've already said – it bears being said again – even the art of it, for me, is wasted.

Incidentally I may say that even before the book came out there was further evidence for Robert's forewarning and my own predicting. I'd seen fit to write the novel in the form of a private diary – an honourable enough tradition, one would have thought. I'd found, when I told certain literary persons about it, that the temperature of the conversation dropped with a thump. Honourable enough the tradition might be: they signified unhesitatingly that it was dead.

Forewarnings, predictions turned into established fact. It was impossible not to see that the book, one of my best – one of my very best? – had totally failed. My American agent hadn't got me a publisher in the United States. I packed up a copy for my former American publisher who found the book so adorable that she wanted a copy to keep for herself. One copy in the USA? At least it was a copy adored, when there were obviously many copies in the United Kingdom that were unadored – come to that, un-bought.

My London publisher couldn't find anyone who was prepared to publish the book in paperback. Once in a lifetime I'd had a modest best-seller in Penguin; but that was in the days before selling a million copies of *Lady Chatterley's Lover* made all previous Penguin best-selling look, as Tom would say, like chickenfeed – or should it be peanuts? (Perhaps chickens feed on peanuts?) There were no serial rights, no televison rights; I made no bones about accepting that – the book wasn't cut out for either. No translations into other languages: that didn't surprise me, in view of the pretty familiar way in which I normally expressed myself in the English language – imagine a Japanese confronted by, Let Henry James put that in his pipe and smoke it!

So the deadly blow began to fall, the feel of disaster.

The arthritis in my hip had been getting worse: the pain kept waking me up during the night when I turned over in bed. And when I awoke in the night I thought of the book, and felt – arthritis in the soul.

Had I been guilty of a semantic self-deception, I asked myself in the dark hours, a lapse in comparative thought? (I always was the first person to condemn a lapse in comparative thought on the part of somebody else.) The book might be one of *my* best books: that was only by internal comparison among my own books. If one threw open the judgement on it to external comparison among everybody's books, all my books might be at the bottom of the scale, my best merely being at the top of what were the generality's worst.

Elspeth tried to cheer me up. She said:

'You'd better start taking those anti-depressant pills again.'

'How can *they* make my book *sell*?'

We were sitting on one of the sofas in our sitting-room. We were alone. It was evening, a summer evening.

Dark though my mood was, I realised that the room, now it was finished, looked very pretty. In evening light from an open sky such flaws as there were seemed to fade. The curtains, the pictures, the pieces of furniture, the carpet . . . the mild colours among which the pictures shone. We could now start living in the room, forgetting about it now that it pleased us. I could sit in it thinking about disaster – would the book sell even 1,500 copies?

Elspeth said: 'Just look at those clouds!'

Across the blue sky there were three stripes of thin, flocculent clouds, in the sunlight shining pink and gold.

'Yes,' I said glumly.

After a few minutes she tried again. 'Come on,' she said. 'Think how nice the flat looks!'

'It does.'

'You can *live* in it,' she said, making fun of me.

'We can *afford* to live in it,' I said, getting back at her.

'Of course we can.'

'If Stewart says so, it probably is so.' Stewart had made his first appraisal of our finances. Our straits, he told us, were not dire. (They were nearer to what Elspeth had been telling me all along.) Far from dire, he said. In fact he thought I ought to be encouraged by them – we had enough money for holidays! Stewart, it was already apparent, was interested in us as people.

Elspeth didn't take up the argument. I went on.

'It probably is so, provided you go on earning a living for the two of us. As Tom might say, Bringing home the bacon.' (I should never forget, 'On the breadline'.)

'Oh, stop it!'

424

'You can't expect me to contribute much more than I earn from teaching.'

'There'll be *some* royalties.'

'Chickenfeed!'

'All right – they may be less than you'd hoped for from *this* book – '

'You don't think I'm going to write any more books, do you?'

'I hope you will.'

'What's the point? I'm getting near the end of my literary career. There's nothing really to hope for. I'm not going to go on writing novels, even if *I* think they're good, just for them to plop like this one into . . . the well of nothingness.'

'That's ridiculous.'

'It's an artful use of the title of another book.'

'Let's talk about something else!' She thought. 'If you still insist on being worried about money, you must remember there'll be money coming from other sources. Stewart thinks we've done reasonably well with the money we've put into investments and insurance, and he'll do better with it for us.'

I couldn't bring myself to say Chickenfeed again – or Peanuts. She went on.

'There'll be what you inherit from your mother. Then when you're seventy you'll take your pension.'

She meant my Old Age Pension, which I'd deferred taking on the basis of somebody's dubious actuarial calculations. I said: 'I've no idea how much that will be. I've never seen it printed anywhere.'

'You can write to the DHSS and ask. I think you ought to write straight away – Stewart wants to know. Will you, this evening?'

'All right.'

She went on. 'And then there's Robert's Trust.'

'We've no idea how much that will be and I don't see how I can ask him. I think it's best to leave it out of Stewart's computations – just treat it as a bonus when it comes.'

'All right. But I really did hope you were going to stop worrying about money, now that we've got Stewart. I thought when *he* told you, you'd believe it.'

I changed my tack. 'It's funny,' I said, not in the least

meaning that it was comical. 'Everybody has always thought I didn't need to worry about money. Everybody in the Government Service thought I was making a fortune out of my novels; everybody in the literary world thought I was laying up a fat pension from the Government Service. Both wrong!'

Elspeth was silent.

'Perhaps,' I said, 'it was I who was wrong.'

'What do you mean by that?'

'By having two careers. By not staking everything on one or the other. So ending up as a failure in both.'

Elspeth gave an impatient sigh.

'Though it's probable I couldn't have been a success in either. In the Government Service I was constantly saying sharp, bright things that either maddened people or frightened them . . . Also, because I had a career as a writer, they never felt I was one of them.' I laughed sarcastically. 'Though if I *hadn't* had a career as a writer they still mightn't have felt I was one of them.'

Elspeth murmured something I didn't catch.

I went on. 'And it's been exactly the same on the other side of the fence. If I'd staked everything on my literary career, I should have had to buckle to and show myself, if nobody else, I really believed in my novels enough to live by them . . .' I paused. 'I ought to have written many more novels than I have. To be successful your best novels have to float on a corpus of work. A corpus of work is very important: it carries weight . . . I ought to have written short stories, if only to please people who've been constantly asking me to. And do you realise I've spent half of my life thinking about novels, what they ought to be, and how to write them? And I've scarcely put a word on paper about it. I shall depart as if I'd never been.'

Realising that the last sentence was somewhat ridiculous, I went on quickly.

'Furthermore, if I'd chosen to be only a writer, I should have stood a better chance of literary society feeling I was one of them, instead of always standing outside. There's a great deal to be said, whatever the society you're living in, for that society to feel that you're one of them. If they don't, you pay a price . . . I've never written anything I didn't feel a compulsion inside me to write. I've never taken any notice of other people. I've gone my

426

own way, regardless.' I repeated it with heart-rending emotion – at least it rent *my* heart. 'I've gone *my own way!*'

'My darling, this is really getting – '

I was not to be stopped. 'I suspect there's never been a bit of society that's felt *I* was one of *them*. I haven't been. I'm *not!*'

Elspeth took hold of my hands. 'My darling, please don't go on! You are what you are.'

'That's the trouble. It isn't that I could have behaved any differently if I'd not wanted to be a total failure. I should just have had to be *somebody else*.'

Elspeth said: 'I can only think of one thing to say to you, my darling, and I don't know how much it means to you.' She leaned round, so as to look into my face. '*I* love you for what you are. I love *you* . . .'

And I looked into her face. I turned away so as not to burst into tears.

There was a very long pause. We were both looking towards the windows. The stripes of cloud, high and still, went on shining pink and gold, ineffably pretty.

I stirred, turning to get more comfortable on the sofa.

Elspeth said gently: 'Don't you think it's really time you had that hip seen to?'

427

PART IV

CHAPTER J

ONCE MORE INTO THE MAW

I am referring to the maw of the National Health Service; my subject, the hip-joint, replacement of bone by stainless steel and plastic. I decided to go to our GP – I'd now reached the stage when the pain was such that I was avoiding going out.

'It's one of the more successful operations,' she said, with the comparative thought which I regarded as fair encouragement. And then: 'You'll have to decide whether you want to go on taking distalgesic for more years or have the operation now.'

'That seems clear.'

She went on: 'The operation hasn't been going long enough for them to guarantee successful results for more than ten years. 'But that' – she laughed cheerfully – 'should take you into your eighties. Most hospitals have a waiting-list of two years.'

Thinking, Boldness is all, I said promptly, 'I'll go ahead now.'

'Right.'

We got on rather well in a hearty way.

'I'll let you have a list,' she said, 'of three of the best people to go to. Then if I were you, I'd shop around. See what you think of them, and see how long their waiting-lists are.'

I was so struck by the impropriety of 'shopping around' that I just said:

'Thank you.'

A few days later she telephoned me a list of three surgeons and their hospitals.

Mr F R Digby-Waterton

Mr Q Redruth

Mr B J K T Lascelles

I read the names with pleasure – classy names! 'We're obviously at the top of the tree,' I said.

'I suppose Digby-Waterton must be related to Mr Justice Digby-Waterton,' said Elspeth.

I said: 'I rather go for having the solitary initial, Q. That's real class.'

'It must be for Quintin.'

I said, 'It might be Quetzalcoatl.' I tried it over. 'Quetzalcoatl Redruth. An old Aztec Cornish family. It *must* be Quetzalcoatl.'

'Are you going to start with Digby-Waterton?'

'I suppose so.' Digby-Waterton's hospital was one of the largest and most renowned in London. 'But I'm sure "shopping around" is not allowed by the NHS.'

'I don't see why you shouldn't do it.'

'Suppose I'm found out?'

'It'll take so long for your records in the NHS to come together, it'll be too late.'

I saw the force of that remark. 'All right.' I decided, however, to go through all the hoops of each of the processes in series, rather than embark on the hoops of all three processes concurrently. I asked our GP to give me a letter to Mr Digby-Waterton and I set about getting a first appointment – some weeks ahead – with the hospital.

In the meantime there was a film about the operation shown on television – I was in the swim of things! Actually the film was shown on a night when Burke and Steve were giving a party, but if it had been on a different night I'm not sure I should have brought myself to watch it.

The appointed afternoon came and I presented myself at the hospital. There were people everywhere. One of the little girls in the reception found my name on her list and directed me to one of the waiting-rooms down one of the corridors. The name on the door at the other end of the room said –

Mr G E Blenkinsop

That didn't surprise me. I was not expecting to be seen first go by the Great Man himself. (Over my cataract I'd started off with His Majesty in Wimpole Street because I'd gone to him as a private patient.) I sat down as the last-comer to a party of four or five waiting patients. I'd brought a novel to read. Time passed. The patients in front of me in the queue were duly called in to be seen by Mr Blenkinsop. I went on reading. I suddenly realised

432

that patients *behind* me in the queue were being called in to be seen by Mr Blenkinsop. I stood up, preparatory to action. At that moment the little girl from the reception came running in.

'Mr Lunn!' I turned to her. 'Mr Lunn,' she said breathlessly, 'I'm very sorry – we made a mistake. It's Mr Love who's going to see you.'

She hastily conducted me from my first waiting-room to a second one. On the opposite door it said –

Mr T W Love

There were more people in this room. I said, 'I hope I'm not at the bottom of this queue.'

'I'll just find out.' With that she disappeared, never to be seen again. I returned to my novel-reading; till at last my name was called and I entered the room occupied by Mr Love, sitting at a large desk, and a nurse, sitting at a small folding table.

Mr Love was a presentable youngish man, that is to say rising forty, wearing spectacles and dressed in an appropriately dark suit. He had the standard manner for his status. The mantle of greatness had not yet fallen upon him, but I thought there were unmistakable signs now and then of his reaching up to give it a downward tug. At the end of a short interview, obviously standard for this hoop in the process, he instructed me to go and be X-rayed, hand in the film at the reception, and return to his waiting-room.

Centralisation being up-to-date – recommended by The Experts – the hospital had one centralised X-Ray Department, into which therefore flowed all the patients from all the Departments. I was reminded of a pre-Bank Holiday afternoon at Paddington Station. I settled down to reading my novel again, waiting and waiting and waiting. Finally, with my film developed and checked and enclosed in a yellow envelope, I went with it to the reception.

Another little girl received the yellow envelope and me. 'I'm afraid,' she said, 'Mr Love has gone . . .' She looked up at the clock for corroboration: it said quarter past six. 'We shall have to make you another appointment to see him.'

As good as her word, she made me another appointment to see him.

In two weeks' time I was back again, safely in the correct

waiting-room – on the door opposite to me, the name of Mr T W Love. Four or five people were already there. I was now reading a different novel. It was just coming up to my turn when a little girl rushed in – I was used to little girls by now – and said:

'Mr Lunn, have you been X-rayed?'

I said, 'Yes, I have, the first time I was here. What's more, I handed in the film at your office.'

'Thats all right, that's all right,' – she was already rushing out again – 'we'll *find* it!'

Three patients later I was called.

Mr Love was sitting at the large desk, as before. Beside him, this time, was sitting a slightly junior version of himself – I saw how the American term 'side-kick' originated. The nurse was at her little folding table. Mr Love had a few minutes of question-and-answer, from-the-other-side-of-the-table discussion with me; and then made the remark –

'You seem very set on this operation. Is it because you watched the television commercial for it?'

Stupefaction sent me to the peak of haughtiness.

'You do me an injustice on two counts. First, I didn't watch the television film. Second, I'm counter-suggestible to commercials.'

Stupefaction all round! Mr Love looked at his side-kick: his side-kick looked at Mr Love. The nurse dropped her biro on the floor.

A patient had answered back – had answered back not just on equal terms, but on *superior terms*!

For a moment neither of the men knew what to say or do. The nurse picked up her biro. A delicious moment: I thought. Insolent young puppy shot down in flames – a delicious metaphor! Meanwhile I was giving them the opaque, implacable stare of which my mother was such a mistress.

Mr Love began to talk again from an entirely different plane. A mumbling speech which improved as it reached its point – 'In this hospital, Mr Lunn, we aim at treating our patients as individual people.'

I was relieved to hear that I was not going to be operated on as a group of people. I was still giving him my mother's stare, but I began reducing its opacity and implacability.

He said: 'Shall we look at your X-ray?' He put the film in a viewing-machine and switched on the light.

Under the spell of instruction I subsided into normal manners. So did he, though he had further to go. Finally he said:

'I'm willing to put you down on our waiting-list for the operation.'

I didn't feel the speech was warmed with conspicuous enthusiasm. I said, 'Thank you.' He went on.

'But I have to warn you that we have a waiting-list of up to two years.'

I felt it was probably two years for me – two more years of pain. I stood up, preparing to leave. And then devilment inspired me to give his tail a final twist.

'And who,' I asked with utmost innocence, 'will be doing the operation? Mr Digby-Waterton?'

He gave me a cool smile – which I rather respected him for – and said:

'Mr Digby-Waterton. Or myself. Or another colleague of mine.'

Exactly like the Civil Service! Either I myself, or another Under Secretary, will be dealing with your case, Mr Snooks.

'Thank you!' I said.

When I got home Elspeth said, 'Well?' and I said, 'We definitely go to see Mr R. I suspect it's going to be Quetzalcoatl for me.'

She laughed. 'Why are you so pleased with calling him Quetzalcoatl?'

'His initial's Q, isn't it? Also I think one can do with the help of a god in these things.'

'Don't get above yourself!'

Next morning I asked our GP for a letter to Mr Redruth.

So began a career through the hoops of a second process. I was shopping around. I got an appointment at Mr Redruth's hosptial.

Our GP had told me this hospital was small and old-fashioned, but I wasn't prepared for its being quite so Victorian. A small entrance-hall with a crest in the mosaic on the floor; a little old lattice-gated lift – one wouldn't have been surprised to see Florence Nightingale get out of it. To reach the Out-Patients' one had to go down a corridor, then, startlingly, through the oak-panelled foyer of the Board room; then down a flight of stone stairs that must have been terrifying for crocks on crutches. The waiting-room was subterranean and served partly as a thoroughfare. There was a reception office on one wall and along the opposite wall two rows of seats. But at one end there was a large concertina-gated lift; and at the opposite end a pair of double doors above which a screen said in lighted green letters –

OPERATION IN PROGRESS

I settled down to wait. I noticed the name on the door to which we were being called was –

Mr Q Redruth

It looked as if, here, I was going to see the Great Man himself. It turned out that I was.

'My name's Redruth,' he said grandly, and gave me a powerful handshake.

A round head, a strong neck, and biceps that filled the sleeves of his jacket. Clipped grey hair, a very handsome dark suit. Quick on his feet. Another rugger-player, I thought.

'I believe in seeing my patients, myself, on their first visit.'

The room was rather dark and I'd just noticed that there was a nurse there, Indian-looking, pretty.

'Yes,' I said, trying to make the word sound appreciative – which it was. He was very grand but not exactly regal; more like ducal, Duke of Edinburgh ducal.

We sat down for a short preliminary interchange. Then he said, 'Now I should like to examine you.' There was a little annexe to the room, with a bright light and a curtain to pull across. I stripped and climbed on to the bed. He came in and tested my hip in this way and that, compared it with the other hip –

'H'm, I see what you mean.'

He pointed to a dressing-gown, hanging on the wall. 'Now go and be X-rayed and come back!'

I put on the dressing-gown and said politely, 'May I leave my clothes here?' They were neatly piled.

He started. 'Yes. You may.'

When I got outside I saw other people in dressing-gowns, carrying their clothes round with them. Was I the first patient ever to dump his clothes in the ducal consulting-room? What a gaffe! It was too late to go back for them. Would he hold it against me?

When I returned with my photograph his mood was unchanged. 'Let's have a look at you!' I put on my clothes.

'Yes,' he said as we looked at the film, illuminated. The second time round, I was beginning to recognise myself.

'Now this – ' he began. In the nick of time I stopped myself from saying, Yes, I know.

All went well. He pointed out what was wrong and explained what he did in the operation. Then he went back to his desk and we sat down for his final speech.

'You've probably heard this is generally a successful operation. It is. There's only one thing that goes wrong: the chance of that is about one in a hundred. It's if you get an infection.' He paused. 'We have to take the prosthesis out. You can still *walk*. But one leg's two inches shorter than the other.' He gave me a look that was penetrating, roughly amused, unchanging.

Boldness is all. I didn't say anything. The speech was succinct and contained the essential bit of statistical information.

'If you come to me,' he said, 'I'll operate on you in three months. I don't believe in long waiting-lists. In Hove the waiting-list is four years.'

I wasn't thinking of going to Hove.

'My rule,' he went on, 'is that if I can't operate on a patient in three months, I don't take him on.'

He stood up and I stood up. I suspected that I was going to ask him to take me on. The risk: one in a hundred. But I didn't say anything. He held out his hand and gave me another powerful handshake.

'Good morning, Mr Lunn.'

I said, 'Thank you.'

Outside the room, somebody lying under a scarlet blanket was being wheeled by on a bed, wheeled from the double doors to the concertina-gated lift by a man in green overalls and a green cap. Something made me feel it would be unwise to report this to Elspeth when I was giving her an account of the proceedings.

I'd now gone through the hoops of a second process. I gave

Elspeth my account of it and I reported it to our GP, who said, 'You'll have to think about it, won't you? You see why I recommended you to shop around.'

I did see. I also saw that if you 'shop around' you have to make a choice – that's if you mean to buy at all. I did mean to buy. I'd endured the pain for years. I'd contemplated the operation for months. I'd mobilised myself for the crisis. It would have been intolerable, now, to call it off, and only somewhat less than tolerable to postpone it.

I had already struck off No 1 on the list before our GP got a letter from Mr Love saying he had 'reluctantly' put me on his waiting-list of two years. And she had ascertained for me that Mr Lascelles's waiting-list was scarcely any shorter; and further-more his was another big hospital where there was no way of telling if I should be operated on by the Great Man himself: I struck off No 3.

That left me with Quetzalcoatl. Elspeth was doubtful, not about Mr Redruth's skill but about the antiquatedness of the hospital. She proposed that we should find the money for me to side-step the NHS and go to Mr Digby-Waterton as a private patient, when I should be more certain of being operated on by himself after a very much shorter wait. I refused. 'Other people have to go on the NHS. I will.'

We enquired among our medical friends. Quetzalcoatl was acknowledged as one of the masters of his trade. (Our GP happened to have one of his successes on her list of patients, 'an old lady of nearly eighty who's jumping about like a flea!') It was the small antiquated hospital to which Elspeth kept returning in her argument. It was a teaching hospital, annexed to another of the largest, most renowned hospitals in London, and destined to be closed down – Centralisation. Elspeth was afraid I'd get less efficient nursing service. On the other hand, because the nursing-staff was small and not constantly being circulated in a huge machine, its members got to know each other and, so it was said, gave the place an atmosphere that was human and friendly.

What to do?

Elspeth said, 'Poor darling,' sympathetically.

I said, 'Think of the thousands of other people who have to . . .' The end of my sentence was lost in a vision of that

Paddington Station of X-raydom. Throngs and throngs of people, all having to think about these disturbing, wearying, frightening things for days on end, weeks on end, months on end. Suffering humanity.

Actually I'd begun to feel that I knew what to do. Boldness is all.

'Unless you're too doubtful, I shall go to Redruth.'

'I'm not *too* doubtful . . .' she said doubtfully.

'One has to remember that the element of chance probably outweighs any of the things *we*'re weighing up.' It was the sort of remark I found sensible but Elspeth didn't find comforting.

So it was decided. I was accepted by Quetzalcoatl. Within three months. It was now the beginning of July. We had received our invitation from Tom to spend the last week in August at his country house in Kent. If I could persuade Quetzalcoatl to do me in the first week of September, that would leave a month before the University teaching term began. ('Don't worry at all, dear boy.')

I wrote a polite letter about dates to Quetzalcoatl and got a friendly, sensible reply – to my astonishment not from a secretary but from him. Elspeth said:

'You really must stop calling him Quetzalcoatl.'

I had to admit that he didn't look at first sight like a plumed serpent. Yet wasn't the Royal Army Medical Corps' symbol the caduceus, that staff with *two* serpents entwining it?

I could see it wasn't going to be easy.

CHAPTER II

BEGINNING OF A HOUSE-PARTY

The white Mercedes we'd been told about was waiting outside the railway station. A young man in his early thirties jumped out of it as Elspeth and I appeared at the exit.

'Hello! Joe and Elspeth? I'm Tom's secretary.' He held out his hand. 'Jim.'

We looked at him. Veronica had told us he wasn't what she expected; nor was he what we might have expected. First of all we observed that he couldn't be more than five foot three inches in height. He was dressed in a close-fitting denim boiler-suit, and nobody could miss the fact that his body was strong and very well-shaped, alert, springy, filled with energy. We shook hands with him.

'Welcome to Hattersley Hall – when we get there!' He glanced round and gave a merry, ringing laugh. 'Welcome to the railroad station – let me take your baggage!'

While he was stowing away our suitcases he went on. 'Tom's waiting to welcome you. Everyone else is here.' He looked up for a moment. 'Robert and Veronica, whom you know. Burke and Steve, whom you know. And two more couples from Boyce Peterhouse New York – Peter and Merrill, and Jack and Barrie. Quite a party.'

Elspeth and I said something, but we were mainly occupied in looking at each other with a question – Merrill, Barrie, were they men or women? If only Americans wouldn't call their children, particularly their girls, by names which gave no clue to what sex they were! Actually I guessed that Merrill was a woman, because Steve had once naughtily told me that Peter was a former 'secretary' of Tom's who had gone off and got married. (Later it transpired that Barrie was Jack's wife, and a strikingly attractive woman to boot.)

'Ready?' Jim looked up from completing his task. He had a very presentable lively face – wide-open bright blue eyes and a firm laughing mouth. His hair was brown, cut shortish and ruffled.

He held the door of the car for Elspeth to get into the front seat. She told him I would sit there as it would be more comfortable for my hip.

'Your hip?' he said. 'I noticed you were limping. Is it arthritis?'

I said it was.

'Then you've just got to have it replaced. It's a great operation – my aunt had it and she's good as new.'

I was settling into the seat. 'Actually I *am* going to have the operation.'

'Oh really?' As he got in beside me he glanced at me with his bright blue eyes and gave his merry, ringing laugh. 'Then you don't need my advice!'

I said, 'I suppose not, but it's reassuring all the same.'

He started the car.

I went on. 'I'm hoping to go into hospital a few days after we leave here.'

'Oh! That's too bad. You won't be able to come back with us all to New York.'

'To New York?' I said. I didn't know how Elspeth, at the back, was taking this.

'Tom will tell you about it.'

I shifted my head so as to see Elspeth's reflection in the mirror. It showed nothing.

Our journey was under way.

In half an hour's time we arrived at Hattersley Hall. We exclaimed with pleasure as it came into view. It was a beautiful, late eighteenth-century country-house, quite small – smaller than I'd expected. The car crunched over a spacious gravelled yard with a coach-house on the opposite side.

The door was opened by Tom himself, our host waiting to welcome us in person. He was looking plump in casual shirt and trousers, his greying red curly hair freshly clipped very short, his pouting smile composed and smooth.

'How nice to see you both!' He turned momentarily from us. 'Now, Jim! If you'll just take the cases up, then we'll all meet for

441

tea in the drawing-room.' A woman-servant quietly disappeared into a doorway. Tom turned back to us. 'I'm sure you'd like to go up to your room. Jim will go with you.'

We looked around us with wonderment and more pleasure. The house was as beautiful inside as it was outside. We went up a broad eighteenth-century oak staircase, where there were bunches of flowers on the window-sills, to a broad landing with a Persian carpet. It appeared that there were two master bedrooms with their own bathrooms; one occupied by Burke and Steve, the other reserved for our host and his secretary. Robert and Veronica were in a bedroom down a few steps at the end of the landing. The two Boyce Peterhouse couples were installed, no doubt in equal comfort, over in the coach-house.

'Tom apologises,' said Jim, as he showed us into our bedroom, 'for your bathroom being next door' – he was amused – 'instead of *en suite.*'

Left alone we looked round our bedroom with more wonderment and pleasure. It was lofty, and the walls were papered in a pattern of dark, sumptuously-coloured leaves and flowers, a pattern which repeated itself at such long intervals that it was barely discernible. There was the same pattern on the material of the curtains. There were two tall sash windows, the lower halves open to let in the warm, sunny, afternoon air. We went to one of them and looked out. Below us was a part of the garden, lawns divided into compartments by clipped yew hedges twenty feet high.

'Coo, what it must be to be rich!' I whispered.

'Tom says he isn't *really* rich,' she whispered back.

'When did he tell you that?'

'That day when he took me out to lunch to talk about our finances.'

I did know about the occasion, but was distinctly inclined to ignore it.

We turned to look at each other. 'I asked him about it.' She went on whispering. 'He says that in America you don't really count as rich unless you're worth tens of millions. And not *very* rich unless you're worth tens of billions.'

'And he hasn't made *that* much?' I was beginning to laugh.

Elspeth began to laugh. 'But he wishes he had!'

I laughed aloud.

'Sh! . .' Her eyes were sparkling. 'I think Burke just counts as rich.' She paused. 'And Tom intends to behave as if he did!'

'What a man!'

Elspeth went on. 'He told me something else that was interesting.' She became serious. 'Burke once confided to him that rich people only feel really at ease with each other. So I don't suppose she feels really at ease with us.'

'Other things must come into feeling really at ease with someone,' I said stuffily. I was thinking again of what I had imagined to be the deeply ingrained self-consciousness in Burke's nature. Self-consciousness to that painful degree didn't seem to me, as I'd ever observed it, to be affected by whether one was born rich or poor, beautiful or plain, intelligent or not.

Elspeth with her thoughts obviously on a different tack, said: 'She seems to feel really at ease with Steve.' A different sparkle was in her eyes now.

'But I'm sure she could never marry him. That somehow just wouldn't be allowed.'

'Poor Burke! . .'

I laughed. 'I don't know about that!'

We turned back to the room. We tried the bed. We thought how pretty the furniture was, and how alluring the selection of bedside books. On one of the little tables there was a small radio set.

'It's a wonder it isn't a television set,' I said.

'Wouldn't that make it seem like a hotel? . .'

'I wonder if we shall get breakfast in bed.'

'I thought you didn't like having breakfast in bed?' She knew perfectly well.

'No. But I love settling down afterwards . . .'

'Darling,' she whispered, eluding me, 'we *must* go and wash our hands – they'll be waiting for us.'

'They won't.'

'Even if they're not, we ought to go down.' She laughed at me. 'We *are* going to be here for a week.'

'All right . . .'

We went down to the drawing-room. With the exception of Robert and Veronica, everyone was there. It was a spacious

443

room, decorated pleasingly and unobtrusively, leading into a smaller room, furnished as a summer-room with white painted furniture and verdant plants.

In the main room Tom was standing with his back to an empty fireplace.

'What a marvellous house you've found!' Elspeth said to him.

I said, 'I didn't know you could rent such places.'

'I'm glad you like it.' He smiled. 'I looked at several houses that were bigger, but this seemed just right – more intimate . . .' For the latter remark he was addressing himself intimately to Elspeth. Then he turned to me and said in a grander tone of voice: 'Also it means one can dispense with having a butler.'

I was delighted – Tom with a butler!

Elspeth said to him: 'It's all so beautifully done.'

'Ah yes,' said Tom to her. 'It's owned by Lord Reresby Willoughby.'

'I'm surprised he can bear to let it.'

'I'm told,' said Tom, 'his agent chooses tenants with exceptional care. They have to be in *Who's Who* if not *Debrett.*'

I continued to be delighted. How could *he* be in either? I wondered. I was reminded of, Everything in perfect taste . . . But I'd forgotten Tom's basic down-to-earthness –

'All the same,' he was saying, 'Lord Reresby Willoughby locks up his best pictures and his oldest silver.'

We were amused. Tom said to Elspeth: 'Now I must introduce you to those of my house-guests whom you don't already know.' We began to move away from the fireplace.

At that moment a good-looking youngish woman came in carrying a big silver-railed tray with the tea on it. 'This is Mrs Birrell,' he said to us, 'who keeps house for me. In tremendous style.' When she had gone he went on. 'Her husband's my chef. The two of them live here permanently and run the place between them. I always want to call him Augustine, of course – his name's Leonard!' And then his silky smile flickered into a private grin for me. 'Actually Len . . .' Unmistakably alluding to his own lower middle-class origin and mine – I grinned back.

'Is he a good cook?'

'Superb! . .' And then he failed to resist adding, 'He'd *better* be!'

The other guests were helping themselves to tea, and Tom took us to meet his entourage from Boyce Peterhouse New York.

They were agreeable people. Peter, intelligent but to my mind slightly softish – I suspected that he must owe his successful career to Tom's dynamism: Merrill, not especially prepossessing but the reverse of softish, and somewhat over-ready to talk about her five children – to whom Tom was most appropriately godfather. Jack, I took to – one of those men who, one gradually comes to realise, are so complex and interesting that one forgets all about their absence of looks and physical charm: Barrie, very satisfied with him. (According to Steve, who told me later, Jack had risen to the entourage as one of Tom's chief lieutenants, not as his 'secretary'. One was pleased to think that Boyce Peterhouse offered two channels for promotion to higher rank.) We all chatted amiably.

Suddenly above the conversation, was to be heard –

'Jim! Where are Robert and Veronica?'

'I guess they went over to watch the cricket game.'

'They're *missing their tea*!'

I tried to catch Steve's eye – he was sitting on a sofa with Burke. Fortunately I failed. I went on talking to Jack.

I gathered that in the previous three weeks the party had included other entouragistes from Boyce Peterhouse New York. It seemed that we, in the final week, when old friends from England had been summoned, represented the pick, the nearest and dearest of the bunch. I have to say that our being there at all was sheerly a manifestation of Tom's personal imperialism. In advance the party had provoked Robert and me to malicious comment. Yet now that we actually were all here, I felt that we were going to enjoy ourselves.

There was a mild bustling disturbance in the company. It was Tom, followed by Jim, leaving for the kitchen, there to discuss with Len the evening meal – we subsequently learnt it was one of the most solemn moments of the day. As the time was six o'clock, most of us promptly went up to our rooms to listen to the BBC News. (In a disgraceful way most of the nation was following salacious references to a leading politician being accused of conspiring to have a male model removed from the scene.)

Afterwards we bathed and changed – our clothes had been laid out for us with exemplary neatness.

When we were coming downstairs again, we met Jim, still in his boiler-suit, running upstairs. He stopped, looking up at us, his blue eyes bright with fun –

'How is it?'

'I think we're going to like it,' I said.

'Don't you think it's real Agatha Christie?'

'I hope not.'

'*How do you know?*' Before we could reply he was on his way upstairs again, leaving a merry, ringing laugh to float down on the air.

The door of the master-bedroom shut. I whispered to Elspeth:

'Do you think he's always in the manic phase?'

She looked amused. 'I like him.'

'So do I.'

We found Tom already down, ready to make the first drinks for his guests with his own hands. The woman-servant we'd seen before, looking like a pleasant middle-aged woman from the village, stood discreetly by while her master performed. Tom handed Elspeth a gin-and-tonic.

'I do hope you'll like a slice of lime in it. We tend to have lime, here; but Josephine will gladly change it for a slice of lemon if you prefer it.'

'I'm sure I shall like lime,' said Elspeth, who had never had lime in it other than when she had been in the USA.

Tom smiled encouragingly at her. He made a drink for me and then, as we were the first down, began a private conversation.

'I hear you've been seeing Stewart.'

I said, 'It doesn't take news long to get around.'

'I make it my business.' He smiled at Elspeth as if the remark were purely social. Purely social, my foot! It contained an element of pure menace. He said to Elspeth and me jointly, 'What did you think of him?'

'Very impressed,' said I.

'And you, my dear?' He made it clear that it was Elspeth's opinion that really mattered to him.

'I agree with Joe.' I wondered if she had intimations of what was going on – it sounded as if she had.

'Furthermore we like him,' I said, 'and I think he likes us.'

'He does like you.' Tom nodded his head grandly. 'I think Stewart will serve you well.'

The conversation was ended by the appearance of Robert and Veronica. Tom turned his attention to Veronica. Robert grinned at me. Tom made a drink for Veronica. Scotch-and-soda.

'Did you enjoy the cricket?' he said to her.

'Yes, Tom.'

'I didn't know *you* were so interested in the game.' He was implying that she was putting up with it because Robert wanted to watch it.

'I don't know what makes you think that, Tom. I was practically brought up on it.' She laughed. 'Ho-ho-ho!'

Tom was taken aback.

'A long time ago,' said Veronica, 'one of my brothers nearly got into the England side.'

'Really, really . . .' Tom's smile was distinctly uncomfortable. 'I hope our local team gave you an enjoyable performance. I should have thought, myself, they were bloody incompetent.' (The local cricket-ground adjoined the garden of the Hall.)

'We enjoyed every minute of it, didn't we, Robert?'

At the cost of missing their tea! I thought. Robert said with lofty amusement:

'It was very nice. Very nice . . .'

More people came into the room, the Boyce Peterhouse contingent, Steve and Burke.

'Now Jim! I think you might take over getting Josephine orders for drinks.'

Veronica, standing beside me, said *sotto voce*: 'What do you think of Jim? I should think he's a little sex-pot, wouldn't you?'

She was waiting for a reply, her narrow grey eyes sparkling with stern amusement. I looked round for help. Making a move towards the small garden-room, I said, 'I don't know.' I was hoping that everybody else would now be out of earshot.

'You must know,' said Veronica.

My technique of saying this was a back-of-a-postcard expression such as I'd never use entirely failed me. Feebly I said: 'Certainly he's got a lot of energy.'

'Energy for everybody, *I* should say. Ho-ho-ho!'

'I should think Tom absorbs quite a lot of it in one way or another.' I was trying to get the conversation on to a broader footing.

Veronica thought about it.

En passant it occurred to me that Jim, with the example of Peter and others before him, must be far from oblivious to the good that Tom's dynamism could do his career in the firm of Boyce Peterhouse New York. (And for my money, Jim was a better man than Peter.) Harking back to the long distant past . . . Tom had done pretty well, for those days, by Steve.

Veronica said: 'Do you think that Jim will go off and get married?'

'I shouldn't be at all surprised, in fact I should think it very likely.'

'Wretched Tom . . .'

We contemplated the fortune of the unhappy man who desired only heterosexual young men. Robert and I had sometimes talked about it, but only on the premise that most of what was to be said about it had already been said by Proust.

Yet there wasn't in *A La Recherche* a character quite like Tom. Through personal magnetism and personal dynamism Tom had managed to live a long life – next month he'd be sixty-seven – without ever lacking the attendance of a clever, personable young man drawn from the same circle in society as himself. One of them had followed another. (To end up with Jim seemed to me pretty triumphant.) When their heterosexuality got the better of them and they went off and got married, Tom's personal imperialism came into force, and they found themselves joining the entourage – themselves, their wives, their children!

Robert pointed out that members of Tom's entourage didn't put up much of a fight against remaining thus. When Tom died he would be leaving a lot of money, a lot of money! He wasn't going to leave it to any of his family, and he wasn't going to leave it to any institution. The future of the special entouragistes was golden – Tom said so, to Robert. Robert and I speculated on how much some of them might get. But alas! alas! not Steve. Steve had got away from Tom when Tom left for the USA – just at the time when Tom took off on his flight to riches. Poor old Steve! . . Steve had lost his chance – Tom said so, to Robert.

I said to Veronica: 'Given the cards Fate dealt him – and some of them were pretty bum cards – Tom has played his hand jolly well. When you come to think of it, consummately!'

Veronica said, 'I suppose he has.'

'That sounds a bit too grudging. He's a very intelligent, gifted man, you know.'

Veronica thought about it. While she was thinking, a gong sounded softly. Tom announced that it was time for us to go into dinner.

On the way to the dining-room we passed one of the small wonders of the house – an alcove-room turned into a library. As we went by I glanced round the shelves and saw book after book that I should like to read. (We discovered later that they'd been assembled not by Lord Reresby Willoughby but by the Birrells.)

We sat down to dinner at a long Regency table on which stood two handsome Sheffield plate candelabra, the candles burning stilly in the faded summer light. Tom sat at the head of the table; on his right, the first evening, Burke, and on his left Veronica.

The serving of the dinner – in the absence of a butler! – was overseen by Len in person. It had better be superb – it *was*. The voice of our host acquired a purring sound. I was too far away to hear what he was saying to the two women, but it was clear from the soapy, pop-eyed looks he was giving them that he was making up to them. I had a presentiment that during the week we were going to see a fair amount of Tom's making up to the women members of the party – suborning *them* into his personal empire while he had the chance.

I imagined Veronica being admired for being so clever and so effective. I thought with distaste of the evening when Elspeth would be sitting up there, being admired for being so sympathetic and so *wise*, my dear . . . I wondered what Tom was admiring in Burke. Her riches, I hoped; her artistic flair in the theatre; her desire to do good with her riches – and I wondered what he was saying to her about Steve. From their facial expressions I could see that, whatever he was saying, both women were lapping it up as readily as the superb dinner, at that stage Romney lamb fresh from the Marshes. Especially the candle-light suited Burke: her pale complexion looked warmer and her black eyes gleamed more softly, as did the square-cut

449

emerald. And Veronica looked more blooming, more at ease: I saw Robert eyeing her from his end of the table, where Jim presided.

If I knew anything about it, Tom's ploy with Burke – though of course the words would never be spoken – would be to the effect that 'We rich people, my dear, *know* each other . . .' If it hadn't been that she was upper class in origin and Tom lower middle class, she Irish in origin and he Jewish (a standard New York juxtaposition), I might have found it easier to judge how he was faring – or what Burke happened to be thinking about it. The fact that Burke's inherited riches were doubtless by several orders of magnitude greater than those Tom had made for himself – according to him, her grandfather had built railroads, 'relatively small railroads, I believe' – only made the ploy more appealing to contemplate.

I was always entertained by the spectacle of rich people together. The quotation from Scott Fitzgerald about the rich being 'different' struck me as wrong. All human beings, rich or poor, are made of the same stuff. On the other hand, in the way the very rich behave, the way they comport themselves . . . there, there is the difference. A slight air of apartness, of truly belonging elsewhere than with the not-rich, their antennae sensitised to recognise each other; of feeling really at ease only with each other, (I recalled Tom's transmission of Burke's confidences to Elspeth). Seeing them, the very rich, pair off with each other in America was, I thought, very like seeing members of the high upper class pair off with each other in England – or, come to that, members of the Party hierarchy's top layers in the Soviet Union. As long as that went on, the human comedy was in no danger of petering out – nor was the grip of people who were in power.

Meanwhile I was trying to fend off questions from Merrill about my views on Northern Ireland, needling questions. (Was she, too, Irish in origin?) As it happened I knew something about Northern Ireland, through belonging to an independent association of people of good-will, mostly Irish in origin though I was not, which devoted its energies to searching for any moves whatsoever that might be made towards composing the conflict. Regrettably I found the current views of many Irish-Americans

450

as ignorant as they were vociferous: they didn't want to *listen* to anybody – Merrill didn't want to listen to me, really – and that puzzled me. I had my work cut out to hold my tongue. I stalled. And Merrill was not the woman to take stall for an answer. The conversation became tense.

I was saved by Steve, who was sitting next to me. (There were two spare men, and Steve had found himself next to Jim, with whom he appeared to be getting on hilariously.)

'Do we overhear the makings of an Agatha Christie situation?' Steve enquired. (A merry, ringing laugh from his left.)

Nothing I might have said or not said about Ireland could have had the same effect. Giving them her most stunning high-and-mighty glance, Merrill ostentatiously turned the other way and started to talk to Jack. Horrid woman!

Steve gave his mock-rueful smile, which was patently appreciated by Jim.

I was saved.

'Quite a party,' I said to Jim.

'*I* said it first!' A merry, ringing laugh again.

CHAPTER III

END OF A HOUSE-PARTY

T he days passed very swiftly. The weather was fine and I should have been content to do nothing but hang about in the garden – reading (I was on the panel of judges for a book prize); writing (I had to do a review); or even thinking . . . The garden, being divided into compartments by the tall yew hedges, was made for such pursuits; or rather, it would have been made for them if Tom had not seen fit to revive a tennis court in one of the compartments, install a croquet lawn in another, and designate a third place where we could play a sort of *boules* with stainless steel balls.

Tom didn't exactly command, but we found ourselves kept on the move by *dromophilia* most of the time. There were some very pretty walks in the countryside, trips by car to local places of literary interest. One evening – the evening being on Len's day off – we were transported to a very grand country restaurant. Another evening we went to a nearby town to a repertory theatre, one of the recent generation of repertory theatres named after celebrated actors and actresses, and created, when the old reps were dying out, to put on interesting and mildly superior lists of plays. (Steve had once directed a play in one of them.)

Robert discovered urgent affairs which called him up to London for a couple of days. Nobody was less given, I thought, to being a captive, least of all a captive kept whizzing about like a bluebottle by Tom.

But then I thought that perhaps I was being unfair to him. I had a feeling that this might be a week when he went down to see Annette – he'd never tell anybody about that. And I wondered how her treatment for diabetes was going. (He'd never mentioned it from that day to this.) I thought they would probably be finding it difficult to treat her for diabetes on top of all the other treatments. Robert must be more worried than ever before.

From time to time I myself managed to escape the company for a few hours at least. Along one of the boundaries of the garden there ran a delightful brook, beside which I could lie peacefully in my swimming-trunks, even if the water was too shallow to swim in. Also there was a small secluded pond, too stagnant to swim in, at the edge of which there was a sweet little tumbledown pavilion. It was a few days before my hiding-places were discovered.

One afternoon, a 'free' afternoon before we all were due to dine at the country restaurant, I was lying reading by the brook when Burke came upon me.

'I'm discovered!'

She laughed. 'I knew where you were. We all know where you are.' She stood before me, looking small and trim in carmine slacks and a multicoloured top – very elegant, very American.

'Don't get up! . .'

I was by now standing up, facing her. She wavered.

I said, 'Let's both sit down!'

'Intelligent proposition.' She smiled, with a piquantly stylised turn of the head.

We both sat down on the grass.

'I wanted to talk with you, Joe.'

The unease, the jumpiness I had noticed the first time we met, were back in force.

'Yes,' I said as gently as I could.

She began.

'I love England so much, Joe. I have so many friends here . . . I've already stayed beyond my schedule. I really have to get back – for my theatre. I stayed on to come to this party of Tom's, but I can't stay any longer. I just have to get back to New York as soon as the party's over. You know?'

I said – feeling slightly jumpy myself – that it had been fun having her here. I hated that word 'fun' as we all used it – it always sounded to me vulgar and trivial.

'It's been fun, being here.' She paused an instant, flickeringly. Then: 'It's been fun, having Steve around.' The more nervous she was, the more she sounded like an actress.

Steve was what she was wanting to talk about.

I said: 'I can believe that.'

'I know you can. Joe, I've had more fun with Steve around than I'd have imagined possible.'

Irrelevantly I was visited by the image of Steve around with her at grand ambassadorial parties up in Regent's Park. Steve! . . Delightful image.

I dismissed the image and looked at her.

'Not just fun.' She glanced at me and then away. 'What I really mean,' she said, 'is happiness.'

I said, 'Steve's a very easy person to feel . . . at ease with.'

'How right that is! How well you know him!'

I wondered if perhaps I was beginning to know her, too. I said quietly:

'Long may the happiness last!'

Too quick on her cue – *'Quien sabe?'*

I said, 'I think you probably know . . .' As I watched her I thought I saw for the first time a faint colour come into her pale complexion – I might have imagined it. Her eyes were very bright.

We stopped talking. Only the brook went on making its watery noise on the pebbles.

Her mood changed. As if getting down to business, she said:

'I suppose you know Tom suggested I ask Steve to come back to New York with me?'

'I guessed.' I grinned.

She laughed with amusement. '*I* don't collect scads of people to take around with me.'

I laughed too.

'There's a lot of things for Steve to do, *independently*, in New York. In my theatre. He was into children's theatre in your country five years back. You know?'

I nodded my head as if I did know.

There was another pause.

'What is the trouble, then?' I asked.

'No trouble. It's just Steve seems uncertain.'

'Do you want me to speak to him?' The minute I'd said it I realised it was stupidly crude.

'No, no.'

'I didn't mean that –

She interrupted me, not worried by my gaffe. 'It's just he's uncertain of himself.'

I said, 'He always has needed someone at hand.'

'That's right. But I want him to understand I'm offering him something independent. Work in my theatre.' She looked at me directly. 'I know he can do it. You know?'

I looked directly back at her, sitting there in her carmine slacks, pale-complexioned, brightly black-eyed. A clever woman, rich and influential no doubt; and a very nice, good woman. I wanted her to be happy.

'I know he's going to talk with you about it,' she said.

'Tom has talked to him?'

We exchanged a glance, agreed in making no comment on Tom's interventions.

'That's all,' she said, and got up. 'I'm grateful to you for this...' And then suddenly, surprisingly, as if her self-consciousness and diffidence had suddenly melted, she said, 'I like you, Joe.'

Before I had time to find a reply she was walking away.

I lay back on the ground and stayed there for a while.

I began to think about the pursuit of happiness. Was ever a pursuit more ill-advised? Happiness is one of the random gifts of Fate: you just happen to find you *are* happy . . . And that's all. It can't be predicted or commanded or caught – pursuing it is about as well-advised as pursuing the end of the rainbow. The most you can do is put yourself in a position where it seems to you a shade more likely that you'll happen to find you're happy. I thought Burke would probably agree with me.

I remained by the brook, expecting Steve to put in an appearance. He didn't.

Finally I went up to our room to change for the evening's expedition. Elspeth was already there. Suddenly there was a knock on the door. Saying, 'What on earth?' I went to open it.

'It's me, Veronica. Can I come in?'

I opened the door and she came in.

'I'm sorry to disturb you just when you're going to change.' She looked at us and we saw that her eyes were darting with light.

'I'm spitting mad!' she cried. 'I can't contain myself. I've got to tell somebody. Positively spitting!'

I moved a chair for her to sit down. She refused it. The colour in her cheeks was brilliant.

'Tom,' she said. 'What do you think Tom's said to me.'

Elspeth and I sat down side by side on the bed.

'He's given me his advice. He thinks Robert ought to marry me. His advice to me is to threaten Robert, that if he doesn't get a divorce I'll leave him. Can you believe it?'

Elspeth and I glanced at each other. I said, 'I'm afraid I can.'

'Did you ever hear such ridiculous advice? The man's a fool!'

'No, he's not a fool,' I murmured.

'*I* think he is. Do you know any advice less likely to achieve the desired result?' She looked at us furiously. 'I know you think I don't know Robert as well as you do, as well as Tom does. Perhaps I don't. You've known him for more than forty years. But in two years I've learnt *this* – I've never met a man less susceptible to blackmail. He'd positively hate it. And he'd hate *me.*'

We were silent in agreement.

'Do you wonder I'm spitting mad?'

'*I* don't,' said Elspeth.

There was a pause.

'I hope to God he doesn't hint something of the kind to Robert.'

I said, 'I don't suppose he will.' Knowing Tom's mania for interfering, I didn't feel that the remark carried unlimited conviction.

'I told him pretty forcibly not to,' Veronica said. 'He's a monster!'

'No,' I said, hoping to calm her down. I smiled at her. 'You could say he's a Force of Nature. You have to take him as he comes.'

'*You* can say that!' She looked at Elspeth as well as me. 'He hasn't tried to break up you two.' She laughed harshly. 'Yet!'

I said, 'In a way he's seeing it from your point of view. He knows you want Robert to marry you. And he thinks that's a good thing – just as we all do. So he goes all-out for the desired result.'

456

Veronica paused to think about it.

I went on. 'He's rash, impetuous. What his mother used to call "mad-headed". He probably thought he was doing his best for you.' Knowing Tom's natural capacity for breaking things up, I didn't feel that this remark carried unlimited conviction, either.

Veronica sat down on the chair.

'The important thing now,' she said, 'is to make sure not a word of this reaches Robert's ears.' She was struck by a fresh idea. 'It's interesting – Tom took the opportunity to do this while Robert's away. I hope you noticed that.'

I said, 'I'm not so sure he wouldn't have done it while Robert was here, if Robert hadn't gone away.'

'Stop! You'll make me spit again.'

I laughed. 'I don't want to make you do that, Veronica.'

Veronica showed signs of grinning. 'I feel a bit better now . . . Good God, look at the time! We've all got to change.' She stood up. 'Thank you, both of you!' And she went quickly to the door.

When the door shut behind her, Elspeth and I looked at each other in consternation, but there was no time for discussion. We began changing our clothes. At one stage in it Elspeth said:

'Do you think Robert will get a divorce?'

I shook my head. 'I don't really think so.'

A little later Elspeth said:

'If Annette were to die, do you think Robert would marry Veronica?'

I felt I was not giving the expected answer – I said, 'I haven't the faintest idea.'

After that we completed our changing and went downstairs to join the party for the restaurant.

I found myself sitting next to Tom in the back of the white Mercedes. He was not in silky, soapy mood: on the contrary, irascibility was unconcealed. His face looked red and puffy. I thought it must be the after-effects of a row with Veronica.

I was wrong. He said bullyingly:

'Have you been talking to Steve?'

I said No.

'I suppose you heard Burke's offered to take him back with her to New York?'

457

I said Yes.

'I hope he won't be such a fool as to turn it down.'

The brutal tone of voice made me look again at him. His eyes were glaring.

I said peaceably, 'I don't think he will.'

'You know Burke means to keep him? *And* he'll have a job in her theatre. *For as long as he wants!*' Tom's voice rose, as at the thought of that length of time.

'That sounds good.'

Tom hadn't finished. '*And,* he'll have *me* to take care of his future.'

I was silent, digesting that information.

'Jim! You should have turned left there.'

There ensued an altercation about the A this and the A that. Jim was obviously on the right road. I was glad when the journey was over.

It was the following afternoon when Steve approached me. I had changed my site to the little pavilion beside the pond. The bushes around it were undisturbed by the breeze, and there were a few leaves floating on the water. I looked up – Steve was carrying a copy of *Happier Days*, one of the two "house copies", as Tom called them. He settled down beside me. I put down the book I was reading.

'I've just finished this,' he said. 'It's terribly good.'

I laughed.

'Honestly, Joe, it is.'

I didn't propose to renew my paranoiac argument about there being only ten other people who thought so.

He opened the book and began to laugh. 'This scene is terribly funny.' It was one of the scenes in which a patient came to ask the GP's advice about a quaint intimate difficulty, quaint, to say the least of it. The doctor told him not to worry – it happened to other men . . . Steve finished reading the scene again. Then he said:

'I think the doctor and the girl are terribly good.'

'I'm quite pleased about that.'

Steve said, 'What does Elspeth say about it? The doctor's obviously you.'

'She expressed general approval of the book.'

'Wasn't she embarrassed?'

I said, 'I think – I hope, she puts art before embarrassment. She tries to, I know.'

'What a marvellous wife!'

'You can say that again!' I thought about her. 'She was my greatest stroke of good fortune.'

We were silent for a moment. I contemplated the still reflection of the clouds in the water.

Steve said:

'Joe, what am I to do about New York?'

I said, 'So far I've only heard Burke's side of it. And Tom's.'

'And Tom's!' He laughed. 'Can I bear being drawn into . . . the circle?'

I said, 'I take it you've realised there are certain practical advantages in being drawn into the circle, as you call it.'

'What?'

'One day Tom's going to leave a lot of money, certain members of the circle are going to do pretty well. He's said as much, to Robert.'

'*Joe*! . .'

I grinned at him – innocently he had *not* realised it. 'It's something to be taken account of,' I said.

Steve said, 'You may not understand it, Joe – one of the reasons for going to New York is that I should have *work* . . . Having work is more important to me than you think.'

I nodded my head to indicate my being convinced.

'The other reason is Burke, of course. Joe' – he looked me in the eye – 'Joe, I'm *devoted* to her.'

'Yes,' I said, respecting his manifest struggle against the flaw of sounding unconvincing. He actually was telling the truth, as he had been over wanting work in the theatre – and also over not having realised that if he went to live in New York some of Tom's money might ultimately come his way.

Suddenly he said, 'I envy you being settled, here.'

I could have made some horrid quip about being settled in failure, but I didn't. Anyway he was probably thinking about Elspeth. I said:

'Yes.'

We were both thoughtful. Finally he stood up.

'You're waiting to go on reading,' he said. He went away.

And so we came to the last evening.

Tom saw to it that this last dinner was the most superb of all. We dined a little later than usual, and there was in the atmosphere that warmth of mutual affection, bonhomie, high spirits at prospective liberation, which characterises the end of a school term. We really did all like each other. (In fact Tom's personal empire comprised likeable people – with the exception of Merrill!) The house-party had been a success.

Towards the end of the meal we started to drink toasts. Tom, sitting at the head of the table, had Burke on his right and Elspeth on his left. (Veronica had been demoted.) Tom, I could see from his gestures, was taking the last opportunity to butter up Elspeth. Robert was now with us again, and Veronica had broken the rules of etiquette by planting herself determinedly next to him. The contingent from Boyce Peterhouse were doing well on the alcohol. Jim had the expression of a man whose staff-work has come off perfectly. We were all happy.

The last of the toasts was of course kept for Tom. We all drank to him with feeling.

And Tom replied:

'There's nothing more heart-warming than to be surrounded by one's friends. I'm deeply honoured by you all, for coming. And I'm deeply grateful . . .'

We made appreciative murmurings. He went on.

'My friends from New York have no option in going back to New York – they've got to get back to Boyce Peterhouse.' He smiled dominatingly at them. 'And I can tell you now that Steve is going to come with Burke.'

There was modest hand-clapping.

'I know that Robert is in the throes of important discussions with his publisher about a new book.' (Nobody else knew.) 'And I know that Joe is going into hospital quite soon. But I make them this offer . . .' He smiled seductively at us. 'Just for the hell of it – a quick return trip to New York, out by one Concorde and back by the next Concorde. Come back with us! Just for the hell of it.' His smiling went on. 'And to give me pleasure.'

Elspeth and I were glancing at each other: so were Robert and Veronica.

Tom said, 'Jim has already made our reservations for the day after tomorrow. If you, Robert and Veronica and Joe and Elspeth, think it's fun, Jim will get reservations for you – we know how to do these things. How do you feel about it?'

In exchanging glances I had observed that Elspeth's was totally non-committal. Robert appeared to be shaking his head.

'Just let Jim know first thing in the morning.'

There were encouraging sounds from the others. 'Do come!' and '*All* go to New York.'

I imagined that Concorde flights were about three days apart. It would be nice to see New York again. Money no object!

The dinner-party ended with warmth, bonhomie – and afterwards, slight signs of drama.

When Elspeth and I got to our room, our room with the dark leaves and flowers on the wallpaper endlessly entwined, I said:

'Well, what about it?'

Elspeth shrugged her shoulders.

'Shall we go?' I said. 'We can just make it before I go into hospital.'

'You can go, if you like. I shan't.'

I was surprised by the remark and the tone of voice in which she made it. I said: 'I shouldn't go without you.'

'I don't see why not.' She was making preparations for going to bed, not looking at me.

I drew back. 'I suppose it wouldn't be a very good idea to cross the Atlantic twice in the week before I go into hospital.'

'I should have thought it would be a very bad idea.'

There was a silence. A long silence. I was sitting on the bed, watching her.

'What's the matter, my darling?'

She said, 'What do you mean, what's the matter?'

'You seem . . .'

She was putting on her dressing-gown. 'Oh.'

I stood up and went towards her. 'What *is* the matter, my darling?'

'I've got a headache.' She was not looking at me.

I stepped backwards. 'I'm sorry.'

She fastened the dressing-gown and went out of the room.

I told myself it must be the effects of alcohol. I began to make my own preparations for going to bed.

CHAPTER IV

'THERE MUST HAVE BEEN SOMEONE'

Afterwards I couldn't think how I'd missed something seriously the matter with Elspeth. The following day we were occupied with travelling back to London, and then, as Viola was away, with getting the flat into working-order again.

Elspeth was distant, tired, unwell.

'What's the matter, my darling?'

In a slow, uninflected tone of voice, 'Nothing.'

The day after that was the day when Tom and his entourage, an entourage augmented by Steve and Burke, took off in the Concorde. Robert and Veronica had turned down Tom's invitation. (Veronica had privately told me she was still spitting mad.) Elspeth went back to work. It would have been exciting to see New York again, but foolish for me to go, on the brink of going into hospital for a major operation.

Was Elspeth desperately worried about the operation? I asked myself. How could she be anything else?

At the height of insensitiveness I accepted an invitation from one of my friends to spend the evening with him at his club, leaving Elspeth to come home from work and spend the evening alone.

At least, I thought when I was letting myself into the flat, I was not over-late coming home. The flat was in darkness. Elspeth had gone to bed. The flat was silent. I crept about as quietly as possible and finally opened the door of her room.

I could tell in the darkness that she was awake.

She was lying on her side, facing outwards, and I knelt beside the bed and kissed her.

Her face was wet, wet with tears.

'My darling, what *is* the matter?'

463

She began to sob.

'You *must* tell me.' I felt a terrible apprehension.

She shook her head.

I began to stoke her forehead and her hair, waiting for the sobs to quieten. At last I said, 'Now? . .'

The bedside clock was ticking. She said:

'Tom told me . . . you didn't invent it.' She burst into tears again. 'There *was* someone . . .'

I suddenly felt rage, fear, despair. 'No!' I cried.

She was weeping without restraint. I said:

'*It isn't true*! My darling, it isn't true! . . He was lying.' I couldn't believe it. 'Did he actually say that? In those words? Or did he somehow make you believe it, by one of his innuendoes?'

She did not answer.

I went on. I scarcely knew what I was saying. 'How could Tom know, anyway? He wasn't even in the country!'

Between sobs she said:

'He got it from Steve – Tom said Steve . . . thought there was someone.'

'*Steve*!' I was appalled. 'Steve couldn't have said that. He knows there wasn't.'

Elspeth said nothing.

'Tom could make anything sound true,' I said. 'But Steve wouldn't lie about a thing like that. Steve will tell you. Steve will tell you it was Tom's idea.'

I suddenly realised that Steve was gone, not there to tell her. And Tom was gone, so I couldn't beat the destructive lights out of him. 'This is horrible!'

She moved her forehead away from my touch.

'Robert knows I invented it,' I said. 'He will tell you.'

'Everyone who reads the book thinks there *was* someone.'

The book. My novel! I couldn't speak.

'Everyone thinks it rings true,' she said.

Art must ring true or it's wasted. 'They don't,' I cried. 'They can't.'

'There must have been someone . . .'

'There *wasn't*!' Suddenly I found myself bursting into tears. I touched my forehead against her. 'There wasn't anyone. There

464

never has been anyone. Since I married you I've never been in love with anyone but you.'

She sobbed uncontrollably. So did I. 'You're my only love,' I cried. 'I couldn't live without you. You're *my life*!'

For a long time we remained still, silent, waiting for the tension to go. I was still kneeling down beside her. I kissed her on the lips: she allowed me to kiss her. Could this ever be repaired? I was wondering, bereft of confidence. I had never been in love with anyone but her since I married her. It was a nightmare sort of night. I couldn't possibly lose her trust, her love . . . She *was* my life.

And so it went on.

Elspeth was the first to recover a little. She said:

'You'd better get off your knees, my darling. They'll be terribly stiff in the morning. And it isn't good for your hip, either.'

I said, 'I'll come to bed.'

She didn't move.

HOW CAN PEOPLE SAY SUCH THINGS?

I thought Elspeth had had a restless night: I knew I had. We sat down to breakfast, at the Breakfast-Bar, with perfunctory exchanges of conversation that might have passed between strangers – only we weren't strangers: we kept eyeing each other.

I could think of nothing more to say than I had said the night before.

I had cooked the breakfast: Elspeth was dressed, ready to go out to work. A radio voice was reading us the News above the whirring of the extractor-fan – something about the Prime Minister deciding to call or not to call a General Election. Between our places lay a picture postcard just arrived from Viola.

What else could I say? What could I do? I realised that I had no idea what Elspeth was thinking – we *were* strangers . . .

'Was that a fresh packet of bacon you opened?'

'Yes. I'm sorry it's so salty.'

'Yes.'

'Sainsbury's.'

For a minute or so we both self-consciously listened to the News. We heard tips on which horses to back in today's races.

'My darling,' I began.

'Yes?'

I hadn't prepared what to say next. I said, 'I hadn't thought what I was going to say.'

'Is there anything *to* say?'

We looked at each other.

'I suppose,' she said, 'it's for *me* to think . . .'

'My love.' I took hold of her hand, on the Breakfast-Bar. She withdrew it, to get on with her breakfast. Then she offered her hand back again.

'My love,' I said again.

The radio told us the time. 'I must go,' she said. 'I'm going to be late for the office and I wanted to be early.' She finished her breakfast.

The telephone rang. It was on the wall beside the door. As I stretched out my arm, I caught Elspeth's glance – we knew it was going to be bad news.

It was the Matron of the convalescent home, ringing to say that the doctor had been to see my mother yesterday and had arranged for her to be transferred to hospital today, in fact now.

'Is she worse?' I was holding the receiver where Elspeth could catch what we were saying.

'Not really, Mr Lunn. But the doctor thought she needed more care than we're able to give her here. It's a new hospital with all the latest things. He didn't know till this morning if he'd be able to get her in. It's only temporary. I'll give you the address and the 'phone number.'

Elspeth handed me a pencil and a slip of paper. I wrote.

'I know she'll be all right, Mr Lunn. We're only sorry to lose her for the time being as a patient here.'

'That's kind of you.'

The conversation ended. 'So,' I said. Elspeth waited. 'I'll go straight down and see her this afternoon.' I'd been intending to go down and see her tomorrow, as it was her birthday.

'Yes, of course.'

A few minutes later I was seeing Elspeth off to work. I held the door of the flat open for her. She hesitated, wanting to say something – not, I knew, about my mother. She said:

'I don't want you to say anything to Robert.'

'All right.'

We kissed each other dryly on the lips. I caught hold of her hand. I simply had to ask her –

'Do you want me *not* to say anything to him because you take *my* word; or only because it would embarrass you too much, in any case?'

She turned back and looked at me.

'I don't know.'

I said nothing. She took her hand from mine. 'I really must go, darling.'

467

At that she went towards the lift, and I waved to her – it was an old-fashioned lift with side-panels of bevelled glass – as it took her down.

Somehow the hours passed till it was time to go and see my mother. My sister had sent me a cheque to buy flowers for my mother's birthday. At Victoria I decided to spend it all on bunches of freesias. (Freesias seemed to be on the flower-stalls all the year round, nowadays – those stunted chrysanthemums in pots actually were there all the year round.) The train, in mid-afternoon, was empty. I tried to read.

My taxi-driver from the station knew the hospital-entrance which was nearest to the ward I wanted. It was a side-entrance. As I went through it I saw that it was the entrance for the mortuary. Really! . .

The hospital was brand-new, mostly only one storey high and consequently extensive. I made my way along a series of well-labelled corridors, some of them having full-length windows opening on to squares of grass. When I reached my mother's ward I was astonished. Relatively small and divided into compartments like an open-plan office, it was close-carpeted everywhere in a pleasing tobacco-colour; the wood of the new furniture was light maple-coloured; the chromium-plated fittings sparkled freshly; and the air-conditioning was above reproach. There were old people sitting around, quietly; nurses, subduedly busy, moving to and fro. A nurse from the reception showed me where my mother was, in a partially glassed-off compartment by herself.

'How is she?'

'She's taken the move very well. We've just given her some treatment, you may find her a bit sleepy. Otherwise she's quite good – we think she's remarkable for her age.'

My mother was dozing. She was lying on a couple of high pillows and not leaning askew. The nurse roused her.

'Who is it? My son?' She opened her eyes. 'Is that you?'

'Yes, it's Joe.' I kissed her on the forehead as usual. 'I've come to see you.'

'I'm glad you've come.'

'I thought I'd come and see you straight away, in your new place. How do you find it?'

468

The question seemed to rouse her. 'Comfortable.'

I pulled up a chair and sat down close to her. 'It seems a super hospital to me.'

She spoke muzzily. 'They didn't seem to be able to get that sore place on my back better. And they weren't very good at dressing my breast, either.' She paused. 'I suppose they were doing their best.'

'I think it'll be much better here.'

'Time will tell that.'

'I'm sure it will.'

'Possibly.'

'And I shall keep on coming to see you.'

There was another pause. She closed her eyes.

I said, 'Good gracious! I've forgotten your flowers. It's your birthday tomorrow and I've brought you a great bunch of flowers from my sister.'

'What's that, flowers?'

'I've brought you some. They're from your daughter – it's your birthday tomorrow. They're from *her* – for your birthday.'

'What sort of flowers?'

'Freesias.'

'My favourite flowers.'

'That's why I chose them.'

I got up and carried them across from a small table I'd put them on, by the door. I undid the paper and held the flowers close to her nose. She sniffed them slowly and deeply.

'What a glorious smell!' She sniffed again. 'Hold them there a bit longer, my dear!'

I held them there.

'That's all right, now.' Then she said, 'Please write and thank her for them. She knows I can't write. Tell her how much I enjoyed them!'

'We'll put them beside the bed and you'll be able to smell them from where you are.' (There were half a dozen bunches of them.)

On the window-sill there was an empty vase, waiting. (The hospital that had everything!) I filled the vase from the tap over a wash-basin and dried the bottom of it with a paper towel. I went back to the bedside and put the flowers on the locker.

My mother said, 'I'm thirsty. Have they left me a drink?'

There was the usual plastic drinking-cup with serrated spout on the bedside table. I said, 'I'll give you a drink.'

I held the cup for her and she tried to grasp it with her arthritic hands. 'There you are,' I said. She clutched at the cup strongly as I tried to guide it.

'You'd make a good nurse.'

'You've told me that before.' I laughed.

'I'll tell it you again.'

I wondered how often that would be.

The drinking was over and I sat down. There was a long silence. I wondered if she was asleep.

'I can smell those freesias from here.'

'I'm glad – that's what I hoped.'

'They smell glorious.'

And then she said:

'If *only* I could have a peep at them! Just one little peep.'

I could say nothing. I suddenly recalled the moment when they took the bandages off my own eye – the impenetrable milky veil, gone. The pink cheek of the nurse, the darkness of her eye, the white oblong of her cap – an unforgettable *sight* . . .

'Oh well, it's not to be,' said my mother.

I nodded my head in agreement, acceptance. My mother was quiet again.

At last I was beginning to think it was time for me to leave when a nurse came in, wanting to give my mother some sort of attention. I said, 'I'll go now.'

I stood up and said goodbye to my mother, touched her forehead, and told her I'd come again. 'It's your birthday, tomorrow,' I said. 'Here's a big kiss for your birthday.' How could I wish her many returns, or even a happy birthday? I kissed her forehead.

To the nurse I said, 'Perhaps I might see the Sister before I go?'

She said the Sister was not available. 'You'll find the Charge Nurse in his office, just next to the reception.'

I went to the office. The door was open and a man in a white coat was sitting at the table, writing. He asked me to come in and sit down, and he went on writing.

I waited for him. He was a toughish-looking man, well-barbered and closely-shaven like a Regular Service-man. There was a framed photograph of a wife and three children on the table in front of him, on the wall behind him a collection of notices, including one roster showing nurses' duties and their time off, and another showing their leaves – rosters that couldn't be missed. He went on writing, and I speculated about him. Ex-Royal Navy, medical orderly? Efficient, male, the sort of man to keep those nurses to their rosters, I was ready to bet.

'Now, sir.' He looked at me. In the manner of a petty official he'd kept me waiting, but his facial expression was not unamiable. I told him who I was.

'Your mother was only admitted this morning,' he said. 'I've still got her file on my desk.' He took it out of a tray and opened it. 'Ninety-three tomorrow.' He looked at me. 'She's a remarkable woman, your mother.'

The atmosphere began to change. I found – and he found, too – that we were beginning to chat. He was interested in my mother; and then in me, especially when I told him how impressed I was by the hospital.

He explained: 'This is what's classified as a short-term hospital.'

'Well, the convalescent home gave me the impression that she was here temporarily.'

He shook his head. 'I don't think she'll go back to the convalescent home.'

I said, 'It obviously got a bit beyond the convalescent home to look after her. They oughtn't to have let her get a bed-sore.'

'Oh, we'll clear that up.'

'What about the cancer?'

'We'll make her comfortable.' He gave me a friendly glance.

I said, 'I presume that means morphia?'

'Something that will make her comfortable.'

'How long will she be able to stay here, then?'

'I'll keep her as long as I can.' He gave me a matey, tipping-the-wink sort of look. 'If I were you, I shouldn't worry about it.' The formal decision about her staying was no doubt to be made by a doctor. I imagined the impeccable NCO's manner in which he might double-cross that doctor.

I said, 'I was struck by the shape she was in, even this afternoon after having had to be moved. She didn't say a thing that wasn't rational. Her voice was strong. And I was surprised by her physical strength when I was trying to give her a drink and she was grasping the cup.'

'You're right, there. There's still a lot of strength left in her.' He looked at me and said:

'It's the cancer that'll get her in the end.'

I nodded my head, suddenly too shocked to speak.

The telphone on his desk rang and he spoke into it. When he finished I stood up to go. He held out his hand. 'Cheers, Mr Lunn. I expect I shall see you again.'

I went away with his words haunting me, 'It'll be the cancer that'll get her in the end . . .' Oblivious to the effect they would have on me – just a natural thing to say in the circumstances.

In the train I attempted to read an evening newspaper. I was longing to get home to Elspeth. And then I began to wonder what *her* thoughts and reflections had been during the day.

Elspeth was already home from work, sitting on one of the sofas, reading. I kissed her and sat down beside her.

'You didn't stop at Victoria for a beer?' she asked, not smelling beer on my breath. 'Why not?'

'I was too reduced. I just wanted to get home to you.'

'Was it such an awful day?'

'It began reassuringly,' I said. And then I recounted the whole story, ending with the *coup de grâce*.

We sat for a moment silently. I said, 'I suppose I'll have to ring up my sister and tell her.'

Then we sat for a longer time, silently, haunted by the *coup de grâce*. Finally I said:

'How *can* people say these things to one?'

She put her arms round me. 'Poor darling . . .'

I put my arms round her – and then, remembering Tom, realised that I could well be saying, Poor darling . . . to *her*.

How *can* people say such things to one?

PART V

CHAPTER I

GOODBYE TO A HIP-JOINT

The remaining days of the week passed. I went on finding myself trying indirectly, because I hadn't the heart to ask her, to take the sense of Elspeth's feelings. I thought it wasn't as if she hadn't been previously warned about Tom's propensity for the warm, gossipy, oh!-so-human remark that was really at core destructive. It was his way. How right my first instinct had been to keep her out of his way! I recalled the moment when I'd given in to the idea of our meeting – seduced, that's what it was, by an invitation to dine at the Carlos. The Carlos. If he'd suggested the Dorchester or the Savoy, Elspeth and I would never have set eyes on him.

There were the questions I still wanted to ask – what did Tom actually say? what words did he utter about me? and about Steve? I tormented myself with imagining oozy, empathising remarks. 'The book is so good, we all know it must be taken from life.' And then, 'But you're so wise, my dear, I know you won't let it affect your happy marriage.' I had the idea that his words might have upset her so deeply that she hadn't registered them exactly; for instance, hearing as direct statement what was his typical half-suggesting, half-exploring innuendo. And the same went for whatever he said Steve had told him. I remembered my conversation with Steve in the little pavilion beside the pond at Hattersley Hall, when he asked me what Elspeth thought of *Happier Days* – he simply couldn't have gone in for immediate perfidy after that.

Where did all this take me? I asked myself. The answer was nowhere. The time one spends on thinking about things that get one nowhere!

However there weren't many more days to pass. I was

commanded to go into hospital on the Saturday, to be operated on by Quetzalcoatl on the following Tuesday.

Elspeth went with me, went up to the ward and waited with me in the waiting-room, which seemed to double with recreation-room – dilapidated armchairs, other people's left-behind magazines, and a noisy television set. The patients waiting, all men, were a very mixed lot. Elderly men, only to be expected; middle-aged men who looked as if they might be ailing; young men, some of them hobbling about after accidents – probably having fallen off their motorbikes. (There was one healthy young man who looked as if he hadn't got anything at all the matter with him. 'Wonder what *he*'s in for?' we speculated. I later discovered he was in to be circumcised, poor fellow.)

Elspeth waited while I underwent the first preliminaries and was put to bed – Quetzalcoatl ordered the week-end's bed-rest – and then she sat with me through the afternoon, a sunny Saturday afternoon when we might have been strolling beside the river, watching the sailing-boats tacking from side to side and the power-boats being driven round in circles, and perhaps ending with the delectable spectacle of cars parked on the slipways by owners too gormless to know the Thames had tides that came up.

Mine was a large ward, with one half divided into compartment wards, then a broad aisle, and then a single row of beds against the wall. Very Victorian. It looked moderately clean and well-kept. I was tucked away in one of the compartments, my bed beside a tall window outside of which there was a little iron-railed balcony overlooking a square – where the gardens were still prettily in flower. Actually there was another smaller part of the ward that one had to go through to get to the lavatories and to the staircase and lift, compartments for beds on one side, the Sister's office and so on on the other. When I paid my first visit to the lavatories, I thought they looked like a Victorian 'conversion'. Below a ceiling that must have been about fifteen feet high, there was one tiny shower-room with a door that didn't fit; one bathroom, with a large cast-iron bath in the middle of the floor and behind it a jungle of pipes rising to disappear in the darkness and dust above; three shaving-cubicles, three WCs with chains that didn't look particularly reliable; and a doorway to the room into which nurses were carrying bottles and bedpans. I thought it wisest, on my return to Elspeth, not to describe the lavatories. I'd made my choice: I knew the place was Victorian.

On the following afternoon Elspeth came to see me again, and later on Viola and Virginia. I noticed the girls having a sharp look round, but nothing was said.

By this time I'd done a first survey of the ward-population. Most of the beds against the opposite wall were occupied by athletic young men who'd had cartilage operations: they were noisy and vigorous, lying on their beds in strange postures, playing their radios loudly, organising games of cards, shouting jokes to each other. (Viola and Virginia didn't pass unnoticed by them. We ignored low wolf-whistles and loud guffaws – there are occasions when it's brought home to one inexorably that Humankind is part of Animal Creation.)

The rest of the patients seemed to be mainly divided between sufferers from hernias and from haemorrhoids: they were mostly older and quieter, especially the latter were quieter. There was one elderly man who'd had a knee-joint replacement – interesting to me. One bed contained a hatchet-faced man who was so emaciated and so yellow that I felt he wouldn't be there for long. And there was a strange stumpy little man, near-dwarf, with some kind of breathing obstruction that caused him to make a continuous blowing noise – having his mouth open all the time, he was inclined to slobber.

As it was a teaching hospital there were quite a few student nurses in the ward, young girls, some of them carrying text-books with them: I saw two of them in a corner, coaching each other. My first impression of all the staff was that they were in amiable mood and on good terms with each other – one of the advantages of the hospital's being small, I'd been told in the first place.

On Monday morning I was visited by Mr Redruth, looking large and powerful, treading lightly. (At Elspeth's insistence I was trying to stop calling him Quetzalcoatl.) He was in bashing form, spruce and handsomely dressed – scales flat and glistening, plume erect – and he brought a small retinue composed of the House Physician, who was a tall, lightly-built, fresh-complexioned man with beautiful thick blond hair (he was called Carroll); the senior of the two Sisters, an oldish, experienced, motherly woman (she was called Holmes); and a couple of nurses whom I hadn't seen on the previous day, one of them carrying the patients' files. The new characters in my life!

'I gather you're in good form,' Q said in a loud cheerful voice.

'So far as *I* know,' I said. I noticed his eyes were a dark grey, making his glance seem slightly opaque. His hair was stiff and straight and plastered down flat.

'So far as *you* know? Is that good enough for us, Sister Holmes?' He glanced at the Sister, grinning ironically at my expense.

'We are satisfied, Mr Redruth.'

'Right. Then what is it we say? All systems go!'

He turned to the blond young doctor – whom I now saw to be in his late thirties – and said to him, 'We've got the two of them. I propose to do this patient first.'

'Yes, Mr Redruth.'

He turned to me, 'You heard that? We'll do you first. Nine-thirty, sharp.'

'Good.'

He took a step nearer, and said in a quieter, though equally cheerful tone of voice:

'When you come round you'll find we're giving you some blood. Don't be alarmed! It's standard procedure. This is a rather bloody operation. OK?'

'Yes.'

He grinned. 'I'll see you, Mr Lunn.'

I couldn't help grinning, myself, recognising that I asked for this kind of cheerful, bashing treatment – after my own fashion I bashed back.

Throughout the day there were more preliminaries. Sister Holmes came and gave me a knowledgeable, motherly talk about the operation. She was followed by one of the nurses I'd seen in the morning, a nice girl who talked to me animatedly. She said something about the prosthesis –

'Haven't you seen one?' she asked. 'Haven't they ever shown you one?'

'No,' I said. I didn't know that I should have been able to look at it, if they had shown me one.

'It looks like a pork chop,' she said.

'Oh!'

From what I'd imagined, I could see that was what it might well look like. Like a pork chop. Exquisite simile!

Later on a bearded young man in a white coat came to see me.

'You'll have to be shaved, Mr Lunn,' he said. 'Shall I do it, or would you rather do it yourself?'

I said, '*You* do it, please! You're the expert. I should be terrified of nicking myself.'

He came back a little later to do it. He surveyed the area thoughtfully.

'I think I shall take it off here.' He traced the boundary with his forefinger.

'What?' I cried. 'You're not going to do it asymmetrically, are you? It'd look ridiculous – not being the same on both sides.'

'All right. I'll take it all off.'

I was surprised by how easily he did it. He really was an expert.

So, after Elspeth had been and I'd been given nothing to eat, I ended with the standard notice, illiterate but comprehensible, hanging over my bed –

NIL BY MOUTH

Next morning I made that journey, though I was too far gone under premedication to observe it properly, being wheeled across from the wide, concertina-gated lift to the double-doors above which the lighted sign said

OPERATION IN PROGRESS

I was talked to by the anaesthetist, in green cap and mask, who had one of the deepest, cosiest voices I'd ever heard. (I thought it was a man – it was only when she came to see me next morning that I saw it was a tall, good-looking woman.) And after that . . .

After that x hours must have passed. (I'd been told how many **x** was but I hadn't bothered to register it.) And then I suppose I must have been wheeled back, under a scarlet blanket, past a row of waiting patients.

y hours passed and I began to come round to a strangely euphoric state, produced by two thoughts that were going slowly and re-iteratively through my returning mind. Euphoric, triumphant –

'*I've not got an infection* – I took a risk and the gamble's come off!' And 'I shan't have to wake up again to realise I've got to have this operation!'

I began to wake up, know where I was, still savouring the two thoughts as they spaced out and disappeared. The lights in the ward were on. I saw Elspeth coming to see me.

'How are you feeling?' she whispered.

'Fine.'

She smiled at me. 'You don't look so bad.'

I looked up at her. 'If there's nobody looking, please kiss me!'

She bent over me.

'Well . . .' I said.

She sat down. I held out one of my hands to her – the other hand was impeded, and I remembered that I was connected up to a blood-supply. She took hold of my hand, and we remained quiet.

Two nurses came up, one youngish, the other very young. 'We want to take your temperature and blood-pressure, Mr Lunn.' They told Elspeth she needn't go away, as she'd only just come. They performed their task. While the very young one was packing up the sphygmometer, the other one said to me: 'We shall want to take your temperature and blood-pressure every hour. Through the night.' She smiled at me. 'We'll wake you up.'

When they'd gone I said to Elspeth: 'Am I in a different bed?'

'They've put you in the bed nearest to the desk where the two nurses on duty sit.'

She kissed me again, and then she went away.

And so I began a long night of being roused hourly. When I was awake I could hear, in the silence of the ward, the two nurses whispering to each other while they measured my blood-pressure and my temperature. I couldn't always catch what they said.

At one hour I thought I heard one of them saying, 'His temperature keeps on going up,' and the other saying, 'It shouldn't . . .'

Well into the night the whispered colloquy was longer. 'His temperature's still going up.' 'It shouldn't be . . .' 'Then *why* is it going up? . . .' I didn't catch the reply, or the remarks that followed. 'She . . .'

At the next awakening there was somebody else there. 'His temperature's still going up, Sister.' (Was the third person the Night Sister from somewhere?) 'Have you checked everything?' 'Yes, Sister.' 'Have you checked his blood-supply? If you're giving it him too fast, that will send his temperature up.'

I missed the next bit. It was hard to listen – was I half-asleep, or partially anaesthetized, or rather ill?

I was aware of one of the nurses moving about at the head of the bed, where the blood-supply was. Her clothes rustled. Then they all went away.

At the next hour I was more alert – I had reason to be. The whispering began while my blood pressure was being measured. 'His temperature's still up.' A few moments later the two of them were rustling near the head of the bed. 'Have you checked the regulator?'

'It doesn't seem to have changed.'

'Are you sure you adjusted it?'

'Yes . . . It doesn't seem to work.' Pause. '*How* does it work? . .'

'It shows you in the diagram.'

'Shall I go and get the diagram?'

'Sh . . . *I* know how it works. I'll have a go at it.' There was a brief pause.

'Is the valve all right?'

Another pause. I could almost hear her fiddling with the controls. Then –

'There! I think I've done it!' Pause. 'Yes . . . That's OK now.'

'Are you sure it's all right?'

'Better stay and keep an eye on it for a few minutes.'

'Yes . . .'

I didn't get straight off to sleep again. After the few minutes, the other nurse came back. 'Is it all right now?' 'Yes.'

At the next hour. 'Has his temperature stopped going up?' 'Yes.'

'Thank God for that! . .'

I went off to sleep.

First thing in the morning I saw that early colloguings were

481

going on at the desk. Sister Holmes was there. I realised that of the two nurses who'd been in charge of the whole ward all night, the older one was qualified, while the younger was only a student.

The blood-supply was in working order. My temperature was now giving no cause for alarm. (Only the chart at the bottom of my bed would give away the vicissitudes of the night.) My blood-pressure had been satisfactory from the start.

Quetzalcoatl came to see me, Dr Carroll in attendance, and Sister Holmes. He asked me how I was. I said, not untruthfully, 'Very well.'

'You look reasonably well.' He turned to the Sister. 'A surprisingly good colour, isn't he?' I appreciated that. I was a bit surprised, too.

He turned back to me, with opaque grey eyes and unchanging cheerful expression –

'The operation went very well. I'm very pleased. We shall get you out of bed tomorrow. And as soon as we're able to stop draining the wound, you've got to try and *walk*!'

At that he went away, giving me a fine example, I thought, of how to walk with a boxer's quick-footed tread.

I couldn't wait for the day when the draining-tubes came out – a nasty sensation, but worth it.

Sister Holmes was there and the physiotherapist handed me the crutches I'd practised with before the operation. I felt a bit odd, to be standing up, staggered nervously, and then made a start –

I could walk *without pain*!

A nurse was walking beside me. I didn't need her. Dr Carroll appeared, to watch me, and he discussed my efforts with the Sister.

'I think that in a day or two, Mr Lunn, you'll be able to try it with two sticks,' he said afterwards. I was beginning to like him.

I was suddenly taken with the idea that I might become a star pupil if I tried.

When I broached it with Elspeth that evening, she said, 'Not too fast . . .'

So I got on to two walking-sticks. I thought I was managing pretty well.

Then came the day for Quetzalcoatl's regular state visit; with Dr Carroll; Dr Carroll's assistant, a bright little Pakistani doctor called Zia; Sister Holmes; the other Sister, who was called Lewell; the male Staff Nurse; and a collection of other nurses.

When he got to my bed, Mr R said, 'I want to see you walk.'

I managed to get out of bed, was handed my sticks, and set off down the broad aisle, diffidently at first and steadily with more confidence. When I thought I'd gone far enough I turned round, to see him with his whole army lined up, watching me.

'Now,' he said. 'I want you to try it with one stick.'

Before I'd properly taken the news in a little nurse came up and relieved me of a stick. I was left with one. I had to try it. I began. I could do it!

Q turned to his cohorts and said, 'If only they were all as easy as that!'

When I reached him, he said, 'You'd better get back to bed. I'm very pleased with you.' There was a pause and then he said to all of us, 'Now I'm going on my holidays for a month.'

CHAPTER II
SOME TURNS OF FATE

The next thing was the removal of the stitches. I felt I was in sight of leaving the hospital. I was walking well with one stick and free from pain. The removal was entrusted to a little student girl under the supervision of a qualified nurse. I noticed, to my surprise, that a couple of small drops of blood appeared: the nurses didn't seem to be surprised.

On the following day Elspeth was spending an hour with me in the afternoon. I found it necessary to go to the lavatory. I kept away from the lavatories, since they were practically always unspeakably awash. The cleaning of the ward, apart from a weekly floor-polishing by external contractors, was in the hands of a party of Jamaican women, by my standards as insolent as they were slatternly: they swabbed the lavatories out, after a fashion, first thing in the morning, and then refused to touch them again – one sometimes came upon a nurse cleaning up the mess, but not often. Anyway I was there, washing my hands at a washbasin, when I felt a trickle of something down my leg. I looked down, saw blood running down my leg, dripping on the floor.

I called out for a nurse. At the end of the passage appeared Elspeth and Sister Holmes. Nurses appeared with a wheel-chair in no time, and I was taken back to the ward. Dressings were put on to staunch the flow of blood – brownish blood, I noticed, not bright red. Elspeth looked pale. What is it? we wanted to know. What does it mean?

The Sister explained and reassured us – it was nothing new to her. After the operation, serous fluid and old blood had collected in the wound: instead of being absorbed internally, it had ruptured externally. It was called a haematoma. (The student

484

nurses wrote the word down and then went away to read up the details in their medical dictionaries.)

I now had to wait for the blood to drain away externally.

'How long is that going to take?'

'It's impossible to say. Perhaps a week. Perhaps a few days.'

(That was the first time I heard, A few days.)

Later, after Elspeth had gone away, miserably to break the news to the girls, the Sister told me she had two private rooms vacant at the moment. 'We keep them for emergencies. I could let you have one of them, if you'd like it. You'd have a bit more privacy.'

I said I'd jump at it, thinking of how I could listen to concerts on my radio without distraction.

'You won't feel lonely, Mr Lunn?'

I didn't think so. After all, I spent quite a lot of time practising my walking, up and down the ward. The star pupil. (I was determined to eradicate my limp.) The haematoma wasn't going to interfere with that. And in the course of my walking I got to know some of the other patients. The young man who'd come in to be circumcised was still with us, looking rather sorry for himself. He was having a painful time – he must have had an adhesion. One day, though, he showed a glimmer of amusement. 'Yesterday one of the student nurses did my dressing,' he confided. 'She put it on *over the end* . . .' I laughed, even if it was unkind. Anyway I thought he had something to look forward to. He was visited every evening by a very glamorous West Indian girl who embraced him passionately before she left – I saw how his operation had become an urgent necessity.

I had to wait for the haematoma to drain itself away into the dressings. 'A few more days.' One morning I heard Carroll say to Zia, as they were going out of the room, 'Imagine having a pint bottle of milk on your hip!'

To make me more comfortable I was given a new way of keeping my dressing in place. A little nurse came in holding a roll of white, woven elastic tubing. She looked thoughtfully at my hip – my left hip, it was – then thoughtfully unrolled a length of this sort-of body-stocking, took up the pair of scissors that hung from her belt, saying, 'I haven't done this before . . .'

To tell the story I shall have to explain – what I then didn't

485

know – how the thing worked. The idea was to cut off a piece of tube of appropriate length; then to make, part way down it, a lateral cut half-way across: one began by thrusting both feet down the tube till they came to the cut; then one thrust the right foot through the cut and went on pushing the left foot down the rest of the tube: one ended up with the lower part of the tube round one's left thigh, holding the dressing; and the upper part round one's loins, thus leaving one's right leg and the lower part of one's anatomy free.

Now for the story. She cut off a piece of tubing and diffidently snipped a very small cut across it half way down. The process began. When my feet came to the cut it was too small for my right foot to go through it, so that *both* feet went *down* the tube. As she hauled the tube up my legs I had intimations of what was supposed to be going on. 'That won't do,' I said. 'If you go on like that you'll have me like a mermaid.'

She giggled and blushed. 'I shall have to make the cut wider,' she opined. She pulled the thing off and lifted her scissors, then extended the cut till it went three-quarters of the way across.

This time the process went quite differently. The opening in the tube for my left foot was too small for me to get my left foot into it, and inevitably *both* feet went *through* the cut. As she hauled the tube up, the piece intended for my left thigh dangled at the side.

She stared at it, and for minutes we were both too helpless with laughter to go on. Then I said:

'I think we'll start all over again and you'd better let *me* do the cutting.'

So began my regime of regularly doing it myself. A fresh dressing was put on the wound every night: every morning I looked at it to see if any more blood had seeped out. (Imagine a pint bottle! . .) It took me back to those long-lost days when the children were babies in nappies, when we looked hopefully each morning to see if the nappy was dry.

A few more days. And a few more days. 'Not more than a week, now,' said Sister Lewell.

My friends got into the way of sick-visiting me regularly.

Robert came with books for me. Veronica came and disapproved of my having a haematoma. It was no use my

486

telling her it was fortuitous: Veronica's temperament was not given to recognising the fortuitous – that was not the way of the Civil Service. '*Somebody* must be responsible,' she said.

George Bantock turned up, to tell me not to worry about my classes. That was comforting.

The girls came together, one day, to consult me.

'We think we ought to go and see Granny,' said Virginia.

'It's ages since we saw her,' said Viola.

'It might be,' said Virginia, 'the last time we can.'

'If we didn't go,' said Viola, 'we might always regret it . . .'

They were fond of my mother, but Elspeth and I hadn't suggested that they should go and see her because it was so daunting. Viola had of course heard the reports of my own visits, (with the *coup de grâce* excised.)

As my mother was now in the least daunting hospital I'd ever seen, I didn't discourage them as I'd discouraged my sister from coming over from America to see my mother for the last time – in my sister's case my mother would have realised it must be for the last time; and that, it seemed to me, would have been too heart-rending for both of them. I said to the girls, 'I think you might go.' They began making their plans.

Elspeth, trying to look bright and cheerful, came to see me day after day.

Day after day I went for my walking practice, up and down the wards, learning now to go up and down the stairs by the lift, sometimes merely carrying the stick. Otherwise I stayed in my room, reading my way – like the Noble Lord Balderstoke in similar circumstances – through the Palliser novels; and listening to concerts on my radio.

I was getting onto friendly terms with the two doctors and the two Sisters. I was seeing more of Sister Lewell – oval face, long nose, high colour in her cheeks, dark hair; and a subtle, fluid smile . . . Who did she remind me of? Answer: that early love of mine, forty years ago, who wanted me to marry her and whom Tom, in the midst of passionately pursuing Steve, had thought of proposing marriage to, out of sympathy with her ill-treatment at my hands. *Myrtle*! . . A very strange coincidence. I didn't mention it to Elspeth. When I speculated on why she was not married, Elspeth pointed out that she was wearing an engagement ring. Sister Lewell . . .

Sister Holmes became confidential. One day she told me, 'In your operation and the other one,' – the other patient was a woman – 'Mr Redruth used a new spray they've brought out. It inhibits the flow of blood, so that the surgeons can see much better what they're doing.' She paused. 'Both patients got haematomas. I don't think he'll use it again.'

I thought, Two-out-of-two may strike into the feeling heart but it doesn't go very far with the statistical head. (What you want to know is, How many out of two hundred?) I resolved not to start a row by telling Veronica.

Meanwhile I began to see what Sister Holmes had said about my feeling lonely. In my private room it was easy not to go out and join in ward-activities, for instance not to join the team of ambulant patients who helped with the trolleys of morning-tea and the day's meals. (They thought I was a snob.) I began to notice the symptoms of hospital anxiety-neurosis – 'Have they missed me with the morning coffee?' 'When are they coming to change my dressing?' 'How late are they going to be with the last drug-round? I'm waiting to go to sleep.'

One day the little dwarf came in, blowing and slobbering – I was pretty sure he was one of the causes of the WCs being awash. He had a pack of cards and was obviously going to show me a trick. 'Oh no!' I cried, 'I hate card-tricks!' I felt very ashamed, afterwards.

I became friendly with two men near the aisle, whom I constantly passed and re-passed. They were down from Birmingham, where there were immense waiting-lists for admission, to have hernia operations. They were in their early forties, intelligent, sensible, fathers of families, called Chris and Geoff. Chris, being the nearer one to the aisle, was spokesman for the two. When I asked them what they did, he said:

'Oh, we're only engineers . . . with British Leyland.'

'*Only* engineers,' I said. 'You shouldn't think that.' I told them I'd spent most of my official career among scientists and engineers – the backbone of an industrial nation. 'What sort of engineers?' I asked.

'We're the lowest of the low.' He smiled at me. 'We're on the production line.'

488

Perhaps he was teasing me, yet his self-deprecation was genuine. I was pretty speechless – that the anti-technology element in our culture could bring men like this to such a pass! Insane.

On the other hand Geoff's sixteen year old son had gone into BL – that very morning, in fact: Geoff had telephoned him at 6.30 am to wish him Good Luck. I was touched. The sort of men they were, the sort of lives they lived, rarely found its way into current novels. So much the worse for current novels!

They had their operations and I saw them sitting up in bed the morning after they recovered. 'How now?' I asked.

As usual Chris replied for the two. 'We're OK. But they didn't tell us . . . after a hernia operation your thing swells up and turns black.'

'How alarming!'

'It was. I called the nurse. But she said it was all right.'

'What about Geoff's?'

'The same,' said Geoff.

'He called the nurse, too,' said Chris.

'What did she say to him?'

'She said, "Oh God! Have I got to look at another one?"'

I burst into laughter and glanced at Geoff. With momentarily lowered eyelids he had an unconcerned look. I went on laughing. On the evening before their operation, I'd come upon Geoff drying himself unconcernedly outside the door of the shower-room. He had something to look unconcerned about.

I left them to go on with my walking-practice, but I smiled every time I thought about it. However when I recounted the incident to Elspeth, she took a high line. 'Men in hospital,' she said haughtily, 'always think the nurses want to look at their you-know-whats.' I didn't enquire how she knew.

Nearly dry, my dressing in the morning. 'Two more days,' said the youthful orderly whom I could sometimes catch, as he was passing my open doorway, to change the dressing. 'Only two more days, I promise you.'

Dry enough for Dr Carroll to tell me I could have a bath, my first bath.

The shower was now out of order; so it had to be the big cast-iron Victorian bath, in the room which towered upwards into darkness and dust. (It would need scaffolding for anybody to get rid of all that grime.) Two nurses were filling the bath for me. Had the bath been cleaned? It didn't look like it. 'That's all right,' they said, showing me that they were emptying into it two sachets of Savlon, to which I already knew I was allergic.

'First of all, think! Mr Lunn, how you're going to get into the bath. And then you'll get out the same way.'

'In reverse,' I said.

'Yes.'

So I was bathed by two nurses. A few hours later the allergic irritation began in exactly the zones where it might have been expected.

However the bath was considered a success, and in a couple of days' time Carroll permitted me another. As a result of my protests, the sachets of Savlon were replaced by sachets of salt. 'Just as effective,' said the senior of the two nurses.

I think it must have been a day or so after that – I'd now been in hospital for five weeks instead of two – when Elspeth was sitting with me in the evening. We were both looking forward to my coming out. Suddenly the door slid across.

Who should be standing there but Steve!

'*Steve!* . .'

He came in, smiling. 'It's all right. I haven't come back!'

I glanced at Elspeth, wondering if she would go straight out of the room. She stood up, saying, 'I'll leave you, now.'

'Oh no!' said Steve. 'Please don't go away! I can only stay a few minutes, and I haven't got anything to say that I can't say to both of you.'

Elspeth reluctantly sat down again.

Steve was wearing a pin-striped suit instead of denims, and he was carrying an up-to-date flat brief-case. He looked well, if a little tired. There was no trace of embarrassment in his manner.

He began to draw up a spare chair. 'You must wonder why on earth I'm here.' He sat down. 'As soon as I left the country, my dear wife decided we should have a divorce. Can you believe it? So I've had to come back to see lawyers.' He looked at Elspeth and me. 'Have you ever had to see lawyers? It's terrible . . . They go on and on. And one's paying for their *time*.'

I was smiling at him, but I saw that Elspeth, though she had stayed, was not smiling at him.

'I found out where you were from Veronica,' he said. 'Robert wasn't to be found.'

'What did Veronica say?' I said.

'She gave me the address of the hospital.' He paused, and smiled in recollection. 'She told me she hates Tom, but she wouldn't tell me why. As if I couldn't work that out!' He laughed. 'He must have interfered between her and Robert. He tries to do it with all of us. You're lucky if he didn't have a go at you two . . . It feeds his lust for power over people.'

I glanced at Elspeth, trying to signal with my eyes, *Steve doesn't know what Tom said to you.* I was sure he didn't. Nor could I square his present manner, easy and careless and honest, with his having deliberately done harm to Elspeth and me. I hoped Elspeth was beginning to feel the same – thank goodness! she was showing no signs of leaving now. I must say I thought it was a test of her amazing spirit.

Steve chattered on. As he wanted to hear, half-wanted to hear, about my operation, I demonstrated to him how I could now walk easily *without* a stick. 'Marvellous, Joe.'

Then we returned to his divorce, which, after so many years, seemed as remarkable to me as it obviously did to him.

'Do you *want* a divorce?' I asked.

Steve laughed with his rueful expression. 'Not much.'

'Does she?'

'She's told her lawyers she does.'

There was a pause. 'Lawyers!' said Steve. And then, 'But I mustn't go on about them. I'm just waiting to get back to New York.'

'How're things going?'

'Burke's theatre is smashing. And with a bit of luck I shall carve myself a niche in it – which is what Burke wants me to do. Think of that, Joe!'

'I think of it with pleasure and satisfaction, Steve. And *hope*!'

Steve laughed and picked up his brief-case. 'I must go. But first of all I want Joe to sign something for me.' And out of the brief-case he took a copy of *Happier Days*.

'It's super, Joe,' he said, and handed it to me to sign with his biro.

I took it from him. While I was opening the pages, he spoke to Elspeth in a quiet tone.

'I think you've been super over it all . . . I mean, the way you've gone calmly on, when you must have guessed what snide people must be saying about Joe behind your back. What *Tom* was saying behind your back.'

Elspeth said coolly, 'Was he?'

Steve smiled at her. 'You don't know Tom as well as we do. He tried to get Robert and me to say that we knew that Joe had been –' Her expression made him stop. 'I'm terribly sorry, I've embarrassed you, Elspeth . . .'

I intervened. I looked up from the book. 'You and *Robert*?' I said. 'When was that?'

'On the last morning at Hattersley Hall. You two had gone. Tom opened a bottle of champagne – he opened a lot of bottles of champagne. It got him into a lascivious mood – lascivious isn't the word, but you know what I mean. When he started to talk about *you* again, Robert put him down in a way I've never heard Robert put anybody down in before. Elspeth will forgive the schoolboy language' – he smiled at her – 'Robert shat on him from a great height. Gave him to understand that he was being a fool, a knave and a liar.' He looked at me. 'I agreed.'

I couldn't speak. I didn't trust myself to look at Elspeth. I finally managed to say:

'Well, here's your copy of *Happier Days*, now increased in value out of all recognition.'

'Thank you, Joe.' He playfully held it up as if he were going to kiss it, then put it into his brief-case and stood up to go.

'Get well soon, Joe! Don't limp any more!' He turned to Elspeth. I wondered if he was going to attempt to kiss her – he did – and if she would allow him. She did.

When he had gone I held out my arms to her, and she came to the bedside and rested her face on my shoulder.

'My darling . . .' she said.

I closed my arms round her. 'My love.'

We didn't discuss it any more.

People clattered about in the doorway, serving the supper.

Elspeth said, 'I must go home and prepare some supper, I suppose. What are you going to do?'

I thought I might well just lie on my bed, thinking of what we had been through. I said:

'There's a lovely concert tonight. I shall listen to that.'

And that was what I did. The concert was in two parts and I listened all night to it. I switched off the light and listened, lost in emotion.

When the concert was over I had to get out of bed. I pushed back the sheets – I still slept with a cradle over my feet – and swung my legs round.

As I swung my legs round I felt a riveting pain. I tried to stand up and couldn't bear to put my foot on the ground. In my leg, my hip, my groin, pain of an intensity I'd never experienced before.

Standing there in the darkness, holding on to the bed, I felt terror. I *knew* what was the matter.

CHAPTER III

THE DARK SIDE

For a minute I held on to the bed in the darkness. Then I managed somehow to find my stick and I set off, half-hopping in a few steps at a time, for the Sister's office. In the corridor everything seemed unusually silent. To my relief when I got to the office door I saw both Sister Lewell and Doctor Zia. 'I can't walk.'

They came out instantly. 'You must go back to bed.' They supported me on the way back to my room. 'Where's Doctor Carroll?' I asked. 'He's in the operating-theatre,' said the Sister. At this time of night! I was not surprised, though: he was unmarried and worked all hours. 'He often operates at night,' she said. (The two of them were friends: I'd heard them call each other by their Christian names – I'd even wondered, at one stage, if it was Carroll she was engaged to.)

In my room Zia said, 'I want you to try and stand up as straight as you can, with both feet on the ground. I want to look at your two legs together.'

The Sister stood beside me while he walked a few paces away and I hitched up the operating-gown that I persuaded the nurses to let me wear in lieu of pyjamas. (It did up at the back – sometimes, to Elspeth's disapproval, it undid without my noticing.) 'Please hurry up!' I begged. 'Please! . .'

'Now lying down on the bed.'

He and the Sister eyed my legs carefully, as it were measuring. They glanced at each other.

He delicately tried to test my hip. He was small and clever and sensitive – sometimes over-sensitive. 'The pain's terrific,' I said agitatedly.

He went back to the bottom of the bed. 'There is no difference ın the length of your legs,' he said. 'I think I can tell you, Mr Lunn, that it is nothing dramatic.'

Nothing dramatic! He must mean no displacement of the prosthesis –

'But haven't I got an *infection*?' I could hardly utter the word.

Sister Lewell was about to take my temperature.

'That is possible.'

'Is my temperature up?' I asked when she took the thermometer out of my mouth.

'Yes.'

I said to Zia:

'What happens next?'

'Dr Carroll will see you first thing in the morning, and decide.'

'Aren't you going to start treating it now?' I was near to hysteria.

'I will make sure it is OK to give you some distalgesics. That will help you to get some sleep.' He went out of the room.

What I needed was antibiotics, not distalgesics. Sister Lewell followed him.

A minute or two later she came back with two distalgesics and held up my head while I washed them down with a drink of water.

'When is Mr Redruth coming back?'

'Not till next week, I'm afraid.'

She settled my pillow, for a moment laid her hand on my forehead. And then she went away finally.

I spent the night in pain and sleeplessness and agitation. I was convinced they were not treating me with antibiotics now because they couldn't get me any. This hospital drew its supply of drugs from the main hospital – centralised for efficiency – and I'd come to the conclusion earlier, from watching ward-activities, that after a certain hour at night our hospital couldn't draw any fresh drugs till first thing next morning. Sister Holmes had told me that was not so. I supposed it couldn't be so. Yet in the night I was sure it could.

First thing in the morning Dr Carroll came in. After operating till midnight he looked tired. His eyes looked tired – he had what Robert and I called cerebrotonic eyes; smallish and transparent, eyes that seem to perceive and apprehend instantly. But his

golden hair was gleaming and his complexion looked as fresh as
ever. Dr Zia was with him.

He examined me, discussed me with Zia, ordered me to be
X-rayed – and prescribed antibiotics.

'Have I got an infection?'

'It may be, but you shouldn't react over-hastily.'

'When I'm in riveting pain?' I thought of Quetzalcoatl's, One
case in a hundred.

'We shall do something about that.' He closed my file and
handed it to Zia. 'I will come in and see you again this evening.'

This evening! That meant a day to pass. Actually a fair slice of
it passed in my being carried down to the basement and being
X-rayed. The radiographer wanted to repeat one of her
photographs: through an open doorway I saw her studying the
negative.

'Does anything *show* in them?' I asked, as she handed the
envelope to the orderly who'd wheeled me down.

'I don't see anything. The prosthesis looks all right.'

I wondered if Carroll would see anything. What were the
things that might be seen? I was so ignorant. The only things I
could imagine them seeing were facts about whether anything
had gone wrong with the prosthesis – whether anything had
happened to the pork chop.

In the late afternoon Elspeth came to see me. Having only just
been told, on her way in, she hadn't had time to cover up her
distress. She sat down beside my bed and simply held my hand.
As luck would have it, or perhaps wouldn't have it, the
antibiotics arrived while she was there. After I'd taken my first
dose I lay back on my pillow –

'Thank God for that!' I'd now made a start.

'Twenty-four hours late,' said Elspeth.

I thought, Twenty, but felt too ill to say it. She must be
wanting to remove me from this hospital forthwith. (When I
came to think about it, much later and without hysteria, I
realised that it was the bureaucratic machine that had absorbed
the time, not an ineffective hospital staff.)

Elspeth just remained holding my hand for a long time.

So I passed another night, and next morning felt worse.
Carroll came and examined me, carefully round my groin, but

496

he had nothing more to say. I asked how long it took for the antibiotics to take effect.

'It varies.' He glanced at me obliquely. 'We shall see.'

That morning I had two visitors, not knowing of the change in my state. George Bantock and his Administrative Dean.

I was lying still, with the sheets drawn up to my chin, feeling iller than I'd felt before.

'We've come to say,' George began, 'how welcome back you'll be, dear – ' The word 'boy' disappeared from his lips before he uttered it. He and the other man looked at each other.

I managed to say something; they remained motionless with embarrassment for a second or two, then made a rapid exit. Embarrassment or shock?

When one's ill, time seems to pass in a sort of haze. Nurses came and went. Carroll and Sister Lewell seemed to be in the offing: I felt the better for their being in the offing. Elspeth came. It would have been bad enough to be in pain, if only through the haze I had not kept recalling, 'You'll still be able to *walk*, but one leg will be two inches shorter than the other'.

Next day the antibiotics had definitely begun to take effect. The haze dissipated and I began to feel compos mentis – if one can be said to be compos mentis when still near-hysterical with anxiety and depression. Anyway I was in a sane enough state to begin asking Carroll medical questions, questions buzzing like bees round the central topic in my imagination, infection.

He answered my questions. For one thing I asked them so directly, no patient's inferiority about it, that he'd have had a job not to answer them. For another he was – to me, anyway – beginning to seem an interesting man. And for yet another, he saw that I was able to comprehend his answers.

I learnt some central facts. You could have an infection of the wound – I'd got one. It could be treated with antibiotics – I was being treated. You could have an infection of the bone: that could not be treated without taking out the prosthesis – leaving the leg two inches shorter.

'Can the infection get from the wound into the bone?'

'Sometimes it appears to do so.'

'How often?'

'I can't say. Occasionally.'

(I wanted to ask him to go and look up the statistics, some-where.) I said:

'If it does, how long does it take?'

He closed the file he was holding. 'I don't know who could answer that, Mr Lunn.'

'Mr Redruth?'

A distant look came into his eye. Then he smiled. 'I'll come and see you tomorrow morning.'

That left me with another twenty-four hours before I could ask more questions. I reflected on his patience, and then on his nature. He was a man of quick nervous apprehensions, I was sure; yet there was a smoothing-out layer over them, a layer that made for equanimity, optimism, which might have been professionally assumed but seemed to me genuine.

I had a bad day. Elspeth came and gave up trying to converse. I just wanted her to hold my hand, indefinitely.

Last thing at night, when I was still wakeful, Sister Lewell brought me an unexpected cup of tea. She helped me to lift my shoulders from the pillow while I drank. She said:

'I do wish you didn't get so depressed, Mr Lunn.'

I finished the tea and gave her the cup to put down. 'Wouldn't *you* feel depressed?' I looked up at her. 'I keep thinking over and over again, *Is it going to be all right?*'

Impulsively she held my head against her body. 'Oh! Mr Lunn, I don't know what we're going to do with you.'

Later I went off to sleep, thinking, If only Elspeth were here!

In the light of the next day I realised that I had changed over from being a star pupil to a problem-patient.

Carroll seemed to be spending a lot of care on exploring my groin, where I felt the pain was most intense, on prodding gently in one place after another.

'What are you looking for?' I asked him.

He answered with equanimity and patience, while getting on with the job.

So I was introduced to the subject of lymph nodes; their function – or absence of function – their liability to infection; the possibility of their treatment. Under the spell of instruction, I felt eased. (How to treat a problem patient!) He ended my catechism when he thought it had gone on long enough, and assured me that the antibiotics really were taking effect. Consoling.

When I reported it all to Elspeth in the evening, she said thoughtfully: 'H'm. . . I think he's a bit of an Aunt Martha, myself. Sunshine Sally . . .'

I was indignant, but not well enough to argue. I asked her to read to me, and it was in reading *The Duke's Children* to me that she spent her visiting-time during the next week.

The following day Quetzalcoatl was back from his holidays. He came in with retinue, stepped up to my bedside and said, with his opaque look – but with something less than his former bashing manner:

'I'm sorry about this.'

I murmured something.

'Your X-ray looks good.' Back in louder, more cheerful form. (The X-ray showed that the prosthesis was all right – the main part of *his* business.)

I murmured something else.

'The pain seems worst in the groin? I should like to have a look at you.' He drew back the sheets – with special care, because of the audience, for my modesty – and repeated Carroll's exploration. (Not the occasion for asking questions about lymph nodes.) He demonstrated to the audience that the haematoma was healed. Then he put back the sheets without comment.

As he stepped powerfully and lightly away from the bed, he said, 'We shall keep you on the antibiotics.' And he led his retinue out.

He had not been quite as he used to be, I thought. Something told me I was going to see rather less of him. It occurred to me now that behind the loud, cheerful bashing, there was something sensitive. Professional pride, perhaps, I thought ungraciously.

So I felt I was from now on really in the hands of Carroll and Zia and the two Sisters. I had to concede that the antibiotics were reducing the pain, and after a few more days I was allowed to get out of bed and walk across the room. (I took the opportunity to sneak a glance at my record-chart and see that my temperature was subsiding.)

I found it hard to believe that I could be out of the mire until there was evidence that the infection had been killed off completely, but Carroll and Sister Lewell were steadily more hopeful. (Aunt Martha, Carroll might be – I liked him.) I began to be able to walk up and down the wards. I was X-rayed again. I came to the end of the course of antibiotics. They assured me that the danger was over. I could scarcely believe it, still.

I was walking down the passage-way outside the Sister's office – it was a Saturday afternoon and there were empty beds where patients had been discharged before the weekend. I came upon Sister Lewell and Dr Carroll, chatting outside the office-door.

Sister Lewell looked at me with a happy smile. 'You're walking well again.'

I wasn't totally free from pain and stiffness, as I'd been before, but, I supposed, near enough.

'At the beginning of next week,' she said, 'I think we shall have to discharge you.'

'Really!' I looked at Carroll, who nodded his head in agreement – they must have been discussing me.

'Yes, really!' She gave me a fluid, subtle smile.

'Oh!' I cried, flung my arms round her neck – after all, she did remind me of someone else – and kissed her enthusiastically.

I stood back – we were laughing at each other.

'And now,' she said, 'aren't you going to kiss *him*?' And she glanced at Carroll.

For once my wits deserted me. I couldn't think what to say – to say No would sound beastly. He was standing, looking at the ground. I muttered something unintelligible – 'I don't know' or 'I don't think so' or something. (I thought of really witty answers *afterwards*.) I turned to Sister Lewell – she was laughing at me with subtle enjoyment.

I felt I came out of the incident badly.

CHAPTER IV

IS IT GOING TO BE ALL RIGHT?

Home again! It was marvellous, even if my hip was not quite as perfect as I'd hoped – I was still needing a stick, after having once been able to do without it. But I should be able to do without it again in a little while. I began to pick up my life. I telephoned George Bantock to say I'd be back – perhaps my class could come to the flat? 'What a splendid idea, dear boy!' And I arranged to resume meeting Robert in the pub. And so on.

The weather was awful but I decided I must go out every day. On the fourth day I crossed the road, to walk by the river. As I stepped up a pavement, I felt a sharp pain in the groin –

It was back: the infection hadn't been killed: it was still there.

I telephoned the hospital and was able to get Carroll. Come in straight away! Forty-eight hours' observation.

I telephoned Elspeth at her office and told her. 'I'm back at Square One.'

And then I got a taxi back to the hospital.

Is it going to be all right, or isn't it? Who could say that it was?

At the hospital Sister Holmes found me a bed – it was one of the beds the two engineers had occupied. She sent me to be X-rayed. 'Dr Carroll will be in to see you later.'

It was late when Carroll arrived. He drew the curtains and examined me, and he looked at the X-ray photographs. The pain was mostly in the groin and I felt him exploring the lymph nodes – I knew about *them*.

He said, 'Your X-ray looks all right.'

I said, 'If the bone becomes infected, does that show in the X-ray photograph?'

'It does ultimately.'

'How long's that?'

'It takes some time to show.'

I paused. My agitation was surging up. I said:

'I hope to God you'll *tell* me, if and when it does.'

'Oh yes.'

'Because if it does,' I said, 'I'm for the high jump, aren't I?' I meant another operation, permanent lameness.

He suddenly stood up straight, leaning backwards away from me.

'Look here! Mr Lunn, you must *stop* looking on the black side all the time.'

He'd never spoken to me like that before – it hadn't occurred to me that he had it in him, Aunt Martha.

I stared at him. He did have it in him. He was *not* an Aunt Martha ... My agitation was dismissed: I felt I ought to apologise. He went on.

'I'm prescribing you different antibiotics.' He produced two bottles from his white coat-pocket. (I immediately suspected that it was because they couldn't be procured through our hospital at this time of night that he'd brought them with him.) 'It's a three-week course,' he said. 'I'll finish my round and come back – I want to do a tissue test.'

When he came back the curtains were drawn again round my bed; Sister Lewell held my left foot and a nurse held my left shoulder, while he inserted a series of hyper-fine needles into my hip. At one point he said, 'That's got down to the steel.' I didn't know why the other two were holding on to me, as it didn't hurt.

So I spent forty-eight hours during which the pain began to subside. This time it was nothing new. I tried to think about my plight sanely. If I had to have another operation and was permanently lame, it was not the end of the world – what had become of my courage? I should still have my loved ones, and they would have me. There were lots of things I could go on doing. I could go on writing. (I had momentarily forgotten that the fate of *Happier Days* had made me threaten never to write again.) I could go on teaching if I wanted to. There were some physical activities from which I should be debarred: there were others from which I shouldn't – very definitely shouldn't!

It was Carroll's opening words that had done the trick. 'Look here! Mr Lunn.' His patience had come to an end, and who was I to say it shouldn't have? So far I'd only thought about myself being independent as a man. Well, *he* was independent as a man, too. In this bizarre medical situation we were getting to know each other.

After the forty-eight hours I was discharged again, this time with a three-week supply of antibiotics. I set about resuming my lawful occupations.

I held some classes in the flat. My pupils much preferred it to their classroom, and my teaching went with a swing. In one class I was inspired – though not by anything that had anything to do with my pupils. I was enthusiastically repeating to them Wilkie Collins's advice on novel-writing to Charles Dickens –

Make 'em laugh! Make 'em cry! Make 'em wait!

What better advice could one have? And then suddenly I realised that time after time in my own novels I'd made 'em laugh: it had never occurred to me to set about making 'em cry.

For a moment I was carried away – that's what I mean by inspired. That's what I'm going to do! I thought. If ever I write another novel I'll make 'em cry as well as laugh. I'll make 'em laugh and make 'em cry in the same chapter, on the same page! (You see how inspiration makes a novelist get above himself.)

I went on with my class. *They* didn't notice anything.

I resumed other lawful occupations. I went down to see my mother. I met Robert, who, apart from being pleased to see me out, was in low spirits that I didn't understand – it seemed that all was well with Veronica. Viola got us some tickets for Carreras and Sass in *Un Ballo In Maschera* at Covent Garden. I watched Elspeth preparing our suppers – a very lawful occupation.

I came to the end of the pills. The state of my hip was just about what it had been when I was discharged the first time. What happens now? Is it going to be all right or isn't it? The first day passed, the second, the third . . . I was awakened in the night –

The pain in the same place.

I let Elspeth sleep on while I waited for the morning, to telephone the hospital.

The routine was the same. Come in immediately, for forty-eight hours' observation! This time I was received by Dr Zia, who drew the curtains and examined me himself, incorporating, before I realised what was happening, a new test of his own – I thought it would serve him right if *I* felt *his* . . . I was X-rayed again. And late at night, as usual, Carroll appeared.

'Your X-ray's all right,' he said.

'What about the results of the tissue-test?'

'They haven't come in yet.'

'After three weeks?'

'They often take longer than that.'

I thought, in that case a patient could have died in the meantime. But I was resolute in behaving myself. I said nothing.

'This time,' he said, 'I shall try another pair of antibiotics. And I want you to take a course of three months.'

'Good Lord! That'll take me to the New Year.'

'Yes.'

I looked at him: he looked at me. Neither needed to say anything.

The new antibiotics were huge capsules, bi-coloured as usual – the size of horse-pills.

In the following forty-eight hours they took effect. I was discharged for the third time. Sister Holmes saw me off and we chatted about my antibiotics. She was in her sensible, motherly, confidential form.

'Antibiotics are a marvellous discovery,' she said, 'but there's still an element of hit-or-miss.' She looked at me. 'But *you* will be able to understand that.'

(I supposed the news of my medical catechising had spread round.) I said:

'Please God this is a hit!'

She said, 'I've seen what he's prescribed for you, one general and one specific. The general's a very good one. The specific one has come out under test with flying colours.' She paused an instant. 'I think you stand a good chance.'

I said, 'Thank you,' and kissed her motherly cheek.

'We shall miss you,' she said.

Such a thought had never occurred to me. I kissed her again on the strength of it. I said:

'Goodbye. You've all been very good to me.'

And so I embarked on a three months' course of continued

wondering, *Is it going to be all right or isn't it?* But I found that in the passing of three months, some of the steam goes out of wondering. I returned to comparative thought. So obsessed with myself, I'd never thought of other people being lame and surviving. They had to put up with it, and they lived their lives all the same. I felt ashamed of having let my courage desert me.

After a few weeks I was free from pain or discomfort, walking without a stick again, forgetting that I might really be under sentence. I kept renewing my supplies of the multicoloured horse-pills – it was only occasionally that I thought, when I woke up in the mornings, *What's going to happen when I stop taking them?*

Then one day came the news that the fine new hospital, where my mother was, could keep her no longer. She was to be transferred to a cottage hospital not far from the convalescent home. My spirits sank. 'I'll go and see her straight away,' I said to Elspeth.

It was a horrible December afternoon, with a dark sky and rain beating against the window of the railway carriage. I had a taxi out to the cottage hospital, which looked to me like a collection of wartime huts. As a nurse showed me in one direction down a narrow passage-way, I glanced back in the opposite direction and saw a large common-room in which nurses were entertaining geriatric patients sitting smiling in chairs.

My mother was in an equally large room. It was bare – a few ancient hospital-beds round the wall, half of them empty; some vases of fading flowers on the window-sills.

During the last weeks I'd seen my mother deteriorating. Her voice was no longer resonant, her grasp on the drinking-cup had disappeared.

Now, as I looked down at her, I saw that she had gone further. The nurse had difficulty in rousing her. Her mouth moved but she was not speaking. I said, 'It's Joe.'

I sat down beside the bed. I thought, Thank God! she can't *see* this place. I watched her breathing. Her mouth was still moving.

Without having thought about it, I'd always taken it that you were either living or you weren't. It seemed to me now that my mother was somewhere between the two.

A nurse came back to give my mother a dose of medicine out of what resembled an eye-dropper. Morphia? This time my mother looked as if she might understand that I was there. I bent over her. 'It's Joe. I'm here.'

'Joe? .' Her lips formed the word.

'Yes, my dear. Joe. *I'm* here.'

I could scarcely catch any sound from her, yet I knew what she said. *'That's good . . .'*

Impulsively I began to stroke her forehead and her hair. I couldn't remember ever having done it before. For a while her mouth went on moving; then she relapsed into drowsiness, into sleep.

My arm began to ache. I saw, through the window, the roof of a taxi driving up to the door for me. The rain went on pouring throughout my journey back to London. Was this the last journey?

Yet it was not the death of my mother that we heard of next.

One evening there was a telephone call from Robert. Elspeth and Viola and I were eating our supper at the Breakfast-Bar. I took the receiver from the wall.

'I wanted to let you know, old boy . . . Annette died.'

'When?' Half-baked question. I saw Elspeth and Viola listening to follow the conversation.

'The funeral was this morning. I didn't bother you with it — you've got enough troubles of your own.'

'There's nothing for me to say.'

His tone of voice changed. 'It's a little awkward for me, that I've got to go abroad immediately.'

'Where to?' The USA again! I thought.

'Didn't you know? . . I thought I'd told you. I'm going to the Soviet Union. I shall be away some weeks — I'm going down to the Don, among other places. I shall be making speeches, meeting writers — the usual . . . I'm desperately tired. I could well do without it.' There was a pause. 'I'd like you and Elspeth to cheer up Veronica now and then. If you will . . .'

I said that of course we would.

There was a longer pause. Then he brought himself to speak about illness.

'How *are* your troubles, old boy?'

'I came to the end of my antibiotics,' I said.

'When?'

'Ten days ago.'

'Then – then it looks *all right*?'

'I daren't even think so, yet.'

'Bless you!'

I put the receiver back, and I was thoughtful about something else: when he returned from the Soviet Union would he marry Veronica? We should see.

SAILING AWAY

One breakfast-time soon after that, we got the telephone call about my mother. The formula: Your mother passed away peacefully in the early hours of this morning. Peacefully? I supposed it might be called that.

'Now,' said Elspeth, 'do you know what you've got to do?'

'Yes. The Staff Nurse told me. I've got to go down to the hospital and collect a doctor's certificate and take it to the local Registrar.' I thought I'd made a pretty good start.

Elspeth smiled. 'Do you know what else? *Did* you read the booklet?'

I couldn't lie. It was a booklet called *What To Do When Someone Dies*. It had been purchased by Virginia years ago, a sensible move when Elspeth and I went on holiday, travelling from place to place in Canada and the USA by air. I said:

'I'll read it now.' I meant my tone of voice to say, That's time enough, isn't it?

She went into another room and found the booklet. She put it on the Breakfast-Bar and I opened it. Actually I had previously glanced through it. I read through it now. It told you simply, sensibly, usefully, what to do.

Elspeth was sitting beside me. 'I'll telephone your sister just after mid-day,' I heard her saying. 'That'll be just after seven in the morning there.'

'Thank you,' I said, going on reading.

I'd come to the section about undertakers.

Many years ago I'd received my instructions about all this from the person in question, inimitable instructions –

'You don't need to spend any money on me when I'm gone. You can have me cremated. But don't go to Glossop's.'

Inimitable instructions springing from pride and diffidence – pride and diffidence to the end, I thought, and beyond it . . . (She had had my father's body cremated, and she had gone to Glossop's.)

'You have to watch out with undertakers,' Elspeth was saying.

'You don't need to tell me that.' I'd read Jessica Mitford's *The American Way of Death,* unforgettable book.

I could see that the booklet, in its quiet useful way, was not conveying a substantially different message from Jessica Mitford's.

'They take advantage of people being incapacitated by grief,' Elspeth was saying, 'to run them in for all sorts of incidental expenses.'

I'd suffered most of my grief, I thought, along the way during the last few years. My feelings now were mainly relief for all concerned, my mother being first among them – called at last. Elspeth went on.

'Poor people who don't like to say No, who can't afford it. It's sometimes quite shocking.'

I said, 'I think you can take it that I'm not lacking the power to say No.' I smiled at her with amusement.

She smiled back at me. 'That's all very well. But just you watch out! They'll ask if you'd like this or that, and clock up everything you say Yes to.'

'Then I'll say No to everything.'

She laughed. 'Darling, you can't do *that*.'

'Watch *me*!' She'd put me on my mettle, she and Jessica Mitford and the writer of the booklet.

'Watch *me*!' I repeated.

I was going off to make arrangements for my mother's funeral in the indomitable spirit of one going off to do battle with sharks. I felt a passing spurt of exhilaration.

Elspeth said: 'Remember, you can't say No to having a funeral at all!' She was laughing at me.

I laughed back at her. 'We'll see about that!'

As I was leaving the flat she called after me, 'Don't let them take you anywhere by car – they'll charge you up to twice as much!'

'All right.'

509

I needed cars throughout the whole day as it was pouring with rain again. What a New Year! As well as with the possibility of a monetarist Conservative Government coming to power that year, 1979 began with awful weather. Storms and floods – 'unprecedented' the daily newspapers called them, with journalistic disregard for historical records and the meaning of words. (We seemed to read of *unprecedented* storms and floods every few years.) Squalls of water sloshed against the windscreen of my taxi on the way to the cottage hospital.

I collected the doctor's certificate and my poor old mother's belongings – or rather, I took the broad gold wedding-ring for my sister and told the Staff Nurse to dispose of the clothing among the other patients. And I experienced a tremor of dismay. Slackly, or perhaps because I'd jibbed at facing death, I'd instructed the hospital to call an undertaker for me. I asked the Staff Nurse. Glossop's it was. I was dismayed. I'd let the poor old dear down.

The taxi was waiting and drove me down to the Registrar's Office, where everything went according to what the booklet had told me. I was briefed about how many copies of the Death Certificate I should need. Sometime I had to go back again to the hospital: I told the taxi-driver to take me instead to Glossop's.

It was time to join battle with the sharks.

Glossop's had a little over-manicured front garden, always the subject of my mother's distaste. I dashed through the rain up to the front door and was let into a panelled hall and then a panelled waiting-room – all very chapelly, I thought. There were flowers and a respectful atmosphere. Mr Somebody-or-other would see me in just a few moments.

In just a few moments I was shown into the room of Mr Somebody-or-other. I noticed that he was fairly tall, fairly young, sober and sedate and respectful; but there seemed little else to notice – it was as if all noticeable features had been wiped off him, perhaps for the purposes of his profession. He sat down at a big desk. There were flowers somewhere nearby.

He wrote down some of the details necessary for the occasion, ascertained that it was to be a cremation, told me where the crematorium was – I knew, of course, having been to my father's funeral there – and then got down to business.

'You'll be wanting a Service?' he said. 'Most people do.'

'Do you mean a religious service?'

'Yes . . . '

I said, 'Then, No. There'll only be my wife and myself and our two daughters present, and none of us have any religious beliefs.'

'Ah, yes.' He paused. 'But sometimes the deceased would have wished – '

I interrupted him. 'My mother didn't have any religious beliefs to speak of, either. So I'm afraid it's still No.'

'I understand,' he said. 'In that case,' he went on, 'perhaps you'd like a short reading?'

'No, indeed,' I said. 'Glossop's arranged my father's funeral and had a reading. My mother objected to it. Very strongly.'

Very strongly seemed to me only the truth. ('They had somebody *reading*. I don't know what they'd got to do that for. *I* didn't tell them.') This was one of the reasons I'd been told *not* to go to Glossop's.

'I think you'll feel you need *something*,' he said. 'You'll have some music?'

'Yes,' I said with éclat. And then I added, 'I suppose it will be piped music?'

'Yes.' He had an apologetic expression – not knowing what I was briefed to reply if he'd suggested somebody playing an organ for which one had to pay a fee.

'I should like you to play some Bach,' I said. 'But not organ music or choral music.'

He made a note of it.

I was feeling pretty pleased with the number of things I'd said No to. Elspeth and Jessica Mitford and the writer of the booklet might have been proud of me. I felt exhilarated yet slightly tense. The heights of the battle had yet to be scaled.

The heights of the battle were immediately before us – he raised the subject of the coffin.

'Our quote for the coffin is inclusive of the whole funeral,' he said, 'with the exception of the crematorium fee and the doctor's certification fee.'

'Yes,' I said, remembering Elspeth's observation that I couldn't say No to having a funeral at all.

'Now,' he said, turning over the pages of what appeared to be a catalogue of coffins, 'our Charlwood is very popular. I think you might be very satisfied with it.'

'And how much does it cost?'

'Including VAT, £437.'

'No,' I said. 'I should like something that costs less than that.' (I hadn't much idea whether £437 was a lot or a little, but I didn't doubt that I was right to say No to it.)

He looked thoughtful. 'I think perhaps we can do you one for something less than that.' (Perhaps, indeed!) He paused and turned over some pages. 'Yes. Here's one. Our Ruvigny. That costs rather less.'

'Oh yes?'

'We can do you our Ruvigny for £285.'

As I gave no sign, he began to describe the Ruvigny, what wood it was made of, what metal the handles were made of –

'Brass handles!' I interrupted. 'What on earth do we want brass handles for?' I went on. 'Come to that, do we need handles at all?' The booklet had prepared me for brass handles: no handles was entirely my own inspiration. I felt really exhilarated.

He looked at me.

'If you'll excuse me a moment, I'll make an enquiry,' he said, and went out of the room.

I supposed that he must have gone out to consult some higher authority. I should have loved to think he was beginning with 'I've just got a customer in my room who's a shark . . .'

When he returned he said:

'I think we *can* manage something less for you. It's our Rock-Bottom – £242.'

At first I thought Rock-Bottom must be the name of another coffin. I said:

'Thank you. I'll accept' – I suppressed the impulse to say, Your Rock-Bottom, and said – 'your offer'.

He did some more writing. Then he proposed the date and time of the funeral. The rendezvous was here. 'Will you be coming by car?'

'No. We shall be coming by train from Victoria.'

'Would you like us to have one of our cars to meet you at the station?'

'No, thank you. We can easily get a taxi at the station when we're ready.'

'Of course.' He paused. 'And flowers? Would you like us to order some flowers for you?'

'No, thank you. I know the flower-shop just along the road, here. I'll go in and see them about it after I leave here.'

'And then you have to go up to the hospital again?'

'Unfortunately yes.' It was still pouring with rain.

'I believe one of my colleagues is going up to the Crematorium shortly. If you'd care for it, he could pick you up at the florist's and drop you at the hospital – it's on his way.'

I nearly said Yes, just to give him a break. However I said truthfully, 'I hadn't planned to go up to the hospital immediately.' There was a pub near the florist's – I needed it.

'I understand.'

Poor sod! He did some final writing, which seemed to take him a long time.

I gave my attention to an enormous vase of flowers about a yard away from me on my right. It was what's called a flower *arrangement* – very rightly called so. Another squall of rain dashed itself against the windows. I heard him say:

'And now, would you care to see the deceased?'

Just before I'd left home Elspeth had said to me, knowing that I had never seen anyone who was dead, 'You realise that they'll ask you if you want to see her?' I hadn't known what to say.

Now it was easy. I heard myself saying –

'Yes, of course.'

He said, 'I'll just make sure everything is ready,' and he went out of the room again.

I waited. The rain dashed itself against the windows again What had I *said*? . . He came back.

'Yes. Will you come this way, please?' And he opened another door.

I followed him through it. He stood aside. I saw her.

'*There* she is!' I exclaimed, my feelings suddenly lit with affection and warmth – I might have been looking for her in a room where there was a party going on, and have suddenly spotted her talking among friends. There she was!

She was lying in the middle of the room. Her feet were towards the windows at the end of the room, the back of her head towards me. Her hair was sweetly done up into the knot on top of her head — one sometimes saw it done up just like that nowadays on ladies walking along Knightsbridge.

I went forward to look at her. She was lying quite high in what seemed like a little wooden box on top of something; pale as when I'd last seen her, composed, still — called at last.

I heard the undertaker go out. I moved round. The little wooden box made me think of a boat. She was lying in it as if it were just about to float off. She was covered in what looked like a white satin nightdress with an embroidered bodice, embroidered in multicoloured silks and lurex gold thread — there'd have been a row, I thought, if she'd known they were going to do that! The long white dress, the silks and the flowers round about, and above all the way she was lying as if she were floating, suddenly made me think of Sir John Millais' painting of Ophelia – which I hadn't seen for donkey's years and couldn't even remember well.

So *there* you are! I thought. Floating, ready to sail . . .

It was the moment when a superstition of my childhood, over half a century ago, sprang up in me. I'd heard people saying – I recalled it exactly – that you must touch a corpse if you didn't want to dream about it.

'Goodbye, my dear,' I said aloud, and touched her forehead.

Her forehead was cold, much colder, whether from death or refrigeration, than I'd expected. Poor old forehead . . . I remembered stroking it that last time while she was still alive, just alive – '*That's good* . . . '

No more, now. I'd said goodbye, I'd touched her, it was time to go.

As I turned away I looked at her for the last time. There she lay, floating in the little boat, ready to sail away. Ready to sail away to nowhere. Nowhere . . .